THE IDOL OF
THE DARK TOWER

~~~~~~~~~~~~~~~~~~~~~~

Cautiously, Joe and Marge crept up the stairs in the Dark Tower of Witchwood. Finally they emerged into a brightly lighted chamber. There were no furnishings, but at the far end of the room was a huge, hideous, multi-armed idol made of some dark stone.

Its face was a travesty of a human woman's face. It sat in the lotus position, and eight arms came from its distorted torso. Each of the hands held a different deadly weapon. Its eyes were blazing red rubies of nearly impossible size and perfection.

"Look at those stones!" Marge gasped.

Joe shook his head. "I wouldn't touch it. It's probably cursed a thousand ways from Sunday."

"Actually, I'm not," the idol said. "If you looked like this, would you need much in the way of curses?"

By Jack L. Chalker
Published by Ballantine Books:

THE WEB OF THE CHOZEN

AND THE DEVIL WILL DRAG YOU UNDER

A JUNGLE OF STARS

DANCE BAND ON THE *TITANIC*

DANCERS IN THE AFTERGLOW

THE SAGA OF THE WELL WORLD
Volume 1: *Midnight at the Well of Souls*
Volume 2: *Exiles at the Well of Souls*
Volume 3: *Quest for the Well of Souls*
Volume 4: *The Return of Nathan Brazil*
Volume 5: *Twilight at the Well of Souls:*
        The Legacy of Nathan Brazil

THE FOUR LORDS OF THE DIAMOND
Book One: *Lilith: A Snake in the Grass*
Book Two: *Cerberus: A Wolf in the Fold*
Book Three: *Charon: A Dragon at the Gate*
Book Four: *Medusa: A Tiger by the Tail*

THE DANCING GODS
Book One: *The River of Dancing Gods*
Book Two: *Demons of the Dancing Gods*
Book Three: *Vengeance of the Dancing Gods*

THE RINGS OF THE MASTER
Book One: *Lords of the Middle Dark*
Book Two: *Pirates of the Thunder*
Book Three: *Warriors of the Storm*
Book Four: *Masks of the Martyrs*

Demons of the Dancing Gods

Jack L. Chalker

A Del Rey Book

BALLANTINE BOOKS • NEW YORK

A Del Rey Book
Published by Ballantine Books

Copyright © 1984 by Jack L. Chalker

Library of Congress Catalog Card Number: 84-90859

ISBN 0-345-30893-X

Manufactured in the United States of America

First Edition: June 1984
Fifth Printing: May 1988

Cover art by Darrell K. Sweet

Map by Shelly Shapiro

For Ken Moore, Dan Caldwell,
and the rest of that crazy bunch,
along with a gift certificate for
a presmoked cigar.

TABLE OF CONTENTS

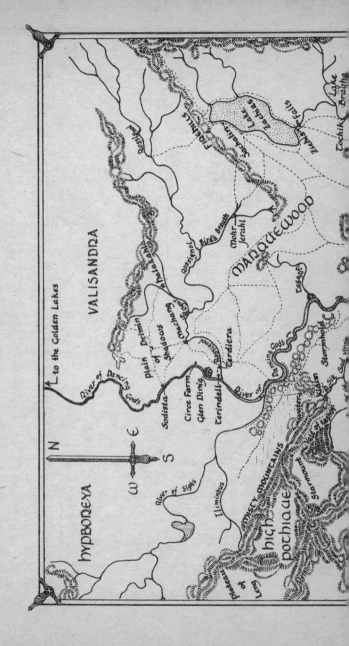

CHAPTER 1

ENCOUNTER ON A LONELY ROAD

The road to Hell is sometimes paved with good intentions.
—The Books of Rules, CVI, Introduction

IF HE HAD TO GO TO HELL, WELL, IT WAS BETTER TO GO dressed in expensive clothes, drinking good wine, and smoking a fine cigar.

The small figure walking slowly down the road was hardly visible in the darkness, and any who might have come along would probably not even see, let alone notice, him. He stopped for a moment, as if trying to get his bearings from the stars, and sighed. Well, he thought to himself, the clothes weren't bad for being nondescript, and the wine was long gone, but he did have one last cigar. He took it out, sniffed it, bit off the end, and stood there for a moment, as if hesitant to light and consume this one last vestige of wealth. Finally he lighted it, simply by making a few small signs in the air and pointing his finger at the tip. A pale yellow beam emanated from the finger, and the cigar glowed. Such pranks were really pretty petty for a master sorcerer, but he had always enjoyed them, taking an almost childlike pleasure in their simplicity and basic utility.

He found a rock and sat down to enjoy the smoke, looking out at the bleak landscape before him, invisible in the darkness of the new moon to his eyes, but not to his other, paranormal senses.

The darkness was in itself a living thing to him, a thing that he sensed, touched, caressed, and tried to befriend. He found it indifferent to him, interested instead in its own lowly subjects—the lizards, the snakes, the tiny voles, and other creatures that inhabited the desolation and knew it as home. For these and all the nameless citizens of its domain, the night was life itself, allowing them access to food and water under cooling temperatures, sheltered from greater enemies by the cool, caring dark.

The road seemed empty, lonely, desolate as the landscape itself, a track forlorn and forgotten in the shelter of deep night; but as he sat there, nursing the last cigar, he extended his senses and saw that *this* road was different, *this* road was for those with beyond normal senses and training. *This* road was inhabited, used in the night; as he let himself go, he could hear the groans and lamentations of those who used it now in the depths of night.

Even he could not see them, not now, but he could hear them, hear the crack of the whip and the cries of hopelessness and despair from those who moved slowly, mournfully, down that lonely road.

For in the dark, at the time of the new moon, he knew—perhaps he alone knew—that this road had a dark and despairing purpose beyond its utility to the travelers of day and full moon.

They were walking, crawling, along that lonely road, he knew, going toward a destination they dreaded yet had richly earned.

The month's quota of damned souls was a bumper crop, judging from the sounds.

One night, he knew, he'd be there, reduced to the same level as all the rest, walking or crawling down that road himself. One night, he, too, would be brought as low as the lowest of those now moving down that road, paying a due bill he had willingly run up. Perhaps, just perhaps, it would be this night, if his tongue and quick mind failed him for once. He was willing to go, he tried to convince himself, but not yet, not just yet. He had surrendered much to travel that road one day, not the least of which was his honor, and he certainly was loath to pay without at least attaining the goal for which he'd sold his soul.

The cigar was almost finished now, but he continued to nurse it along almost to the point of burning his fingers, as if the end of the cigar would also be the end of his hopes, his dreams, his life, and his power. For the first time, in the dark, with the sounds of the damned filling his bargained soul to its core, he had doubts and fears about his course and his own well-being. Was the great goal worth this sort of ultimate price? Did it really matter one way or the other what he did or didn't do, or was he, like the cigar, a momentary brilliance turned to ash and of no more consequence than that in the scheme of things?

He got up, dropped the stub, and crushed it angrily with his right foot. Such melancholy was for fools and failures, he scolded himself. He had not failed yet, and in his setbacks he had learned a great deal. Now was not the time for self-deprecation, self-doubt, and inner fears to consume him—no, that was what *they* would want, not merely his enemies but his unhuman allies as well. They, his allies, were the cause of this, for they dealt in such matters, traded in doubt and fear, sowed the seeds of turmoil inside you, and, in that way, they fed and grew stronger.

He began to walk along the dark, lonely road in the wastes, conscious now of being among the milling throng of the damned on their way to perdition, and conscious, too, that they knew he was there, a living, breathing man of power. He could feel their envy, their hatred of him for still cheating what they now faced; he could feel, too, the pity in many of them, not merely for their own sorry fates but for him as well.

Turn back, he could hear them crying. *Do not walk this path with us, as we have walked. You still live! For you, there is still time . . .*

Still time . . . Until his corpse rotted as theirs now did, until his cold and silent soul received their summons, there was always time. Time to set things right. Time not to repent, nor turn back—never!—but time, instead, to complete the work.

Within the hour he had passed through the slow-moving throng and stood at a point in the road where, in the light of day, it went through a narrow pass and emerged in greener, more beauteous regions beyond. Any who dared this path on a night so dark would still pass through to that other side, oblivious to that which lay before them, only slightly out of phase with the world they knew. But he—he was a sorcerer and he saw the many plains in his mind's eye and in the magical energies that flowed through all the world.

The colors of the valley's magic were crimson and lavender,

the colors of its district prince, and they flowed along the road with its great traffic of once-human misery, flowed with a curious and subtle beauty to the head of the pass, then seemed to pause a moment before beginning a swirl in the air before him, as if, somehow, these great colors were some sort of liquid, here reaching a great drain.

And, in fact, it was so, for through him passed the souls of the damned, screaming in terror, unable not to press forward, reaching the great swirling mass of magical energy and falling in, their cries and pleas for a mercy now forever denied them cut terribly short as they were sucked down the great outlet from the real world in which they had forged their fate to Hell itself.

Not that Hell was actually so terrible. He had visited there on two occasions and found it more a place of curious fascination than the abject horror of the old tales and mystic religions. Yet it was still an unhappy place, fueled with hatred and revenge, its most terrible punishment a constantly available vision of the glory and beauty of absolute perfection that could always be seen but never experienced. They walked in Hell, always avoiding the vision, their eyes averting from it as men's eyes averted from the sun; yet they were always aware it was there, a place of indescribable joy and beauty that was held tantalizingly before them, just out of reach—always out of reach. It was this vision that had been denied him on his visits, for no living being was permitted to see such a sight as Paradise, lest, it was said, he be consumed in the light and desire nothing else. This did not really bother him; everybody in his past whom he knew, liked, or admired was in Hell anyway, along with all the other interesting people.

The swirl was changing now, becoming more irregular, as if disturbed by some great power or form arising within it, going, as it were, against the flow of the thing. It was less a drain now than a spiral. He saw the four arms of the turning swirl break from the main mass and fly upward above it, then form in a diamond. The light of these four shapes was no longer nebulous, but instead took on the form of wraithlike faces, demon faces, looking down upon him with cold interest. Now from the center of the magical mass shot two more bright lights, out and up into the diamond-shaped phalanx of faces, the demonic captain and the equally demonic sergeant of the guard.

Finally, out of the mass, so large it almost *was* the mass, walked a vaguely humanoid form. The creature was terrible to behold, one who had once been a creature of near perfection, an angel, distorted by hatred and an unquenchable thirst for revenge into a vaguely manlike thing that oozed the rot of long-dead corpses and whose face, twisted in an expression of permanent hatred, was set off by two huge pupilless eyes glowing a bright red.

The creature was dressed in royal robes of lavender, set off by a crimson cape, boots, and gloves. It halted in front of him and looked down menacingly. He bowed low and said, "How is my lord Prince Hiccarph?"

The demon prince gave a bull-like snort. "You really blew it, didn't you, Baron Asshole?"

"*We* blew it," he responded calmly. "Despite that cursed dragon and the very considerable powers of Ruddygore, it was the lack of the Lamp that did us in. We had it in our grasp—and, in your august presence, a brainless hulk and a slip of a halfling girl stole it right out from under your nose. All that when one wish would have carried the day and the war for us. You can't make me take all the credit, not *this* time."

"I can make you take whatever I wish," the demon prince hissed. "You're mine, Baron. I own you, not merely when you get here but right now. I think this fact bears reminding."

He smiled. "If that is true, my lord, and I am your abject slave, then the fault is truly yours for the loss, for you chose the instrument and you played its string."

"You *are* an impudent bastard," Hiccarph commented, his tone softening. "Perhaps that's why I like you. Perhaps that is why I just don't strike you down and take you with me tonight."

Inwardly, the Baron relaxed a bit at the comment. Still time . . . still time . . . Aloud, he asked, "Have you determined why those two were able to ignore your powers? At first I thought it was the Lamp, but I soon realized that the magic Lamp of the djinn would have little authority over you."

"I have done much research on the matter," the demon prince told him, "and still I have not the answer that is true. Dozens of explanations have occurred to me, but which one is the right one? Unless I know the exact means by which Ruddygore accomplished this, I can take no measures to counter it. We know very little about them, after all; and, if I peer too deeply into it from my side, it will certainly alert his Majesty, and I would prefer *he* in particular learn nothing of our little project, at least not yet, for understandable reasons. Since they worked so well for Ruddygore, though, it is likely he will continue to use them, and in that we might ultimately learn the secret through your offices. Remember, Baron, that we are in a sense kindred in this matter. Neither of us can afford to fail, and both of us will suffer terribly if we do."

The Dark Baron nodded. The harsh and rugged land of Husaquahr, dominated by the great River of Dancing Gods, had never been totally conquered by force of arms and, as such, it was the key to the domination of the entire continent. The continent, in turn, was the key to the entire world, since a bare majority of the Council of Thirteen, the most powerful necromancers in the world, lived on it—including, of course, himself. Control of the Council meant the ability to rewrite the Books of Rules, which governed the lives and powers of all who lived on the world, and that meant absolute control. From this world, formed by angels in the backwash of the Great Creation, Hiccarph and the minions of Hell could launch an invasion of Earth Prime, an Armageddon that might well have a different ending from the one everybody and every holy book of both worlds predicted.

Of course, there was more to it on a personal level than merely giving Hell a great advantage. Hiccarph might be a prince, but as his sphere of influence was Husaquahr and not any place on Earth Prime, he was a decidedly minor one in the Hellish hierarchy. If Hiccarph could deliver *this* world to his Satanic Majesty free and clear, his standing in the royal pecking order would be second only to great Lucifer himself.

But Hiccarph was taking a terrible gamble himself. For over two thousand years there had existed a compact between Heaven and Hell, a reordering of the rules of their great war. No longer would angels and demons walk directly upon the planes of the worlds, but would, instead, act through intermediaries native to those planes exclusively. Thus balanced, the minds and souls of the worlds would themselves choose sides and do the work freely and for their own motives. To break the compact would be tantamount to a formal declaration of war, the second War of Heaven called Armageddon, a war Hell did not wish to fight unless it believed it could win.

And yet Hiccarph had in fact broken the compact and directly intervened in Husaquahr. With his powers, unconstrained by the man-made Books of Rules, he had built and backed the forces of the Dark Baron and conquered over a quarter of the entire land. They had been stopped, though, in a great battle in which Hiccarph's powers were blunted by his inability to act against the two from the other plane at a key point in the battle, and by the subsequent skill of opposing sorcery and swords. Because of that defeat, the Dark Baron's forces had had to withdraw, and both the Baron and Hiccarph were in pretty deep trouble.

The longer it took, and the more direct involvement by the demon prince, the more likely his activities would be discovered by his own king, who might not approve of such a premature and unilateral breaking of the compact by a comparatively minor underling. But the more open and direct Hiccarph's involvement, the more the enemies of the Baron would be strengthened, since those opposing Hell would be able to rally all the most powerful sorcerers to their side—a combined power Hiccarph alone could not block. Worse, proof that the compact was being violated would raise even the hands of evil against the Baron—for who, living in decadent splendor and enjoying the power and possessions that evil brought, would like to take a risk on Armageddon, at which point their wonderful wickedness might be destroyed for all time, when they had sure things in the here and now?

"Those two saw you," the Baron pointed out. "Live witnesses now exist that know you personally intervened."

"They are of no consequence," the demon prince assured him. "After all, Ruddygore already knew. But the others—particularly those who are already in the service of Hell—will not want to believe. They will find the idea that any might violate the compact unthinkable. Only if faced with proof so clear and incontrovertible that they can not help but believe will they do so. That's the only thing that's saving our collective asses, Baron, but it's a big thing."

He nodded. "So what do we do about these two you can't control?"

"They are no longer any threat, now that we know their looks and boss. Remember, while they are immune to me, they are vulnerable to the Rules of Husaquahr; thus, they can be easily handled by such as you. It is ironic, my dear Baron, that, had you actually gone to attend to them instead of me, we would have won. While my far greater magic was powerless against them, you could have frozen them to statues or turned them to toads with a flick of your wrist. Ruddygore is clever— he foresaw in the Mazes of Probabilities that such a situation might occur and prepared for it—but his advantage is now known. Once known, his schemes are of no consequence. I think we have seen Ruddygore's bag of tricks. He will not expect us to act again so soon, and we will not give him the time to prepare more tricks and traps."

"You have a plan, then?"

"You still control a quarter of Husaquahr. Your army is a good army, perhaps the greatest ever raised here, and it retired from the field intact and in good order. In the end, it was geography that defeated us, as it has defeated all past conquering armies here. Even without the Lamp, we almost carried the day, nor could our enemies mount a credible counterattack. They won in the end because geography told them where we must meet and they were there, well fortified and in the defensive positions of their choice. Eliminate the geographical factors and we will carry any battle."

"But how do you eliminate geography?" the Baron asked, fascinated but skeptical.

"With me, you are the equal of six of the Council," Hiccarph told him. "We have the power. Now listen, my impudent instrument, as to how it will be used."

CHAPTER 2

VISITS WITH OLD FRIENDS

The fairies may belong fully to no human orders, nor their political parties.

—The Books of Rules, LXIV, 36(b)

THE GLEN DINIG WAS A PLACE OF MAGIC AND MYSTERY. THE sacred grove of trees along the banks of the River of Dancing Gods was but a few hours north of the great castle Terindell at the confluence of the Rossignol and the Dancing Gods, yet it might as well be on another planet. Legends abounded concerning it, but few had actually seen it and fewer still dared to penetrate its depths. Even those who scoffed at the legends and tall tales nonetheless admitted that there was a strong spell on the place; no human male could enter it, no matter from what direction or means, nor male fairy, either. Only a few steps into the tree-covered area and a man felt his breath become labored and hard; in a few steps more, he would be gasping for air, with the choice of suffocation or fleeing outside the invisible but tangible boundaries.

Legend said that a great witch, a virgin power who was the daughter of Adam and Lilith, had finally tired of the world and its struggles and created this place, perhaps on the spot where, a world away, Eden had once stood; and here she remained to this day, never aging, never changing, in some strange and wondrous world of her own creation, echoing imperfectly the Garden she once actually saw so long ago. Exiled, as her mother had been, to this new and alternate Earth, unable to die and unable to forget, she was in a state where, at least, she might not go mad.

Some said she *was* mad, of course, while others said she

had transformed herself, and that she was not in the Glen Dinig but rather was the magical forest now. All that was agreed upon was that she was there, that her name was Huspeth, and that even those who really didn't believe in her still feared and respected the name.

The woman who rode into the forest confidently had a great deal of the respect and awe that Huspeth and the Glen Dinig radiated within herself, but she did not fear either the witch of Glen Dinig or the forest itself. She knew them well, as old friends and great teachers, and she owed them much. She *did* have fears and concerns, though, and she dreaded this trip for what to the superstitious outsiders would seem amazing reasons. She was coming to ask of them that they separate her from this wonder and magic forever, because she had no choice.

The woman had a strange appearance, both human and fairy, with a beautiful, almost unnatural face and figure set off by enormous, deep, sensuous eyes that no human ever had. Her skin, too, was a soft orange, and her hands and feet, with their length and clawlike nails, were pure fairy.

Huspeth met her warmly at the small glen in the center of the forest and tried her best to put the newcomer at ease. The cauldron outside the hut where the white witch lived was bubbling with grand smells, and Huspeth would hear nothing serious from her visitor until both had supped and the sun had vanished far beyond the trees.

Finally, by fireglow, the legendary witch gazed sadly at her strange-looking visitor and sighed. "Well, my daughter, time has caught up with thee, and thine anguish I share."

Marge smiled a sad smile and nodded. "I owe you everything," she said sincerely, "and I'm pained by this—but I can put it off no longer. It's—well, it's driving me crazy!"

Huspeth nodded sympathetically and gave her hand a motherly squeeze. "Already thou art burdened with living in two worlds, not truly a part of either yet very much a part of both," the witch said soothingly. "That is a far greater burden than any should bear, yet to live in three is impossible."

Marge stifled a tear, knowing that at least one other understood. Two worlds and not truly a part of either, she thought sourly. A Texas girl who'd failed at a career, failed at marriage, even failed as a hooker and as a waitress, who'd hitched a ride on her way to Hell with a crazy trucker drafted by a sorcerer to fight a war in another world. Joe was *supposed* to be here in Husaquahr, at least, although he might argue the point. Ruddygore had needed a hero not born of this world and thus immune to the demons of this place and he'd plucked Joe from Earth just before Joe was to die in a crash. She'd hitched a ride with Joe that dark night, thinking of suicide and expecting to make El Paso. Instead, here she was, in the land where fantasy was real, the origins of all human fantasies and myths, across the Sea of Dreams. And here the sorcerer with the impossible fictitious name of Throckmorton P. Ruddygore—Huspeth had taught her that none of the Council of Thirteen used their real names, since knowing the real name of someone in their class gave an equal opponent some kind of advantage—had sent the hitchhiking Marge to Huspeth in the Glen Dinig, to be trained as a healer and white witch. After the training, she had done her job well and contributed to keeping the powerful magic Lamp out of the hands of the marching Dark Baron, but there had been a catch. The order of white witches to which Huspeth and she belonged drew power from their virginity and celibacy—and Marge had once again been virginal in Husaquahr—but the more magic she had used or been subjected to, the more she changed.

"Aye, thou art a changeling sure," Huspeth told her, echoing her thoughts. "It is he whom thou dost call Ruddygore who did this knowingly. Is there hatred in thy soul for him for this?"

She thought a moment. "No, not really. Not at all. Just for a moment there, I was back on that lonely west Texas highway, not caring if I lived or died. Without him I'd be dead, either in that wreck or not too long after by my own hand. Whatever he did, he had a right to do. I've got no kick coming."

Huspeth smiled and nodded. "Thou hast learned much, my daughter, and thy wisdom becomes thee. I do not much like him, as thou knowest, for he trafficks in demons, yet his heart is good even if his soul be impure. He had very good reasons for bringing thee and thy companion to this world, and his skill at the art placed you both in the place where you were most needed. It may seem cruel to send thee to a celibate order and then make thee a changeling, but I divine strong purpose in it. Thy string is complex and far from played out. At first I thought him taking a subtle jest at me, but now I see it is not so. He needed thee as a witch of the order, but the clouds of Probability change with events. The first act is done, the curtain is down, but the play is far from completed."

Marge felt a little better on hearing this. "Then—whatever I'm becoming—is what is needed next?"

The ancient witch nodded. "It is clear now."

"Then—why? What must I face?"

"That is unknown to all save the Creator," Huspeth told her. "The future is not fixed but is all probabilities. One highly skilled in the arts may see that a thing is needed while not knowing why, or when, or how. But it is now clear that the curtain must rise on the next act of our play. A conference of the Sisterhood was already held. Thy vows are lifted, as they must be. Thou art free."

Marge frowned. "Just like that?"

Huspeth laughed softly. "Just like that. And why not? For all the magic of the initiation which confers the power, a vow is a vow and not a spell. It is not a command but a contract. Thou hast not broken thy vow, so there is no dishonor. Release is needed and granted freely and willingly. The war against the forces of Hell needs thee." She sighed. "But stay the night with me. Enjoy the Glen Dinig. In the morning, perhaps, we shall visit the unicorn and say thy farewells. Then shalt thou ride forth to a new destiny."

Marge was almost overcome with emotion, and tears welled up in her eyes. "May I still—return? For a visit?"

"At any time, my daughter, for my daughter thou shalt remain always. The Glen Dinig shall sing whenever thou dost approach, and here thou mayest always find rest and comfort."

That made it much better, much more bearable. "Mother— what shall I do now?"

"Travel to the east along the Rossignol," Huspeth told her. "Ten days' comfortable journey will bring thee to the tributary called the Bird's Breath, and so thou shalt follow it to a forest called Mohr Jerahl, a place much like this one. There shalt thou find the fairy folk called the Kauri, who will complete the process and instruct thee in thy nature. Thou art bright, and so it will take some doing inside thee to trust thy feelings at all times, even over thy head, but this is the way of fairy folk, and they live lives far longer than humankind."

"What about Joe?" Marge asked. "Can he come with me? I think I'd like some moral support."

Huspeth gazed off into space for a moment, seeming not to hear, then turned back to her visitor. "He may accompany thee to the edge of Mohr Jerahl, but he must wait there for thee. There is mortal peril for a human to enter the home of a fairy folk; should he enter, he will almost certainly have to kill many Kauri or be consumed by their power. It would not be good to begin thy relationship with thy new people with death, for the fairies do not age as humans do, but exist in their soul-state, and death for any fairy, including thyself, is the true death, not the transition of the humans. If he must come, then make him wait. Time to the fairy folk in their own land is not like time elsewhere, so his wait will not be long, no matter how long dost thou tarry."

"These—Kauri. What are they like?"

"An ancient folk of great power over mortal flesh, which is needed to safeguard their fragility. Their nature is quite elemental and is best experienced firsthand. Don't worry. *Thou* wilt find peace and confidence as one of them."

CHAPTER 3

A NICE LITTLE BUSINESS TRIP

For a barbarian, image is the most important thing.
                              —Rules, LXXXII, 306(b)

THE MAN WALKING ACROSS THE CASTLE'S INNER COURTYARD would have stood out in any crowd. He was a huge man, well over six feet and so totally muscled that those looking at him generally expected him to crash through stone walls rather than be bothered to walk around them. His face, which he himself described as vaguely Oriental—a meaningless term in Husaquahr but not back in his native Philadelphia—was handsome and strong, with piercing eyes that seemed almost jet-black, the whole thing set off by a thick crop of truly jet-black hair that hung halfway between his shoulders and waist. His skin was tanned a magnificent bronze and looked tough enough to deflect spears. He wore only a flimsy white loincloth, hung from an ornate hand-tooled leather belt, and a hat, made to his specifications by the milliner in the nearby town of Terdiera. It was a cowboy hat, brim sides turning up in starched salute, and on the front was a strange symbol and the word, in English: "Peterbilt." The hat, which had shown great utility in deflecting the elements, had been widely imitated in the land around Castle Terindell.

He approached a low building separated from the castle proper and knocked at the wooden door. It opened, revealing a tall, sinister-looking elf whose thin-lined face, penetrating eyes in perpetual scowl, and cold manner were in stark contrast to the small, happy groundskeepers always working on the castle itself. This was a warrior elf, an Imir, a professional soldier and deadly fighter.

"Hello, Poquah," the big man said cheerily. "Is he in?"

"Downstairs, working on cataloguing his sculpture collection," the Imir responded. "Come in—the lady is already waiting inside. You can go down together."

Joe entered, having to bend his head slightly to clear the door, and looked around the familiar study of the sorcerer Ruddygore, its sumptuous furnishings complementing the walls of red-bound volumes that seemed to go on forever—the Books of Rules, which governed this entire crazy world and were constantly being amended.

Marge was standing there, just looking at the huge books as she always did, probably wishing she could read them. Although the trading language they now used routinely as a first language bore an amazing resemblance to English, at least in many of the nouns, adjectives, and adverbs, its written form was pictographic, like the Chinese of their old world, with over forty thousand characters representing words and ideas rather than letters. It took an exceptional mind to learn it, starting from childhood. Total literacy meant power and position, no matter from what origins one came; but there was far too little time to learn it, once one was an adult.

She looked around as he entered and gave him a mild wave,

then turned back to the books. "You know," she said, "they still remind me of the U.S. Tax Code. Thousands of years of petty, sorcerous minds constantly making Rules on just about everything they can think of. And every time there's a Council meeting, there's another volume of additions, deletions, and revisions. I bet nobody knows or understands it all, not even Ruddygore."

He just nodded and shrugged. The whole world was nuts, but people still acted like people, and that meant nutty, too. He'd long since stopped being amazed at much of anything in this world and just accepted whatever came. "So how are you doing?" he asked her, trying to start a more normal conversation.

She turned and shrugged, and he couldn't help but reflect how she seemed to get more beautiful and sexy every time he saw her. "Not bad. You?"

"Bored," he said honestly. "The first time I bent a three-inch iron bar into a pretzel, I was like a little kid and I went around bending all sorts of stuff, lifting horses, wagons, you name it. But now it's all just nothin'. I mean, it's no big deal any more."

Nothing, in fact, was any big deal any more. He was used to stares and people scrambling out of his way—so used to it that he pretty well took it for granted now. Just going into a town was an experience only for those with him for the first time—the women all gaga over him, no problems with service, conquests, you name it. There wasn't even any fun in claiming that he could outdrink and outfight anybody in the town. Hell, he *could* and he knew it. In the two months since the battle, he'd become totally bored, jaded, and itchy for anything new, even if it was risky. Just a couple of days before, two thieves from out of the area had attacked him in a back alley. One had hit him over the head with a club while the other had swung a board into his stomach. Both the club and the board had broken on impact—and so had the two thieves.

Just now he'd come from the practice field down by the river where several trainees had tried to shoot arrows into him. Without even thinking about it he'd twisted, turned, and knocked those arrows that still would have hit him down in midair. Gorodo, the huge, nine-foot, blue, apelike trainer of heroes and military men, had asked him for permission to have trainees try to kill him any time. So far, none had shown the least promise. He feared no man and no physical threat; only against sorcery was he powerless and, even in that department, he'd used his brains and quick reflexes to dodge most of it.

That had been the plan, anyway, since the start of all this. He would be the brawn and Marge would deal with the magic, aided by this Huspeth she always talked about and by Ruddygore, of course. They made a near-perfect team. But since the Dark Baron's defeat, there had been little to do.

Poquah appeared—he had the habit of doing that, without any sound or sign until he spoke up—and said, "The Master says to come down. He's in the middle of the catalog and he doesn't want to lose his place."

Marge joined them, and they walked out a back door and down a corridor which led to the sorcerer's magical laboratory. They were not going there, though, but to a basement beneath the main hall and study, where Ruddygore kept many of his more personal valuables. She looked up at Joe and whispered, "Ever seen this collection?"

He shook his head negatively.

"Don't crack up or make jokes when you see it," she warned him. "He's pretty sensitive about it."

Before he could ask any questions, they were in the basement and surrounded by what she was talking about. For a moment he looked around, trying to sort out the collection from the junk—but it didn't take him long to realize that the junk *was* the collection.

There were thousands, perhaps tens of thousands of them—in every size, shape, color combination, and in just about every style. It was, he had to admit, the largest grouping in one spot of tacky plaster sculptures short of a Hong Kong factory. Here they were—the monkey contemplating the human skull while sitting on a plaster book labeled "Aristotle," plaster dogs, plaster cats, pink flamingos, lawn jockeys, and just about every other expression of the tacky art ever "won" by contestants at Beat-the-Guesser stands and fire carnivals the world over. The souvenirs were there, too—the plaster Statues of Liberty, the U.S. Capitols, even ones with a foreign flavor like the seven Eiffel Towers, half a dozen Big Bens, and three different Mannekin Piss statues from Brussels, one of which had a definitely obscene corkscrew imbedded in its painted plaster.

He was about to say something when a shaggy head popped up from the midst of the statuary that virtually filled the room, looked at them, and beamed. "Marge! Joe! How good of you to drop in! How do you like the collection? I daresay it's the finest of its type on any world!"

Joe was about to make a comment on just what he really thought of the junk when Marge kicked his shin. "Um, I'll agree that nobody else has a collection like this one," he managed, trying to sound diplomatic.

Throckmorton P. Ruddygore got up slowly from the floor, where he'd been working, then started looking for a way to get out of the pile that surrounded him without breaking anything. This was no mean task for him, since the sorcerer looked like nothing so much as the classical depiction of Santa Claus, although, at a height of more than six feet, his proportionate bulk was certainly over four hundred pounds.

Joe and Marge carefully helped to make a path for him by moving statuary where they could, and at last the sorcerer was able to reach the entryway. Usually dressed in fine clothes or majestic robes, he allowed few people to see him in the gigantic T-shirt and Bermuda shorts he was now wearing.

After greeting them warmly, he looked at Marge with his piercing blue eyes and asked, "What is it you want, my child?"

"I think you know," she responded. "At least, you'd *better* know."

"Well, I don't know," Joe grumbled.

Ruddygore just nodded. "I think it's best you go and do it as soon as possible. Events are moving at a far faster pace than I had anticipated. Something very odd is going on in the Baron's lands, and that spells trouble. I may need you both at any time."

That interested the big man. "You mean another battle?"

"Not like the old one, Joe. I think the Baron has learned his lesson on that one. But there are disturbing reports from the south. Whole military units seem to have vanished or been broken up and re-formed elsewhere. Boundary defenses have been strengthened, although obviously we can't possibly mount a successful counterattack, and it's getting tougher to get in and out of his areas. Something's up, something new, and we can't get a handle on it; but it's certain that the only reason for such ironclad border control, other than to repel invasion, is

either to keep your own people in—and he has other means
to do that—or to keep the flow of information to a minimum.
Our usual spies have been next to useless, I'm afraid, so I'm
hoping to learn something at the convention."

"Convention?" Marge prompted.

The sorcerer nodded. "Yes, the annual meeting of the sorcerers, magicians, and adepts of Husaquahr. It's a rather large,
elaborate affair lasting five days, and it's only three weeks
away. This year it's in Sachalin, Marquewood's capital. I leave
in ten days for it, since it's a long way. Everybody will be
there, though—the entire Council, as a courtesy, including
those members, both greater and lesser, from the Baron's lands.
I might learn something useful."

"Wait a minute," Joe put in. "You mean to tell me that even
the Baron's side will be there? In a country they just tried to
conquer?"

Ruddygore smiled. "Yes, it *does* sound odd, but the Society
is above politics, and politics often intrudes but never interferes.
They'll all be there—but on their best nonpolitical behavior,
I assure you. The guarantee is that there will be so much magical
power and skill present that any side in a dispute will be in the
minority—and the majority will act decisively and ruthlessly,
I assure you, if the bond of the society is violated."

"The Dark Baron—he'll be there, too?" Marge asked, tem-
porarily forgetting her purpose.

"Oh, yes, but not under that guise. He'll be his usual self
and impossible to detect by normal means. It's interesting. He
may greet me warmly, then buy me a drink—or I might buy
him one. All the time he'll know, while I'll just wonder at
each and every one of them. But, no matter, some slip, some
slight thing, might be betrayed in such an atmosphere, and we
must be on the watch for it."

"We?" both of them echoed.

"Oh, yes. I certainly want you there as my guests and part
of my entourage. Poquah will also be there, along with other
interested members of the household, but they'll all have been
there before. You two will be fresh, unknown to other attendees
and they to you; you might pick up something that familiarity
misses. If you leave tomorrow, you can make Mohr Jerahl,
then take the old road through the Firehills and get there in
plenty of time."

Joe frowned. "Now, one of you want to tell me what this is all about?"

Marge laughed and turned to the big man. "Poor Joe! I'm sorry! I'm going to the home of—well, my people, I guess I could say. I want to complete the transformation quickly, just get it over with."

"The way is possibly dangerous, Joe," the sorcerer added, "although probably no more than any place else in Husaquahr. The perils are more likely thieves and the like than any really magical dangers, though there might be some. You must remember by experience what sort of things might lurk off every trail. Going, Marge will be extremely vulnerable to such dangers, which is why I'm asking you to go. Once you get there, *you'll* be in more danger than she, so when you reach the edge of Mohr Jerahl you'll have to camp and wait for her. The kind of magic the fairy folk have on their own home turf is beyond you or most others, Joe, and I don't want to lose you. I'm going to need you when the time comes again for sword and spear."

"Well, I don't know . . ."

"Trust me, Joe," Ruddygore urged sincerely. "Even I would think twice about going in there without all the armaments of the magical art, and you have none. The Kauri are particularly powerful, which is why, once the transformation is completed, you and Marge will make the perfect team. You will complement each other almost absolutely, and that will make the two of you among the most dangerous pair in all of Husaquahr."

Joe thought that over. "The most dangerous pair . . . I kind of like that. And I've been bored stiff, anyway."

"Then go with my blessings and heed my warnings," the sorcerer told them. "We will meet again three weeks hence at the Imperial Grand Hotel in Sachalin."

Much to Joe's disgust, the journey was without incident and through rolling farm country. They decided to skip the long and treacherous trollbridge near Terdiera and made their way along the Rossignol and its good trading road to the much larger town of Machang, which, being at a particularly sharp and inward angle of the river, was a convergence of many roads and trade routes and had a bridge there built and run by the government.

The Rossignol at this point was barely a hundred yards wide, but the channel was still more than ten feet deep, hardly fordable. The falls to the east of the town offered too risky and slippery a crossing on horseback; beyond that, the river was heavily patrolled and the border strongly fenced, as the water was shallow enough for anybody to walk across.

The formalities on the Valisandran side of the border were few; a small shack contained an official and a sorry-looking soldier who barely seemed interested in checking anybody going out. On the other side, though, was the tiny Marquewood town of Zabeet, a poor and rundown little place that seemed to subsist on cheap tourist trinkets sold to those who, coming along the trade routes for one reason or another, wanted to say they'd been to Marquewood without actually having to go there. The people were poor and dressed in rags; many of the children weren't dressed at all, and everybody seemed anxious to sell travelers something petty and crude that they had no desire for.

Still, for such a forgotten part of the country, it had one hell of an official entry station—a gigantic building entrants actually had to ride through, complete with officious clerks who were dressed in uniforms that suggested they were chief generals in some big army. The little man with the ten stars on each shoulder and the fourteen stripes down his blue uniform's sleeves was at least thorough.

"Names?"

"Joseph the Golden and Marge of Mohr Jerahl," Marge responded, already a little bit annoyed.

The eyebrows went up. "Mohr Jerahl? Then you are a citizen of Marquewood?"

"In a way I guess I am," she admitted.

"Documents, then?"

"The fairy folk need none, as you know."

"And if you were truly of Mohr Jerahl, you wouldn't need this bridge, either," the clerk responded coldly. "Insufficient documentation. Entry refused. And you?"

Joe was growing a little irritated at the man's manner and drew his sword. It was an impressive weapon, being one of the last of the legendary dwarf-swords and thus magical, with a mind and personality of its own. To the consternation of all, Joe had named it Irving, after his small son a world away; but looking at the thing induced only respect, not derision.

The clerk was unfazed. "Striking a customs and immigration official with a sword, magical or not, is an offense punishable by not less than ten years at hard labor and/or a fine not to exceed fifty thousand marques," he said casually. "Undocumented and threatening. Entry refused." He turned to go back to his station, and Joe roared.

"How are you gonna impose that punishment if you're dead?"

The clerk stopped, turned, and looked at the big man as if he were a small child or an idiot. "I am only a small cog in a great bureaucratic machine. What happens to me will not alter things one bit. It will simply trigger the crossbows now aimed at you both and, if you survive them by some miracle, will make you wanted fugitives. It is not my job to bring you in or punish you. We have police and army units to do that."

"Why, you cold little—machine!" Marge snapped, and started for him.

"Wait!" Joe shouted, sheathing his sword. "As an old trucker, I should have realized that you don't fight his type with weapons." He saw Marge stop and look hesitant and he turned back to the little man.

"Tell me, Mr. Official, what is the penalty for bribing an officer of the government at an official entry station?"

The clerk thought a moment. "It would depend on the amount."

Joe reached into his saddlebag, found a small pouch, opened it, and removed two medium-sized diamonds. He dismounted and walked over to the little man and handed him the two stones. "How about for this amount?"

The clerk reached into a shirt pocket, pulled out a jeweler's magnifier, and looked them both over critically. He placed both the stones and the magnifier back in his pocket, then took out a small pad and scribbled something on it that neither of them could read, handing two sheets to Joe. "Documentation all in order. Have a pleasant and enjoyable stay in our beautiful country," he said. He turned and went back inside.

Joe grinned, looked at Marge, and said, "Let's mount up."

They were through the little, shabby town and out onto the Eastern Road before they slowed and pulled alongside each other. Joe was still grinning. "No doubt about it," he said. "People really are the same all over."

She shook her head wonderingly. "You know, he wasn't

kidding about those crossbows. I spotted them all over, on some kind of lever and spring mechanism. Either he or a buddy could have made pincushions of us. What made you sure he'd take the bribe and not just arrest us for violating some rule thus-and-so?"

The big man chuckled. "Because people *are* the same. The more straightlaced and officious they are, the more corrupt they wind up being. That fellow had no flexibility at all, yet here he is at the only major border crossing to a town dependent on tourists. He wouldn't last long there if he was for real—the people in that poor little town would have lynched him. No, he's an old pro. He spotted us for people likely to have money and tried the good old shakedown. I've seen his type many times, usually at seldom-used border stations."

She was still shaking her head. "But what if he was wrong? What if we didn't have the money or never caught on? I notice he never asked for a bribe, and you never actually offered one."

"Well, if we hadn't gone across, we'd have gone back and stayed in Machang long enough to gripe about him. Somebody would cue us in—bet on it. Somebody working with him, most likely. And that same somebody would find out if we had no money and offer to get us across for something—say one of the horses. Don't worry—that fellow will spend the end of his days either a very rich and comfortable man or in jail. Bet on his being rich. Don't believe what they told you in school—crime pays real good. That's why so many people are in the business."

She thought about that for a minute. "Uh—were *you* ever in that business?"

He laughed. "At one time or another, I think most everybody is. For truckers, it's maybe half the time. Not even the most honest, flag-waving Jesus man doesn't run an overloaded rig once in a while and skip the coops—weigh stations—or maybe run at ten or twenty over the speed limit. About a quarter of us haul stuff we shouldn't in addition to what's on the waybill, to make a few bucks. You talk as if you never did anything illegal, either."

"Let's not talk about that," she responded, and they rode on.

Again the road followed the river for a long way; but midway through the second day out from the border crossing, the main road diverged into three branches, one heading west, one south, and one southeast. Joe looked at Marge quizzically. "Which one?"

She didn't hesitate. "None of them. We go due east now. That way." She pointed.

He looked in the indicated direction and could make out a not-very-worn dirt path that went out over the meadows and toward a wild forested area far to the east. "You sure?"

She nodded. "Forget the maps and road markers now. I can—well, I can *feel* it. It's kind of like a—magnet, is the best way I can say it."

He shrugged, and they set off on the primitive path.

And yet it wasn't so much a magnet as a presence, she decided. There was something there, something warm and alive, something that she could feel with every step now. It was an odd, indescribable feeling, and she could only hope that Joe would trust her.

Joe really had no choice. He let her take the lead, although the path was still clear enough to follow, and just relaxed.

They camped well into the forest that night. It was a pretty peaceful place, but he didn't want to take any chances; he suggested they alternate sleeping, with Marge going first. She tried it, but soon was back by the small fire.

"Trouble?"

She shrugged. "I don't know. We're very close now, Joe. We'll reach it easily tomorrow with time to spare."

"Cold feet, huh?"

"Something like that. I mean, I don't know what to say, what to do. I really don't know what's going to happen to me—what I'm really turning into, if that makes any sense."

He nodded sympathetically. "Yeah, I think I know. It's been pretty rough on you here."

"Oh, no, not really. Remember, I was a total washout back home. I was on my way to kill myself when I ran into you, you know. No, it's the other side. I've been *happy* here. For the first time in my life since I was a kid, I've been happy. I really like this place. And now, somehow, I'm afraid again. This—whatever it is—is forever. What if I don't like it? Or what if *they* don't accept *me?* What if I change into somebody you and all my other friends don't like or can't relate to? It seems that every time I have something right, it goes wrong."

He squeezed her hand tightly. "Don't worry so much. You'll have a real home here, with people you can call your own. None of the people of faërie I've met are any kind of holy terrors if you just treat 'em as people. Besides, Ruddygore said we were gonna be a super team, and he wouldn't say that if we couldn't stand each other, right?"

She smiled and kissed him lightly. "You're right, I guess. But I can't help worrying."

She was able to go to sleep after that, but she started him thinking in odd directions, some of which he didn't like. He wished for one thing that he were as confident of this changeling thing as he made out. He really cared for her, and that made her special in more than one way. He also valued her because she was his only link back to Earth, to the world in which both of them had been born and raised. Oh, sure, Ruddygore went back and forth all the time, but he was still a man of this world, not of the other, and he was hardly around all the time. Joe needed Marge, he knew—she was the one link he had to all that had been his world. He couldn't help but fear that she would have no such need of him—not after this.

No matter how he sliced it, after tomorrow she *would* be at least as much of this world as of their native land, and she would have roots, family, tribe, grounding. Not he. Even here he was the outcast, the outsider, the barbarian from a far-off land that didn't really exist.

The Kauri would be her new roots, her anchor, he knew— but she was the only family he'd ever have here. He wasn't like her. He'd never read all those books, dreamed those fancy romantic dreams, the way she had. He hadn't wanted to be here and had never felt at home here.

He wondered what all those trainees who watched him knock their arrows from the air and all those people who cleared the streets for him would say if they knew that this big, hulking brute of a muscleman was scared to death.

CHAPTER 4

BECOMING AN ELEMENTAL SUBJECT

Faërie seats of power may not be invaded by mortals without permission without exacting severe penalties.
—Rules, XIX, 106(c)

THEY REACHED THE BIRD'S BREATH, LITTLE MORE THAN A creek at this point, about midday. The air was hot and thick and insects buzzed around them in constant frenzy, setting up a cacophony of buzzing sounds. Marge halted and turned to Joe.

"This is where we split up," she said a bit nervously. "Make camp somewhere along here and wait for me." She turned back and pointed to a dark grove of trees beyond the small river. "That is the start of Mohr Jerahl."

He stared at it, but could tell no difference between the forest they'd been traveling through and the one on the other side. Still, he knew, there was little to distinguish the Glen Dinig from the surrounding countryside, either, and it was certainly a real and, for him, deadly place. "I still think I should go with you, at least as far as I can," he argued. "You don't know what's there, really."

"No. Absolutely not. First of all, you remember Ruddygore's warning. That's magic over there, Joe—a place of enchantment."

"If you remember, Irving and I have done pretty good against enchanted places and things. As for Ruddygore—he's not my father, whom I never listened to, anyway. I paid my dues to the fat man; he don't own me any more—just rents me for a bit."

She grew alarmed at his stubbornness, remembering Huspeth's very dark scenario. As best she could, she tried to explain the position to him. It was possibly true that Joe could survive, even triumph, but not without dire cost to her. "For *my* sake, Joe, stay here. Promise me. Give me your solemn word."

He sensed her genuine concern and, although he put up something of a front, he knew from that point on that he'd lost the argument. He glanced around. "Okay. Two days from right now—then I'm coming in looking for you."

"Two days! Joe, I don't know how long this is going to take! It could be going just right and then you'll come in and screw it all up!"

"Thanks for the confidence," he grumbled, "but two days is it."

She thought a moment. "How about this, then? If I'm delayed for any reason, I'll send a message somehow. One that could only come from me. Fair enough?"

He considered it. "Maybe. But remember, we've got a hard way to go to that wizard's convention yet. We'll see. That's the best I'll do for now."

And, in fact, it was the most she could get out of him, and she decided it would have to do. She realized that his attitude was entirely based on his concern for her safety, and that made it really impossible to go further. She got down from her horse and turned toward Mohr Jerahl.

"You gonna walk?" he called out, surprised.

She nodded. "I think it's best. I *know* it is, somehow."

"No weapons or food or stuff?"

"No, Joe. This one I walk into clean. You take care of yourself. You're going to be a sitting duck out here for a couple of days, and this kind of place holds who knows what kind of dangers."

"I can take care of myself," he assured her. "Just make sure *you* can."

She blew him a kiss. "I think I'll be pretty safe once I get across the creek." With that, she walked down to the riverbank and into the water. It wasn't very deep; even at the center, it did not come up beyond her waist, and the current was weak and lazy. She had no trouble making the other side. Emerging, she turned and saw him, still there atop his horse, staring after her. She waved at him, then turned and disappeared into the forest.

* * *

That feeling that she'd had since they diverged from the road less than two days earlier was tremendous now. She'd felt its overpowering influence from the first time she'd looked at the place across the river, but now she was in it and the feeling was all around her. For the first time she sensed, at least, what the nature of that strange sensation was.

It was raw power.

Mohr Jerahl was in some ways an analog to the Glen Dinig; it was a place of enormous magical power, power that could be seen, touched, felt. But while Huspeth's small realm was under tight and absolute control, Mohr Jerahl was not. The term "raw power" was literally correct—this was no tame and obedient magic, neatly tied into complex spells, but a force of supernature, an unbridled power that just *was*. It was incredibly strong, yet it had a single defined center, a locus, that she instinctively headed for. There, at that central radiation point, would be Kauri. There she would meet what she must become.

It seemed to take forever to get anywhere in the forest, and the sun was passing out of sight and influence by the time she was sure of any real progress, yet she felt neither hunger nor thirst, nor did she feel the least bit tired. The tremendous magical radiation went through her, tickling and even slightly burning not only her skin but *inside* as well, yet she knew it could not harm her. How she knew this, she wasn't sure, but it was a certainty that she was feeding off the radiation, drawing strength and whatever else she needed from it.

Darkness fell, in a land where the trees were so thick they would block the sun in daylight, yet she had no problem with that darkness. In fact, fed by the radiation she could now see as a bright, bluish glow that illuminated everything and bathed it in its eerie light, she saw every object distinctly and without shadow. In many ways it was a clearer vision than normal sight, although a more colorless one.

She knew that, somehow, she'd been delayed until darkness fell, that the magic was strongest then, and that the Kauri, as was the case with a majority of the fairy races, were more in their element.

She heard all sorts of stirrings in the trees; once or twice, she thought she caught girlish laughter from above and sensed the sudden shift of mysterious bodies, but they kept too far away for her to tell who or what was making the sounds. She was beginning to regret leaving her bronze dagger and bow back at the river, though.

And then, with a suddenness that startled her, she broke through the trees and saw the locus of Kauri power.

The clearing was enormous, composed entirely of some gray lava base that seemed permanently rippled, as if built of a frozen river rather than a hard-rock base. It rose slightly for perhaps a half mile, forming a cone-shaped structure, and at its center was a perfectly circular opening through which bubbling, roaring sounds and heavy, sulfurous smoke billowed upward. The crater was not only the source of the radiation but also a source of tremendous heat, and she knew that, somehow, this was a perfect miniature volcano.

Again she heard the girlish laughter, this time behind her, and she whirled and faced five of the Kauri.

The thing that struck her first was that they were absolutely identical; some fantastic, fairy quintuplets. Their basic form was human; all were female and might be called by many voluptuous. Their rounded, cute, sexy faces were marked with large, sensuous lips and huge, playful brown eyes. Yet the faces had a quality that could only be described as elfin, and through short-cropped hair that was a steely blue-black color, slightly more blue than black, protruded two cute, pointed elfin ears.

They were under five feet tall, but not by more than an inch or so. Their skins were a deep orange in color. Looking closer, though, she could see some familiar yet quite nonhuman differences. Their fingers were abnormally long and ended in clawlike nails; their toes, too, were a bit longer and more regular than human toes and ended in similar sharp, pointed, animallike nails, pointing slightly downward. Between digits on both hands and feet was the webbing that had first appeared on Marge back in the mountain town of Kidim. But their most distinctive feature was their wings, sinister and batlike, yet somehow less threatening in deep crimson than in demonic black, although, she saw, the crimson was only on one side; the back of the wings was a deep purple color. The wings were not merely attached to their backs but seemed to be woven into and between their arms and their bodies, so that, when an arm moved out or forward, the membranes fluttered and acted something like a natural cape. The Kauri just stood there, watching her, not so much with hostility, but with a sort of playful puzzlement on their interminably cute faces, and she sensed she was supposed to make the first move.

"Are you the Kauri?" she asked.

"We better be, dearie, to be here," one of them responded in a voice that was soft and somewhat childlike. "So what's it to you?"

"I was told to come here," she explained lamely, trying to decide how best to put all this. First meetings were always a problem for her. "The sorcerer Ruddygore of Terindell said I was a Kauri changeling. I am supposed to complete the change here, rather than let it go in little bits and pieces."

"A changeling!" another exclaimed, sounding exactly like the first. "Well, I'll be damned! Been a long time since we had one of *them* for a Kauri!"

Suddenly there was a tremendous babble of voices—or, as it seemed, the same voice repeated hundreds, perhaps thousands, of times, all at once, and saying different things. She whirled around and saw that the crater was filled with Kauri, all looking and sounding the same and all talking at one another. There was nothing to do but let them run down; nobody could ever get them quiet any other way.

One of the original five broke away from a conversation and came over to her. "Well, I sure hope you *are* a Kauri changeling," she almost shouted over the din.

Marge frowned. "Why's that?"

The Kauri took her hand and led her back toward the wood for a bit. The grip was feather-light, and the fairy creature moved as if she had almost no weight at all. She still had the moves, though—they *all* did. If there were fairy hookers, this was their convention.

The combination of forest and the slowly diminishing din, as Kauri ran out of things to say, helped a bit.

"Whew! It's always like that around here," the fairy woman told her. "I'm Aislee, by the way."

"I'm Marge," she responded, glad to find some kind of friend. "This is all pretty new to me, so thanks."

"Oh, no problem. You got to learn how to cope around here, anyway. I was *born* around here and it still drives me nuts sometimes."

"I'm afraid I don't know enough even to comment on that. In fact, you five were the first Kauri I'd ever seen."

"Yeah? Well, I guess that's natural. Most of us stay around here or in the Firehills region and east. It's kinda the pledge, y'know; keeps us pretty bored most of the time."

"The pledge?"

Aislee nodded. "Yeah. You know—we won't do to others if they don't do to us, that kind of thing. They're scared of us and we're scared of them, so we take it easy."

"You mean nobody ever goes far from Mohr Jerahl?"

"Oh, some go a long way. We're always in demand, y'know. Conventions, banquets, troop entertainment, that sort of thing. But it's strictly temporary and real limited, y'know."

No, Marge *didn't* know, but in fits and starts she began to get a picture of just who and what the Kauri were.

The Kauri flew, of course, like many other fairy folk, and were very light and hollow-boned. Still, they were tough—their skin was covered with a substance that had the feeling and texture of felt, while their wings were soft and satiny. This covering protected them from almost everything—it was waterproof, even fireproof, and it somehow acted like a major shock absorber. The Kauri were also extremely fluid in internal construction, so they could bear almost crushing weights without problem—yet they themselves were so light that they had trouble staying grounded in a strong breeze.

While hard to damage or kill—except with iron, of course—they were by nature quite passive and found it impossible to cause permanent injury, let alone to kill anyone or anything.

Although without any magic powers or spells themselves, they were controlled empaths in both directions. The emotions of any human were an open book to them, and they could instantly tell fear, love, sincerity, or falsehood. This had its drawbacks—sorrow would flood into them and they would find themselves crying uncontrollably; hilarity or joy around them would make them so manic they'd be higher than kites. They could, however, project desired feelings to others—humans, certainly, but also many of the fairy folk, particularly the most dangerous. It could be conscious, especially in a one-on-one situation, but it could also be instinctive. If a threat were perceived—and it usually could be from the empathic input—then they became impossible to harm or kill. The more intense the negative emotion, the more the counter was radiated.

As Marge and Aislee talked, a couple of other Kauri found them and joined in, like excited schoolgirls.

It was obvious that the Kauri had no self-control over their emotions whatsoever. Emotional seven-year-olds, Marge decided, with the brains and physiques of very adult women.

Naturally, they were in great demand as courtesans, exotic dancers, and everything else that adult physique implied. They could and did mate with practically any male of any species, human, fairy, or animal, and the occasional issue of such matings was an unpredictable hybrid in half the cases, or, of course, a Kauri in the other half. All Kauri were absolutely identical, it seemed, because all descended from an initial mother Kauri back at the start of the world. The laws of genetics often went wild in the magical Kauri world. The Kauri, at least, believed that many of the hybrid races of their world were their children—the centaur, the satyr, the medusae, and just about all other hybrid forms. Changelings, too—those born of one race who turned into another, such as Marge—were their doing, although it was extremely rare that a changeling would become a Kauri.

Marge sat down and relaxed with them, not sure if it was the fairy empathic powers that made her feel at ease or that it seemed she was back with a group of barely post-pubescent girlfriends in junior high school, but not really caring, either. They giggled, they played, and they seemed incapable of staying on a single train of thought for any length of time; but as the hours passed, she did get most of the information she wanted.

In many ways, each of the fairy races embodied some basic, elemental force of nature, and it seemed that these elf-nymphs represented a curious blend of childlike enthusiasm and raw sexuality.

They had no government, no ruling class or council. They could never have gotten organized enough for that, nor could any of them for long follow another's lead. Their lives, in the main, seemed the classic fairy ideal—they awoke, they played, they sang, they danced, they spent all the time having childish fun. Occasionally an emissary from some far-off place would appear at a clearly defined "gate" to Mohr Jerahl and make them a proposition. In exchange for their limited services at some great occasion or function, they would get—well, nice things. Their wing structure precluded clothing, but they loved jewels and jewelry—the finer crafted and the prettier the better. New songs, dances, games, toys, and puzzles for the whole tribe were also highly prized. There was no order or system— whoever happened to be around and felt like going for whatever offering was tendered just went.

Although they had no active powers of their own—save projecting emotion, and that was best done one-on-one—their passivity was no problem in a violent and magical world. Without their knowing how, any spell or physical overpowering was somehow countered. They *absorbed* the strength, whether physical, mental, or magical, from the one trying it on them and retained its power for some time—from a few hours to a day or more. They had no idea of the nature of any of their attributes; they were too elemental to have a science. They had not reached their current point through evolution—they had always been as they were now and would always be so—and, therefore, had no interest in the matter. Marge began to realize what Huspeth had meant by saying she must put reason and logic aside and do things instinctively, unthinkingly.

A top-grade sorcerer, of course, could negate their powers, since the very nature of long studies in sorcery was the scientific investigation of magic and its application. Ruddygore knew how the Kauri's incredible defenses worked and so he could methodically prepare a counter to them—but few others could, and only the best would block all the magical loopholes.

Still, the Kauri were as much feared as prized. If they wanted, they could overload a man's emotional centers so much that they could turn him into a virtual love slave, sapping all self-control and free will. At the same time, that strength or power taken from someone was in a way vampiric; the one from whom it was taken lost it, perhaps for good.

There was danger outside, too, even for such as these. Their power was strong only against or with males; with women they had, at best, a localized and temporary effect. The emotional projection still worked, but little else, and that meant that women, particularly those skilled in magic, could harm them.

Marge began to see at least part of Ruddygore's thinking,

particularly when she considered only the sorcerer's interests. And why consider more, for that matter? After all, Joe and she had both been very close to death back home and, no matter how much they might resent the sorcerer's machinations concerning them, it was, at least so far, much better than the alternative.

As a team, they had what Ruddygore would be interested in most. As a passive shield, she could protect against much of the magic of this world they were likely to encounter; Joe could certainly handle the rest of the problems. What concerned her was just how much of what was truly her would survive in that partnership.

She was still full of questions, though. "If you all look identical, then how do you tell each other apart?" she wanted know.

They laughed at the question. "It's easy. You just *know*, that's all," one answered.

You just know, *that's all...*

The basic schism between human and fairy.

"But come," Aislee—at least Marge thought it was Aislee—said to her. "We can solve this a lot easier by making you totally one of us." They all got up, and the Kauri added, "Uh, you are *sure* you're Kauri, aren't you?"

Marge frowned. "As far as I know. At least, that's what the sorcerer told me, and he should know. You should, too, if you can read me as you say."

"Oh, yeah, we can tell *you* believe it, but not whether it's so. There's only one way to find out; and if your wizard slipped up, it will be real trouble."

"How do we—do it?"

"The last mortal part of you has to be taken off, of course. Come on—this should be interesting."

Marge didn't like the tone or the implication here, realizing that to these creatures she was a game, a diversion, a bit of fun and no more.

The crowd of Kauri was still out there, but now they sensed that the big moment had come and lapsed into near-total silence. They were the spectators in the coliseum now, waiting to see the show.

Aislee and the others led her up the gentle cone to the very rim of the crater. The heat and smoke coming from the mass bubbling not far below were secondary to the tremendous, blinding magical radiation at this point.

"Well," one of the Kauri prompted, "go ahead. Jump in."

She felt doubt and panic flood into her. "You mean—jump in *there*?"

"That's the only way to do it."

She swallowed hard, and her mind swirled with tremendous doubts. What if they were testing her? What if they were trying to get rid of her? What if this were some grisly practical joke of bored fairies?

Behind her, she could hear the crowd shouting, "Jump! Jump! Go on! Jump!" It sounded like some ghoulish cheerleader squad for a virgin sacrificial ceremony and—uh-oh. She'd forgotten that *she* was biologically virgin now. Virgin plus volcano equals sacrifice . . .

"Jump in, jump in! Rah! Rah! Rah!"

She just stood there, petrified with fright, knowing she could not move a step in any direction, not even to run.

"Oh, the hell with it. This is getting boring," one of the Kauri next to her muttered. The next thing Marge knew, she felt a violent shove and she was falling, falling right into the boiling, bubbling magma . . .

There was a shock as she hit the red, bubbling mass that might have a temperature of perhaps two thousand degrees, and an all-encompassing but very brief pain, much like that which an electric shock would give.

And then she was floating, swimming, flying, suspended in the mass but no longer sensitive to it. There was no up, no down, no east, west, north, or south. There was, however, a presence. It was in there with her, all around her and coursing not only through the molten magma but right through her as well. She did not know what it was, but it was undeniably the locus, the source of the magic.

"Be at peace," came a powerful, all embracing, motherly voice in her head. She realized that no words had been spoken, since none could be, under these conditions; but the voice was so commanding, so authoritative, yet so friendly and reassuring that it could not be denied.

It was her long-dead mother's voice.

"Mother?" her mind shot out, trying to reach it.

"I am indeed the mother of the Kauri, of which you are almost one," the voice responded.

"Who? What . . . ?"

"You are troubled, child. The Kauri are not troubled, for were one to be troubled, the race would be troubled. To be troubled is for threats to person or the race, not otherwise. Mohr Jerahl is a place of peace, of art and dance and fun. The Kauri are the creatures of Mohr Jerahl, and so they must reflect its nature. Come to me in the fire, as all those who venture outside our homeland must, and let me ease your trouble. Relax and think not; come unto me and give me your mind."

The creature, whatever it was, hesitated a moment, as if waiting for her, but she did not, could not, yield to it.

"You hesitate. You close your mind to me. Why?"

"I—I'm afraid," she admitted. "A change in form is one thing, but I don't want to be not me any longer!"

"But you will always be you and no other," the voice of her mother soothed. "You come from the world of the Creator. He alone fashioned your soul and its nature, and He alone can refashion it. But the shape of that soul is Kauri, deep down. Your sorcerer knew this when he directed your destiny so."

"But the Kauri are of this world, not mine!" she protested. "How can I have a Kauri soul?"

"Child, the soul is insubstantial, mystical. It exists on the magical plane and on no other. The fairies—all of faërie— are souls bared, souls distilled, unencumbered by human form and fears, for they exist only in the world of supernature. They exist on the plane of pre-creation, before the universes were formed, at the level of elemental, basic magic. Humanity was made by imposing natural law on the soul; natural form, pain, toil, suffering, mortality—these came later, when the Rebels caused the violation of Eden's perfection. All that is now taken from you. All that was mortal and natural in you was borne away when you entered here. The nature of the soul determines the nature of the person.

"The fairies exist in all humankind and are not bound by any world or its rules, only by those rules imposed upon the race by the Creator. We were the models and the overseers in the grand design. Humans who go against their own natures— as many do for a variety of reasons, not all under their control— suffer all the more for it. For, you see, that is the true curse laid upon man after Eden—that he will turn his back on supernature and will fight his own soul. In such a way do misery, unhappiness, and evil breed."

She was startled by this information and its implications. "What you are saying, then, is that we are *all* changelings."

"Yes, all. But when death comes to the mortal and frees the soul, and that soul is purged of its sin, it lives apart from us, within the Sea of Dreams, in a world that is wholly supernatural. Fairies, being of the world, do not have an afterlife. The price is paid—we may achieve the true balance of our natures only by remaining alive until the end of all time, when Creation shall be undone. That is our curse for being lax and allowing the chief Rebel to slip unnoticed into Eden. That is the curse you now share, a fair exchange for shedding your mortality. But a cleansing is needed to make you truly of faërie and allow your full supernature to come out. To do that, you must surrender to me."

Marge understood now the logic of it all, understood the nature of the fairies and the soul as few had understood before her, yet she could not bring herself to yield. Most of her wanted what was offered, but there was still that corner of her that was afraid, that feared tampering with her mind as this world had tampered with her body.

"Or, to put it another way," the goddess of the volcano added, "if you don't yield to me, you'll swim around in this hot muck, frying your little buns off for all eternity." For emphasis, the pain began, and slowly increased.

A Kauri goddess might be somewhat intellectual, but she was the mold of the race and not much more patient than her children. The vision, the sensation, of the classical Hell of Marge's Christian upbringing was a really persuasive argument. As the pain continued to rise, she could stand it no longer. "All right! Take me!" her mind screamed.

The pain ceased, and the entity, whatever it was, assumed complete control. Marge was aware and fully conscious, yet not in control of even her own thoughts. Her memory was triggered and read out in reverse order, every moment of her past flowing from her and into the creature. Her mind was incapable of digesting the minutiae that were stored in her own brain, and she tended to seize upon and partially relive only brief scenes of major events.

She was outside the volcano. She was walking through the forest. She was leaving Joe. She was at the entry station, now back at Terindell, then in the Glen Dinig. In fits and starts and in a sort of backward review, she relived the great battle, the Land of the Djinn, the fight for the Lamp, and the battle at the pass. Backward, ever backward.

She crossed the Sea of Dreams once more and found herself totally shorn of hope, direction, or self-interest, walking along a lonely west Texas road.

His face was a furious red with anger, hatred, and frustration, and he was beating her repeatedly, all the while shouting, "What the hell good are you? Can't even make a damned kid in this Godforsaken hellhole!"

"I, Marge, take thee, Roger . . ."

"I'm sorry, but less kids means less teachers and lower budgets. You know how it is. Now if you'd been in math or science . . ."

She stood on the steps outside the administration building, still in cap and gown, holding the diploma up to the bright, blue Texas sky. "See, Momma? I did it!"

"Mommy! Guess what! Tommy Woodard asked me to the prom! Tommy Woodard!"

It was blood! She was bleeding from *there*! Oh, God! *"Mommy!"*

"There, there! It's just a skinned knee. Mommy'll put a little stuff on it and kiss it and make it all better . . ."

She didn't like playing hide-and-seek when there were *boys* playing. They always cheated or ganged up on the girls. "Eight . . . nine . . . ten! Ready or not, here I come!" She could hear the squeals of laughter and see just a corner of somebody's foot behind the bush. She ran for the hider, who, suddenly knowing she'd been spotted, broke from her hiding place and started heading for the tree base. Marge felt a thrill and whirled, trying to beat Mary Frances to the . . .

Sufficient, a voice said from somewhere. *Freeze*.

Quickly, methodically, she began to come back toward the present. All of the events were there, all the traumas, all the heartbreak, but it wasn't quite the same as it had been. It was real, it was hers, it was even totally comprehensible, but somehow it just didn't matter so much any more. The dark times that had formed her were there, all right, but the good times, the happy times, the fun times stood out. She could reach out and touch any of those dark spots at any time, but, left alone, it was the good times, the fun times, the *innocent* times that seemed somehow forward, filling in the empty spaces.

The goddess of the Kauri had in fact been truthful, honest, and correct. Marge *understood* now, understood the nature of the Kauri and the reason for it. She had recaptured it, with the goddess' help—that essence of childhood that adults could fondly and wistfully remember but never really reexperience, except vicariously through watching their own children. She realized, with a tremendous surge of excitement, that she had indeed buried the horrors of her past, even though she was still and would always be shaped by them. She was new, reborn, free . . .

Free!

She burst out of the top of the volcano and flew up, up into the night, with a feeling of incredible energy and joy. She spread out her arms and let her wings catch the air currents she could easily see. Not even thinking about what she was doing, or how, she did whirls and flips and laughed and giggled at everything like a drunken flyer on a real tear. The world looked subtly different, and very, very beautiful, with every single object, every single substance, in clear focus as far as she could see; yet, unlike her earlier experience, it was also a riot of colors. She began to shift through all the levels she could see, and the world changed dramatically each time.

The colors, the rainbow of colors—*why, the whole world was magic!* She saw below, above, all around, the world of faërie, and it was more beautiful than she could have ever dreamed.

And now others were joining her, playing, looping around in the air. She knew them without having to think at all; her sisters, the Kauri, each radiating a subtly different magical pattern and emotional register. They greeted her, welcomed her, by drawing from her the tremendous feelings she was having, and they played, chased, showed off, and generally had a really good time themselves.

They soared together beneath the stars, protected in the glow of the Earth Mother's radiant embrace, skimming the treetops, then rising upward, ever upward, until the whole magical land was spread out before and beneath them. With no cares, no worries, they soared like superchildren, everything new, everything a wonder.

She saw the treasures of the Kauri and plucked a beautiful, gem-encrusted tiara out of the pile and crowned herself queen of the air; others scrambled for even grander headwear and challenged her reign, laughing and giggling all the while, flittering about and snatching crowns, tiaras, and all sorts of other regal stuff from one another. There were forty or fifty queens crowned that night, all self-anointed—and the same number dethroned by playful, giggling subjects with ambitions of their own.

There were toys and games and maddening puzzles, and all sorts of fun things. And never once was there hatred, malice, anger, or fear.

They plucked ripe fruits from trees and bushes and ate them, often throwing them at one another, and walked on the waters of a deep volcanic lake without sinking in. And they were *all* queens of this mystical, magical, happy place.

When the sun came up, turning the land a new set of colors, they went to the trees, high up and far beyond any ground-dwelling things, and settled into happy, dreaming sleep. For Marge, it was a sleep filled with the happy experiences of childhood and the best and deepest sleep she had had in many long years.

The next night was more of the same. There was total acceptance of her by the native Kauri; like her, they could see and feel inside one another, and she was one with them. This time they ranged far, almost to the Firehills, great ridges in the earth that seemed to hiss and glow from long fissures in their sides—mountains that were at once solid and yet continually on fire.

She did wonder that they never ventured forth by day, but she was told that the brightness of the sun hurt their eyes and could actually blind them for a while. Paradoxically, the Kauri were attracted to light, or, at least, to open flames, and great fires could have a near-hypnotic effect on them. While it could not harm them, it induced an odd sort of catatonia of mind and body, and this, in turn, left them defenseless. It was a hard thing to explain, being more related to brightness than to the size or shape of the light; but, they assured her, she would know the first time she left the protection of Mohr Jerahl. That comment for the first time brought her thoughts back to Joe, who would be waiting for her only this one more night. Tomorrow he would enter Mohr Jerahl in search of her, committing the ultimate sacrilege of bringing iron into the enchanted land.

"I must go to him while the dark still holds," she told them with much sadness and regret. "He must not be allowed to enter here."

"But you'll get rid of him and return soon enough," Coasu, one of her new friends, responded.

She thought about it. "No, not right away. I think I must leave for a time, my sisters. Something pulls me that I can not explain, something that is still important. I am Kauri for a reason, and that reason pulls me away, but only for a time."

They could read her sincerity, but they could not understand it. "Then we will go with you, too," Coasu said. "Aislee, me, and perhaps others. If this matter is so important, then if one Kauri can help, perhaps many can help more. You are sad to leave, and one must never leave Mohr Jerahl in sadness."

Her deep affection for them and their offer reached out to them, so that no words were needed, but she shook her head. "No, I am sad to leave only because I love this place and you all so much. But once I looked in the face of Hell, and I know that somehow I must help defeat it here and now. They all knew this—the Earth Mother, Ruddygore, Huspeth."

"This is getting heavy," Aislee noted, grumbling. "We have nothing to do with that kind of thing."

The thought came, unbidden and from elsewhere, into Marge's mind. "The Earth Mother knows. We have no dealings with the affairs of politics, but this is beyond that. All of faërie is involved in this. Ask the Earth Mother."

They knew instantly that it was not Marge who had spoken, and they became quiet and almost reverential. Marge smiled and kissed them all in turn. "I'll be back," she promised them. "I am a Kauri now, and a Kauri forever, until the end of time. Besides," she added, part seriously, "it could be a lot of fun being a Kauri out there." She laughed. "And I'll bring back a new present and let you drool all over it."

That broke the mood. "Yes! Something really good!" one

cried in anticipation. "Make them pay well for your services! It is a Kauri tradition."

Visions of tacky plaster sculptures came into her mind and gave her a mild case of the giggles, but, she promised herself, there would be none of *that* here.

It was an emotional farewell, a party of sorts that got enough out of hand in the Kauri's usual anarchistic way so that she finally just slipped out on it and flew to the Bird's Breath.

Crossing the little creek and leaving Mohr Jerahl gave her a cold, eerie feeling—a feeling of being somehow cut off from a warm and friendly glow.

She flew down the river a bit, until she saw Joe's camp. Its fire was just a few glowing embers, and both the big man and the horses were fast asleep. It was easy to find him, though— the iron in the sword, deadly to her even in the early stages of her transformation here, was now a tangible and terrible, cold darkness that she would simply have to adjust to. She knew that it gave these sensations to all fairies, save only the dwarfs, whose special power it was to handle iron and its deadly magic, and in that alone was there some comfort. Although all iron threatened her, this was as close as she could come to "friendly iron," and she knew Joe had been well trained and was accustomed to shielding the fairies on his side from its power.

She flittered down near the fire, just across from him, with the unnatural silence that only a fairy could have, and stood there a moment, looking at the sleeping man.

The sword began to hum softly but irritatingly. She took a single step forward and the noise became a terrible, grating sound. In that same instant Joe rolled, grabbed the sword, and was on his feet, at the ready. As with all dwarf things, Irving was far more than a mere sword of iron alloy. Now, unsheathed, it seemed almost to burn her with a cold, deadly radiation all its own, a flow that ebbed and pulsed with the humming sound.

"Who are you?" the big man challenged menacingly.

"Put the sword away, Joe," she almost pleaded with him. "It's hurting me."

He made no move to do so. "How do you know my name?"

"It's Marge, Joe. This is the way I look now. All the Kauri look like this."

He frowned a moment. The creature was incredibly, voluptuously beautiful, but it was not reminiscent of Marge in any definitive physical feature. "Can you prove it? I've had some bad experience with good-looking nymphs and sprites that didn't mean me any good." He thought a moment. "What's the capital of Pennsylvania?"

"Oh, good grief." She sighed. "I don't know. Philadelphia?"

"I was thinking Philadelphia, but it's really Harrisburg," he snapped back. "You're just reading my mind!"

She could feel his anger and suspicion flowing out of him and into her, and it was an ugly feeling indeed. She could counter it, of course, even bring him down, but the empathic projection might not have much power over that damned sword, which had a mind of its own and could protect against some spells as well. Instead she countered, "Joe—what's the capital city of Missouri?"

He was startled. "Huh? St. Louis?" She shook her head. "Columbia? Kansas City?"

"Jefferson City," she told him. "See all that proves? But I'll describe every inch of every truck stop in Ozona, Texas, for you and even describe all the damned tacky sculptures I can remember being in Ruddygore's basement."

He relaxed, and so did the sword, as his face reflected an unthreatened but incredulous feeling. "Marge? Is it *really* you?"

She nodded. "Now put that damned pig-sticker away. Feed it a bone and tell it to be a good dog or something."

He sheathed the weapon, which lapsed back into silence, reading his conviction, but he still could hardly believe it. He walked over to her and examined her closely, dwelling, she noted, on some rather interesting parts. "Damn!" he swore. "This is like coming out of Ruddygore's lab, way back when, all over again. You're—smaller."

That was true enough. Not only was she the four-foot-ten that was the height of all adult Kauri, but her exaggerated shapes and curves gave her an even more elfin appearance.

"But I've grown my wings," she pointed out.

He cleared his throat. "Yeah—and other things, too."

"You called me a nymph, and that's right. In fact, we're the prototype for all nymphs. They say this is my true nature coming through." She chuckled. "No wonder I kind of fell into prostitution back in Texas for a while. But back there I had so many problems and hang-ups, they drove me crazy. Over here, like this, I'm free of all that."

He grinned at the implications of that. They had a long way to go, after all. That did, however, bring him back to the future. "We should be going in the morning. Ruddygore's convention is still a rough ride from here, and it's all paths rather than roads."

That brought her up short a bit. "That could be a problem," she told him. "I'm nocturnal. The sun kind of saps my strength, puts me to sleep."

He laughed and walked over to the packs, then rooted through them for a moment before coming up with an object. "That explains this, then. I didn't have much to do, so I decided to look at what Ruddygore had put in here. Among the things was this." He brought the object over and handed it to her.

It was a pair of sunglasses, a wraparound sort that hugged the face, with cupped lenses that blocked all light not coming through them, almost like goggles. She put them on and was not surprised to find that they were a perfect fit, even adjusted properly for her pointed, elfin ears and the new shape of her face. She took them off again and looked at them, then giggled. "See the printing down here on the frame?"

He shook his head. "It's too dark for me."

"It says, 'Made in Taiwan'!"

CHAPTER 5

A FEW MINOR OBSTACLES

It is best to avoid volcanoes whenever possible.
                                        —Rules, XXII, 196(c)

THE GLASSES PROVED SUFFICIENT FOR MARGE TO ENDURE DAY-light, but did nothing to restore needed sleep. She fitted on the horse fine, though, despite the membranous wings and her smaller size, and found no trouble keeping an almost effortless balance. Finally she just told Joe that she had to nod out, and he told her to do so. Although the fearsome Firehills loomed in front of them, they would not reach them until late in the day, and the land was pretty much a flat semidesert, requiring no real riding skills. Her horse was well trained, although Joe wished often for Posti, the gray mare who was really a transformed dirt farmer. Posti had returned safely to Terindell, but was not allowed to make this trip to Sachalin. Ruddygore had been more than worried about a transformed horse in the midst of a bunch of drunken sorcerers.

Things went smoothly for several hours. Joe was a little bored, but he'd made his living in the old days driving a truck, and this was a lot easier to handle than a fully loaded semi. He *did* wish now, as he had often wished, that saddles came with tape decks, but he compensated by singing his favorite old Ferlin Husky and Waylon Jennings tunes. He had a lousy voice, but it was always impossible to convince him of that fact in this world or the one from which he'd come; as he belted out tune after tune, he hardly took notice of the hordes of insects, small animals, and birds fleeing in all directions before him as if from a forest fire. As for Marge, when she was out, she was *out*, it seemed, which suited him just fine right now. He needed some time to think.

She definitely took some getting used to, he reflected. She'd been okay before; Ruddygore had given her a pretty good figure. But, particularly after that witch in the wood got hold of her, she'd been less of a looker and more like a female jock. This new Marge—or new, new Marge—was something else again. Small, petite, cute, sexy as all hell, and naked to boot. The batlike wings were so beautifully colored that they seemed more like some precious butterfly's than anything negative. She was definitely no longer human—no real person had ever been put together so absolutely perfectly, except maybe in some artist's dreams—but the old Marge personality and an incongruous trace of a Texas accent still came through.

Those wings, they were funny things, he decided. He'd seen her fly and knew that she just lifted off effortlessly, like Peter Pan or something, often hovering as if gravity didn't exist for her, and quite often without spreading those wings at all.

They weren't necessary for her to fly, that was for sure, and he wondered if they were just decorative or whether they had some different kind of function. They definitely made wearing clothes impossible, so her unnatural endowments were out there for the world to see. That, too, would take some getting used to. He wanted her, and he knew that any other man who was the least bit turned on by women would want her, too. He wasn't sure how he'd take that. He'd gone crazy during her whole celibacy period, but at least it had been the same for every other man she knew. Now, though—well, creatures weren't put together that way just for the hell of it. Every fairy he'd run into since being in Husaquahr had a particular role to play and was more or less designed for the part. It didn't take a lecture in fairy lore to tell him what the Kauri's obvious role in the supernatural scheme of things was.

In a sense, it made him feel even more alone, since he knew that there was now a gulf separating them forever. She was no longer human, nor could she be expected to be human again. The fairies always did what they had to do, what they were supposed to do, his teachers back at Terindell had assured him. While that made them somewhat predictable, it made Marge and him more than a world apart.

He continued to brood as they slowly approached the Firehills, alternately cursing Ruddygore for bringing him here and himself for feeling weaknesses inside himself he never really knew were there.

The Firehills looked more intimidating the closer he got to them. Less a mountain chain than a whole line of continuous small volcanoes, their tops were shrouded in white smoke, through which occasional flashes of fire were visible now. He was worried about that fire, and by the fact that there seemed no break as far as the eye could see in that solid, if fairly low, black wall. They had been following the now tiny Bird's Breath all the way, but soon it petered out into a not-very-wet marsh, while the path continued right toward the barrier ahead, with no pass in sight.

There were bushes and many odd-looking groves of trees, but now in the air there was the unmistakable smell of sulfur and the rotten-egg odor of hydrogen sulfide. The path led through brilliantly colored mud pots, some of which occasionally gurgled and bubbled and steamed their foul odors. Here and there were pools of very clear water, but he could see within the pools the discolorations from the settling out of minerals and the steam rising off their surfaces. Clearly the Bird's Breath had its origins in volcanic waters, and probably should have been named Dragon's Breath. It sure smelled like it, anyway.

Off in the distance, a geyser spouted a hundred feet or more into the air with a great rush and roar, and he stopped momentarily to watch it, then became acutely aware that there were a lot of geyser holes all around him. He sighed and pressed on, trying to reassure himself that it had been Ruddygore who had recommended this route. It didn't reassure him all that much, though, since Ruddygore had always been more certain to get them in trouble than out of it in the past.

The sun was low in the sky when, threading his way through a virtual mine field of volcanic manifestations, not to mention leading Marge's horse through it, he finally reached the base of the Firehills themselves. The horses were getting jumpy and acting uncomfortable from all the hissing, roaring, bubbling, smoke, and smells, but they didn't feel anything he didn't feel double. He decided that it was time Marge woke up, no matter how much beauty sleep she needed.

After finding that yelling and shaking her produced only a dreamy reaction and shifting, he finally got fed up and did some obscene and not-very-gentle things to her. She gave a big, dreamy smile and sighed; her fairy eyelashes fluttered a bit, and those great, sensuous eyes opened a crack. Under any other circumstances, he would have been delighted at the reaction, but the fear of being roasted alive had a tendency to drive all other impulses from his head.

"Marge! Wake up!" he screamed as the lids started to flutter back, and he reached over, cursing, and dropped the dark glasses back into place.

From Marge's vantage point, it was at first like being awakened from a pleasant sleep filled with erotic dreams to a disorienting confusion; but when the glasses slid down, she suddenly saw perfectly and sat bolt upright. "Wha—what's happened?" She looked up at the blackish cinder wall rising just ahead of them and the strange and violent landscape behind and grew instantly alert. "How'd we get *here*?"

"We rode," he responded sourly. "The map says there's a path over this damned hill. Not only do I not see one, but darkness is coming on, and I sure don't want to spend the night here!"

She glanced around. "Looks okay to me. Real pretty, in fact." She stopped short for a moment, realizing her reaction and comparing it with her memories. The Kauri were creatures of this earth-fire, but others were not. The land posed no problems for her, yet she could sense Joe's fear and discomfort with that empathic ability and she grew concerned for his safety. She looked up at the Firehills, so dark and featureless to their smoke-covered tops, and she could indeed see the flashes of molten fire through that smoke. It looked as if the whole ridge had a crack most of the way to the top, a crack running horizontally as far as the eye could see. "Let me have the map," she said, suddenly serious. She looked at it for a moment, frowning. "Let me go up and see what's what."

Without waiting for his reply, she rose effortlessly off the horse and into the air, moving straight up until she was out of sight. All he could do was wait there, calming the horses and starting to worry more and more.

She was gone for what seemed like ages; then, as silently as she'd left, she returned and quickly settled, standing daintily atop her horse's saddle. He could see by her expression that things were at least as bad as he'd imagined.

"Trouble," she told him needlessly. "I've been all over the area, and finally I figured out that we took a wrong turn. There's something of a break in the Firehills about twenty miles northwest of here, in a place where they're not very active, and there's an old path to it and across. There's a second branch of the Bird's Breath we were supposed to take and didn't."

He sighed and shrugged. "The thing was so small I never saw any junction. That damned map doesn't show which is which, so I followed what looked like the main course all the way here."

"Yeah, this *is* the source, but it's not the stream we were supposed to follow."

He looked toward the darkening, nightmare landscape to the northwest. "So I guess we'll have to detour."

She shook her head. "Uh-uh. You don't want to go through that mess, I'll tell you. This is a calm and stable part, I'll swear. You could never be sure of the ground elsewhere. It's a good twenty miles back to the fork, then another thirty to the pass. That's two, maybe three days, and I don't think the horses could take it. They're straining now."

He sighed. "So what else can I do? *You* can fly over and be safe and comfortable in bed tomorrow, but I sure as hell can't, and I'm not going to abandon the horses and supplies unless I have to. In this stuff, it would be their death warrant."

She nodded. "Then the only way is to go up. If we can cross over, the horses can get a good rest and watering on the other side." She paused. "You, too."

He wiped sweat from his forehead and looked up at the ominous hill. "So how do we do it?"

"First let me go up and check it out, see if there's any place we can cross. Then we'll risk my horse, with me leading. If the stuff underfoot holds her, it will hold you and yours."

He nodded. "Fair enough. But be careful—I don't want you melted down."

She laughed. "No danger of that. I can swim in the stuff, Joe. I *have* done it." She sighed and looked up at the swirling smoke. "Well—here goes!" And with that, she was gone, flying up the side and into the dense cloud at the top.

This time she was gone for only a couple of minutes, reappearing and setting down in front of her horse. "There's a way, I think," she told him, "but it's going to be a real hairy time for you and the horses. It's cinder most of the way, but I think it will hold. Up just into the smoke, though, the heat comes and goes. There are real nasty cracks all over the place." She pointed. "But in one spot, just over there, it seems fairly cool. It's been hot, though, and the heat has melted and remelted the stuff up there. The surface is almost like glass, and it's bound to be slippery. If you slip, it's pretty nasty on either side."

He looked up and swallowed hard. "Well, let's try it. *Anything* to get out of spending a night around here. I want to get it over with while there's still some light."

She nodded. Taking her horse's bridle, she stepped out onto the cinders. The horse resisted for a moment, then went along when she saw Marge being supported. Then the horse sank a bit into the cinders and ash and thrashed for a moment in confusion. It took precious minutes of Joe's daylight to calm her down and get her to go on.

Beyond, the cinders and ash were so dense that they gave

a surprisingly solid footing. Joe decided to lead his horse as well and was relieved to find that the hill felt, at least at the beginning, cool. He was, however, really beginning to wish he could trade his thick sandals for some even thicker boots. Asbestos boots, preferably.

The slope was rather gentle, and they took it at an angle, but it was slow going, and several times the material gave way, causing a momentary loss of footing. The horses were a big problem here, but, fortunately, none were sufficiently unbalanced by the occasional loss of footing to go tumbling over and back down.

Almost before Joe realized it, they were up to the smoke level and into it. The stuff stank and stung his eyes, causing even more problems with the horses, but the gases weren't very dense, once he was in them, and he could, at least, see ahead to the rear of Marge's horse. One thing for sure, though—the air was getting really hot, and he was sweating as he never had before. The volcanic surface, too, was getting pretty damned warm, although not bad enough to cause burning.

And then they hit the remelted area. He had imagined a smooth slope. In fact, it was rough and irregular, but it *was* shiny and slippery. Only the irregularities in its surface, almost like a frozen sea, allowed them any chance of footing. The stuff was *hot*, too—he felt as if he were in somebody's giant oven, and the bottom of his sandals were becoming very, very warm.

He soon saw why. Only ten feet or so on either side, the glassy surface dropped away to reveal a bubbling, hissing pit.

"I'm already well done!" he called out, coughing at the smoke and miserable from the intense heat. "How much farther is it?"

"Not far," she called back. "Just ten more minutes and we're home free!"

He groaned. He wasn't sure he or the horses could last that long. Right about then he was so miserable he didn't give a damn about the horses.

Suddenly Marge stopped, and he almost screamed out in agony. "*Now* what?"

"We're not alone up here," she responded, sounding worried. "I think you better draw Irving."

"He's so damned hot I can't even *touch* him," Joe called

back in disgust, but he did try the sword hilt—and found he wasn't kidding.

A series of small, dark shapes that looked like moving globs of obsidian formed around them on the peak. Joe couldn't get a good look at them, but Marge had no trouble at all. They did, in fact, appear to be made out of the same stuff as the melted material on which they all stood, but these creatures had definite form. They looked like funny little men—or, rather, statues of funny-looking little men, she decided, with short, stocky bodies, stubby limbs, and huge balloonlike noses. She couldn't help thinking of Grumpy from *Snow White* as she stared at them, and that certainly fitted their expressions and mean-looking gazes.

"Are you union or scabs?" the lead one rasped out in a stern, deep, gruff voice.

The question took her aback. "What do you mean? All we're trying to do is cross this mountain before the man with me and the horses die. *Please* let us past!"

"Are you union or scabs?" the creature repeated, unmoved.

"I am Kauri, and no scab!" she responded angrily. "You should know we have no need of a union!"

"Hah! Sexual exploitation without love or involvement and all for some cheap bauble," another of the creatures muttered. "And they're so dumb they don't even see how they're exploited."

Marge was acutely aware that time was running out, but she decided she had to play their game before they forgot their challenge and started debating among themselves. She'd had enough of that with the Kauri. "We're independent, yet collective! You know that! It's in our nature to be so! What sort of creatures are you that you don't know this?"

"We're kobolds, of course," the leader snapped.

"And we're on strike," another piped up. Joe felt his horse shudder, and began to feel that he was going to pass out on his feet, as well. He couldn't take much more of this.

"Aye," another kobold responded. "No more of them fairy rings and stuff until we get our contract!" The rest of them cheered.

"Your dispute is none of our affair," Marge argued pleadingly. "Please—this man will die if we're delayed even a few moments longer."

The leader looked over at Joe. "How do you stand on unions?"

Right then Joe was not feeling in a fraternal mood. He decided that, if he weren't about to die, he'd like to chop these bastards up into little pieces. He tried to snarl a reply, but only inhaled more of the acrid smoke and started coughing.

"He *is* a union man!" Marge told them, thinking furiously. "He's a Teamster."

The kobolds all looked at Joe critically. "Indeed? He don't look like no wagon driver to me," the leader noted. "Let's see your union card!"

At that moment, Joe's horse gave another great shudder and this time collapsed onto the hot surface. Joe whirled, then fell almost completely over the horse.

Marge yelled in a mixture of anger and panic, "In the name of the Earth Mother, help me get him off this place before he dies and quickly!"

"Religion is the opiate of the masses," one of the kobolds muttered, seemingly unmoved.

"Still," the leader mused, "we can't have a popular workingmen's movement—"

"And women," another added.

"—sullied at its great beginnings by a lack of compassion . . . Hmm . . . You! Imli! Zimlich! Grab his head and feet! You, Kauri—get going! We'll follow!"

Quickly the little men snapped to action. They were extremely strong and powerful, despite their small size. It took only two of them to lift Joe as if he weighed next to nothing, and four more actually lifted the horse and started after Marge and the others at what was close to a trot.

The obsidian bridge thinned appreciably as they went, and it was none too clear just how much longer it could support weight, but Marge's horse needed no urging. They were across, followed by the kobolds, in a few brief minutes. The weight of Joe's horse, though, was the final straw for the weakened bridge; just as they cleared the last of it, the entire center shuddered and collapsed with a rumble back into the volcano.

Joe awoke slowly in the darkness. He had been nearly comatose for several hours, often delirious and out of his head. He felt a cold compress being applied to his forehead and groaned, although it felt really good.

"Joe?" Marge asked tentatively, and he could hear the concern in her voice.

"Yeah," he croaked, his voice a dry rasp. "I *guess* I'm here."

Her joy at his coming out of it was such that not only was it evident in her physical reactions but also was radiated from her into him. It was a strange, warm sensation, unlike anything he'd experienced before, and he was deeply moved by it.

"How bad am I hurt?" he asked her, trying not to show what he was receiving. To his relief, the joyous emotions didn't change.

"You're not bad. A little scorched around the edges, but mostly it was dehydration. I've been feeding you water in small doses all night and getting compresses on you to bring the temperature down." She handed him a canteen, and he drank from it so greedily that she had to pull it away. "Uh-uh. I know something about dehydration, and you take water in slow doses," she cautioned. "Here. Take a little of this."

She handed him a small, crumbly ball of gray-white stuff, and he put it in his mouth, then almost sat up and spat. "That's *salt*! "

"Yeah. I got it from a salt lick. You need it to replace what you lost and help keep in the water."

He took a little more water, forcing himself to go slow, and did feel a bit better. "What about those bastards on the mountain?"

"They finally carried you most of the way here," she told him. "They're a very funny sort, but not bad really, once you get to know them."

"I know what *I'd* like to do to them," he grumbled.

"You couldn't if you wanted to. They're hard as rocks; and since they're related to the dwarfs, iron has little effect on them. Besides, they could melt your sword before it ever got to them, anyway."

"Where'd they get all that militant labor crap, though? They sounded more like *our* world than this one."

She nodded. "I wondered about that, too. Apparently there's been a movement going around to organize all the fairy workers, particularly the heavy-labor types like the kobolds. Nobody's sure where the idea came from, but it's going around and it's catching on with some like the kobolds. I think we better tell Ruddygore about it when we get there, though. There was one thing that really puzzles me."

"Huh? Only one?"

"Well, in this instance, anyway. One of the kobolds quoted Lenin, word for word. Lenin, Joe! Here! Where nobody ever heard of him!"

"You mean the Russians are invading?"

"No, of course not. Don't be silly. But somebody over here is bringing in ideas wholesale from over *there*, that's for sure. That bothers me, Joe. Remember that Ruddygore was worried about the plot to bring guns into Husaquahr?"

He nodded. "I remember. He had that rat Dacaro turned into a horse for suggesting it."

"Well, maybe—but it doesn't add up. Ideas are stronger even than guns, Joe, and somebody's importing ideas. Trouble is, who's the only guy we know who can make the trip between our world and this one any time he wants to?"

Joe, although still dizzy and weak, saw her point. The base of Ruddygore's power was his unique ability to travel between the worlds across the Sea of Dreams. They had never been really sure about the big sorcerer, and this compounded the doubts beyond measure. Ruddygore had fought the forces of Hell head on, yet he conjured up and used demons from the same place for his own purposes. He had fought the Dark Baron to a standoff, which had put him with the good guys, yet— had he fought for the same reasons as the rest of them? Or was he, in fact, taking on a rival challenger to his ambition of ruling the Council and the world? Certainly there were depths and layers to the sorcerer far beyond the funny fat man in opera clothes, depths and layers hidden by his wild personality.

"Let's let it rest for now," Joe suggested. "I'm tired, weak, and dizzy and I feel that I could sleep for a month. But let's remember that we're only doing some work for the old boy. He doesn't own us, and we'll work for ourselves first. Okay?"

She smiled at him. "Okay. You know, though, I—" She stopped in mid-thought, seeing that he had sunk back down into a more normal but very deep sleep. She got up and sighed, looking around. Let him sleep—he certainly needed it.

Joe slept through most of the next day, and it was early evening by the time he woke up. He was sore and stiff and still felt terribly dry, but he managed to go through a series of exercises without doing too badly.

His horse, he found, was dead and already stinking up the place. Marge or the kobolds had managed to get the saddlebags off, though, and he found some salted fish and the few cakes remaining of the hard, extra-sweet Terdieran candy. It wasn't enough, but it would have to do for now.

Marge's horse seemed to have come through the mountain crossing reasonably well, but he thought it best not to push her for another day or so. For now he'd repack the supplies into one load and let the horse carry that. He felt he could walk.

He found what he could of dry wood and, with the flint from the packs, made a small fire. There was a rustling in the trees behind him and he turned warily, but it was only Marge, who'd apparently been asleep up in the tree.

"How are you feeling?" she asked him, settling to the ground. "You look a mess!"

He chuckled. "Oh, I'm okay. I think we ought to press on, even though it's dark. You can see pretty well around here, and my night vision's not all that bad. I've been looking at the map and I figure it's about forty miles to the main road, if we can go due west, then maybe another fifty to the city. It's a long, tough walk, but I can make it."

She nodded. "The land's not bad. I went up and took a look at it. While it's all overland, no good roads or clear paths, it's mostly farmland and forest. Maybe we can hitch a ride when we hit the main road. They might have some kind of coach service or something. At least maybe we can buy another horse."

He frowned. "Do we have enough money left for that?"

"We do now. The kobolds decided it was their fault the horse died, so they gave us compensation." She went over to her own pack and rummaged through it for a moment, then reached in and pulled out a large, blackish rock. She seemed to have trouble with it, so he went over and took it from her, then almost dropped it. It was incredibly heavy.

"What *is* that?"

"Raw fairy gold," she told him. "Worth a hundred horses."

"Well, then, let's get started, now that we're on the same clock."

She laughed. "I think maybe you ought to go down to the

riverbank first—it's really a creek, but the water's fine. You're coal black from soot and ash."

He didn't feel much like it, but he went, and he *did* feel a little better after he'd immersed himself in the cool waters for a while. Coming back out, he checked over his clothing. The belt with his great sword had come through pretty much untouched, but the thick loincloth he'd been wearing was stained and singed. He had spare loincloths, so that was no trouble. The sandals, though, were his only pair, and they were cracked and worn almost beyond belief. He decided to go barefoot until he could buy some new ones.

His cowboy hat, much to his relief, was virtually unscathed, and he stuck it on his still wet hair, fastened the loincloth to the belt and strapped it on, checked to see that his sword was easily drawn, then nodded to himself. "Okay, faithful scout," he called to Marge. "Let's pack up and get on the trail."

"Ugh! Kemo sabe!" she responded playfully, and they went to work. Somehow they managed to get everything of importance onto the horse.

Using Marge's incredible night sight as the pathfinder, they had little trouble going for most of the night. By early morning, although it was impossible to tell for certain, they thought they had made at least fifteen miles. Joe let Marge sleep then on the horse, in front of the pack—since she seemed to weigh virtually nothing, the horse never noticed—and, taking frequent breaks for both his and the horse's benefit, he managed to add over five miles more before deciding to camp out in a small wooded grove.

Marge had been correct—the rough land had given way quickly to rolling farmland, with lots of herd animals idly grazing and, here and there, red-roofed farmhouses and fields of neatly planted wheat, corn, and other grains. He remembered somebody telling him once, after some big eruption down in South America or some place, that the reason people lived so close to volcanoes was that they only went off once in a lifetime, while the stuff they spewed out was the best farm dirt in the world, and he could see that, at least here, it was true.

Occasionally they stopped at a farmhouse along the way. But, while there were a few draft animals available, there were no horses. Finally giving up, they settled for a mule and loaded most of the supplies onto it, allowing Joe to ride Marge's horse, while she sat atop the packs on the mule. Now they would make better time.

He kept to his modified schedule, remaining awake through most of the night and into the morning, then joining Marge in sleep for the afternoon. He didn't really need as much sleep as she seemed to, and certainly this was the most peaceful and uneventful part of any of their journeys in Husaquahr.

They reached a farm road which, they were assured, led to the main highway, and it was in the early morning, with Marge barely dozing on the mule's back, that they met their first odd or unusual experience.

Joe stopped both animals, reached over, flipped down the dark glasses, and shook her awake.

"Hmph? Uh? Something the matter?" she muttered drowsily, still mostly asleep.

"I'm not really sure," he responded a bit cautiously, "but unless I've gone nuts, the road ahead is being blocked by a pig."

"So? Shoo it away."

"Uh—this pig is standing up like a human on its hind legs and is holding a cutlass, and I really don't like the mean glint in its eye."

CHAPTER 6

THE TROUBLE WITH MAGICIANS

Once a thief has committed himself or herself to that vocation by deed rather than by inclination, the thief is bound by that nature, regardless of consequences, and the Rules apply for life.
                                          —Rules, VIII, 41(b)

MARGE SUDDENLY SAT BOLT UPRIGHT AND STARED AHEAD OF them. Sure enough, there in the middle of the farm road was the biggest pig she'd ever seen, impossibly standing on its hind legs. The creature was easily Joe's height that way and must have weighed in at half a ton or more. Around its middle was a belt of some sort, its only clothing, and again impossibly, in its right foreleg it gripped a menacing-looking cutlass, apparently held mittenlike between the two parts of the unnaturally pliable split hooves.

"Halt! Stand and deliver!" the pig grunted menacingly.

Joe sat back and shook his head in wonder. Of all the sights in Husaquahr, this was certainly the most ridiculous he'd ever encountered. "So, pork chops, what do you need with money?" he called back.

"You think I *like* being like this?" the giant pig retorted. "It takes money to hire somebody good enough to break a spell like this."

Joe reached down and took hold of the hilt of his great sword, which hummed in anticipation of action. "Well, porker, it will take more than a pig with a pig-sticker to get anything from us. Stand aside and pick an easier victim."

"Your choice," the pig grunted back. "We take what you have from you now and you escape with your lives, or we pick over your bodies."

"We?"

There was a rustling from the underbrush on either side of the road ahead of them, and there appeared the most incredible trio of creatures they could imagine. One had the head and torso of a chimpanzee that blended into the body of a large snake. The second had a giant duck's head on a cow, udder and all, while the third looked like nothing so much as a human-sized catfish whose fishy body merged into that of a crab, complete with pincers. The monkey-thing had a broadsword, while the cow-thing held a bow. The fish-crab needed no other weapons than those pincers.

It was hard to take such monstrosities seriously. "What in *hell* happened to you?" Joe asked them, as Marge just gaped, open-mouthed.

"We were lying in wait for the Sachalin night coach, which was late as usual," the cow-duck quacked, "when we saw this guy coming, all alone, decked out as if he was king of the gem mines. It just got the better of us, I guess. The sight of all that wealth made us forget about the sorcerer's convention."

Joe nodded. "I see. And when you jumped him, he turned out to be somebody powerful and he zapped you. I must say he had a real sense of humor."

"Hilarious," the pig snorted. "Now that we've had our introductions, can we get back to business?"

Joe sighed and sat back a bit in the saddle, positioning himself. "Your bad luck continues, my odd thieves. As you can see, neither my fairy companion nor I have much to hide, and we are going to that same convention. I think, again, you'd better wait for safer game."

"Says you," the monkey-snake retorted. "You don't look like a sorcerer to me, and it's clear *her* magic powers, whatever they are, aren't for fighting." It chuckled. "Care to kiss me, honey?"

"It's true, we're not magicians, although we serve Ruddygore of Terindell, whose power will find you no matter where you are—and you look to be pretty easy to find in any case. But I *do* have one bit of magic, and it is of the most fatal kind." Joe paused and whispered so low he could only hope Marge could hear. "Be ready to charge when I do."

"Yeah? And what kind of magic's that?" the pig sneered.

Joe drew his sword, which began to hum even louder. Its blade seemed like something alive, pulsing a glowing bronze. "This," he told them, "is my very good friend Irving."

"Irving!" They all started laughing and sniggering. "What sort of name is *that* for a sword?"

The great sword's hum rose in pitch, as if it were angry and insulted by the remarks. The sword was, in fact, a semi-living thing of sorcery and iron, as only the dwarfs could make it.

"Irving doesn't like to be laughed at," Joe said quietly, then suddenly kicked his horse and sprang forward with a yell. The attack took the thieves by surprise, and he was on the pig before any of them could react, bringing Irving down on the cutlass and slicing through the thief's weapon as if it were butter. With his foot, he kicked out and sent the great pig sprawling on all fours.

The monkey-snake screamed in anger and launched itself at Joe, but he whirled around and this time was not so gentle, slicing off not only the sword but the arm that held it.

Needing no more of a cue, Marge charged on her mule right

through the mêlée, the mule jumping over the pig.

Joe reined in his horse, reared back, and looked at the other two creatures. The duck-cow had seen enough, dropped its bow and stepped back. The fish-crab, however, looked uncertain.

"Well, fish-face? Do we see what Irving does to those claws?"

"Uh—I think Irving is a real nice name for a sword," the fish-crab blurbled and backed off.

By this time, though, the pig had gotten back up behind Joe and now reached to unhorse the big man. Joe saw the move from the corner of his eye and pulled back on the reins, causing his horse to rear up on its hind legs. The pig, startled, fell backward and Joe came down and had his sword at the creature's throat before it could recover. "Be thankful I spare your lives," he told them. "If I meet the man who did this to you all, though, I'm going to buy him one hell of a good drink." With that, he whirled and rode off, following Marge, who'd stopped to watch about a hundred feet farther on. He passed her, slowed, and called out, "Well? What are you waiting for? Run for it before they get their wits back!" Then he was off.

She shrugged and kicked the mule, proceeding forward at a lesser pace.

They kept it up for almost a mile before Joe slowed to a walk and relaxed, allowing her to catch up. "Close one," he commented. "If they'd had any guts at all, they'd have had us, Irving or not."

She burst out laughing. "Somehow I don't think they'll *ever* have the guts. A pretty poor lot of robbers they are, even as monsters."

"Don't laugh too long, though. Remember, we're riding into a whole city just crammed with magicians, and most of 'em with the power won't think any more of us than they would of bugs."

"That's more your worry than mine, I think. I'm not really sure of my powers, but they seem made for a situation like that."

He cleared his throat. "Um, yeah. I've been meaning to ask you about that. I kind of assumed that your powers were in the, ah, lovemaking area."

She laughed. "Well, so I'm told. But that's only the lesser part. Supposedly, I can cancel out magic, even redirect it. I'm not sure how that works, and they weren't very good at explanations. It's just supposed to come when I need it, more or less."

He thought about that. "It makes sense, sort of. No great powers, like a lot of the fairy folk are supposed to have, but you'll have the power of whatever is used against you. Seems to me, they'll think twice about using you for a subject with that in mind."

She nodded. "If they know it. Kauri are better known for the other thing we do best, and I don't think it would work well against somebody like Ruddygore or the Dark Baron or even Huspeth. Still, most magicians aren't on that level, so I feel fairly safe. Truth is, I might not have much offense, but I'm a catalog of defenses, which is what I think Ruddygore had in mind. You're the offense and I'm the defense." She saw him frown at that. "What's wrong?"

"The old bastard hasn't done anything for us or to us, unless it's for some reason of his own. That magic Lamp business was big, but I don't think it's what he really brought us here for and made us what we are today, whatever that is. He's got something big planned for us, and I don't like the smell of it."

"You were the one who was bored," she reminded him. "I would think you'd like a real challenge."

"Challenge, yeah, but if that Lamp business was just practice, what's he *really* got in mind, and can we survive it?"

"You're unusually gloomy today! Huspeth said Ruddygore could see the direction of the future and planned accordingly, and those silly Rules said we were destined for at least three great adventures. Me, I'm not going to worry until the third one. Instead, I'm going back to sleep."

And she did.

The main road was wide and well traveled, as they expected one of the primary routes between the capital of Marquewood and the rest of the nation to be. Not only were there the usual wagon trains of goods going to and from Sachalin, but there was much traffic by individuals and small groups. Joe noticed that most of the people going away from the city looked rather ordinary—merchants, deliverymen, carpenters, all the people a capital would be expected to have. The traffic in the city's direction, though, beyond the commercial trade, seemed a different sort. Old women in black cloaks and hoods, small groups dressed in varicolored robes, and mysterious, mystical, even sinister folk were the rule.

Joe stopped at a roadside inn that was doing a large business and went inside. He was getting really tired and he figured that they would most likely have a room available at midday. Few landlords could resist the possibility of renting a room twice in one day, and he could use a bed after so long on the road.

The innkeeper, a big, burly man named Isinsson, didn't disappoint him, although a large eyebrow was raised at the sight of a groggy Marge wearing only dark glasses.

The price was reasonable, and Joe agreed readily to leave by eight in the evening. The room was small but adequate, and the double bed had a genuine feather mattress. They looked at it groggily, and Joe said, "Too bad. If we weren't both so dead, we could make real use of it, as the landlord thinks we will."

"Maybe we'll wake up early," she muttered and lay face down on the bed. Joe looked at the velvety wings sticking out from her back and, with a silent wish that she didn't toss and turn in her sleep, he secured the door and joined her in slumber.

When he awoke, to his great disappointment, it was after seven. Marge, he saw, had already arisen and gone from the room. For a second, he was worried about that, remembering the last time she'd disappeared from a hotel, but she hadn't been fairy then. He was pretty sure she could take care of herself. At least, he hoped so. The next dragon they met might not have a neurotic fear of fair maidens.

He packed up and went down to the main floor, which was fairly crowded with traffic. He didn't see Marge anyplace, but he decided not to get really worried until it was time to leave.

There were no empty tables; but with such a crowd, any empty chair belonged to the first person to sit in it, and he picked one with a small group of ordinary-looking people and ordered a heavy meal.

The people at the table were a little taken aback by the giant barbarian in their company, but they soon relaxed and warmed to him as the place filled with those more mysterious sorts and various kinds of not very pleasant-appearing fairies.

The squat, middle-aged man with a light beard and no mustache was Jeklir the grainer; the pudgy, middle-aged woman with him was his wife Asarak; and the teen-ager with them who looked every bit their progeny was their son Takgis.

"So you're from Sachalin," Joe noted. "On your way home from a trip?"

"Going on one, rather," Jeklir responded. "Time to visit the wife's relatives in Mobadan, at least for a week or two."

Joe's eyebrows raised a bit. "I would think this would be your busy season. I came through a good bit of farmland, and it looked as if the harvest was just coming up."

Jeklir's eyes darted nervously at the crowd around the inn. "Um, usually you would be right, barbarian, but ordinarily merchants would welcome a convention, not close up shop and leave as it dawned, if you get my meaning."

Joe did. "I guess the ones coming will be a pretty scary group, if what we've seen is any indication. My—partner— and I ran into some unlucky thieves this past morning who had run afoul of a sorcerer."

"You have no idea," Asarak assured him. "Every time this convention comes to a town, horrible things happen. Be just a trifle slow with the ale, and they turn you into who knows what; and the adepts—they're the worst, practicing spells on all the honest people with abandon. If you're going into the city, you watch your step, young man. They pour love potions in the punch, make people bark like dogs, and worse, just for the fun of it. The authorities can't do a thing, either."

"I'm surprised anybody will have them, if what you say is true," Joe noted between bites of the first really good, solid food in a week.

"What choice do they have?" Jeklir responded. "I mean, it's always sponsored by a master sorcerer, and if your local sorcerer decides to host it, what can anybody, even the government, do?"

Joe nodded sympathetically. "Yeah, I can see that. But you mean the whole town will be closed up?"

"Oh, no. First of all, the government can't close, so all those people have to stay and they have to have their services. The hotels can't close—they're booked. And the bars, restaurants, and shows will be open, of course. Many of the owners will keep a low profile and send their families out of town, but they hire a lot of farmers and contract for a lot of serf labor to be out front. There are always the ones who do so good they get special favors, too, and some of it can be put right after, particularly the stuff done by the adepts. That doesn't help the embarrassment and degradation while it's happening to you, though."

Joe understood. Like all conventioneers, these magical ones would let their inhibitions down and have a totally good time—for them. In the process, they'd drive the town nuts, but there was always a cleanup crew of powerful sorcerers around to fix things. He wondered how long it took and whether everything ever got fixed, but he suspected that, within the confines of the host town or city, anyway, things were under more careful watch than they seemed to be. In the end, it was mental anguish applied to ordinary people that was the real price—but the rewards, too, were great. Few groups had conventions this large, and while some might get stuck a hundred times with phony money or gems that vanished, others found overly generous rewards. It really meant millions to the city, too.

Not, however, for a grain merchant. Joe couldn't blame the family for getting out for a while.

He finished his meal and settled his accounts. But after saying luck and farewell to the temporary refugee family, he still hadn't caught sight of Marge and he began to grow a little worried. He found the innkeeper and asked if he'd seen her.

"The sexy fairy lady? Yeah, I seen her. Don't worry. She'll be back down in a little while, like she has been."

Joe stared at the man. "Like she has been?"

Quickly and a little bit nervously, the innkeeper described Marge's activities of the past couple of hours. Joe was incredulous and more than a little hurt. He stalked outside to the stable area, got the horse and the mule, saddled them, and reset the packs, brooding all the time.

Marge came out of the inn entrance and spotted him, then walked over to him with a very light and sassy manner. She stopped short, though, about ten feet from him, and the smile faded as she sensed his emotional turmoil. She instantly understood the problem, but couldn't really sympathize all that much. "Well? What did you expect?" she asked him. "You just kept lying there, snoring like mad."

"Yeah, but . . ." he tried lamely. "It's so . . . *cheap*."

"It's not that," she told him, stepping more into the light and putting out her hand. He looked at it and saw two large and obviously very valuable rings on her fingers. He saw, too, that she wore a very expensive-looking gold necklace. In her left hand she held a small velvet case. "I found out a lot of things already tonight, and one of them is that you *must* give a gift to a Kauri or she owns your soul. The first man practically fell all over himself finding something to give me."

"Well, at least you'll always be able to buy what you need," he grumped.

"Oh, Joe—it's just in my nature. It's one of the things I *do*."

"Yeah, but—so many?"

She shrugged and got on the mule. "It was like eating peanuts. Once I got started, I just couldn't stop."

He sighed and mounted his horse. "Well, you ought to have real fun in convention city up ahead."

"I intend to," she told him. "But don't be so damned sanctimonious about it all. I heard Houma and Grogha talking in little-kid whispers about the virgins of Kidim. It didn't matter when it was you men against scared, defenseless girls, now did it?"

"But that was different!" he protested.

"How?"

"Well, um, the damned town deserved it, that's all. They staked you out for the dragon, remember!"

"Even if that were a good excuse for the seduction of innocent kids, which I doubt, it certainly wasn't true that first night. You didn't know about it."

"But you were celibate then! A virgin witch!"

"And you weren't then and aren't now. The only difference is that I'm not now, either. Deep down you're just like all men, you know. It's okay when *you* do it, but women—uh-uh. And I'm even more of a threat—a woman who can control the emotions of men. A woman in command, you might say. No, Joe, don't pull that hurt act on me. Not until you can explain to me why I'm an immoral prostitute while you're just having a boy's night of fun out on the town." With that she kicked the mule and started out onto the darkened road.

He waited a moment, not at all agreeing with her position but unable at the moment to figure out why she was wrong, then followed her.

*   *   *

It took two more days' ride to reach the city, and during that time he still hadn't really figured it out, but he'd partially come to accept it. He did more or less understand why he took it so personally, though. It was one thing for him, say, to meet a woman he didn't know and have a fling in the hay, but Marge was something else, somebody special and important to him. People he knew and cared about just didn't do things like that.

Except, of course, once he'd known and cared about a very special young woman, who'd even borne him a son, but now, in another world and in another life, she was living with another guy and probably griping about never getting any more alimony. And he'd tried more than once to pick up truck-stop waitresses and lady truckers, some of whom he knew very well indeed, and sometimes he'd succeeded. In a sense, he realized, he'd taken refuge in Marge's former self. She'd been safe, dependable, nobody else's, even if not his.

But, irrational or not, he couldn't shake his sense of hurt and perhaps jealousy, at least not yet, and he consistently refused her advances as if, somehow, at least that could be preserved between them. She would remain, then, somehow, his partner and his friend and nothing more, in the same way that, were she a male and a womanizer, he might accept but not approve.

It was, damn it, just that she was so damned *desirable* . . .

Sachalin was truly deserving of the term city, rather than the less important designation of town. It spread out for miles along the shores of Lake Zahias, a lake so huge that it resembled an ocean or, at least, one of the Great Lakes, and had tides.

The city was built up against a series of low hills that were, perhaps, the moraines of the great glacier that carved and became Lake Zahias. Also deep, the lake actually made Sachalin a major port, since at its southern end the River of Sorrows began, winding its way through deep gorges to Lake Bragha, then slowly between the mountain ranges to Lake Ogome, until finally, as a great river, it reached the Dancing Gods itself. A parallel canal had been built between Zahias and Bragha, but two great falls prevented full access to the sea. Still, it was a simple transfer of goods from ship to barge to ship to get materials easily into the interior of Husaquahr, and this made Sachalin a rich and important city indeed.

The volcanic soil from the Firehills covered hundreds of square miles to the north and west of the city and lake, meaning that a tremendous amount of food, principally grains, was sent back down from the port all the way to the City-States and beyond.

Sachalin was set only slightly inland from the port and the white, sandy beaches, and it seemed to be constructed of uniformly blocky buildings, two to six storeys high, built of some white stone and masonry materials, topped with characteristic red shingle roofs. Unlike most cities and towns in Husaquahr, it was not walled, being far too large and sprawling for that, but it did have big, open arches at its entrance that served a strictly decorative function. The road led along the lakeshore after that, where Marge and Joe could see countless fishing vessels tied up in neat rows for the night, as well as occasional yachts and luxury vessels. The heavy-goods commercial port was north of the city, leaving the center for public beaches and pleasure use and not spoiling the view.

They arrived in early evening. The city did not die after dark as most towns did, but took on a whole new character. Uniformed men of the watch, as they were called, walked every street, lighting lamps with long lamplighter torches. The glass containers for the streetlamps were irregular and often multi-colored, their bright flames inside producing not only more than ample light but also colorful, dancing patterns against the white stucco buildings. It was, in a sense, fairyland by engineering rather than by magic, but it was no less effective.

Although neither Joe nor Marge could read the language, the pictograms on the signs were easy enough to follow. When they reached a broad park with beach on one side and town on the other, the road formed a circle around a huge monument to some very odd-looking creature. Leading into the circle from town was a tremendously wide avenue, paved with tiny little bricks and lined with trees the entire way. It seemed to have a series of circles through town to the hills in back, each one with a small park and monument in the middle, but far back, against and seemingly either carved out of or sitting on a ledge in the hills, was the great capitol building itself, looking less like any capitol building they had seen than a huge, columnar, Grecian-style temple to some ancient gods, bathed in great lights.

They turned toward the capitol and started into the city proper, following directions on the small map Ruddygore had sketched for them of the city center. The large buildings behind the trees on either side seemed to be mostly banks and offices—shipping brokers, the grain exchange, and other such institutions. This was the financial heart of the city, it was clear.

"It's *beautiful*," Marge said, mostly to herself. "And everything's so *clean*."

Joe understood what she meant. Even the best of towns they'd seen in Husaquahr had been straight out of the Middle Ages, with sanitation to match. Here, though, it looked as if an entire crew of workmen came out each night and scrubbed the place clean, removing trash, droppings, and just about everything else, then even polishing the brick and scrubbing the building facades. The air was crisp and clean-smelling, with no hints of garbage or even horse droppings.

At that moment, Joe's horse relieved herself on the bright roadway, and he felt suddenly very guilty for her doing so. He hurried on a bit, and they were a couple of blocks up and at the next circle before he halted at Marge's call. "Hey, Joe—look back!"

He looked and saw dozens of tiny fairy gnomes emerge from the trees up and down the whole block where his horse had violated the scenery. They hurried quickly to the center of the street, swept up the droppings and took them away, then scrubbed the whole area and vanished once more into the tree-lined sides of the boulevard. "It figures," he muttered, then turned and continued on.

Although the hotel and entertainment district was in the dead center of the city, the fancy hotels for the business clientele who would be visiting those financial centers were all directly on this main, wide boulevard, and the grandest of them was the Imperial Grand, a huge, fancy structure that took up more than a square block. Like all the buildings, it wasn't really very high—though at eight storeys it was one of the tallest buildings in the city—but it was fancy.

The front, in fact, was almost entirely of glass, rising from street level up four full storeys, creating a massive atrium and lobby which was like a glass-covered right angle viewed from the side. This connected to a solid four-storey stone and stucco block with balconies sculpted on its face, so that anyone coming out of any room would have a free view of the open space area. On top of this were three four-storey cubes, giving the whole building a distinctive look. It reminded Joe of some fancy American hotels, as if designed by Mayan temple designers. There was even a parking entrance on the side, which led down below the hotel to an underground stable that looked fancy indeed. Liveried attendants helped Marge and Joe off their animals, unloaded saddle and packs, put small collars on both horse and mule and a sticker on the saddle, then handed Joe three embossed leather claim checks. Another packed up their meager luggage in an odd-looking cart, and they followed him to a wide, beltlike structure rising at a steep angle. Strong, thin boards were spaced about eight feet apart going up. They were instructed to sit down, and the attendant then went over and rang a large bell.

"A real bellman," Marge noted dryly.

Suddenly the belt started moving slowly upward. It so startled them, despite the obvious intent of the gadget, that both almost fell off. The bellman, as soon as they were clear, rolled his cart onto the next plank below them and hopped on himself. Joe looked nervously around and saw that they were going to be raised just above lobby level, followed by a steep drop. The ascent wasn't very fast, but they were traveling backward.

When they were most of the way up, the bellman reached over and grabbed another rope, ringing the bell below once more; just as Joe rose up so that his feet were clear of the floor level, the device stopped and he and Marge jumped off. It then moved again, and the bellman and his load were lifted up.

Joe looked at the bellman with unconcealed curiosity. "How does it work?"

The bellman smiled, telling them both that this was his most asked question. "There's a treadmill down there. Put some mules on it every once in a while and it winds up a tremendous spring. When we need to run it, we just take the brake off and it goes up until we hit the brake. During the busy periods, we just keep the treadmill going all the time. Smart, huh? Wait till you see what else this place has. There's no other hotel like it anywhere."

They looked around the broad, glass-enclosed atrium, but there were few people about, and Marge remarked on it. "Oh, they'll start coming in big tomorrow," the bellman assured her. "We're full up the next seven days. Tonight we'd normally be about half full, but with most of the businesses down the boulevard taking a holiday during the convention, there are only some early arrivers like you now. Ah, you *are* here for the convention, right?"

They nodded. "We thought we were late. I guess we made better time than we expected," Marge commented.

They followed him to the registration desk, a massive horseshoe-shaped affair of stained and polished oak. The desk clerk, dressed in almost regal splendor, eyed both of them with some suspicion and a nose high in the air. "Yesssss . . ." he virtually hissed at them, trying to avoid any sort of eye contact.

"We may be a little early, but we're supposed to have rooms reserved for us here," Joe told him.

Now the beady little eyes focused first on Joe, then on Marge. "Are you certain you have the correct hotel?"

"This is the Imperial Grand Hotel, I presume."

"It most certainly is."

"Well, we're in the right place, then."

The clerk gave a bored sigh. "Very well, then. Name?"

"Joseph the Golden, Castle Terindell, Valisandra."

"How original," the clerk muttered patronizingly. "A barbarian with a mailing address." He checked through his large card file, then checked again, and finally said, "As I suspected, there is nothing, and our hotel is booked for the next week."

Joe thought a moment. "We are with Ruddygore of Terindell," he told the clerk. "We are a part of his party."

The clerk was unimpressed and yet he dutifully checked and cross-checked his file cards once more. Finally he nodded to himself. "Ah, yes. Ruddygore, Throckmorton P., party of seven. Let's see . . . Yes, an Imir is already in as the advance man for the party. I will send a runner up to approve you." He turned and tapped a small bell on the desk. From a place somewhere beneath him, a tiny pixie, no more than two or three inches high, popped up and waited for further instructions, its transparent multiple wings beating so fast they were virtually invisible. The clerk jotted something on a pad, tore off the top sheet, folded it in quarters, and handed it to the little creature. "Lake Suite," he told it.

The creature was off in a flash, flying into one of a number of round tubes that seemed to go into the wall in back of the clerk.

"Those tubes go to every room in the place?" Joe asked a little suspiciously. If pixies could use them, so could other things, and they made nice sound conductors as well.

"Oh, my, no!" the clerk huffed. "They go to each floor of each wing, and the messenger then rings a bell."

Joe nodded, feeling a little better. He didn't trust hotels at all, and his experience with any of the larger ones in Husaquahr had been less than pleasant.

"Madam," the clerk said as they waited, "we would appreciate it if you would, ah, cover up while in the public areas. The Portside, down at Lake Boulevard and Pier Six, is more, ah, suited to your sort."

Marge got mad fast. "And what exactly is my sort? Do you discriminate against fairies? Are we not good enough for you?"

"Oh, of course not! That's not what I meant at all."

"Then make your meaning plain. I am a Kauri, and we have very short tempers."

"Exactly my point. I mean, with the convention coming in, it's very bad for the hotel's image."

Joe, too, got a little rankled. "With what I hear about this convention, you'll be lucky to have a hotel left when it's over. Are you going to be working through the next week?"

"Why, uh, I expect to. Whatever do you mean?" The clerk was uncomfortable when the topic got personal and forced him to the defensive.

"When the adepts get through with you, you might wish you'd gone on vacation with an attitude like that. Now you've insulted my partner and friend, and we weren't doing anything but following your rules and making no trouble." He put his hand to his sword hilt, but Marge stopped him.

"No, Joe. Just stand to one side for a moment. This is *my* little problem."

Curious, the big man moved over and just watched. Marge stared hard at the clerk, then brought her two arms up over her head, fully extending her magnificent, soft wings. The clerk started to say something, then stopped and became suddenly dull and glassy-eyed. She smiled at him, and he smiled back, although Joe was surprised that it didn't crack his face. She rose, floated over the desk, and landed just in front of the transfixed man, whose gaze never left her. Marge nodded, still smiling, put down her arms, and began systematically to undress the clerk. Joe—and, he couldn't help noticing, the bellman and other employees in the lobby area—watched with a mixture of awe and amusement. Within two or three minutes, the clerk was completely nude.

At that moment, the pixie shot back through the tube, flew up to the clerk, and stopped short, the look on its face one of total incredulousness. Marge reached out and took the small paper from the pixie and glanced at it, then turned and handed it to Joe. It was a scrawled mess, but they recognized Poquah's distinctive calligraphy and guessed what it said. "Well, we can go up now," Joe suggested a bit nervously.

"Awww..." Marge pouted, sounding disappointed. She leaned over, kissed the clerk lightly, and said, "You'll wait right here just like that until I get back, though, won't you?"

The clerk nodded dreamily.

Marge smiled, floated back to the other side of the desk, and looked at the bellman. "Let's go."

The bellman led them around the big registration area to a hallway and into the main building in back. On one side was an opening in the wall, revealing a small, gondolalike car. They could see a second about halfway down the hall, and guess a third at the end.

The thing proved to be something like a ferris wheel, but very, very slow and driven, apparently, by the same sort of treadmill-gear-spring device as the escalator from the stables. They went to the top, then had to transfer to a smaller, similar device and do the whole thing all over again. "Uh—you *do* have stairs," Joe said to the bellman hopefully.

"Oh, sure. This is mostly for the bigwigs and the luggage. The top two floors of each tower are suites only, and the kind of people who have 'em not only usually have tons of baggage but they don't walk no place."

"Um—just out of curiosity, what do you think of that little scene down there?" Joe wanted to know as they reached the top floor of the south tower.

The bellman chuckled. "Some people, they run outta town when this convention hits. Me, I love to stick around. I mean, I gotta work under guys like that for most of the year."

Both Joe and Marge grinned. "And you're not scared of something happening to you?" she asked him, trying to sound nonthreatening.

"Naw. I been around magicians and stuff a lot, and overall they're a pretty fair lot. Mostly they stick it to people who really need it, and, I mean, most of us can't, right? This convention's the payoff to all them types who do the same to everybody, and I love it."

They both chuckled and followed the little man to a large and ornately carved set of double doors. The bellman pulled on a satin rope that dangled from a small recess. In a few seconds, the door opened, and the familiar face of the warrior elf Poquah looked out at them. The Imir was as outwardly impassive as always; but when he saw Marge, his thick, ruler-straight eyebrows that flanked his cat-shaped eyes at a forty-five-degree angle went up about an inch. It was as much of a rise from him as either of them could remember. He looked at Joe, nodded, then turned back to her. "And this is our old Marge?"

She grinned. "No, it's the new one. Hello, Imir."

"Hello, Kauri. Come in, both of you."

They entered, and the bellman followed. Marge stopped short when she saw the suite and gave a low gasp.

It *was* impressive. The walls were entirely of some sort of tinted glass, apparently going all the way around the top of the tower. There were drapes, controlled by long, thin ropes, that could be lowered from recesses in the ceiling to cover them, but Poquah had left them open in this large parlor.

It was furnished with thick sofas, ottomans, and luxuriously padded chairs. The tables were of carved and beautifully stained hardwoods, each one a handmade work of art. The entire suite was carpeted in thick, soft wool, dyed in patterns of reds, yellows, blues, and greens. Facing the inside of the parlor, against the wall parallel with the hall, was a huge bar on one side and a mini-kitchen on the other, complete with a small stove, wood for that stove, and a chimney leading up.

The bellman looked questioningly at Poquah, who simply said, "Just set them down here. We will put them away when we arrange who's to go where."

The bellman did as instructed and turned to go. Joe fished in the pack, brought out a small chunk of Firehills fairy gold left over from their road transactions, and called after him, "Here—catch!"

The bellman did so and realized almost instantly that he had more than an ounce of fairy gold in his hands. It was certainly a bigger tip than he was used to, but he suppressed his surprise and joy and tucked it in a pocket. "Thank *you*, sir and madam, and if you need anything, just go to the middle of the hall and call the messenger." With that he was gone, shutting the door after him.

"That was an abnormal tip," Poquah noted. "It sets a bad precedent."

"Well, it was mine, not Ruddygore's, and I liked that little guy," Joe told him. "Besides," he added a little sharply, looking at Marge, "he's going to have to clean up a bit after us, isn't he?"

She gave him a "Who, me?" sort of innocent look, and Poquah was quick to sense that there was something he'd better know. "What have you two done already?" he asked suspiciously.

"We had a little run-in with a stuffed shirt at the front desk, and Marge got mad," Joe told him.

"What did you do?"

"He told me to get out of his hotel and go down to the docks, as if I were some kind of tramp," she responded defensively. "I just gave his libido a nudge so he only had eyes for me, that's all."

The Imir sighed. "And I suppose he's standing there behind the desk right now, stark naked, just pining for your return."

"Why, yeah. How'd you guess?"

"As hard as it might be for even me to believe, the Imir and Kauri are rather closely related, and I have had some experience around you as well. Combining your rather odd sense of humor with the Kauri's almost total lack of self-control, it was obvious. Is it permanent?"

"Oh, no. Oh, he'll still have a thing for me, but he'll snap out of it in an hour or so, get real embarrassed, and put his pants on again."

The Imir nodded. "Ah, yes, you Kauri *do* have that nice little trick, don't you?" He looked over at Joe. "You see, her victim will still have 'a thing,' as she put it, for her even after it's over, so he'll take it out on the staff, on everybody else, even on himself, but he'll *never* be mad at, let alone blame, her. Hmph! Totally useless in a fight, but with those defenses nobody ever lays a glove on them." He thought for a moment. "The Master and the others will be in sometime tomorrow. The master bedroom, with the harbor view, is through there, so that will be his. The room on the other side will be shared by myself and Durin, his personal chef. There are two more rooms down the hall that interconnect with each other but not with this apartment, and we have Macore and Tiana to take care of as well as the two of you."

"Macore! It will be good to see him again!" Joe cried. "But what's he doing here?"

"The Master has his reasons," the Imir replied enigmatically.

"And who's Tiana?" Marge wanted to know.

"Tiana—oh, yes, you might not have met her. She fled from Morikay and has been under the protection of the Master for years. He sent for her to meet him here. You'll learn more, perhaps, when you see her." He looked thoughtful again. "I assume the best course is to put you, Marge, and Tiana in one of the rooms, with Joe and Macore in the other. I regret that, but I do not think Macore is the correct sort of person for many reasons to put in with the young lady."

Joe looked a little sourly at Marge. "Suits me," he said. "Why not just give each of us a key now?"

Poquah nodded, walked into his own room by sliding back a door, and soon returned with two large brass keys. Each key had a small leather tag attached with a welded brass ring. "If you use any of the hotel's amenities, the key will be all you need for payment," he explained. "Outside, use what money you have. From the bellman's tip, I assume you do not require any more at this time."

"I think we're okay for now," Joe told him. "At least, I am."

"I have no need of money," Marge said, "but I'm going to have problems carrying this key around. I'll leave it either at the desk or with you when I'm going to be gone for any length of time."

The Imir nodded. "Very well, then. Come over here." He walked to the wide windows that looked out on the town. "Below there, and for several square blocks on either side, you see the entertainment district, which usually goes all night. The restaurants and bars are quite expensive, but all of high quality. There are also stage shows, strolling entertainment, and other amusements down there. On the other side, opposite this hotel, is the central market, which is quite extensive and has some of the finest craftspeople in all Husaquahr, and which also has for sale almost anything you might wish. Please keep your expenses down if possible. Prices always double or more when a convention is in town, and our coffers are not unlimited."

Both of them knew that this was more the Imir's nature speaking than any policy or problem from Ruddygore. The fact was, to somebody on the Council with his own castle and more, wealth was virtually limitless. Poquah, though, was not only the sorcerer's chief bodyguard but also the manager of Castle Terindell, and he took every expense personally. He was also, contrary to the traditions of his race, an accomplished sorcerer himself and, because of that, was somewhat in exile from his own people. Being of faërie, he could never gain the power and control of a human sorcerer, but he was nonetheless a very, very dangerous man in all respects.

Joe picked up the bags, and he and Marge walked out of the suite and down the hall. Poquah shut the door behind them. Joe realized almost immediately that the Imir had failed to tell him which room was which, and the pictogram on the keys was very little help, so he tried his on the first door they came to; naturally, it didn't work. Marge unlocked the door with hers, and they stepped inside.

The room was large and comfortable and had a huge bed and a mini-parlor with sofa, but it was nothing like the master suite. It was still better than either of them had seen in a long, long time, though. Marge turned and looked at Joe questioningly. "Sure you don't want to sleep here tonight?"

He sighed. "No. Not yet. Let's let things go a bit, huh? Besides, you ought to enjoy a solo room for one night. What do you want from the packs?"

She thought a moment. "The glasses, I guess, and my trinkets from the last couple of nights." He put the packs down, and she rummaged through and got the few items. "That's it," she told him.

He shrugged. "Okay. Well, let me get settled in next door. After that, I guess I'll find a restaurant and then hit the sack.

I think I want to move myself back to a little more of a day schedule."

"Suit yourself," she told him. "The night's still young." He turned to go, but just as he cleared her door, she called out, "Joe?"

He stopped and actually hesitated for a moment, but shook it off. "Look—that stuff you did with the clerk. Never do anything like that to me. Never. Promise?"

She nodded, looking suddenly serious. "I promise, Joe. You know I'd never do anything like that to you."

"I don't know anything about anything any more," he responded and walked down the hall.

His room proved to be a mirror image of hers, but with two slightly smaller but still plush beds. He put the packs down and looked around, for the first time noticing a small sink in one corner, with a pipe coming out of the back and angling down like a spigot. Looking a little closer, he discovered a rod and handle on the floor next to the sink that actually went through the floor. Curious, he pushed down on it, finding it something like a bicycle pump. Pumping it a bit harder, he saw water coming out of the spigot and into the basin. He checked and found it cool but not cold and marveled anew at how clever the people who designed and built this place were. The pump took very little effort, so he wasn't bringing water up from anywhere. Probably there were tanks on the roof, he decided, so the pump only opened some sort of valve when it was pushed—it *had* turned halfway around when he'd pushed it down the first time, and twisted back at rest—and the pump's suction just drew water a short distance into the sink line. It was clever. More than likely there were huge cisterns up there catching rain off the lake, supplemented when necessary by hauling water up to the top.

The water closets were at either end of the hall, and he was tempted to find out if they had flush toilets, but that would wait. He'd know soon enough.

Using the water and towels, he gave himself something of a sponge bath and turned two bright white towels almost black doing so, then changed into his last clean breechclout. He reminded himself to find out about laundry services here and that he had to get over to that market the next day and buy a new pair of sandals, or, perhaps, boots. Maybe both, he thought after a moment. After all, he was here on Ruddygore's expense account, and to hell with Poquah.

Satisfied as he could be, and with his hair combed and fastened by a headband, he left the room and went down the hall, stopping at Marge's room. He knocked. When there was no answer, he tried the door. It opened, and he peered inside, but the room was empty.

Well, he thought, so much for company for dinner. That brought him up short for a moment, and he frowned. Come to think of it, in the days since she'd come out of that forest with wings, he'd never seen her eat. He wondered if she did, and, if so, what.

CHAPTER 7

ON THE CONVENTIONS OF UNCONVENTIONAL CONVENTIONS

It is permissible for a white magician to buy a black magician a drink, or vice versa, openly at convention, without poisoning it.
—Rules, VI, 201(b)

RUDDYGORE ARRIVED IN THE MIDDLE OF THE AFTERNOON OF the next day, accompanied by Durin and Macore and also by an extremely large retinue. He made a grand sort of entrance, being carried in in an ornate, gold-embossed sedan chair on the backs of four dark, burly men wearing loincloths and turbans. They brought him right up in the chair on the lifting stairs from the stables, so that the proper impression was actually enhanced as he rose into view. Besides, the whole thing wouldn't have fitted through the front doors.

The sedan chair was the immediate object of interest for all in the lobby area, and there was quite a crowd by this time. Joe had been sitting in the lobby bar for about an hour, waiting for this, having been awakened by Poquah, and even he had to admit it was really impressive. The rest of the people checking in had been a pretty weird lot, with robes and strange chants and bizarre animals and birds accompanying the costumed magicians, but this one had real style.

A clearly prompted Macore, looking resplendent in scarlet and silver noble's dress and leading the parade, walked solemnly back to the door and opened it. After a dramatic pause, the huge sorcerer got out, looking imperiously neither to the right nor to the left, instead just standing there waiting to be admired. He wore formal opera clothes best suited to the nineteenth century on Joe's own world, including a full opera cape, and carried a brilliantly polished mahogany walking stick with its handle a magnificently carved, solid gold lion's head in full roar. He snapped his fingers and Macore scampered around him, reached inside the sedan chair, and brought out a flat disk which he then shook with his wrist, causing the disk to form into a great top hat matching the formal outfit. The little thief, playing the part to the hilt, handed the hat to Ruddygore, who idly placed it on his head, then snapped his fingers once more.

Durin, his fairy chef, a very round and cherubic figure, who looked like a five-foot-tall version of a Disney dwarf, was attired in splendid white fur. He walked from behind the sedan chair and around Ruddygore and Macore to the front desk. The uniformed desk crew, already accustomed to serving all manner of humans and creatures, nonetheless was gathered together awaiting what came next. "Throckmorton P. Ruddygore, Master of Castle Terindell, Vice Chairman of the Council of Thirteen, Grand Master of the Society of Thaumaturgists, Keeper of the Threshold of Worlds, Th.D., Ph.D., M.D., and D.O.G." Ruddygore smiled and bowed.

The desk clerk was not officious but also not all that impressed. A hand went down and he called out, "Front, please!" Several bellmen engaged in a pushing and tripping contest to see who could make it first to what was obviously a big tipper.

"Show Dr. Ruddygore and his party to the Lake Suite," the clerk instructed the winning bellman.

That one grinned, went over, and bowed to the master sorcerer. "If you will follow me, sir," the bellman intoned and started off with his body militarily erect, aware that he was leading a parade.

Macore followed, adapting the same manner of walk, then

Ruddygore, and finally the little chef, obviously having the time of his considerable fairy life. Joe chugged down the remains of his tankard—it was full of straight hypercaffeinated tea, anyway—and decided he'd take the stairs. Even if he didn't hurry, he knew that, by the time they all took that set of elevator contraptions, he'd be ten minutes ahead of them. As he made for the stairs, he heard the clerk snap, "You muscle guys! Get that rig back down where it belongs!"

Joe was certainly ahead of the game as he knocked on the suite's large door. Poquah answered, looked at the big man's face, and said sourly, "I assume he's arrived?"

"And how! Did he come all the way here with that outfit?"

"No, actually he had me rent it a couple of days ago here in the city, and they picked him up on the edge of town. Cost a fortune, too, not to mention a lot of my time. Do you know how hard it is to find four men who not only can bear that kind of weight but also are about the same size?"

"I can guess," Joe sympathized. "Whoops! I think I hear them coming now!"

It was pretty unmistakable, hearing the clanging and clattering of the car arriving and then the bunch of them getting out of it. Joe chuckled. "I hope they have a really heavy-duty set of springs on that gadget."

Poquah went over, opened the double doors wide, then did a double check of the bar stock and of several large trays of pastries sitting on the kitchenette counter. Satisfied, he waited. Soon the batch of them walked in, led by the bellman. They stood there a moment while the sorcerer looked over the place. When he nodded, Poquah went over to the bellman. "Arrange for the bags to be delivered as soon as possible," he instructed, "and do not touch or disturb the seals on them if you value your life."

The bellman, not easily intimidated, just stood there. Finally, out of the corner of his mouth, Ruddygore ordered, "Tip him, you idiot!"

The Imir sighed, took a pouch from his belt, and gave the bellman three gold coins. Joe didn't know how much it was, but it certainly was less than the hotel man had expected, judging by his expression. "More if the bags arrive quickly and in perfect condition," Poquah told him. "Now—go!"

The bellman nodded glumly, turned, and left, and Poquah

shut the doors behind him. At that moment they all relaxed, and Ruddygore broke into hearty laughter. The big man went over, grabbed a pastry, and plopped into one of the plush chairs, which groaned and sagged noticeably. "God!" he exclaimed. "I've been wanting to make an entrance like that ever since I saw *The Thief of Baghdad!*"

Joe was the only one who even slightly understood the comment, although he'd never seen the movie. Ruddygore, with his ability to go between the worlds, was equally at home in either one.

"So what's a D.O.G.?" he asked with a smile.

Ruddygore's eyebrows rose. "Why, hello, Joe! A pleasant, successful, and uneventful trip, I trust?"

"Not exactly," he responded, "but that will wait."

"Yes, I *do* want to talk to you in a bit, after we're settled in and I find out what godawful stuff they have me doing at the convention. Poquah, did you get a program?"

"They were late, as usual," the Imir replied. "They only finished carving the plates the night before last. Naturally, they had lots of last-minute changes."

The sorcerer sighed. "I suppose we ought to give them the idea of the Gutenberg press, eh? I think movable type's time has come for Husaquahr. It's almost impossible to have anything accurate when it takes a team of scribes a month to carve out each page." He turned back to Joe. "A D.O.G., if you must know, is a Doctor of Oddball Gimmickry. It's irritating at times, but a lot of titles, particularly in academia and the Society, have rather unfortunate initials. Try not to laugh at them when you hear them if you don't want to be turned into a toad."

"I'll remember," Joe assured the wizard.

Ruddygore reached into his inside jacket pocket and took out a cigar, lighting it by pointing his index finger at the tip. A tiny spark jumped, and he was puffing away. He sighed. "It's been a wearing trip, I fear. With a week to go, I really should just take it easy today and get a decent night's sleep, but I probably won't. That was one of the reasons for the grand entrance down there, though. If I just walked through the door, I'd run into three dozen people, all of whom are either old friends not seen in a long time or people who have to talk to me or to whom I have to talk. I'd be hours just getting across the lobby."

"It *was* effective," Joe told him. "You overawed everybody except the desk clerks."

Ruddygore shrugged. "Can't win 'em all. I assume Marge is sleeping during this pretty day?"

"I guess," Joe answered. "I don't know. We had private rooms last night."

The sorcerer frowned and looked thoughtful for a moment. Finally, he sighed and got up. "I think perhaps we'd better have our little talk now. Come on into my room." He looked questioningly at Poquah, who indicated which door, then grabbed several more of the gooier pastries, opened the side door to his bedroom, and walked in. Joe followed, deciding he might grab one of the pastries himself on the way.

The master bedroom was truly huge, with a massive bed, a full parlor area, its own water closet, and a mini-bar. Ruddygore slipped off his coat and boots and tossed the hat on the bed. Almost as an afterthought, he turned back and stuck his head into the parlor. "Poquah, when the bags come, prepare some of what's in the red canister," he instructed. "Then have it brought in." He then slid the door closed, indicated a chair to Joe, and took one himself, sprawling comfortably. For a while he said nothing, just looked at the big man across from him. Then he sighed. "I gather you do not approve of the new Marge."

Joe shrugged. "What can I say?"

"Just be honest, that's all, particularly with me. Joe, before I started this operation, I consulted a series of oracles who are pretty good at seeing future trends. Trends only—I've yet to find a reliable perfect predictor, and I'm not sure I'd like the implications of one if I found him or her. The trend was entirely the Dark Baron's way, and it was highly unpleasant in the extreme. The threat went far beyond Husaquahr to the entire world and from it even to yours. It's an end-around to millennia of darkness, even if it fails beyond this world. At the very least, millions of lives were at stake, their children's lives, and their children's children's, not to mention my own ancient hide. Most of what I organized to fight them—and it's a vast and complex system—is better for you not to know, but in all those predictors I kept hitting a blind spot, an irregularity that skewed anything that might be in my favor and reinforced the Baron. It took no great deduction to see that he was being backed by forces from Hell itself, directly, on stage, in violation of every agreement between Heaven and Hell ever made, but it was so clever, so subtle, I couldn't get the proof I needed."

Joe nodded. "I met that demon, remember."

"Indeed you did and you escaped when none should have. That's what I saw as well. If the Baron had a joker, a real demon prince, to help him, then I needed a wild card of my own. That wild card, Joe, is you."

"So you've said. But I'm not magic, and I'm no match for demons."

"Oh, but you *are*, Joe," the sorcerer told him. "You are indeed. And so is Marge. I couldn't stand up to a demon prince, Joe—but you not only could, you did. He had no power over you, and, if you had been able to strike at him, you might have actually wounded him. That's because any demon prince coming through to Husaquahr is attuned to Husaquahr. Things, people, even souls are very subtly different between worlds, Joe, and they must be on the right frequency, so to speak. The demons of your world could harm you, but not one here. That's what I was looking for when I went shopping, as it were, over Earth way."

"But magic works on me here," Joe pointed out. "I'm as vulnerable as anybody else."

"No, Joe. Your body is vulnerable, since flesh is flesh. But if the flesh were all that mattered, then the Baron would have no need of a demon prince, would he? No, Joe—the demon can't even perceive flesh, believe it or not. He sees that permanent part of you, your soul, your true self. It's on that level that demons get you, twist you, corrupt you, often in spite of yourself. Not you, though, Joe—or Marge, either, for that matter. That doesn't mean you can't be corrupted, but you can't be reached on that level against your conscious will here, and that's a vital but very fine point. When that demon saw you both, it reached out to command your souls—and it couldn't. Thus, you were able to break free, use the Lamp, and escape. And, because of that, the Baron was deprived of the Lamp and its powers, and we were able to win the battle. All because *you* were there, Joe, as predicted—you and not one of this world."

"Yeah—but why me?"

"You fitted the bill. You were a big man with a strong ego, an independent with no real ties, and the probabilities said you would be killed in an accident that very night we met. I set up the conditions to divert you to me, and you were diverted. Somehow, inadvertently, those conditions also brought Marge first to you and then to me as well. I didn't expect her, but I couldn't complain, either. But I was prepared for you, not for her, and that caused some problems. Unlike you, her ego, her self-esteem, and her self-image were extremely weak, and never so weak as at the point when we crossed over. Forces that are too complex to explain operated, and while you, with a little help from me, were able to shrug them off, they took hold of her. This is a world of magic, and magical forces are strongest on the nonintellectual level, on the emotional line, as you can see in your own world, in the example of religious fervor. To Marge, back then, the intellect had failed. Her college availed her nothing, her knowledge and skills went unneeded or un-appreciated, and the only thing she'd done, once she'd sunk very low, that worked was selling herself, turning herself into an object, a thing for the momentary gratification of strangers. This was the pattern she brought with her as she crossed the Sea of Dreams."

Joe nodded, following him on at least the intellectual level, although finding it impossible to see how somebody so bright and capable could have sunk so low. He said as much to Ruddygore. "I sure had everything thrown at me and I just kept fighting."

"That's true, but you already had a profession, a skill, and the tools to get by. You were also older, more experienced, and had traveled all over the country. She'd never been out of Texas."

"Yeah, maybe, but I never got to college, either. In fact, the army was the only reason I got my high school equiva-lency."

The sorcerer sighed. "Joe, you're like a lot of smart but uneducated people. You always had that little glimmer of in-feriority when you met somebody with all that education. I can tell you right now that most people with degrees, even doctorates, are dumber and less qualified to make their way than people like you. Consider the fact that I have been educated up the rear end, and a lot of it was interesting but very little was useful. One of my degrees is in music, for example, although I'm only adequate at the piano. It gives me a better appreciation of opera, for example, and opens up new entertainment pleasures to me, but it's just that—pleasures. It's not worth a damn in the real world, not even as entertainment, since I lack the inborn talents that would require. My talents lay in a different direction, and the way I learned how to use those and master the intimate secrets of magic was not by any university experience but by a lot of hard, degrading, and backbreaking toil as an apprentice—read that as a virtual slave—to somebody who'd learned it the same way."

Ruddygore could see that Joe wasn't quite accepting this, and knew the man never really would, but it would have to do.

"All right," the sorcerer continued, "let's just say she blew it both because of her own wrong choices and because of things beyond her control. The fact was, the forces that played on her played on those parts of her that were the most primal, the most basic. They reinforced those elements, while everything else about her was weakened. As a result, despite my efforts to keep her human, she entered here a changeling, and there was nothing I could do about it."

That was interesting, not only because it implied that Ruddygore's powers had real, clearly defined limits but also because Marge and everybody else believed it was hardly natural. "Everybody thinks you caused it. Even the witch she likes so much."

Ruddygore chuckled. "She would. No, I had no idea at the time—since I neither knew nor expected Marge, and knew nothing about her. When I realized it, after acclimating you to this world, I tried to block it by sending her to Huspeth and her witch order, which are, as you well know, celibate."

"Yeah, I know," Joe said glumly.

"Well, that only slowed the changes a bit, and the time she spent among the djinn broke the last restrictions. That's why I decided to get her to Mohr Jerahl to complete the process as quickly as possible. Otherwise she might have gone quite a long time, perhaps years, with a Kauri nature and a basically human body bound by that celibacy oath. She would have either gone nuts or had her newly established self-esteem crushed. By completing the process, it's all right for her to be that way, you see. It's the Kauri nature. And so her self-esteem is intact, her confidence actually strengthened, and she's whole and healthy. She *belongs*. Now do you understand what happened?"

"I guess so," Joe responded hesitantly. "I think I follow you, anyway. You're saying that, if this hadn't happened, she'd have gone nuts or killed herself, and I can follow that, but it's really not my problem. She belongs, sure, but *I don't*. I dunno, maybe it was mean and rotten of me. I guess it was. Sort of misery loves company, I guess. As long as she was, well, somebody else who didn't fit . . . Oh, I like Macore, and Grogha, and Houma, and even Poquah—although I'd never tell him that. But they've never seen a football game, don't know Pittsburgh from Peoria, and think Clint Eastwood's a magic spell for curing warts."

The sorcerer nodded. "Joe, you may find this hard to believe, but I do understand. Yet I think you're missing the point yourself here. Let me ask you something, and I want you to be absolutely honest with me."

"Shoot."

"Are you in love with Marge? I mean, really in love with her?"

Joe thought a moment, searching his feelings, and he had to admit that he'd never really thought about it before. *Was* he? The fact was, he hardly knew her. He'd picked her up, at least partly with the idea of maybe making it with her, and he'd wound up feeling sorry for her. That was—how long? A couple of hours' drive between Ozona and Fort Stockton, and she'd been asleep half of that. Then they'd gotten waylaid by Ruddygore, slept most of the way across, gone through his magic stuff, then separated. He'd spent many long weeks in training; she'd spent them off with Huspeth learning to be witchy or whatever. In fact, the only real time he'd had to get to know her, and this was the new her, so to speak, was on the expedition to Stormhold, and off and on after the battle. They'd had maybe two or three serious talks during that whole time. Once back, she'd taken off again for the Glen Dinig, returning only for what they'd just gone through.

He didn't really know her at all, and she didn't really know him, either. Yet he'd treated her as wife, girl friend, consort, whatever, in his own mind at least. But—love?

"No, not love. At least I don't think so. I'm all mixed up about that," he answered truthfully. "I guess it was more that I needed her, particularly here, and she needed me."

Ruddygore nodded. "And now you still feel a need for her, but she no longer needs you. That's what it's all about, Joe. It gripes your independent trucker's soul that you need somebody and it gripes you even more that they don't need you. But it's not Marge you're really mad at, Joe—it's yourself."

Joe sighed. "I guess you're right as usual, Ruddygore."

"Not guess, Joe, and you know it. I *am* right, and you'd better face that fact, if only for your own sake. Don't let your ego, your self-esteem, get low, Joe, or you'll sink into that same pit she did way back when. I need you, Joe. This world needs you—and you have a real opportunity here to carve out anything you want. Anything, Joe! Pirate or king, merchant or adventurer—you have the potential for all of it. The only one who can stop you is you."

There was a knock at the door, and the sorcerer called out for whomever it was to come in. It proved to be Durin with a pot of something on a silver tray and two mugs. Joe sniffed it, and his face showed total amazement. "That's *coffee!*"

Ruddygore grinned. "Yep. Good stuff, too. A private blend. I had to duck over to New York a couple of weeks ago; while there, I picked it up just for you. I bought a twenty-pound sack and I brought five pounds here."

It was the perfect gesture and it was well timed. Although it was possible to grow coffee in this world—in fact, it was supposedly grown on other continents—it was not native to Husaquahr, and there was nothing Joe had missed more. He savored the mug as if it were filled with some fine, expensive wine, and his morale was lifted accordingly. Ruddygore was able to resume the talk after a bit with the atmosphere much relaxed.

"Joe, we're having this talk because I have some important work for you to do," the big man told him.

Joe nodded. "I figured as much."

"Let's wrap up our discussion of the lay of the land, though, first. You ever wonder why the fairy folk exist?"

"No. I haven't given it much thought. Kind of like why everything else exists. Just the way things turned out, I suppose."

"Nope. When things were set up, evolution was supposed to be the perfecting mechanism, such as it was, but some hedges were included. Intelligently directed redevelopment, it's called in my trade. To ensure that vital pollination was carried out, there were more than a hundred and sixty different races of pixies, each ensuring that certain types of plants grew and dominated in certain areas. The land was protected, particularly in the key areas, by the kobolds, who control vital volcanic areas and can make certain that soil is renewed, especially in areas where there is heavy erosion. I could go through the catalog of thousands of fairy types, but you get the idea. I admit that sometimes it's tough to figure out the vital service of a particular race; in a few cases, like the Imir, they are the guardians and protectors of other races performing essential services, but they all have their niches. That's their primary function—one thing each that guarantees that things will develop in certain ways."

"Seems to me, bees pollinate things pretty good," Joe commented.

"But that's the way things were *supposed* to work. In the early days, though, they needed a nudge. That's what the original fairies were for on your own world. Of course, they weren't that needed, and now those who are left are hunted, oppressed, or hiding out and coping. That's part of my job—finding them and bringing them over here, where we still need them. You see, Joe, this world wasn't as thoroughly planned out or carefully formed as yours, so compromises had to be made. Not only are the fairies vital, but the wild card is magic, which fills in the holes, so to speak. It's actually a more awkward system, but it's worked out pretty well so far."

"This is all leading somewhere."

"Smart lad. First, I want you to remember and accept what I've just said. Marge is still culturally and intellectually of your world, so there's still somebody around to talk to. However, she's also of faërie, an elemental, and that controls her actions and attitudes from here on in."

"You talk as if she's some kind of smart bee or something."

"Well, that's close. Faërie nature and function is instinctive.

It's in the genes, if you will. The intellect is imposed over that, and is subservient to it. Not that fairies are any dumber than humans—many are far smarter—but they have less control. Instinctive behavior, of which we have almost none, comes first. That's why you're going to have to be both patient and understanding with her, Joe. I don't want you two at each other's throat or mad or upset at one another. I can't afford it."

"I'll try. But I notice you keep dancing around the subject without actually coming to it. Don't you think it's about time you stopped discussing the troubles I have and start telling me about the troubles you're going to give me?"

Ruddygore grinned, but the grin faded quickly. "I'm after the end game, Joe. The *coup de grâce*. The Baron's planning something and we don't know what it is. Whole armies have simply vanished, and we don't think they've been disbanded or used internally—he has far too many troops and far too much magic for that."

"And, somehow, you want me and Marge to find out what's going on."

"If you could, it would be a bonus, but I have others working on that. No, Joe, if all goes as planned here this week, I'm going to play my own end game, my separate table. Even if we find out what's up and stop it, it will only be another short victory before something else is tried, then another thing and another. But if I can take out the chief player in this game, I can set these demonic plans back for a generation or more, until they find a new Dark Baron and properly corrupt, train, and position him or her. It's the Baron I want, son—nothing else matters as much."

Joe nodded. "So you're going to try and smoke him out here, then send us against him. The demon can't interfere, so Marge vamps him and Irving runs him through, huh?"

The sorcerer chuckled. "I wish it were that simple. I really do. But Marge would be powerless against somebody of the Baron's strength. In fact, that's her biggest danger. Right now she's feeling her powers and she's cocky and overconfident, which is to be expected. But her powers are really quite limited and easily muted—probably by half or more of the delegates arriving here."

That worried Joe. "Uh—I've seen the results already of

what one of you boys can do when you get irritated."

"I'll talk to her. Hmmm . . . No, that wouldn't do it. I know—I'll set her up."

"Huh?"

"I'll have a couple of old friends get to know her. Either one will become as nasty or obnoxious as the situation permits, and she'll find herself powerless to defend herself. Maybe we'll stick a harmless spell on her, like compulsive singing and dancing or something like that. It will take her down a peg, make her more cautious."

"Well, I'll leave that to you. But if she's powerless against the Baron—and I *know* he could turn me into a toad before I got close—then what are we going to do?"

"During the convention, I, along with Poquah, Macore, and several others not obviously with me, will pursue various lines of investigation. With any luck, we're going to be able to narrow down the Baron's probable identity."

"Good trick. How many real high-class magicians are here? Two thousand?"

"Closer to ten thousand, but that doesn't matter. The Baron cannot conceal the fact that he is one of the top masters of the art in the world. I took him on, you remember, and I *know.* He fought me to a draw, and you get where I am today by going head to head in some very serious contests of wills and magical talent. More importantly, all the talent in the world won't help you achieve true command unless you have these contests with the masters. Why, here I'll probably take on a dozen challengers for my Council seat. It's the only way they learn and, eventually, the only way they get on the Council. The Baron got his skills through such sorcerers' battles, since there is no other way to get them. Consider—he became that good, good enough to tie me, without ever having taken me on before. I'd know if he had, believe me. A battle technique's like a fingerprint. And since the only truly powerful wizards I've never taken on are those on the Council who have made the Council *after* me, I deduce that our Baron is not only a councillor but one of the newer ones."

"All right, that makes sense, I guess. So it's one of thir—ah, twelve people."

"Uh-huh. And it's easier than that, since six of the twelve do not live in Husaquahr, and I'm certain that the Baron must.

We have pretty good records of where the others were, considering the distances involved and magical transportation means, while the Baron was active here. He simply *must* be on top of things through his expanding empire, and that means a Husaquahrian. So now it is one of six, and we shall try to narrow that down further as we go here."

"Uh-huh. And if you do?"

"Then it's your turn. I need proof, Joe. I need absolute, incontrovertible proof that the Baron is a tool of a demon prince. Only with that proof will the Council act against one of its own, and only the Council can do the job."

"Are you sure even of that? I mean, there are several of the Council working with him, aren't there? Don't a bunch live in lands he controls?"

"Quite true, but you misunderstand the seriousness of the affair. The more truly evil and corrupt a sorcerer is, the more stake he has in making certain that the covenant between Heaven and Hell remains unbroken. If Hell breaks the covenant, then the Creator's forces are free to do the same, and that means total war to the finish between the two sides. Armageddon. The end of all the universes. And on whose side will those evil and corrupt ones find themselves?"

Joe's Sunday school was a little weak, but he thought he had the idea. "Uh-huh. So they've got their cushy evilness here, kinda like the Wicked Witch in Oz. They have their own crazy idea of Heaven now, and they won't be anxious to pay the bill."

"You have it. I'm convinced Hell, too, doesn't really know about this. I don't think they're ready for the final battle, which, of course, they intend to win by picking their own time and place. Last I checked, old Lucifer's still got his heart set on nuclear war over on your side. But since he started his whole career on disloyalty and treachery, it's little wonder that his underlings echo that, even to him. He's so busy spreading his little bombs all over Earth, he's not paying any attention to our side, and that's his mistake. So you see, Joe, the odds aren't totally stacked against you. It's few people who have both God and the devil on their side. Maybe you can also now appreciate the real stakes. You have a son, I recall?"

Joe nodded. "Yeah. In Philadelphia. I think about him a lot. That's why I named my sword after him."

"So don't let your emotions get the better of you. A lot hangs on you and Marge getting along and working together. I'll have a little chat with her later on in the convention, perhaps after she's learned her lesson."

Joe knew it was a dismissal and he was glad for it. Besides, the coffee was all gone here, but there was more in the parlor, he was sure. Still, one thing bothered him. As he got up and turned to go, he suddenly turned back to the big sorcerer. "Uh—you say you're gonna have to fight a bunch of up-and-coming sorcerers here?"

Ruddygore nodded. "That's the way it is."

"Any chance you'll lose?"

"There's always a chance, but I've already looked over this group and it looks like a pretty lean crop this season. Not that some of 'em don't have potential—maybe in twenty or thirty years they'll be up to it, but not now."

"Now, don't you get cocky, either."

"Point taken, swordsman to magician." Ruddygore snapped his fingers. "Oh, I almost forgot. Has Tiana arrived yet?"

Joe shrugged. "I don't know. I wouldn't know her if I bumped into her."

"Oh, if you bump into her, you'll know, Joe, I promise you. You two should get along very well, actually. Ask Poquah for her background when you get a moment."

"Okay, I'll do that. See you later?"

"Perhaps. Perhaps not for some time. Relax and enjoy yourself here. Consider it a vacation with pay and relax. In another week you're going back to work."

"I'm going to do just that," Joe assured him and left.

"This your first one of these things?" Joe asked Macore over coffee and pastry in the parlor.

The little thief nodded. "You better believe it. Man, I wouldn't try to hustle any of *these* babies. Their rooms and belongings have magical guardians. You run a con on 'em, even if it works, and they send out the spirit world to get you wherever you are. Uh-uh. This is *one* convention that's safe as a holy temple."

"So how come you're here?"

Macore grinned. "I was asked. Well, more than asked. Better you don't know any more, for your own sake as well as mine. If the old boy wants to tell you, then we'll talk."

"I think I get the idea." Ruddygore was at least the equal of any of the top sorcerers here, so he could offer major protection to a thief—and a master thief, able to tap magical powers through his boss, would be quite an asset here. Looking for—what? Joe wondered. A suit of ghostly armor? Certainly something, anything, that would lead to the identity of the Dark Baron, probably through the adepts. They wouldn't have as good protection, and they'd be overconfident here. Any adepts working directly for the Baron had to know, and, if they did, there might be something telltale somewhere. Joe didn't envy the little thief his job, but he appreciated the risks involved. For some of these more-than-human sorcerers, death wasn't the worst thing to fear.

They had begun talking about old times when there was a sudden, sharp pounding on the door, and all conversation ceased. Poquah emerged from his own room and went to the door, opening it. After a glance, he admitted the newcomer.

At first sight of her, all other topics were forgotten by Joe. As Ruddygore had said, if he ever bumped into Tiana, he'd know.

She was, quite simply, the most beautiful woman Joe had ever seen; from the expressions on the faces of the others, he wasn't alone in that assessment. It was hard to go beyond that. Everything about her was absolutely perfect—perfect figure, perfect proportions, and a beautiful, sensuous face. Her skin was tanned a deep and very dark brown, matching her eyes, but her lips were curiously light and very enticing. Her jet-black hair hung down almost to her narrow, perfect waist, while her skin was as smooth and blemish-free as polished ebony. She looked, Joe thought, like some stunning Italian movie star; there was a Mediterranean cast to her features, as if she belonged somewhere romping on the beaches of the Riviera, and that thought was enhanced by the fact that she was wearing only a breechclout made of the hide of some furry brown animal and a halter of the same material that did nothing to hide her obvious attributes, as well as a necklace of what looked like gold chain to which small, carved pieces of bone had been attached. From a sword belt, a broadsword nearly the size of Joe's hung in a leather scabbard. The belt was worn loosely, emphasizing the curve of her hips.

Probably the most outstanding thing about her was that she was barefoot, yet stood well over six feet tall. In fact, when Joe stood up, transfixed, he found her to be perhaps a half inch shorter than his own six-six—and he was wearing new sandals.

For a moment, nobody said anything, so she walked briskly into the room and looked around. "Well? Is everyone struck dumb?" she said irritably, her voice deep and rich. She spoke with a trace of what sounded like a German accent to Joe; but, considering the fact that this was a world with languages different from his, it might only seem that way.

Poquah was quick to recover. "Tiana, I presume. I am Poquah, the Master's chief associate. These gentlemen here are Macore, Joseph, and Durin, respectively."

She looked them all over, then settled on Joe and frowned. "That is an unusual name here, Joseph. Where are you from?"

"Philadelphia," he told her.

"Oh, that is in the United States of America, I believe," she responded, literally shocking the hell out of him.

"Uh, yeah, it is, but how . . . ?"

"I was never there, but for seven years I was in hiding in Basel, Switzerland."

This was too much at one time. "Switzerland! How?" But instantly he knew the answer. Only one person he knew could hide a Husaquahrian in Europe, and that person was in the next room.

"I was the oldest daughter of Hapandur of Morikay. When I was but nine years old, he was defeated at a gathering just like this one by that pig Kaladon, whom my father had befriended and treated as a son." She went over, looked at the pastries, took one, then sat down on the couch and sprawled out.

Joe sank back into his chair. Suddenly the coffee didn't seem a strong enough drink right about then. He'd once described Marge's moves as catlike; Tiana was a tigress.

"So you had to make a run for it, huh?" Macore prompted. Barely five foot five and perhaps a hundred and twenty pounds, he couldn't help feeling like a little child who'd just come across a ten-thousand-gallon chocolate sundae.

She nodded. "Yes. Kaladon had dreams that he would marry me as soon as I was old enough, thus legitimizing his rule, since everyone knew the bastard won only by cheating. He actually made advances to me, an innocent of nine!"

Joe just followed along, but couldn't help wondering how Tiana could ever have been an innocent nine-year-old.

"Well, with the help of some fairies loyal to my poor father, I escaped, but Kaladon pursued. Fortunately, the faërie network got me to Ruddygore, one of my father's few very close friends who could be trusted, and he took me out of reach for a while."

"But you came back," Joe noted. "Why?"

"I was discovered. Kaladon is in league with Hell itself; in exchange for certain favors here, ones which involved aiding the Dark Baron, the demons of Earth sought me out and attacked. It seemed pointless to remain there when this was my native land, so I was returned. I have been in hiding since, these past eight years, moving with the wild tribes and studying and training when I could in both the magical and the combat arts. I have grown quite good." That last was said without any trace of boasting, and they believed it.

"But now you're back, and in the same hotel as this Kaladon," Macore pointed out. "Why? Are you ready to take him on?"

"No, I do not believe that I am ready for him yet. One day I will be and I will reclaim what is mine by rights. I was summoned here by Dr. Ruddygore, and, considering what I owe him, I could not refuse. It makes no difference. Kaladon had found me out, anyway, and killed many of those who were closest to me."

"Then you are in great danger here," Macore suggested. "Kaladon will know you are here."

"He dares do nothing at the convention unless he wishes to challenge Dr. Ruddygore," she told him. "And that he is not up to doing under any circumstances."

"Quite true," came a voice behind her, and they all turned to see the great sorcerer enter the room, resplendent now in his golden robes. "He has already been informed that any move against Tiana will make in me an enemy he can not avoid in this public place."

"Ruddy!" Tiana cried out joyfully. In a flash she'd gotten up, turned, and actually jumped over her chair, finally reaching and embracing the sorcerer, who, if he'd been of lesser size and bulk, would certainly have been bowled over.

Joe looked at Macore. "Ruddy?"

The little thief tried to suppress a laugh, and it was clear that Ruddygore was not amused. Still, he tolerated the display and attempted to pass it off. "Tiana, it is good to see you once again. I must be going downstairs to find out my schedule, but I can spare a moment. Come—sit just a bit."

She moved obediently back to her chair and settled there. Joe bet a bundle to himself that nobody else could ever get such meek obedience from her. Ruddygore did not sit, but stood facing them all. "That spell I sent you—I gather it worked?"

She smiled and nodded. "Very well indeed. In fact, I passed the usurper in the lobby here and he never recognized me."

Macore looked crestfallen. "You mean she really doesn't look like that?"

Ruddygore chuckled both at the question and at the mean look Tiana gave the little thief. "Oh, my, yes," the sorcerer assured them all. "The spell is a particularly powerful and undetectable one, since it's tailored strictly to Kaladon and affects no one else. To him, and to him alone, Tiana looks quite different, although still rather striking. Basically a blond, blue-eyed, and fair-skinned priestess from the northern wastes, if I remember correctly. It's just enough of a change so that she is definitely not Tiana to him in looks, voice, or habit, but close enough that the reactions of those around him will be consistent with what he sees. It's a thin disguise at best, but I don't expect him to crack it easily, since he's very confident that no one can put an undetectable spell over on him. Don't rely on it too heavily, my dear."

"I am not worried about him," she said confidently. "Not with you around, anyway."

He just shrugged. "Well, I must get down there. Tiana, I've had you preregistered as Uma of the Golden Lakes, just as an extra precaution. Why make it any easier on him, after all? I'm also curious to see how long it's going to take him to find you out."

"That is fine with me," she told him. "I will see you later, then."

With that, Ruddygore turned and, accompanied by Poquah, left the suite.

"Have you any luggage coming?" Joe asked her.

She shook her head. "None. I travel as light as I possibly

can. You learn that most of all after eight years in hiding. Always I carry my sword with me, and in the belt is a hidden compartment in which there are some coins and gems. The only thing I don't have with me is my bullwhip. I was forced to abandon it a few weeks ago, so I will have to get another here."

"The market is excellent for just about anything," Joe told her. "And, right now, we're on Ruddygore's expense account."

She nodded. "Good, then. I am also starved. Will you show me this market? Then we can perhaps get something to eat."

Joe got up and she did, as well. Again there was an eerie sensation in him at her size. "Delighted," he responded, trying to sound as Continental as possible. "Shall we go?"

They walked out the door, leaving Macore sitting there. Durin chuckled from the kitchenette. "Left you alone, huh? I guess you're just not big enough for her."

Macore got up, walked over, took some of the fabulously rich iced pastry from the tray, and, without a word or a wasted motion, pushed it into the fairy cook's face.

Joe was absolutely delighted with Tiana. Although of this world, she had some knowledge of a different corner of his and she was certainly a fascinating person indeed. It was also a relief, after all this time of putting up with Marge's vegetarianism, to find a woman who obviously enjoyed real meat.

Slowly, over the meal, he told her more about himself and about his doings since arriving in Husaquahr. Gradually, the rest of her story came out, as well.

Her father had been of royal blood, but a third son with no chance of inheriting position or title. His obvious talent for the magical arts, however, had taken him in the direction of the Society in the same way that second and third sons of European nobility during the Middle Ages had gone into the Catholic church. He also married a wealthy noblewoman he'd known since childhood, and they were very much in love. In due course, they had a daughter, Torea, but she died mysteriously in infancy of some disease or spell her father was powerless to do anything about. They tried again, of course, at about the time Hapandur won the Council seat and became ranking sorcerer in Zhimbombe, but the pregnancy was well along before he discovered that his first daughter's death had been due to a strange and powerful curse laid on his children by someone unknown who hated him very much. Just who was unknown.

The curse was so well constructed that he could not dissolve it, nor find its key, but he did manage to unravel it "at the corners," as Tiana cryptically put it. The result was that her mother was able to make the decision—either her life or her child's—and she made it. The distraught wizard pleaded with her, but she had taken the death of their first daughter very hard and she was adamant.

"What my father did was complex," Tiana told Joe. "Basically, though, my birth was a magical event of sorts. The soul, I am told, enters at the first commands to the body to give birth. My father, or so it is said, blocked that process, against my mother's strong wishes, so that I might be stillborn, but so strong was her resolve that she died at the moment of my birth. My father would never speak of it, but others have told me that her soul, because of her will to bear me, entered me instead of another."

Joe was startled. "You mean you're your *mother*?"

She shrugged. "I do not know. But it is certain that I have always had strange dreams, and memories of people and places that I have never seen, and I have always been told by those of Morikay that I have my mother's mannerisms, habits, and even turns of phrase. Physically, I resemble more others on both sides of the family than her, but it does seem, sometimes, when I look into a mirror, that another, different face should be there."

Still, her father never remarried, nor, as far as anyone knew, ever even looked at another woman sexually; but he doted on his daughter, to whom he gave his dead wife's name. She had a very spoiled and pampered childhood, she freely admitted, and was totally unprepared for what came after.

Kaladon, a handsome young man with a great deal of talent, became apprenticed to her father and proved a more-than-worthy adept. He was treated as a member of the family—in fact, as the son the old man had never had. She liked him at the time, considering him an older brother, and she had no idea that, even back then, he was arranging for her to get as little education or training as possible, particularly in the magical arts.

"Then came the great convention, at Coditz Green in Leander, where we knew Kaladon would challenge for a leadership position. How proud we were of him—the son of a pig! He was so trusted and so close that it was a shock when he challenged my father, and an even greater shock that he won."

"You mentioned that he cheated," Joe noted.

She nodded. "Later I was told how it was done. He had drugged some of the food my father was served. He could easily do this, because he was a household member and very trusted. It was also a very light drug, one that you would not even know you had taken, but it was enough to slow my father's thinking and speed of action and reaction. After he won, while still at the convention, the usurper's true nature came out, and we knew that we were in the hands of and at the mercy of the blackest of black magicians."

Joe hesitated a moment before asking the obvious question, but he really was interested in the story and anxious to know. "Uh—what happens to the losers of these challenges?"

She gave a slight shudder. "Horrible things. That is why even very powerful magicians do not challenge for the Council. True adepts, not going for a position but simply testing themselves, are prevented by the umpires of such matches from going too far, and so there is no penalty; but if a councillor is deposed, he or she must be utterly reduced so that no rechallenge is possible."

"Your father is dead, then."

She nodded sadly. "Yes, but not by Kaladon's hand. They do not work like that, particularly the black magicians who dominate the white, nor, in fact, the white who dominate the black, but my father had many friends and one was merciful."

He whistled. "Are these contests open to the public?"

"If you mean can you see one, the answer is that you can see as many as you wish here, but it can be a very dangerous thing to watch. The forces involved are tremendous."

He could understand that. "Still, I think I'll see one of Ruddygore's matches if I can. I should know everything I can about the kind of people I'm actually facing here. The fact is, except for some of Ruddygore's stuff with me, the fairies, and the magic Lamp, I've seen very little real magic here. Not the kind they talk of the sorcerers having, anyway."

"Then you should see one, in fact," she agreed.

After the *coup* she was returned, a pampered prisoner, to

Morikay, entirely in the hands of her father's betrayer. Kaladon began a purge of all those, human and fairy, loyal to the deposed sorcerer, but some had gotten the word and arranged for escape routes. Two winged elves from Marquewood, who had worked at landscaping in Morikay, managed to flee with Tiana, as well.

It was a harrowing, risky escape, the material for an epic or two, but finally she was passed along from fairy race to fairy race until she reached Castle Terindell. It was Ruddygore who took her in; when he realized that she would be a virtual lifetime prisoner inside the castle as long as Kaladon lived, he took her across to Earth. Ruddygore, it seemed, had a major interest in a bank in Switzerland, and, since that was where he was heading, that was where she wound up, with loyal guardians in his employ taking her in and providing an identity for her as the daughter of deposed Romanian royalty killed later by the communists there. Having been magically prepared by Ruddygore, she took to languages easily, quickly acquiring a fluency in German, French, Italian, and even Romansch. Her tutors were both of Earth and of Husaquahr, imported for the occasion by Ruddygore on frequent visits, and it was during those years that she threw herself into her studies with but one long-term object in mind—revenge.

By this time, though, Kaladon had fallen in league with the Dark Baron, whose demonic master could talk to and deal with the demons of Earth, and it was as a bribe to Kaladon that the Baron had the demonic forces seek her out and find her. A well-financed Satanist organization in western Europe then was called in for the actual deed, and again she barely escaped back to Husaquahr.

"Ruddy decided that, if they could find me once, they could certainly find me anywhere, now that my appearance was known. As you might have guessed, I had grown and turned from girl into woman."

She had, in fact, been a fairly normal-sized girl, but with puberty came tremendous growth, far beyond anything in her ancestry. "Ruddy has a theory that it was the diet, eating such a different balance of things in Switzerland from what our bodies are used to here. I believe it was probably a spell of some kind put on me before I left Husaquahr, although by whom I am not sure. It might have been my father, of course, or any one of the fairy races who aided me, or a combination of those things. It does not matter, because this is how I am and this is how I like being."

"*I* certainly see nothing to complain about," Joe told her honestly. "You are certainly the most beautiful woman I've ever seen."

She smiled. "That's very nice of you."

"I mean it, too."

She sat back a moment, holding a slight grin. "You know, because of my size I have been very intimidating to men. I wonder if perhaps Ruddy is not engaging in a bit of match-making."

He wondered that himself. If so, he hoped that she had the same attraction for him that he felt for her. It certainly was a very convenient meeting, just after his troubles with Marge, and it *had* been arranged by the sorcerer. Well, if so, it was the best thing the old boy had done for him, even if it didn't work.

Tiana's history for the past eight years had been far different from her earlier life. It was only among the barbarous nomadic tribes of the far reaches of Husaquahr that she could blend in, somewhat, with the large, burly denizens of those places, and it was only among them that she could feel relatively safe from Kaladon's spies and the threats of civilization in general.

At first, she had rebelled at the primitive, hard existence, and there had been a period of tremendous adjustment until she'd learned to accept it. It was a kind of existence that Morikay and Basel had not prepared her for, and she was flung into it much as Joe had been flung into his existence. She had been taken under the wing of some very powerful warriors who owed Ruddygore a favor. She became, however, strong, powerful, and athletic and, because of her size and conditioning, she trained with swords and took the tests of a warrior usually, but not exclusively, reserved for the men. She had excelled at all of it in the end, particularly when she saw the value of it in having some personal freedom in Husaquahr and, perhaps, one day leading a rebellion in the south.

She also trained in, and worked on, the magical arts with the help of Ruddygore and knowledgeable ones he sent to her, first in Basel and later in the northern wastes. She had her father's talent, of that there was no doubt, but she began formal training very late in the game and on an intermittent basis. "It gives me an edge, but not more," she told Joe. "It means, also, that I can often ward off or undo some spells, but the more complex spells are still beyond me, for I have not had the mental training for it." She could, however, read the pictographic language fairly well, and with the proper volume and section of the Books of Rules open in front of her, she could probably do very well indeed. "It is, you might say, the difference between being a good cook and being a chef. A great chef does not need recipes."

They finished, he paid the bill, and they made their way back into the market. There were several leather shops selling whips, and she tried one after the other, impressing the hell out of him, the proprietors, and the passers-by with her skill, but rejecting whip after whip until, at last, in a small second-hand store, she found one that seemed just right to her. "With the others I can do many things," she explained, "but with a whip of perfect balance such as this one, I can work miracles."

She looped it on her belt, on the same side as the sword, in a clasp apparently designed for the weapon, and they walked back to the hotel.

"No shoes or other clothing?" he asked her.

She laughed. "It is odd, but I have been with the barbarians so long that most of those things feel unnatural. If I need furs, I will buy them, but for now I am enjoying for the first time in a long while a comfortable climate. It is not easy to explain, but in order to survive in the wastes, something had to be killed inside me, and that was my sense of civilization, you might say. I find myself preferring to be a barbarian woman, thinking like one, acting like one. All this which was once my own sort of world seems now so soft and decadent. The sword, the whip, and a good horse are all that are really needed, and all that I have or intend to have."

"You seem pretty cultured and civilized to me."

"Because I want to be. That is my veneer, my coat which allows me to go anywhere and do anything. It is the inside that matters, and I have proof of my conversion, as it were. The applicable parts of the Books of Rules that apply to me now are those governing barbarian women; before, they were of the civilized classes. Even the Rules recognize my change, you see."

"But if you depose Kaladon, you'll have to rule Zhimbombe," he pointed out. "That will take more of a change."

"I think they deserve a barbarian queen. We will face that if it comes about."

He noted that she had used the word "if" instead of "when" and nodded to himself. Just how realistic her dream was, even in her own mind, was in question. She had as much as admitted that she could never be the equal of Kaladon and, unless he was finished off, she had little hope of having any kind of control over the country. Kaladon, of course, had probably intended just that—she would be his puppet queen and consort, by which he would consolidate the country and its popular old families and his own rule as both sorcerer and temporal ruler. Joe decided that he'd like to meet, or at least see, this fellow at close range. Certainly, if nothing else, Kaladon would be one of Ruddygore's prime suspects for the Baron's true identity. How easy it would be to pretend to ally with the Baron for favors when actually he *was* the Baron—and Zhimbombe was the first nation of Husaquahr to fall prey to the Baron's forces. A prime suspect indeed. If Joe's suspicions were so, there was a chance through Kaladon's elimination to give Tiana a crack at control by clever politics, sword, and whip.

They reentered the hotel, which was teeming with crowds of people of all shapes and sizes, garbed in every imaginable way. "Shall we register?" Tiana asked him.

He nodded. "Might as well."

She thought a moment. "You are called 'the Golden,' is that not correct?"

"Yeah. Mostly because my last name's de Oro."

"And I am Uma of the Golden Lakes. It gives me a thought. We are both dark-skinned giants, you might say, and we certainly look as if we belong together."

He wondered what she was driving at and just nodded.

"Kaladon will not expect a pair. Let us, at least for disguise purposes, register as mates."

"Huh?" It took him aback, mainly because he'd love it that way, but he hardly wanted to risk alienating her by suggesting it. He just wasn't used to women *this* aggressive.

"You don't wish it?"

"Oh, sure. I think it'll be fun," he answered hopefully. "Let's go."

* * *

It was like waking up from some really strange dream, although she knew it was no dream at all. She wasn't physically tired, but she'd come back up to the room for a little break and found herself just sitting back, relaxing and thinking, and she realized thinking was something distasteful. She certainly hadn't been doing much of it over the last few days, that was for sure.

It was funny how this reaction had hit her, like something out of the blue, but suddenly, after being almost frantically active, she no longer felt the desire. She walked over to the mirror in the room and looked at herself. It was still strange to see the fairy reflection there, to understand that this unnaturally sexy, kittenish, winged figure was herself. But it wasn't the exterior that was troubling her; it was what had happened inside to her head and heart.

She'd been to every bar and bistro in the city, she felt certain, but they all blended into one. And the men—so many of them—all blended into a faceless crowd as well. Not a single one stood out as a real human being. Instead, they were objects, things, nothing more. She went over to a dresser and pulled out the top drawer. It was crammed with junk—small items of jewelry, ornaments, little carvings, even toys. She was afraid to count them and slammed the drawer shut and went back to the bed to think.

Had she enjoyed acting that way? Yeah, she had, she had to admit to herself, but it wasn't really *her*; at least, not the way she always saw herself. Her whole body still tingled, and on that level she had never felt better in her whole life. But was this what she was to be for the rest of her life? How long did a fairy live if not killed? Until Judgment Day, it was said, and nobody knew how long that could be. Hundreds of years, perhaps. Maybe thousands. All like—this?

She remembered the magic time when she had emerged from the volcanic fires as a Kauri and she remembered her sisters of faërie. At the time, they had seemed radiant, magical children at play, but they didn't seem quite so exciting or magical any more. Instead, they now seemed like what they must be—permanent fourteen-year-old girls, locked forever in the state of irresponsible and irrepressible adolescence and freed of all inhibitions; a female version of the Lost Boys, without even Peter Pan, let alone Wendy, to give them any sort of control or direction, and each one more or less exactly like the others. Even she had become exactly like them, and that bothered her only because the Kauri didn't know any other existence or any other way, had never faced or understood responsibility or had a single serious thought in their playfully empty heads. She had, and that alone set her apart from them.

But she *had* been that age once and had been frustratingly restricted by her mother, the school, and the rest of those forces that kept folks in line. Still, life had been unhappy enough since adulthood that she had grabbed onto the chance to return to that state of not-so-innocent grace, to become again that giggly adolescent without any rules or restrictions whatsoever. Who wouldn't love that sort of chance—but as a chance, a lark. It was only now that she realized that this wasn't some second chance but rather a permanent condition.

Already she had hurt poor Joe, the first man in years to be a real friend, the one whose kindness and pity gave her this second chance in the first place. She'd not only hurt him, she'd mocked him, and that was far more painful. Her practical jokes and funny exercises of her strange powers had frightened rather than amused or reassured him. Worse, she knew deep down that she might not have the self-control or willpower to keep those impulses from dominating her again and that each cycle would make them even easier and more natural to accept. The more she lived as a Kauri, the more she would become one inside as well as out. This she knew, although not really from any faërie insight, but just from knowing herself. Conditioning *did* work—as Pavlov's dogs had proved—particularly when there were no alternatives and an endless future of such conditioning. The Earth Mother knew this, and counted on it.

Kauri awoke with the setting sun. Kauri played games, danced, sang, flew around, and soared through the skies playing tag, then went to their toy box and played pretend with their pretty toys. At sunrise, Kauri went to sleep and dreamed only happy dreams, awakening again to do the same thing with minor variations the next day and the next. If they felt like it, on impulse or whatever, they ventured out of their faërie Never-Neverland and played with the boys in the real world that was still nothing more than an extended playland to them, with the inhabitants merely toys like those on the scrap heap.

Kauri didn't need to think. In fact, thinking was something that was an absolutely bad thing for them. Oh, they needed to talk—but innocuously and as vacuously as possible. That, in fact, was an advantage among the kind of men they liked to play with. Marge wondered how long she would be able to have this level of introspection, or even remember words like innocuous, vacuous, or introspection. Certainly her spoken vocabulary already seemed to switch to something more childlike and basic. Following the period of her binge, she now realized, she was speaking in a sexy variation of little-girl speech without even thinking about it.

Without even thinking...

At that moment, she heard a commotion in the hallway and went over to her door. To her surprise, she heard Ruddygore's booming baritone and then the sound of the door of the adjacent room opening and closing.

The old Marge would have hesitated to disturb him and would have just sat and brooded, but she literally didn't think about it in this case. She opened her door, went down to the big double doors of the parlor suite, and just turned the handle and walked in without knocking.

Both Ruddygore and Poquah turned in puzzled surprise at her entrance; but when the big sorcerer saw her, he broke into a grin and sat down in the chair. He looked very tired, but he said, "That's all right, Poquah—leave us alone."

The Imir looked a bit concerned for his boss, but bowed slightly and did as he was instructed, sliding his own door shut behind him.

Ruddygore beckoned her over with his hand. "Pardon me for not rising, my dear, but I'm about done in."

"That's all right," she told him. "I guess I should have set up some better time to see you, but I don't seem much in control of myself any more."

"I think I understand," he said sympathetically. "Don't worry about me. Although I hadn't intended to seek you out until another day or two, this is fine, since I'm not getting any younger and this pace is telling."

"I just want to know why."

"Huh?" The comment took him by surprise. "Why what?"

"Why am I a Kauri? I was happy the way I was, after coming here. Why did I have to change?"

"Those are two different questions, my dear. You seem to imply that I had something to do with it."

"Well? Didn't you?"

"Not a thing, I assure you." As quickly and as clearly as possible, but with more detail on the fine points, he explained to her, as he had to Joe, why she had been made a changeling from the moment they crossed the Sea of Dreams. "I made you neither changeling nor Kauri. You did that to yourself."

"Me!"

He nodded. "Oh, with your mental state, I should have known from the start that you would be a changeling—but what sort was really up to you." He thought a moment. "My dear, what is your vision of Heaven and Hell?"

She shrugged. "Harps on the one side, fires on the other, I guess."

"Uh-uh. Would it shock you to learn that Heaven and Hell are actually the same place?"

"*Huh?*"

He nodded. "That's why Hell is such a curse. You can look around and *see*, with little difficulty, just what you missed, but you're stuck as you are, permanently. And the way you are is what you built for yourself. Let's see if I can explain it. If Joe should die, his soul would be re-formed according to the chain he forged in life, with his own mind, conscious and subconscious, creating his own Heaven or Hell. Most folks, as you might expect, wind up somewhere in between. Then, at the end of time, there will be a Judgment. Those of Hell will at that time suffer the true and total death, while those judged worthy will be able to perfect their own existences and live happily ever after in total communion with the Creator. That's the way it works."

"But not for me?"

"Not quite. As a changeling, your physical form was burned off in the fires; and because you, as a fairy, exist in the physical world, you became what your mind said it should become within the limits of our world. You never wished to harm anyone, so you became something that can not consciously harm anyone. You felt that the world was out to do *you* harm, so you became something that can defend itself against the evil, cruelty, and malice of the world."

She sighed sadly. "I see. With a bad world all around, I

wanted only to give and get pleasure," She stopped for a moment, suddenly feeling stunned. "And since I ran down my education as getting me nowhere and nothing and being a real waste, I became something that didn't need any of that. Sweet Mother! I *did* do it to myself, sort of. But this wasn't what I had in mind!"

"It seldom is," he told her, "for anybody, and not just changelings. It's wonderful to see some of those Holy Joes permanently sitting on clouds, forever singing hymns and hosannahs, bored out of their skulls. You very seldom get what you really want, but you usually get what you deserve, based on your own life and thoughts and desires, both expressed and suppressed."

"Then that's it, I guess. I'm stuck until Judgment, and by that time I'll be as empty and bubble-headed as my sisters and probably just keep on going, like somebody with a lobotomy."

He looked serious. "So that's what it is. I should have guessed as much." And he *did* see. The Kauri form was exactly what that lonely loser on her way to suicide in Texas would have wanted; and, since it was from that woman that the forces of magic took their cue, that was what she'd become. But now Marge was not that woman; Husaquahr had given her a whole new life and outlook, and she was no longer a perfect match for what she now was.

"The best I can offer," he told her, "is some hope, with work on your part, for something a little more than that. You are Kauri and you will remain Kauri. There is nothing anyone can do, since you of faërie may be destroyed but not transformed. But the fact that you're talking to me, here and now, shows that there's still *you* inside there."

"Yeah, but me, the Marge that's talking, is losing. I mean, I think I figured out that Kauri are elementals, not like the elves and gnomes and other creatures. There are water elementals, and wood elementals, even fire elementals, but we're a different kind, since we're out of Earth, Air, and Fire. I don't know about Water."

"You swim like a fish," he told her. "Go on."

"We're—emotion elementals. Only certain kinds of emotions, though. The good ones, I guess. Singing, dancing, playing, even sex."

"That's close enough." Briefly he told her the function of

fairies in the scheme of things, as he had told Joe. "Now, Kauri, they have a very important place in the scheme of things. You may not know it, but each and every man you were with so far had some sort of problem. You're attracted to them without realizing it. They're not evil or nasty or anything like that, not in the main, but they have totally lost touch with that sense of childlike innocence and wonder. They're troubled by all sorts of things—business pressures, deadlines, deep depression, that kind of psychiatric illness—and you, believe it or not, help restore to them a sense of fun, of life worth living. That's the Kauri function."

"All I can say is there are a lot of men with hang-ups," she noted acidly. "That and the fact that never have I felt less like a shrink and more like a homebreaker."

Ruddygore chuckled. "Homebreaker? No. You leave no guilt. That's part of the magic. Those men, like all who receive fairy gifts, take with them only the positive. They become better husbands, better fathers, better in their work for it. Believe me when I say that *Kauri can do harm to no one* unless that person attempts to harm them. *Any* kind of harm. The magic knows.

"Look, Marge—don't downplay your importance. Maybe if they had Kauri on Earth, they would have a lot fewer problems, although there are—counterparts—for the other side as well, you know. Incubi and succubi, they're usually called, and their purpose is the opposite of yours. They are elementals of a far different sort and they are your sole true enemies."

She considered that. "Then is there a male form of Kauri? It seems only fair."

He nodded. "Yes, there is such a race, the Zamir. But let's get back to the Kauri. Tell me—what have you eaten in the past few days?"

She thought a moment, then realized that, while things were a blur, she was pretty sure of this answer. "Nothing. Nothing at all."

"Feel hungry?"

"Not in the slightest."

"Because what you eat is the collective terrors, insecurities, and nightmares of the men you serve. In an ironic way, they power you, as the succubus devours the good and leaves corruption. That's why you feel both physically wonderful and mentally down right now. In time you will transform that spiritual decay and it will lessen, but often it gets too much to bear. Then you *must* return to Mohr Jerahl and cleanse yourself in the fires of the Earth Mother. Otherwise it will tire you terribly and weaken you to a tremendous degree. You see the system now? I always thought it was rather nice."

She *did* see the system, and that made her feel better, to a degree. It explained the very substance of Mohr Jerahl and the reason for the uninhibited innocence they all had there, as well as why they were concerned about her going outside it the first time.

She gave a dry chuckle. "So what you're saying is that I do my job, then revert to this adolescent level, only to build it up again. And because I've eaten my fill, so to speak, and because ol' Marge is really a collection of hang-ups, I'm only me when I'm carrying around everybody else's burdens."

"If you want to put it that way, yes," he told her. "And the longer you go without eating, let's say, the more you will revert. It's actually a tough job, since you, the mistress of emotion, will be on an emotional roller coaster. That's why so many Kauri stay at Mohr Jerahl as long as they can, until their instincts force them out. No, Marge, you don't have to worry about forgetting yourself. Your big problem, particularly if you overdo it, will be carrying the extra weight of depression, neuroses, and anxiety."

She thought about it, and it did make life sound a little better. "Does Joe know this?"

"No, not specifically, but I'll make certain he's instructed. Tiana will probably explain it all to him."

"Tiana?" Very oddly, she felt a slight tinge of jealousy at the name. That made her feel a little guilty, considering how she'd chided him for that sort of feeling.

Ruddygore nodded. "They've hit it off very well." He smiled. "You see? You just felt jealousy and guilt—I can tell. They're inside you now, until you transform them into energy as needed, but they are familiar to you from your past experience. In fact, I'd say that you can handle a far heavier load than a born Kauri, because you have experienced such things firsthand and know how to deal with them. No, Marge—you're not going to lose yourself, just take on a new set of problems. I'm counting on you to be able to handle a great deal in the weeks ahead, more than I'd ever ask a born Kauri to handle."

She got interested in spite of herself and lost some of her self-pity in the process. "So this *isn't* just a vacation or a shakedown for me."

He shook his head wearily. "No, hardly. I hesitate to say this, Marge, but the odds are you might be the only one left at the end of this to tell the tale."

CHAPTER 8

THICKENING PLOTS

The convention shall be limited to members of the Society and their authorized guests.

—Rules, VI, 29(a)

TIANA WAS PROVING A GOOD GUIDE TO THE COMPLEXITIES OF the convention, but it was still a confusing blur to Joe. He felt like a truck driver at a convention of nuclear engineers celebrating Halloween.

Registration proved to be no problem. Their names were on file, their single room number raised no eyebrows, and both were suddenly handed large bags full of written material and silver necklaces from which hung a bronze rectangular pendant with various cuneiformlike letters on it, some large and some small. When they were away from registration, he got Tiana to translate.

"Well, the top row gives the name of the Society and says it is their four thousand two hundred and thirty-first meeting, which is abbreviated as Sach-con Nine Hundred and Two. Below that it says, 'Hello, my name is Joseph the Golden.'"

He looked at the last little figures. "So that's my name in this chicken-scratch writing. I'll have to remember it, or keep this as a reference, in case I have to sign my name and pretend I know it all."

She laughed. "Keep that thing on whenever you are in the convention areas," she warned him. "Each one has a spell personalized to the first wearer that admits you tc all public areas. Try and get in without it and you will get a nasty shock."

"I'll remember," he promised. "Where to now?"

"Let us go back into the exhibition hall. I want to see how much has changed since I was a child."

They went back, both clutching their bags, and Joe felt a little absurd. *Mr. and Mrs. Barbarian go shopping*, he thought. "Any reason why I should lug all this stuff around when I can't read a word of it?" he asked her.

"It is hard to say, but probably not. Why not just put it over in that coat room there and get it on the way back, if it is still there?"

He did just that and felt at least a little less foolish. They then entered the exhibition hall, and Joe was surprised to feel it comfortably air-conditioned. "A minor housekeeping spell," Tiana told him.

So this was more of the magic of Husaquahr. "Pretty tame magic," he noted. "I kinda figured that magic lands like this one had all sorts of stuff going all the time."

"Oh, of course not. It is true that magic is all around us all the time here, but it is not intrusive. In fact, the less it is used or has to be used, the better. It is sort of like a balance of power. Earth is a world dominated by nuclear bombs, yet I would say you have seen more magic in this world than nuclear bombs in yours."

She had a point there, so he let it pass. The exhibition hall was huge and filled with large numbers of creatures, both human and fairy—and some he wasn't quite sure about—all in booths or behind long display tables. There was no logic or order to the arrangement, so the old crone selling the latest chemical advances in aphrodisiacs was right next to the bright young fellow selling the Handy Miracle Pocket Indexer, which was apparently less hype than a description of a portable quick-file system that could be clipped onto a belt or carried in a shoulder bag and that allowed the average magician to access and classify spells by all sorts of cross-indexing methods.

They went on, passing a group of salesmen peddling a condensed Books of Rules—only three hundred volumes—complete with the magical Codex, a cross-indexed compendium allowing anything needed in the three hundred volumes to be found easily. Tiana tried to beat off one of the salesmen and finally got rid of him by commenting, "You are already four years out of date, and by the time I received my volume a month on your plan, you would be twenty-nine years out of date." Arguments that a new edition was in preparation fell on deaf ears.

Some of the exhibits were downright disgusting, like the demonstrations by the Entrail-of-the Month Club. Another service offered fresh bat's blood and monkey's eyes. There were also countless protective gadgets and amulets being sold—all worthless, Tiana assured Joe, since any value they might have had was compromised by their being so commercially available.

Some of the salespeople were disconcerting, too. He didn't really mind the centaurs and their variations so much, nor the Panlike satyrs, and certainly not the nubile nymphs, but some of the creatures selling various artifacts and substances, the purposes of which could only be guessed at, were like nothing he'd ever seen before. There was that creepy blue creature, for example, with the wiry hair and buzzardlike beak whose huge, unhuman eyes kept following them, and the things that looked like giant swamp logs with eyes at the tip of each branch.

There were also memory and concentration aids for sale, voodoo dolls and substances to make more—"free demonstration on request"—and much, much more. Small fairy elves were hawking clothing spun in the fairy way out of fairy gold, "for the wizard who truly wants to look the part."

There were booths representing specific interest groups as well. At one booth an old black-clad hag straight out of *Snow White* was apparently representing the Wicked Witches Anti-Defamation League; at another an extremely fat sort of pixie in a blue Keystone Kops-type outfit offered membership to qualified individuals in the Elves, Gnomes, and Little Men's Chowder and Marching Society; while at a third a tough-looking mermaid was half sunk in a tank of water, smoking a big cigar, and representing something called the City-States' Benevolent Protective Organization. Tiana explained that traders bought insurance from them or their ships mysteriously sank somewhere.

Joe could only shake his head in wonder and say, "Gee, I always thought mermaids were real pretty and lovey and all that."

"Oh, many are, particularly the sirens who lure ships onto the rocks by bewitching the sailors. She is just one of the sirens' minor godmothers."

It also took a little adjusting to get used to some of the titles, whose stated acronyms were more than a little disconcerting. Tiana was in a nostalgic mood and kept pointing out luminaries with a disquieting lack of understanding for the way his own mind worked. He decided that maybe it was the similarity of the common trade language to English that was doing it for him.

"Oh, there is Sargash!" she breathed excitedly and pointed. "She is a famous idiot."

Joe looked at the red-robed woman and frowned. "She doesn't look like an idiot to me. She looks pretty smart."

"Oh, you *are* strange, Joseph! I meant she is a famous I.D.I.O.T.—Iconological Doctor of Incantations, Obturations, and Transudations."

"Oh. Yeah, sure."

"And there is Mathala, ogre."

"Actually, she's sort of distinguished."

"No, no. She is head of the Order of Geomorphic Reification and Exuviation."

"If you say so," was all he could respond. Even though he was getting the idea, he *still* didn't know what those words meant.

"Ah, and that man all in black over there is a world-renowned nutcase."

"Do I want to ask questions about that one?"

"Notater of Ultravires, Transubstantiations, Casuistry, Alchemy, Soporophics, and Ephemerides," she explained. "He will be one of the referees in the sorcerers' matches."

"First get me a dictionary—one that I can read," he grumped.

She stopped and gasped. "There—there is the evil bastard himself!"

He waited, noting a tall, distinguished-looking sorcerer in red and green velvet garb, catching up to and talking with Mr.

Nutcase. "Well?" he said after a moment. "Aren't you going to tell me what evil bastard stands for?"

"It stands for usurper, cheat, murderer, and harlot," she spat out.

Joe was trying to figure out how that fitted the title when she added, "That is Kaladon."

He looked again with new interest. "He's a lot older than I thought he was."

"He is five years my senior. The aging that you see is the wages of his art. He is in fact still the youngest of all the Council members by more than three hundred years."

"Spell or not, I think we'd better be on our way out of here," Joe suggested. "As I understand it, everybody else can see you normally, and you stand out in any crowd."

"As do you," she responded and squeezed his hand playfully, but she also wasted no time heading for the nearest exit.

Back out in the corridor, he looked at her and asked, "Now where?"

She shrugged. "Let us go up to the room and sort through this material. Somewhere in there is a program that will tell us what is going on with whom and where."

He nodded and retrieved his untouched bag from the cloakroom. They headed out into the now jam-packed lobby and up the long series of stairs.

As they walked down the hall, the door to the suite opened and a small figure stepped out. They both halted as the figure turned and looked up, first at Joe, then at Tiana.

"Hello, Joe," she said.

"Hello, Marge. Uh—this is Tiana."

"So I gather," the Kauri answered a little coolly.

"Joseph has told me much about you," Tiana said, trying to break the ice a little. "You have had many great adventures."

"You don't look like much of a slouch in my sort of adventures yourself," Marge responded cattily.

"Uh, Marge—you'll be sharing with Macore," Joe put in.

She looked up at him strangely. "I thought as much."

He shrugged. "*You* called the tune, remember. I'm just playing along."

"Yeah. Well, have fun, you two," she replied, then turned and walked back into her own room.

Tiana didn't quite know what to say, so Joe just moved

forward down the hall, unlocked his door, and the two went inside and closed the door after them.

Finally Joe said, "You know, I'm really going to hate myself for that tomorrow, but right now I just have that feeling that there *is* justice in the world."

"She looked so hurt and lonely."

He nodded. "Yeah. She looked, somehow, almost like that scared, lonely kid I picked up back in Texas. Funny. If she'd been like that the last couple of days . . ."

The big woman thought a moment. "Joe, I think I can explain it. I was just sort of putting myself in her position now." Briefly she described the true nature and function of the Kauri and their strong shifts in mood.

He nodded, understanding to a point. "Well, that explains it, I guess."

"No, Joe, not completely, judging by your expression. You and I, we feel grumpy sometimes, happy other times, as all people do, and as she used to. Now, though, she has no control over it. She can fix the souls of others, but only by taking the hurt inside herself."

"Yeah, but you said the effect wears off—she eats it or something, or she can take the cure back home. That's more than *I* can do."

"That is true—as far as it goes. But tell me, what do you do when you feel very mad about something, perhaps about something you yourself did that you wish now to take back and can not?"

He thought a moment. "Smash my fist into a wall, I guess, or pick a fight."

She nodded. "But the Kauri, they have no release. There is no Kauri to clean *them* up, and they can not harm anyone, not even themselves. It must be particularly difficult for someone with a long human past, I would think. And you should be flattered rather than upset that she did not make love to you."

"Huh?"

"It means you do not have as many problems as you think you do. The only opening she had to help you was your feeling of loneliness, and now that, too, is gone, I think. I hope."

"You're making me feel like a heel right now."

She smiled. "No, you are human, and that is a wonderful

thing to be. She is not human, but she is still your friend. I think perhaps she needs you more than you think, and you need her far less than you think, if that makes any sense."

"Yeah, I guess so. Think I ought to go over and try and smooth it out?"

"It might not be a bad idea, particularly if, as Ruddy implies, we three must go a long way together. I will look through this mass of material we have collected while you are gone."

He smiled, got up, kissed her, then turned and walked out of the room and down the hall, stopping at and knocking on Marge's door.

For a moment he was afraid she was gone; but finally the door opened a crack, then wide, and he entered.

"Hey, look, I just want to say I'm sorry for the smart remark," he told her honestly.

"Yes, I know," Marge replied. "I don't really hold anything against you, Joe—I couldn't! Not after what we've been through. I deserved it and I know it."

He sat down on the side of the bed. "Hey, look—I've had this whole thing explained to me. You're going to find this hard to believe, but Tiana understands the problem and she was a pretty good explainer."

"Oh, I know she's probably a wonderful person and everything, but it's deeper than that. I mean—oh, I don't know what I mean!"

"You mean you'd rather be her than you. *The Chronicles of Joe and Marge*, right?"

She said nothing, but he knew he'd pretty much hit it on the head.

"Well, you're not—and you never were," he went on. "You're you, that's all. Hell, I'm still not sure I like this crazy world much and I'm really not sure I like this barbarian business at all, but I'm stuck with it."

She looked at him curiously. "What would you rather be, assuming you'd still be in Husaquahr and not back home?"

"No thinking there. One of these wizards. Somebody with magic at his fingertips. Swordplay skills are handy here, but all that fighting's like being in the infantry. Cannon fodder for the magic boys—and no match for magic, but a hell of a lot of work, all the same, not only to get the skills but to keep 'em."

She slowly shook her head. "You don't want any magic, Joe. It's not power—it's a curse. For anybody under the master sorcerer rank, it is, anyway—*it* controls *you*, really, and it costs too much. And even the masters—well, every one I've met has been more than slightly nuts."

"Ruddygore?" He paused a moment. "Hmmm... Yeah, I see what you mean. And your witch, Huspeth, has sealed herself off from the world. The more I hear about the others here, the more I think we've met the nicest and sanest of 'em all, too."

"It's the power, Joe. It corrupts most of them, makes them evil beyond redemption, even if they don't think of themselves that way. I can feel it, just walking these halls. Those very few who were so strong it didn't corrupt them, like Ruddygore and Huspeth, it drove into tremendous loneliness. The responsibility's so *huge*, Joe! And as for the fairies—I know now that we are imprisoned by our powers, not free. Like bees and ants, deer and wolves, we're programmed like robots to do one job each and we have to do that job just like the animals. The only difference is, we can think, so we know we're not free. I always used to wonder why those European elves of legend always drank so much. Now maybe I understand."

"Well, maybe. But a little magic might be nice, anyway. It doesn't matter—I'm not magical, that's all, except through Irving. Tiana's an adept. Daughter of a big-shot sorcerer who got killed by another one."

"Yes, Kaladon. Ruddygore told me the background. You know he's the prime suspect for the Dark Baron."

Joe nodded. "Yeah, I know. I'm not sure if I'm hoping he is or he isn't, though, for Tiana's sake."

"What do you mean?"

"If he is, and we manage to polish him off, then she's bound and determined to take over Zhimbombe. That may be her birthright, but it's not her style. On the other hand, if he isn't the Baron, he's just a superpowerful, evil black magician she can never hope to get rid of, so it will eat at her until she tries it, anyway."

"You really like her, don't you?"

He nodded. "A lot. And I think it's mutual, at least so far. Hell, we've just met. We'll see how it goes."

"I'll try and be nicer to her then, Joe, I promise, if you'll be a little understanding with me." She paused a moment. "Still partners?"

He grinned and stood up. "Still partners—and still friends. Uh—I'd give you a hug if I didn't think I'd crush your pretty wings."

"You won't. They're kind of funny, but they have no bones in 'em. I can lie right on them face up if I want to."

So he did hug her and kissed her, too; then he winked. "Three adventures—remember?"

She thought of Ruddygore's gloomy assessment and forced a smile. "Yes, Joe. *At least* three."

Macore sat in Ruddygore's room, still wearing the one-piece black cloth outfit he'd used in his work, his face and hands black as pitch from the material he'd smeared on them.

Ruddygore studied the various papers and objects before him and frowned. "This is pretty tough, I'm afraid. Two are definite servants of Hell and the third must be, to keep his own holdings. Hmph! I always thought of Boquillas as a hothead, but an idealist. I wonder what his price was?"

"Well, we know for sure that this Kaladon is a head man with the whole Barony movement," the thief noted. "I'm positive the units in that report were all involved in the battle at the Valley of Decision."

Ruddygore nodded. "They were. There's no question he's a leading figure in this, but he makes little secret of it. Still, I find it hard to believe."

"He's incredibly young, or so he says. Much too young to have won a Council seat on his own and just the sort to fall into this kind of campaign."

"That's true, but it makes him so bloody obvious. I don't see him as a leader, somehow, with the skills to keep an alliance like this together. He's also pretty weak, really—there are any number of adepts here who could challenge him for position. The only reason they don't this time is that they fear the Baron's wrath, and that bastard can marshal three others of Council rank to back him up in this. The one I fought over the plains of the Valley was as strong as I am, and that's strong indeed. I'm pretty sure Kaladon cheated to win his spot, and he's dependent on the Dark Baron to keep his position. If the Baron loses, he's done in. He has no choice."

"Unless he's diabolically clever," the thief responded. "He's a smart one, I think, and real ambitious. Hell, you know you can become a hawk or a wolf or anything else you want to be. Maybe this Kaladon's not any spring chicken but really an old pro."

The sorcerer considered it. "You mean he created Kaladon as a *persona*, lived as Kaladon those years in Morikay, then made it seem as if he beat the old man, huh? What a fascinating idea! Diabolical! Why didn't it occur to me before?"

Macore grinned. "Because you're a square, that's why. Oh, you can be pretty devious, but only in response to evil. Who do you listen to? A puffed-up, straight-arrow Imir who thinks the only way to get something is to fight your way through a mob? A muscle-bound ex-Teamster? A fairy who used to teach kids?"

Ruddygore thought about it. "Well, more than that, but your point is well taken. Maybe I have been neglecting my true education and perspective of late. Perhaps I should talk more often with thieves and politicians."

"There's a difference? Oh, well, let's look at the others."

Ruddygore nodded. "Esmerada. I had just about written her off because she was a woman, but now, with your new perspective, I see that I can hardly do that. Any of us could be anything we wanted to be at almost any time, so having a male Baron would be a near-perfect red herring."

"I thought the same way. And she's well positioned, too, with a long history in the black arts. She's got tremendous power, even if she is a little kinky about the ways she uses it. Certainly that stuff I found in her adepts' rooms is interesting, if only because it's in no language I've ever seen before."

Ruddygore reached over and picked up the two books. "But I have. You'll have to get these back later tonight."

"No problem. They secured the important stuff real solid, but you sometimes learn more from the stuff they don't consider important. Those books—what are they?"

"An interesting set. This one is a condensed version of a major theoretical work by V. I. Lenin. This other one is almost an opposite, in one sense. *My Battle*, by Adolph Hitler. This fits in some ways with information I've been getting from all over. Even Marge, earlier this evening, told me about a kobold quoting Lenin."

"Never heard of either of 'em."

"And you shouldn't have. Neither should the adepts, for that matter." He studied the books. "Not originals. These are of Husaquahrian manufacture. From one of the City-States, I'd say. Fascinating. I wonder how the original text made its way from one world to the other, where it's certainly not appropriate."

"You mean those things are from the place Joe and Marge came from? Huh. I thought only you could get over there and bring things back."

"So did I, my little friend. So did I. But both angels and demons can dictate, and have done so in the past to a variety of people. This is more diabolical than I thought possible! That damned demon is to blame for this!" He calmed down and sighed. "Well, at least I know part of the plan now. That much is clear."

"Well, *I* don't."

"And you don't have to. That's a separate problem to be attended to besides the one on the table. What of Count Boquillas?"

"He never showed. In fact, word around is that he hasn't showed in the last six months just about anywhere. Rumors in his home district of Marahbar say that he left for his castle hideaway on Lake Ktahr a couple of months ago and hasn't been seen since. Good suspect, though. Idealistic, ambitious, very powerful, and a City-States man to boot, which ties him in to your books, with a castle in Zhimbombe, which puts him directly in the Baron's lands."

Ruddygore frowned. "Still, I would be a little more inclined to him, had he not vanished. He had reservations here?"

Macore nodded. "Him and a whole entourage. But he didn't show—didn't cancel, either, according to the hotel records."

"I don't like this at all. Esmilio Boquillas is an old and valued friend of long standing and a most unusual one among our fraternity. He has a strong conscience and he is an idealist, if somewhat hotheaded. He has been appalled by the carnage of the Baron's conquests—this I know—and has been outspoken against them. He *is* the sort of fellow who might well be influenced by such books as these, if he had a way to know about them in the first place; but, although he was an excellent fencer in his youth for strictly sporting goals, he can't even bring himself to kill a deer or fowl for sport. He is extremely powerful, but not, insofar as I know, a black magician."

"But he's in the Baron's back yard."

The sorcerer agreed. "Indeed he is, and that worries me. He worked out a tacit understanding with the Baron early in the game—indeed, he was the one who negotiated the open-city concept for the City-States, so that trade and commerce could continue—but he's always been disparaging of conquerors. He actually wrote a long dissertation a couple of years back, showing the futility of force in conquering Husaquahr, and it was aptly reasoned out. He is, in effect, our hostage to the Baron to keep the river open."

"Some hostage. Skips out and doesn't even show up here."

"Yes, and that's a worrisome thing. I can't conceive of anything short of defeat and death that would keep him from a meeting of the Society, but he's gone. And I cannot imagine any way that one of his strength could be subdued and taken, unless . . ."

"Unless?"

"Unless the Baron holds him responsible for the defeat in the Valley. Kaladon has often argued, according to my reports, that Boquillas was a dagger in their midst, a spy to those of us in the north, despite his word that he would observe the understanding. With the defeat, Kaladon's paranoia might be taken more seriously."

"But what could they do to him?"

"Individually, very little. Collectively, they could destroy him, but the rest of the Council would know of that. They and their pet demon prince might imprison him, perhaps, as they intend to do to me. Together they could have tricked him into a conference and then created a Null Zone. Inside there, no magic of any sort would function. If that Zone were also a prison cell, he would be helpless. It appears that our young friends will be asked to do double duty, then. I must think on it. Summon them here tomorrow evening, after the matches. I'll talk to them then. By that time the Council will have convened, and we'll see if Boquillas is still among the missing."

CHAPTER 9

THE MISSING MAGICIAN AND OTHER WERE TAILS

Even one who is very good and says his prayers by night, can become a werething when the full moon is bright.

—Rules, XC, 106(a)

"HELP ME GET HIM ON THE BED HERE!" TIANA SHOUTED, AND Poquah, Macore, and even Durin rushed out to see the large woman supporting a Joe in pain and bleeding from one calf. His leg was obviously too painful to stand on, not to mention dripping blood here and there on the fancy hotel carpet.

Marge opened her own door, looked out, saw the scene, and ran to them. "Get him in on the big bed in my room!"

They did as instructed, but it was Poquah who vanished and then reappeared with what proved to be a small medical kit and tended to the wound. "A nasty thing," the Imir commented. "What sort of creature did this to you? A wolf? Some monster from the exhibitions?"

Joe shook his head wearily. "No, it was a Pekingese, damn it."

"A what?"

"He means a little hairy dog with a pug face and curled-up tail," Marge explained.

"Ah! A tansir dog. From the size and depth of the wound, I would have suspected a much larger dog."

"It was as big as it had to be," Joe grumbled. "Damned thing nearly tore my leg off. I didn't even *see* it—I just stepped on its tail. It yelped, turned, and, the next thing I knew, it took a hunk out of my leg!"

Poquah frowned. "Where did this happen?"

"At the lecture on theriomorphism. I was trying to find out

122

a few things and I'm afraid I dragged Joe into this," Tiana said apologetically.

"*Umph!* I think we were the only humans in the damned place," Joe added as a salve was applied. "Centaurs, mermaids, satyrs, minotaurs, all sorts of creatures."

"But that is what theriomorphism is all about," Poquah noted. "All of those you mentioned are half human, half beast, which means they are all theriomorphs."

"Well, how was *I* to know? And since when do those creatures keep fancy pets?"

"They don't," the Imir replied, sounding wary. "Not usually, in any case. Let me examine that wound again." He leaned down and let his curious almond-shaped red eyes focus for a moment, keeping very still. "Hmmmm . . . Marge—will you look at this?"

She was startled to be the one he called, but she moved forward and bent down to see what the elf was talking about. At first it looked like a nice, large dog bite—they *did* have big mouths for such little dogs, she noted absently—but then she saw what Poquah was talking about.

Very faintly and very subtly, the entire wound gave off a soft blackish glow, like a negative almost, but not quite, superimposed on a positive picture. It was so faint it was no wonder nobody had noticed it before, but it stood out clearly now. "That's a spell of some kind," she said, puzzled.

Poquah nodded absently. "And in the black band."

The pain had faded, but Joe started to feel a different sort of discomfort. "What's that mean? How the hell can a dog bite be magic?"

"I'm not sure," the Imir told him, "but it most certainly is a black band spell, transmitted *through* the bite."

"He means," Marge explained, "that the dog that bit you wasn't a dog."

"It sure looked like a dog, acted like a dog, and bit like a dog. And what's this black band business?"

Tiana sounded worried and tense. "It is the color of the spell that tells its nature. Magic is a very colorful art, Joe, made up of a tremendous variety of colors. Which colors are combined, and in what fashion, determines its mathematics and thus what it does."

"Okay, I follow that. What's a black band spell, then?"

It was Marge who answered. "It's a curse, Joe. And because it is only in the base color, it is transferable."

Joe sank back on the bed. "Now, let me get this straight. The dog had a curse, and because the dog bit me, I now have the curse, too. Is that about it?"

"That's about it," Marge agreed.

He considered it. "And I suppose if *I* bit somebody, they'd get it, too?"

"Most probably," Poquah said. "I believe the Master should examine this, although he's fast asleep right now, and I'm not going to awaken him. The wound is still a wound, no matter what else, so we will bandage it, and then you should get some sleep yourself. Tomorrow at the dinner hour the Master would like to see all four of you in any case, so that is plenty of time to find out more of this. In the meantime, I will try to learn something about this dog."

"Sounds good to me," Joe told him. With the usual pleasantries, all but Tiana and Marge left him. He looked from one to the other. "Well, if this isn't any trucker's sex fantasy, I don't know what is. Trouble is, it hurts too much in the leg to do anything about it."

They both smiled, but neither could conceal her concern. He had to admit he didn't exactly like the idea of a curse, either—they were always pretty bad things, and in this crazy world—and particularly at this crazy convention—they could mean anything at all.

Joe awoke feeling pretty good. There was still sunlight outside, but from its angle he could tell that the hour was pretty late and he'd slept a good, long time. He looked over and saw Tiana stretched out beside him, still sleeping. All scrunched up in a chair, Marge was out, too. He knew that Marge, at least, would be out until sundown and he quietly brought himself to a sitting position, then examined the bandages. It was odd—the damned thing had been so painful earlier it wasn't funny, yet now he could swear that there was no wound at all. Cautiously, he put his good foot on the floor, then the bandaged one, and stood up. There was no sensation, except the tightness of the bandage. Otherwise, his leg felt and moved just fine.

He went down the hall to the john with no problems and then walked back. When he re-entered the room, Tiana turned and woke up. She saw him standing there and looked surprised. "You all right?"

He nodded and grinned. "No fangs or funny ears, either. The bandage is tight and it itches like hell underneath, but otherwise no problem. Want to go next door and get Durin to make us a pot of real coffee?"

She got up, yawned, and stretched, her hands actually touching the rather high ceiling as she did so. "You go on over. I need to go next door and get myself a little cleaner and brush my hair."

"Okay. Marge'll wake up and join us at sundown." He went over to Tiana, nuzzled her, then kissed her. "Good morning or afternoon or evening, whatever."

She smiled. "Conventions do that sort of thing."

"Being partners with a Kauri does it, too."

She patted him on the rump and went to the door. "See you in a few minutes," she said and left.

He turned, scratched, sighed, then went out and down to the double doors and knocked.

Poquah opened the door, looked at him, and said simply, "You're early."

He shrugged. "No place else to go—unless there's business going on, in which case I can think of a way to pass the time down the hall."

The entendre went unrecognized. "No. In fact, the Master is not even here right now. He's in a Council meeting."

"Um. Then I can get Durin to make—oops! I already smell it brewing." He walked by the Imir into the room, and Durin's elfin face grinned at him from the kitchenette. Joe got a mug of coffee, then sat down comfortably on the couch.

"How is your wound?" Poquah asked him, after checking on things on the bar.

"Good. In fact, the bandage is the only problem."

The Imir pulled up a stool, stretched out Joe's leg, drew a sharp knife from its sheath on his belt, and slit the bandage cleanly. Then he removed the whole thing with a single, swift motion.

"Ouch!"

"Just the dried blood. It cemented your leg to the bandage, so to speak. Durin—some hot water and a cloth, please."

The chubby little elf was ready for him and brought the

cloth over and handed it to the Imir, then scampered back to the kitchenette.

Poquah carefully washed away the very ugly-looking caked blood, then frowned and rubbed some more.

"Hey!" Joe exclaimed. "Watch it! You're taking leg there!"

The Imir took no notice, but continued until the last of the blood was off. He motioned to the area of the wound with his head. "Most interesting."

Joe looked down and felt sudden amazement. "Hey! There aren't even any teeth marks! That skin's as smooth and unmarked as glass!"

Poquah nodded. "Indeed. That confirms it."

"Huh? Confirms what? Did I get bit or didn't I?"

"Oh, yes, you were bitten, all right, just as you say. The blood alone proves that, does it not? No, it just confirms what I was able to find out from others around and at the meeting where it happened. I would like to get a second opinion, of course."

"Cut the weaseling! What *is* it?"

"Well, last night was the last night of the full moon, which should have alerted me right away. Then, as you said, there is the question of what a dog was doing in a seminar. Now we have the total disappearance of the wound. Tentatively, I would say that you were bitten by some sort of were."

"Were? You mean as in werewolf?"

"And a lot of other things. Weres come in all types, really. It certainly explains why a tansir dog should be sitting in at a seminar on theriomorphism, which means human into beast, does it not?"

Joe sat back, remembering all the werewolf movies he'd ever seen, and this didn't fit the image at all. "You mean every time there's a full moon from now on, I'm going to change into a *Pekingese*?"

"Possibly. Possibly not. Although the spell is totally concealed now, I am positive that it was *strictly* black band—most unique for any sort of werebeast. A werewolf or weredog would also have to have the codex for its particular creature, and this was not at all evident. My tentative diagnosis is that you have become the most rare of all theriomorphs, a true and pure were."

"Huh? A were *what*?"

"A were, period. As there was no codex, it must be externally supplied."

"Plain speech, please. Short words, too, so I can understand what you're saying."

The Imir got up, took the bandage over, and discarded it, then returned and took a seat opposite Joe. "All right. You've been through this before, if I remember. The Circean turned you into a bull."

Joe nodded, recalling the incident with a slight shiver.

"Well, were curses are generalized forms of that sort of thing. Volume Four Sixty-Four of the Rules, if I remember correctly, treats them in some detail but never actually comes to grips with them. Nobody really knows how such curses originate, and the Rules prohibit originating new were curses of a communicable nature. Think of them as diseases, perhaps—not only skin contact, but actual saliva or blood transfer is required."

"But you or Ruddygore can read this volume whatsis and give me the cure, right?"

Poquah shook his head sadly from side to side. "No. Since their origin and exact nature are unknown, so is their cure. They can mostly be arrested through the regular injection of exotic herbs, different ones from different types, but this is unique to me."

"Get to the point."

"Well—" At that moment the door opened and Ruddygore entered. At first he seemed preoccupied, but then he noticed Joe over on the couch.

"So! Feeling better, I hope. Now, what's this about a were-wound?" He walked over, bent down, and looked at the area on Joe's leg that was now distinguishable only by the marks left from the bandages. He nodded, then turned to Poquah. "You've told him?"

"No, he hasn't!" Joe snapped. "He's done everything but. Would *you* mind telling me what all this is about?"

"Well, you stepped on a were's tail, it bit you, and you caught the disease. Of them all, I'd say you were the luckiest, Joe. It's incredibly rare."

"That's what Poquah keeps telling me, but nobody tells me what it is I've got a rare case of! You guys are worse than doctors!"

Ruddygore nodded. "I managed to get hold of the woman who bit you. If it's any solace, she's very, very sorry about it, but she just reacted in pain. She's actually a very nice person, and you're the first person she's ever bitten."

"She's a bitch as far as I'm concerned," Joe growled.

"Well, she was last night, or she wouldn't have been able to bite you, but that's beside the point. Joe, you always said you wanted a little taste of magic, and now you have one. A rather unusual one, I admit, effective on only three nights a month on the average, but somewhat controllable. You see, Joe, you are now a were, but you're not a were anything. Just a were."

"Huh?"

"To put it bluntly, for every night of the full moon you will turn into whatever you're closest to at moonrise. It might be a good idea to carry an almanac from now on."

Joe sat bolt upright, a funny feeling growing in the pit of his stomach. "Let me get this straight. Whatever I'm *closest* to?"

Ruddygore nodded. "It's very unusual, but there's only the were curse, no codex attached; so when the curse is activated, it derives its form from whatever is closest."

"So this one who bit me—she was nearest a Pekingese at moonrise last night? And if she'd been nearest a cow, she'd have turned into a cow?"

Ruddygore nodded again. "An exact duplicate, with everything in place. The curse works on a modified fairy pattern, so you won't turn into a tree or grass or anything like that; but if it's animal or fairy and that's closest, you're going to duplicate it from moonrise to sunrise—unless the moon's already out in the daytime, in which case it will be sunset to sunrise. If you remember your lunar calendar, you can usually control what it is, anyway. It's not a good idea to be riding a horse when it happens, for example. The change is pretty well instantaneous."

Joe whistled, not quite believing what he was hearing. "This woman who did it—how'd she get it?"

"Oh, the fellow was a spider and she walked into the web. He felt so guilty about it afterward he courted and married her. That pretty well solved their problem, since most of the time

they just turn into each other. They seem to think it's fun. At
least it's appealingly kinky. Unfortunately, her husband fell ill
yesterday and she had to go get some medication in town. She
lost track of the time, there was this fellow with a dog nearby,
and, well, you know the rest."

"Oh, great. This is all I needed. Hey—wait! Poquah says
there are herbs and stuff to keep it off, right?"

"For most types, yes. But pure weres are so rare, thanks to
their conscious control, that nobody has ever done any research
on them. I'll put a couple of good people on it right away,
though, so we might get lucky. Unfortunately, I can't wait for
the results of the research."

"Oh, no! Wait just a minute, here! You're not sending me
out on some mission with *this*. I mean, it'll happen in—what?"

"Twenty-seven days, for three nights. So? It might actually
come in handy, if you can learn to control and use it. Look on
the bright side, Joe. You've just increased your survival factors
by a tremendous amount. There's no external sign on a pure
were. Even a top sorcerer would have to know exactly what
he was looking for to see it at all. But for all practical purposes,
you're invulnerable."

Joe brightened a bit. "Oh, yeah. Silver bullets, right? And
they don't have bullets here. Hmmm . . . Maybe this thing has
possibilities, after all. And this invulnerability works all the
time, even when I'm not, ah, you know?"

"All the time. But don't feel totally cocky about it. A truly
powerful sorcerer will spot it after a while, or deduce it the
first time your invulnerability shows. You're still subject to
certain spells from the fairy folk and other sources, too. Silver
is the key, not just bullets. Silver of any kind can wound you;
if it hits a vital spot, it can kill you. A silver sword or dagger—
or the silver hilt of a weapon or walking stick used as a club—
will be more dangerous than any blade you've known."

Joe thought about it a moment. "Well, the club might be a
problem, but I don't remember seeing any silver swords around
here. Silver would make an expensive and pretty lousy blade,
except for show stuff."

"True. But total security lies in an enemy's not knowing
until it is too late." With that the sorcerer stretched out his
hand; there was an electricallike flash, and he held in his hand

a broadsword of what appeared to be solid silver. "Otherwise, a transmutator can do this." He lowered the sword, twirled it, and it became a wooden cane.

Joe heard someone coming down the hall. "Uh—listen. Okay, I'll go along with you, at least for now, but promise me you won't tell anyone else, huh? I want to break it to the others myself."

Ruddygore nodded. "That's all right with me, but—be cautious! Telling the wrong person might prove fatal; but if you tell no one, then you're going to have a tough time explaining it when it happens."

"I'll cross that bridge when I come to it. I—"

There was a knock on the door. Poquah sprang to open it, and Tiana walked in. "Hello," she greeted Joe. "How is it?"

"All well," he told her.

She frowned. "All well so soon? And the curse?"

"Some other time," he responded nervously. "Let's relax for now. It's nothing I can't handle."

"As you say." She sounded uncertain and worried, though, and it didn't escape Joe that her mother had died from a curse, one that she feared she carried but did not know for certain.

Marge joined them within another few minutes; last to arrive was Macore. Durin set an excellent table, and all ate, enjoying the truly magical touch of the elfin chef, except, of course, Marge. After Ruddygore's promptings, however, she found she could still enjoy good wines and the taste of fancy desserts, even though she didn't need them and couldn't fully metabolize them. Still, it made her feel a little more human and a part of the social group that a fine dinner formed. She was also inwardly very grateful to Poquah for calling her in for consultation on the wound. It was, she knew, because they were both of faërie and he had known instantly that she could see the fine magical pattern that most could not because of that fact, but that was a very important thing to her.

Although fairy races usually didn't get along very well and were rife with jokes and rivalries, when it came down to practicality, it was *we faërie* in Poquah's mind. It meant a lot to her, although she was sure the Imir hadn't even realized he was doing her such a service. She was Kauri, yes, but she was more. She was a member of an entire family of living, thinking creatures. She was *faërie*.

There was conversation at dinner, of course, but it was of a social nature and generally concerned with the convention. Joe told the sorcerer that he'd seen two of his matches against adepts. "Nothing like that battle over the Valley of Decision, though."

"Oh, no, this was a lot of sound and fury and clever parries and thrusts, but little more," Ruddygore responded. "None of the challengers were very taxing, and all of them have a long way to go to get any real command, if they ever do. In a sense, it's like giving two people a math problem to solve, only one of them has studied and practiced calculus for years, while the other is just learning algebra. That's all magic really is—topological mathematics combined with concentration and willpower. First you must have the talent to be able to understand and construct the complex patterns which we call spells, then the concentration to hold them at all cost against all distractions, and finally the force of will to impose those patterns on a person or object precisely as you wish. An adept can impose such things, usually from the Rules and other references, by memorizing a lot of standard stuff, but that's about it. A true magician can form what he or she needs without references, and tailor it to the specific requirements of the situation. The best can hold and create multiple original patterns. The more you can do at the same time, the stronger you are. One like Kaladon, for example, might be able to create and maintain as many as ten separate temporary and permanent spells at once."

"Kaladon! He is a pig and a usurper!" Tiana spat.

"Sorry to spoil the food with a bad name, but when you consider that he's the weakest on the Council, you see what a poor adept is up against. Kaladon is good at it, but he's not one of the best."

"My father could maintain fifteen or more," the large woman bragged.

"He could indeed, but not on one particular night."

"The food was drugged!"

Ruddygore sighed and signaled for the table to be cleared, which it rapidly was. "I see it's time to get down to business." He lighted a cigar as Durin served coffee for those who wished it. "First of all, Tiana, your father was not drugged that night."

"What! That is a lie!"

"You said it yourself. He was capable of fifteen or more

spells. No pro in this business goes into action before doing a static purification spell on himself, not to mention a series of mental tests, even against the weakest of opponents, to ensure he is in his best physical and mental shape. No, Tiana, I'm afraid your father was, in fact, in his usual fine form."

"But it must have been the food! Otherwise that pig would have been ground to dust!"

Ruddygore drew on his cigar, sat back, and relaxed a bit. "Well, that was the story the Council more or less allowed to spread around Zhimbombe. It was a face-saving gesture, really; although it was rather insulting to Kaladon, even he went along with it. You see, after the death of any Council member, there is, shall we say, a psychic post-mortem by the remaining members which includes an examination of the winner and his testimony, those of the referees, and others. It is a matter of concern to all of us when one of us goes, as you might imagine, and we are most interested in seeing that it doesn't happen to us." He paused again, then added, "The official judgment was that your father threw the match."

Tiana stood up and glared angrily at him. "I will not remain and listen to this, not even from you! My father would never commit suicide!"

"Oh, sit down, Tiana. *That's* why you'll never be more than a weak adept. No self-control, no discipline. Even if you know all the magic I know and can handle fifty spells at a time, you'll challenge Kaladon, he'll make some off-the-wall remark about your father, you'll get so mad your concentration will crumble, and he'll have you."

She hesitated a moment, then sat back down, but she continued to glare at him.

"Kaladon was, I'm afraid, your father's weak spot. He considered him his son and heir to his Council seat. You knew that. You remember what it was like—before."

She nodded, but did not seem to mellow.

"He had no reason to suspect treachery. Kaladon was quite clever—he fought the match in such a way that it looked very natural and very accidental that it escalated to that point. He must have spent years planning those exact moves. What happened was that he pushed things just over the edge, so that there was so much psychic energy in that hall that it could not be easily canceled out. Likewise, Kaladon had spent some effort making you look very untalented in the arts in your father's eyes. So there he was, faced with the choice of killing Kaladon, letting Kaladon kill him, or hoping the referees would realize the problem and step in. All the evidence suggested that the referees *did* move to cancel; but for some reason, the attempt was not effective. Either the spells were too personalized, or not all the referees were in agreement; but the hesitant ones weren't willing to admit their error later. Regardless, your father weighed all the factors and decided to will his seat to Kaladon."

She shook her head unbelievingly. "I know how he regarded Kaladon, but I can not believe he could do this. He would not do this to *me*."

"If it's any help, Kaladon did cheat. I know how he did it, but I could never prove it."

"What?"

"It would have taken all three referees in tandem to stop the match. All three claimed to have tried and failed. One of them, however, was Esmerada, who is now a close ally of Kaladon and the Baron. The fix was in, and that sort of energy couldn't have been held for long. Your father was backed into a corner and forced into a split-second decision. In a sense, Kaladon's victory was legitimate in that, as I mentioned, his opponent allowed an extraneous factor to divert him. It is entirely possible that your father was simply unable to solve his moral dilemma and thus broke his concentration. The most talented sorcerer in the world can be beaten by a middling-fair magician if his concentration is broken, even for an instant."

She considered it. "You are probably right. But—even with all his deceit and Esmerada's complicity, that means he was the legitimate and legal winner under the Rules! That is terrible!"

"Is it? He still schemed and took advantage of your father and you to get the seat, and he's an even blacker magician than ever now. He must be removed, eliminated—and Esmerada, too. We must stop his cancer of the Barony for all time."

"Can't you just take him on?" Joe asked. "You said he was weak."

"Oh, I could finish him, yes, but he would sense the attack and call upon Esmerada and the Baron for support; and the

Baron almost had me last time. As for a challenge in a formal context, the Rules specifically prohibit one Council member from challenging or fighting another within the rules of the Society. Nor can I enter the castle of a fellow Society member without his or her permission, just as none of them can enter Terindell."

"And I guess they aren't too likely to invite you in for tea and cookies," Marge put in.

Ruddygore nodded. "But I've been studying the proper volume of the Rules pretty closely, and there are other ways. It seems that if someone is in my service and is invited in, he may then invite me. That I find most interesting."

"Uh-oh. I just got a funny case of indigestion," Joe grumbled.

"It's not a very easy or pleasant task, but I think you see where I'm leading with this," the sorcerer continued. "We must strike at the heart of the Barony. We must eliminate Esmerada, Kaladon, *and* the Baron. If I can reach the first two, I can take them. That will leave our Baron, if he is indeed not one of those two, alone and out front. I can tell you right now that I cannot take the Baron; but if I can find out who he is, perhaps he can be goaded into trotting out his demon master. If I can get him to do that, with the Council looking on, they will destroy him as a matter of survival."

Joe whistled. "You sure aren't asking much, are you? We're to get into these castles and call you in, somehow, all without getting killed or turned into toads or something; and if we happen to unmask the Baron in the process, we're to get him to trot out a demon prince for us."

Ruddygore shrugged. "I didn't say it was going to be easy. In fact, tricking the first sorcerer should work out because of the element of surprise in the plan. The trouble is, in the inevitable post-mortem, the loophole will be exposed, so the second one will be ready for you. As for bringing out the Baron's demon, I hardly think that will be difficult if you meet him. Remember, his demon couldn't do a thing to either of you, and he's probably just panting and drooling to do a whole set of things to see why and how he can get around it."

"What army are we leading?" Joe wanted to know.

"No army. It would do no good. I'll supply the army if and when it's necessary. You and Marge are involved, not only for your skills and complementary abilities but also because, pardon me, you are perfect demon bait. All that I have been able to teach you, and all that you have become, have been oriented to this purpose. Tiana will join you for several other reasons, although she, too, is well trained and dedicated, with a bit of both your skills to boot as a backup. But, most importantly, she's a native of Zhimbombe, and I've had her traveling in and out of the area for the past month before coming here."

Tiana nodded. "I wondered why you asked, and only hoped it was for an assault on Kaladon. Much has changed, particularly the people and the very atmosphere of the place. It used to be a happy place. But the roads still go where they once did, and the towns and cities are the ones I knew in my youth. It was strange how it all came back to me, although I have traveled those roads ten thousand times in my mind."

Joe was used to Ruddygore by now, and he was thinking ahead of the plan. "Uh—in what order do we tackle these fearsome giants?"

"Geographically. Esmerada's Witchwood is on the way to Morikay, so she is certainly first. She is the stronger magically, which is why she is the best start—the best to take by surprise. And she is the most hidebound and rigid. My, how she loves the old clichés!"

"Uh-huh. And then Kaladon, all forewarned."

The sorcerer nodded. "But in known territory, with a native guide even to the castle passages and entryways."

"He's likely just to have us killed on sight," Marge pointed out.

"No, not all of us," Joe responded, turning back to Ruddygore. "Right?"

"Well, uh, that's true."

"I would have no problem getting invited into *that* castle," Tiana said, stating what the others were thinking. "That is it, is it not?"

"Well, yes, as a last resort," the sorcerer admitted. "However, I hope we won't have to use that method. I'll be with you all the way, in a manner of speaking, anyway."

Poquah got up from the table, went into Ruddygore's room, and returned with a very pedestrian-looking, Earth-style briefcase. Ruddygore made several passes over it with his hands and then went into an almost trancelike state staring at it. In less than a minute, though, he relaxed, then opened the case. They all realized that the case had been guarded by spells so great they might have destroyed anyone trying them other than himself.

He reached inside and pulled out a small jewelry case, set it before him and opened it, then pushed it across the table to Marge. Inside was a necklace of what looked like solid gold chain; from it, a small but distinctive ruby pendant hung. She looked at the chain, then picked it up and stared at it in puzzlement. "Where's the clasp?"

"I had it made without one," he told her. "Don't worry. Allow Poquah to put it on for you."

The Imir reached over, picked it up, and she felt his long fingers on both sides of her throat and the cold of the chain. There was a hissing sound; for a brief moment, the necklace felt very hot, but it cooled quickly.

"The thing is made of fairy gold and a combination of alloys that make it almost impossible to slip off," Ruddygore explained. "As it has no clasp, it's on for good, I hope. While the blend is strictly Husaquahrian, it was created at Cartier's in Paris to my specifications."

She chuckled. "Cartier's at last."

Again he delved into the case, brought out a jewelry box, and opened it, this time pushing it in front of Tiana. She looked, then reached in and picked up one of the two objects inside. They were attractive, if slightly large, earrings of the same fairy blend, and suspended from each was a finely crafted charm in the shape of a gryphon. Except for being oddly thick, the charms looked to be made of the same stuff as the earrings. Again, there was no break or clasp in the earrings themselves. "Think you can stand wearing them more or less permanently?" the sorcerer asked her.

She nodded. "They are beautiful. Also Cartier?"

"Oh, yes. Well, if you're satisfied—Poquah?"

The Imir went behind her, but this time he took one earring in each hand; pulling back her hair, he tugged on the lobes with his fingers. There was a slight hiss and a wisp of smoke, and Tiana exclaimed, "Ouch!" That, too, was quickly over— and the earrings were through the lobes as if she had been born with them. She reached up with her right hand and felt one of the dangling charms. "It feels strange."

"You'll get used to them quickly." Again Ruddygore repeated the process, pushing another open box toward Joe. The ex-trucker frowned and grumbled, "Oh, no. I'm strictly straight!" Inside was a single small earring with a golden gryphon attached, identical to Tiana's.

Ruddygore laughed. "Joe, it doesn't necessarily mean that back on Earth and it definitely doesn't mean that here. Almost all the barbarian tribesmen wear 'em."

"Well, I don't!"

Tiana looked over at him with an amused expression. "Joe, among the Cagrim tribespeople with whom I lived for some time, when a woman and a man mated, they wore matching earrings. Two each."

"I don't care! What's so important about these fancy pieces of jewelry, anyway?"

Ruddygore grinned. "Inside the jewel Marge is wearing, and inside the left gryphon in Tiana's set—and in your lone one—is the latest miracle of Japanese electronics."

"Electronics! Here?"

"Exactly. Oh, I know, I know. I'm the one who has kept guns and other modern ideas out, and I admit it. However, you must understand that, more than anything, that is my advantage, Joe. It's why this plan will work! This sort of technology is as alien and magical to this world as my magic is to yours. The tiny little power cells in those jewels will last a year and, because they broadcast a simple signal, they carry quite far. You will never be out of range of my messengers, Joe. Although the cells will broadcast only a couple of miles at best, that's more than sufficient for signals to be received *outside* any of the castles—far outside. That's Macore's part of the job."

The little thief nodded. "I don't understand it, but I never did understand spells, anyway. All I know is that I'm going to be able to track you with those things and that you can call Ruddygore with them if you need him. The rest of how it's done I think best to keep from you, and he agrees. What you don't know you can't divulge, and that will keep me safe. I'm also your backup, though—if real problems develop, I'll help where I can."

"Those measures are needed because the things were designed to work in connection with directional receivers that would be large and impractical here," Ruddygore explained. "However, their tiny, very inaudible signals will reach Macore and his, uh, messengers, and that's enough."

"And if we want to call you?" Joe asked. "Then what?"

"This may sound odd, but just take the object—jewel or gryphon—in your hand and say my name. It is triggered to change its signal at that, and that will alert us."

"How soon could you reach us after we needed you?" Joe pressed him.

"I will be publicly and visibly here and in Terindell. There must be no suspicion whatsoever. I feel bound to tell you that it might be many hours before the message gets to me. After that, I will use my unique transportation abilities to reach you very quickly. Now, this is important! While my name alone, uttered in that way, will bring me, you must say, 'Ruddygore, please enter castle such-and-so,' wherever you are. I can be summoned through the device, but I will require the invitation to circumvent the Rules."

"Uh-huh. And what are we supposed to do for the hours it takes you to come to the rescue?" Joe asked him.

"The best you can, of course. After the message is off, Macore will be available as an outside party to help, and he will have other resources to draw upon."

"You won't see me after tonight," the little thief warned, "but I'll never be far away. Count on it."

"Do we have a—ouch!" Joe was startled by a burning sensation on his left ear. His hand went up, and he felt the ring already in place there. He whirled, rising at the same time, and faced an impassive Poquah. "Damn you!" the big man cursed.

"Don't blame him, Joe. I expected some, ah, resistance," the sorcerer told him. "Don't worry. I can hardly see it under all that hair, anyway."

Tiana reached over and pushed Joe's dark hair back. "I think it looks very swashbuckling."

Joe sat and fumed. He said nothing, but it was clear what he was thinking.

"Now we'll work out briefings and strategy sessions," Ruddygore told them. "You should be as prepared as possible. And henceforth, by the way, we will *not* mention the radios. That will remain our little secret—and our little advantage."

They talked on through most of the night, the enormity of the task not escaping them in the least. Finally Ruddygore handed Joe a small, round portrait of a distinguished-looking man of middle age with gray hair and a bushy gray mustache. He had dark, piercing eyes that the artist had caught exactly, and it was clear to look at him that he was one of those lucky ones who aged so well they were even more handsome than they had been in their youth.

"Count Boquillas," the sorcerer told them, explaining the background. "If you happen across him, or can determine his whereabouts, then be sure to tell me. He is the mystery player in this game, in that we don't really know which side he's on or what his game might be. All we know is that a powerful and outspoken critic of the Barony has suddenly vanished, and it would be of great value, not only to find him but to prove how little the Baron's word is worth, if Boquillas is in fact a prisoner."

"So when do we start this death march?" Joe asked.

"I think tomorrow, about sunset," Throckmorton P. Ruddygore replied.

CHAPTER 10

SAILING DOWN THE RIVER

Piracy need not be a dishonorable vocation if bound by the Rules.
—Rules, CLIX, Introduction

THE PORT DISTRICT OF SACHALIN WAS BUSY ALMOST ALL THE time. Although much trade had closed down for the convention, ships kept to schedules as they had to, and that meant those depending on those ships must be ready when they arrived.

Ruddygore had arranged passage for the trio on a merchant-man carrying what seemed to be thousands of neatly racked amphoras of whiskey made from the unusually large harvest surplus in the region. Accommodations were not the most gracious or comfortable, but the ship's captain, who was also half owner, was being well paid and neither asked questions nor even raised an eyebrow at the sight of the unlikely-looking group.

Lake Zahias was huge, and by midmorning there was no land in sight as they moved out to the deep center and proceeded south. The ship was close to three hundred feet long and had a slightly rounded hull that accentuated any rough water but allowed it to take full advantage of the wind, which was quite brisk. Twin masts each held a single, enormous square sail, bright orange in color and with the ship's identification symbol inside a round yellow circle in the center of each. Joe had to admire the way the crew seemed to anticipate every little shift in wind and water and do just what was necessary to keep the speed steady and the ship relatively stable. The sight of so much water reminded him of the ocean, although there was no smell of salt in the spray and the large number of sea birds trailing the vessel betrayed land off somewhere within flying distance.

There were long, empty stretches, but other areas seemed filled with small fishing boats trawling for fish, shrimp, and whatever else these waters held; here and there, they passed a ship like theirs headed the other way and watched the semaphores on both send greetings and news of conditions to each other.

One such passing was followed by a sudden flurry of activity from the crew, each sailor hurriedly falling to one or another task. Joe, who'd been getting very bored playing a local version of backgammon with Tiana, grew curious and soon learned that there was word of a major storm ahead. At the time, it was sunny and fairly warm with just a few fleecy clouds in the sky, and both he and Tiana found all this haste hard to justify.

Within an hour, though, a huge front seemed to move in on them. Not long after, the wind picked up until it quickly became a roaring gale, complete with monster waves, thunder, lightning, and tremendously heavy rain. It soon became impossible to walk even below, the ship lurching and turning in what seemed all directions at once, and Joe found himself wishing for boredom once again.

He and Tiana both became violently ill before too long and just strapped themselves to their too-small bunks, trying to hit the chamber pots when they had to.

Marge came in, looking very comfortable and seemingly unaware that she was being tossed about with the ship. She spotted them both and regarded them with some pity. "You should *see* it up there!" she said excitedly. "Waves just about swallow half the ship, then up it comes again. It's real exciting—and the crew is wonderful."

They looked at her with misery and irritation in their eyes. "You don't feel—anything?" Joe managed.

"A little wet, maybe. I'm sorry for you both, but I guess I just don't get seasick. Hell, I've never been out on a body of water this big before and I think it's exciting."

"Well, go enjoy it, then," Tiana groaned. "Return when the sun shines and the water is like a mirror."

Marge took the hint, but the storm did not abate during the night or into the next morning. Through it all, except for trimming sail, the captain kept his ship fairly well on course and seemed reasonably pleased with the speed he was making. "It will take more than a little blow like this to make me run for safe harbor!" he told Marge proudly.

By the next evening the storm had slackened off a bit, but not enough to allow either of the seasick sufferers below any sort of recovery. Joe was more miserable, he believed, than he'd ever been in his whole life and he would have gladly ended it all if it wouldn't take too much effort. Even his great sword Irving, strapped to a handhold, seemed to hum a mixed and discordant series of notes.

Three days out, the storm passed, although the skies remained overcast and the air was a bit chilled. Joe, feeling weak and miserable, nonetheless had the need for fresh air; the small cabin stank of the remnants of two very large people's innards. He managed to pull himself dizzily up the stairs and onto the deck. The cool mist struck him, and it felt very, very good; he luxuriated in it for a few minutes before taking any sort of a look around. When he did, he was surprised to see land off to the left, even a few houses and animals. The ship was, in fact, close in to shore.

Marge spotted him before he could look much further and came over. "Feeling better?" she asked, sounding genuinely concerned.

He shrugged. "Well, I feel as if I want to live again, but I'm not sure I'm going to."

"How's Tiana?"

"Worse, I think. What's this over here?"

"We'll be in tonight. Zichis is only a few miles up ahead, and that's the end of the line."

"Suits me. Land again," he added, almost dreamily.

"Don't get too comfortable. Tomorrow we just go down and get on another boat, remember."

He groaned. "Don't remind me!"

"Well, at least it's a riverboat."

By the time they berthed, it was well after dark, but both Joe and Tiana showed renewed strength when the idea of setting foot once again on dry land was staring them in the face.

Zichis was a lot smaller than Sachalin and far different, too, in architecture and ambience. This was a working town with no pretensions to anything political and no thoughts of tourism. It was here because, just below the town, at the start of the River of Sorrows, was Zichis Falls, and all commerce heading in either direction had to portage around it. The ships, of course, did no such thing, so all cargo had to be transferred to the next ship in line on the route south. In the meantime, the three were to stay over at one of a dozen or so guest houses, as they were called.

These turned out to be large wooden structures with a hundred or more rooms apiece, all built of the same weathered wood as were the other buildings in the town. The rooms were not much larger than those aboard ship, nor any more comfortable, but they were in solid buildings on solid ground and they neither rocked nor swayed. Marge explored the town while both Joe and Tiana recovered enough to get and keep down a heavy cream seafood chowder at a small restaurant and then to sleep it off.

The next day remained chill and overcast, but the seasickness that had totally immobilized the two humans passed as quickly as it had come upon them, and they both felt cheerful, if weak, and ate heavy breakfasts while Marge slept.

The system for moving cargo down below the falls to a

river port consisted of an ingenious series of water-filled locks that lowered the huge crates and racks on large wooden flats a hundred feet or so at a time. The falls were large and highly impressive, although no Niagara, plunging more than eight hundred feet into a whirling mass below.

People, however, were expected to walk down an apparently endless series of wooden stairs. They soon learned that, to get information on their next watercraft, they would have to descend to what the natives called the Lower Port, despite the fact that there seemed to be no guest houses or any other services there.

Joe looked down, sighed, and said, "Well, I need the exercise."

"What of Marge? She is sleeping right now, remember," Tiana responded.

"Well, she knows the schedule, and the guest houses make it their business to see that people make their connections. I don't think we have to worry. It's several hours until sailing time."

After a seemingly endless descent, they found themselves at the Lower Port and quickly located the shipping offices of the line Ruddygore had told them to use. When they got there, though, they discovered only bad news.

"The *Pacah* is delayed at least eighteen hours," the agent told them, "perhaps more. There have been pirates on Lake Bragha, and shipping has been delayed while protection is arranged."

"Pirates? Up here?" Tiana asked, looking puzzled. "I have never heard of pirates on Bragha before."

"These are bad times, lady." The clerk sighed. "The border runs right through the lake, remember, and even the ownership of the falls is in dispute down there. It's impossible to police anything any more."

"But surely both Marquewood and Zhimbombe patrol the area!"

He chuckled dryly. "Patrol? How long has it been since you have been in Zhimbombe?"

"Many years," she admitted. "Why?"

"They invaded us not too many months ago down south, remember. They're not nice or cooperative people—if all of 'em are people, which I doubt. You goin' there?"

"Down the river, anyway," Joe put in smoothly. "Actually, we're headed for the City-States."

"Yeah? Well, you're both big enough to fight it out, I guess. Me, I wouldn't get any nearer the border than this, let alone go through their territory."

Joe gave him a sour smile. "You're implying that they don't exactly mind the pirates?"

"Hell, who could tell the difference? You watch it, though. When the *Pacah* gets here, it's one of ours and a good ship. You'll be treated well. But from Tochik, you'll be on one of *their* ships, and I wouldn't go to sleep on one of them things if I were you."

Joe looked over at Tiana, but she just shrugged. "We're staying at the Cochis Guest House. Will we be notified when the ship comes in?"

"Oh, sure. No problem there."

They left and walked back to the falls. Joe stared at the huge set of stairs rising up into the mist of the falls and sighed. "Well, I *said* I needed the exercise."

Tiana nodded glumly. "I wish I had a spell for levitation right about now."

They began the long walk up.

It was, in fact, three days before a small group of ships arrived at the Lower Port, four merchantmen and two rough-looking craft manned with archers, bowmen, and even fore and aft catapults.

These were quite different craft from the Lake Zahias freighters—all shallow draft with large single sails and side slots for a dozen oarsmen on either side. In point of fact, the merchantmen were really large rafts with boxy wooden structures fore and aft like small houses and a pilothouse atop each. Clearly the helmsman at the rear could not see what was going on and depended on a crew with an elaborate series of signals forward for direction. In contrast, the two warships resembled sleek Viking craft. They reminded Joe of canoes—the biggest canoes he'd ever seen—with a single sail in the middle.

According to those getting off, the voyage had been a rough one, not only from the usual natural hazards but also from pirates, who had actually managed to separate a ship from the convoy near the mouth of the river, take it, and get it across the theoretical border in the middle of the lake. At that point, as usual, an armada of nasty Zhimbombean warships had come virtually out of nowhere to keep the convoy warships from giving chase.

The captain of the *Pacah* was more than happy to see two large, tough-looking barbarians come aboard, although he wasn't so sure about Marge. He neither liked nor trusted fairies very much, it seemed, no matter how small and cute and sexy they were, but he tolerated them.

There was almost a complete crew change at Zichis, but the officers remained aboard, where they lived below the forward pilothouse. The ship was a co-op, with each of the officers owning a share commensurate with his relative rank. The crewmen coming aboard were paid wages and looked large and tough, as they had to be in order to control oars and poles on the river portion. This, however, would be a far easier trip than the northbound had been—they were going with the current.

Navigating such a craft down a winding and not very wide river was a skill that made the crossing of Lake Zahias seem like child's play. It was clear that the pilots depended not only on years of experience but on a certain necessary sixth sense to avoid the eddies, bars, and other hazards of the river, whose current was strong enough to change things just about every trip.

The land, too, changed dramatically as they moved down the river. There were few trees and great expanses of savanna going off in both directions. The yellowish grasslands were broken here and there by isolated groups of trees, and only the area right along the riverbank was overgrown and green. Off on the grassy plains beyond, they could see legions of wild beasts grazing or running about.

Still, the slow, cumbersome craft, built for tonnage rather than for speed or maneuverability, took two days to reach the lake.

By this time Joe and Tiana had gotten to know each other quite a bit; if Ruddygore had been playing matchmaker, his scheme seemed to have taken. By the time they reached Lake Bragha, Joe had to admit to himself that it was already a problem to remember what it had been like before he met her. Marge had the good sense to realize that this was going on and intruded as little as possible. Although she couldn't really bring herself to make friends with the huge, strangely accented woman who had joined them, she managed at least a professional relationship, which seemed enough for now. Joe felt sufficiently secure now to return to a platonic but cordial relationship with Marge, and that made it a little easier, too.

And, of course, ship's personnel had plenty of problems to keep Marge reasonably busy, particularly after she flew over to the nearest military guard ship.

Lake Bragha was only a third the size of Zahias, but it was still a pretty big lake, although quite different from the almost oceanlike parent that fed it. The river here flowed so gently into the lake that there seemed no seam in the transition, and Bragha, shallow and gentle, was virtually mirror-smooth and highly reflective.

It was only forty miles or so across from the river's entrance to its outlet, but that was the danger area. They could have avoided much of the threat by sticking to the coastline of Marquewood, but that added more than a day to the sailing time, and time was money. Still, the first mate admitted, if losses continued to mount, it might be the only alternative. "Either we go bankrupt taking the slow and safe way, or we get captured and killed," he remarked gloomily.

Although they reached the lake in the early morning darkness, they decided to lay over until sunup before crossing. The three hours or so might put them even further behind, but sailing would be a little easier in daylight. "Not that the pirates don't attack in daylight—they do," the mate told Joe. "But at least we and our protection can see what we're fighting."

The day dawned sunny; while there was still a slight chill in the air, it was clear that the sun, unseen for so long, would warm things considerably by midday. They proceeded as soon as they had good, clear visibility, since at the speed of the flatboats it would take almost nine hours to cross, even with a decent wind. There was no current. "A good wind at our back and a lake mist would have been best," the mate told them. "As it is, I feel like a very big target."

The tension mounted as they started across, and both Joe and Tiana could feel the strained nerves of these peaceful merchantmen. Still, they'd be no pushovers—anybody who could row a craft that size could break a neck in two with a flip of the wrist.

At almost the halfway point, a lookout from one of the other merchant vessels called out, and suddenly the tension became so thick that it was almost a tangible, visible thing. Tiana looked over at Joe, who said, "I'm going to get Marge." She just nodded and continued staring where everybody else was looking.

Marge, even with her goggles, was grumpy and irritable when awakened, but all that fell quickly away when he told her that an attack was possible. Both of them rushed back on deck.

The mate, a big, bearded man, was strapping on a weathered old cutlass. He yelled out that this was in fact an attack, and Joe felt a rising sense of excitement within him. Although he knew that many good people might die in the fight to come, he couldn't suppress an almost boyish anticipation of battle. Damn it, it was what he was trained to do in this crazy world.

He climbed up to where Tiana stood atop the crew's quarters and looked at the oncoming enemy, then frowned. There were clearly five ships coming in, but all five were extremely small and shaped much like the two far larger escorts the convoy had. On those escorts he could hear the barking of orders and the sound of battle drums.

Tiana looked over at him. "What is the matter? You look disappointed."

"Yeah, well, I dunno, but when you say pirates, I kind of expect a big galleon or something flying the skull and crossbones, not five big rowboats with sails."

The mate overheard. While he didn't really understand the reference to galleons, he got the idea. "Don't let them fool you, lad. A single big ship would be easy pickings for the navy boys here. But those little things can really move—easily three times our speed, if they're handled right in a fair wind like we're now getting, and perhaps twice the escorts'. They're hard targets to hit, but they have a single catapult apiece that can sure as hell hit *us*. They can turn in a few hundred feet, and three of 'em will engage the escorts while the other two try for one of us."

Joe nodded. "Will they try to board?"

"As soon as they can. Counting you two, there's twenty-two of us, probably about the same in the two that will try for us. Don't hesitate on any of 'em, remember. They're professionals at this sort of thing."

Joe turned and looked out at the approaching small fleet and smiled. "So am I," he said softly. "So am I."

The pattern was pretty much as the mate had predicted, with two of the small boats separating from the group and bearing down on the lead escort vessel. When they were barely in range, both suddenly seemed to catch fire. Tiana gasped at that, but it was quickly clear that what was being lighted were flaming masses attached to the catapults, both of which were launched with a military precision at the lead naval boat, after which both attackers turned hard in opposite directions. Both shots missed, and the larger military boat proceeded full ahead, aimed straight between the two smaller vessels, which now turned back in.

Two more broke off, going unexpectedly right at the warship, creating four closing attackers on the one larger craft. The bigger ship adjusted slightly, then let loose her forward catapult, which was apparently filled with half a ton of small rocks. It was the machine-gun approach, Joe thought. Nobody could hit the broad side of a barn with a machine gun, but it pumped so many bullets in the right general direction that it was impossible to dodge them all.

By choosing one attacker and firing the tremendous onslaught of stone, the navy couldn't miss, and it was clear that the strategy was successful as the target attacker turned desperately to avoid the mass and could not do so.

But at the moment the rocks were striking the craft, the other three all let loose with fireballs. One fell short, one struck the side of the naval craft, rocking it but otherwise sliding back off and into the water with a great hiss, but the third struck against the rail, splintering into a series of small fires. While the bulk fell into the sea, several small fires and some black smoke were visible in the bow of the convoy's protector.

Undaunted, the naval craft swung around and let loose a second volley of stones as the stern lined up with another of the attackers. Clearly the pirates were paying a stiff bill for this one. As the stones rocked the small craft, a cheer went up from the four merchant crews watching the battle.

Suddenly the second naval escort came gliding past the *Pacah*, closing on the attacking boats. As soon as it cleared the merchant convoy, it loosed its own rocky attack.

Joe frowned and looked around. "Where's the fifth one?"

"Huh?" Tiana, like Marge, was entranced by the battle and was startled by the question. "It is right—where *is* it?"

There was a sudden shout from the lookout of the *Tolah*, just behind them, and they turned back to see what was going on. *"There!"* Joe shouted. "They're already boarding the *To-lah*!"

The mate turned, grabbed a megaphone, and shouted at the pilot in the aft wheelhouse, "Bring her around slow! Make fast for collision! Crew at the ready! Prepare to board aft!"

Joe suddenly saw what the mate was doing. He meant to bring the *Pacah* about slowly, causing the *Tolah* to run into their ship's side. At that point, the crew was prepared to jump to the defense of their sister ship before any of the pirates could gain control of the *Tolah*'s wheel and take her out of the convoy or avoid the maneuver.

Joe looked at Tiana and Marge. "I don't know about you, but I'm going over there!" Without waiting for a reply, he went down the ladder to the deck and made his way aft, drawing Irving as he did so. The great sword gleamed in the warm sun and began to hum expectantly.

Tiana followed, drawing her own nonmagical but still lethal bronze blade. They joined the dozen crewmen, armed with a variety of swords and pikes, waiting to jump over.

Certainly the fighting was furious on the *Tolah*, and yells, curses, the sound of clashing metal, and an occasional cry of pain or anguish could be heard.

One burly crewman looked at the two newcomers and grinned. "All right, barbarians—as soon as you hear the bump, over the side we go. We have at best only a few seconds before the force of the collision separates us again."

They nodded and braced for it. It came almost immediately, nearly knocking them off their feet. But in an instant, and with a joint cry, the *Pacah*'s men stood and made for the boat just on the other side of the rail, already moving backward a bit as it recoiled on the placid water from the shock of the collision.

The pirates were not expecting the attack, and three lost their lives just by turning at the wrong time to see what new enemy was screaming so. The rest recovered quickly and arranged to meet the newcomers. The fight was soon joined, and before long it was a mass of people. Joe was painfully and suddenly aware that he could hardly tell the human pirates from the crew of the *Tolah*, but that didn't bother him right away. At least half the pirates were nonhuman, some in the extreme.

A reptilian creature fully as tall as he, with burning yellow eyes and a mouthful of sharp teeth in its lizardlike head, turned and hissed at him. The creature was a rather sickly blue and covered in scales, and Joe had no time to reflect on what the hell the thing might be. The gleaming sword in its humanoid right hand told him his job, and Irving came up to parry a blow. They were joined.

He concentrated on fancy footwork and positioning as usual and let Irving do the work. This thing, whatever it was, was no pushover, though; it was incredibly strong, and he reeled under the force of its blows, even as Irving parried them. Still, he had greater maneuverability and was able to jump once he got the rhythm of the attacker's sword strokes. He leaped sidewise and let Irving sweep out of the way; the creature missed, and its own momentum carried it forward. Joe brought his great sword down quickly and sliced right through the creature's scaly neck. Greenish ichor squirted out from the gaping wound, and the creature roared and reeled backward, dropping its sword. Joe pressed forward, plunging Irving into the creature's abdomen several times and drawing even more green blood.

Satisfied, he turned and saw Tiana taking on a squat, solid humanoid. The thing was a head shorter than she, but totally hairless and built like a tank, with huge, clawed hands grasping a lethal-looking sword. Joe paused to note the expression of sheer joy on her face as she swung her sword again and again, matching the pirate blow for blow. She was *good*, he decided.

At that moment, he felt a sudden, sharp pain in his back and cried out, whirling at the same time; this maneuver brought him face to face with a thing he could only think of as a four-armed creature from the Black Lagoon. Each of its four hands held a weapon, but one held a broken-off staff, telling Joe that he had been pierced with a spear.

Too mad really to feel the wound, he screamed and swung Irving up and at the creature, who lifted one of its two swords to parry.

This was a tough adversary, since it could use all four arms separately and had the strength to wield its own broadsword with only one hand. Joe knew that this sort of creature was deadly to most opponents, but he'd been trained by an equally ugly, four-armed monster named Gorodo and he knew the tricks, moves, and weak spots.

The creature, too, was damned good; in the hack, slash, and move attack Joe employed, trying to get position, he suffered a wound for every one he scored—but soon two of the thing's arms were flopping on the deck, and it was roaring in pain and flinging its swords wildly in front of itself in a hopeless defense. Joe easily moved under the swords and struck deeply again and again into the thing's armored chest, so strong his anger and so powerful his sword that the armor proved no protection at all.

The creature howled in agony, dropping both swords, and Joe rushed it, pushed it against the rail, then shoved it over. He heard a thud rather than a splash and took the time to look over the side. The creature had struck the pirate ship and now lay sprawled on the deck.

He turned again and saw Tiana engaging a large, tough-looking human swordsman. Praying that it wasn't a crew member, he looked for more game. His eyes went up to the aft pilothouse, where he saw a hairy man climbing the ladder to the wheel. It was clear that, if the pilot was still up there, he'd been felled by a bolt or an arrow. Using his sword as a passage through the deck fighting, Joe made for the ladder himself.

Any doubt that the man now up on the wheelhouse level was a pirate was dispelled as the fellow shouted down to the pirate craft to pull away, then headed for the wheel.

Joe appeared almost in front of him; for a moment, the two just stared at each other. The pirate, Joe saw, was as cold and nasty-looking a character as he'd ever faced, but the man didn't seem to have any weapon. "Come out from behind that wheel or die there!" Joe challenged.

The pirate chuckled and spat. "Goodbye, barbarian!" he snapped and raised his hand in a motion suggesting he was about to throw something. Joe ducked as a small fireball sped past him, right through the spot where he'd just been standing.

Joe knew now that he was dealing with at least a low-level adept and was at risk, but he couldn't wait for reinforcements. The pirate was already turning the wheel hard, bringing the *Tolah* about and separating it from the convoy. Crouching, Joe made his way around the back of the wheelhouse and prepared to rush the pirate. Taking a deep breath, he stood and moved into the wheelhouse with a cry that stopped in mid-utterance. The wheelhouse was empty.

"Nice try, barbarian. Now it's time to die," the pirate said from behind him. Idly, the man made the tossing motion, and Irving, with its own life, began to parry the little fireballs as they came.

Joe at the same time eased back to the door on the other side and quickly ducked around, then pressed himself against the cabin wall. He wasn't sure what to do now.

The pirate walked calmly out from behind the wheelhouse and looked at him, grinning. "Nice work. Too bad I can't afford any prisoners. With a little seasoning, you'd be one hell of a pirate yourself."

Joe tensed and turned to face the man standing only a few yards from him, trying to figure out if he could throw Irving with enough speed and force so that the adept would be unable to parry.

Suddenly a figure seemed to appear from nowhere and come to rest between them, facing the adept. It was small enough that the two men could see right over the newcomer.

"Marge!" Joe cried. "Watch it!"

She spread her wings and looked at the pirate adept. "Want to practice on me first?"

"Out of my way, fairy, or you burn!" the pirate snarled.

"Go ahead."

This time both hands went up, and from the pirate's palms came a tremendous surge of yellow energy. It struck Marge fully, and Joe cried out, "No!"

Suddenly the pirate adept stopped and stared at the Kauri, his expression of confidence fading with his magical energy bolts, to be replaced by a look of sheer fright. "No! Don't!" he cried.

Joe was behind Marge and so could not fully see what the adept was seeing, but he *could* see a huge field of yellow energy shoot from her back at the pirate. The man screamed and was suddenly enveloped in crackling flames. He fried on the spot.

Marge put down her wings, turned, and grinned at Joe, who was just gaping at her. "I thought you couldn't fight," he managed.

The grin grew broader. "But I can defend. *He* attacked *me*, and he got exactly what he gave. Gee—that was kinda neat. I didn't even use all of it, you know. Let me see whether I can release the rest of it down below." She walked to the front of the wheelhouse and looked down at the fight, which was certainly now going the merchant's way but was still pretty fierce. Extending her wings again, she picked out those she could who had to be pirates. Little spurts of yellow energy shot from her; down below, humans and nonhumans alike yelled and screamed in pain. It wasn't nearly enough to kill, only to sting or burn, but the shock of getting hit with a bolt was enough to distract the pirates from the people who were cheerfully trying to kill them and who took full advantage of their added worry.

Joe went back to the wheelhouse. He had no idea how to run one of these things, but he saw the rest of the convoy a thousand yards distant and going away. At least, he knew enough to bring the wheel around so that the *Tolah* was heading back toward its friends. He only hoped that somebody was left down there who knew how to find the brakes on the thing.

That proved an easy task to tell, since the sight of many of their people being killed and of Joe in the wheelhouse was too much for the pirates, who began to break off, close in as a group, and make for the rail where their corvette was lashed.

"Marge—you got any juice left?" he yelled.

She turned. "A little, I think. Why?"

"Fly down there and zap the two lines holding their boat to this one! They'll have to swim for it!"

"Gotcha!" With that she was off, over the side and out of his sight. A moment later he felt a bump and, looking over, he could see the mast of the pirate ship begin to move away from the *Tolah*. He grinned. "Good girl!"

Suddenly he saw a thick plume of inky black smoke appear near that pirate mast. Marge flew back up to him and landed, looking very satisfied with herself.

"They're on fire!" he almost shouted.

She nodded. "I wondered how much juice I had, so after I zapped the ropes, I saw all this crap on their deck they use for the fireballs. It was real easy to light."

He looked down again and saw the remaining pirates leaping over the side. "Damn! Too bad we can't get 'em all, or at least one, alive."

"I'm not sure there's much chance of that," Marge replied. "They had to climb to the top of the rail, which is about five feet, then jump clear of the running board or whatever it is. I make it a jump of maybe twelve feet and I think the water here is only two or three feet deep. The way we're still swinging around, they'll all still be stuck headfirst in the mud when we run over them."

CHAPTER II

ZHIMBOMBE

A percentage of all seats of magic shall be dark towers, said percentage to be not less than twenty percent of all such seats of power at any given time. Practitioners of the black arts shall be given preference for these locations.

—Rules, IV, 203(b) & (c)

BOTH MARGE AND TIANA LOOKED HIM OVER BACK ON THE *Pacah* and did a joint shaking of heads. Joe was almost covered in blood, much of it his own, and Marge swore that she had seen a crewman on the *Tolah* pull the working end of a spear out of his back; yet when the blood was washed off, there seemed not a sign or mark on him, front or back.

"It's a spell, I think," he told them at last, "although just how much I want to push it, I'm not really sure. I don't want to test it by getting my skull crushed or my head lopped off or anything like that, but it seemed to do its job here. Trouble is, a weapon still hurts just as much going in as it always did, damn it."

Both women studied him, skepticism written all over their faces. Finally Marge said, "I've just run through the entire spectrum and I can't see a spell anywhere. Joe—are you holding something back from us?"

He sighed. "Well, you'll find out about it sooner or later, anyway. Um, would it be clearer if I told you that only things made of silver can cause hard wounds or kill me?"

"A werewolf!" Tiana exclaimed, slightly shocked.

"A were Pekingese, more likely, unless I miss my guess," Marge responded. "Is that it?"

He nodded. "Only it's not a werewolf or a weredog." Giving up, he told them what Ruddygore and Poquah had made plain to him. "So, you see, I didn't even want to come on this crazy mission. I've been trying not to think about it since I found out."

"Well, you said you wanted a little magic," Marge reminded him. "Looks as if it's handy magic at that. Either the spear or the sword into your belly might have done you in during that fight back there—or you'd probably be badly infected, at least. As it is, you're sitting here chewing on an apple and feeling fine."

He looked over at Tiana, who seemed very uncertain about this whole business. Aside from a very small nick on the arm, she'd fought through without any problems and without the aid of a magic sword, too. Still, it was she he was most worried about. "Does all this make a difference to you?" he asked her nervously.

She shook her head wonderingly. "I—I do not know. On the face of it, certainly not, but when the moon is full . . . I do not know. The curse is transferable, and who knows how much self-control you might have?"

"A fair amount," he replied. "That's why it's so rare. That Peke wouldn't have bitten me if I hadn't stepped on its tail. I think it's something I'm just going to have to endure, like people with malaria. We'll have to see."

"Maybe it will even come in handy," Marge said thoughtfully. "In a way, it already has done so."

Tochik was another version of Zichis, although it spread on both sides of the falls, which meant on both sides of the border, and each country had its own routing and lift system. The *Pacah* touched port only on the Zhimbombean shore, since all of its passengers and cargo were to be transshipped south.

South Tochik was an immediate contrast to the lands they had known. Entry formalities were officious but correct, although they gave the impression that exiting would be far more difficult. All of the officials, not only at the port of entry but everywhere in the town, wore black military uniforms, and there was a definite impression of being under martial law. The immigration officer asked only routine questions of them, writing in a small book for each; but when all three books were handed to them, he was very stern.

"These are documents necessary for safe passage in the Barony. Keep them with you at all times. It is an offense punishable by imprisonment or death not to have them, and it is an equal infraction not to present them to any uniformed soldier of the Barony, regardless of rank, as well as to innkeepers, transportation officials, or others who might require them. As you are in transit to Marahbar, you will go only to those areas and frequent only those places officials might approve while you are passing through the Barony. Is that understood?"

They all nodded.

"Good. You will proceed now to your hotel. The corporal there will escort you and see that you are properly checked in. As transient passengers, you are restricted to the hotel, its shops, and its restaurants, unless given permission otherwise. Have a nice day."

The corporal was a dour, thin young man with the crispness of a military cadet and the communicativeness of a rock. He was definitely not a native of the region, whose people seemed dark and swarthy, but of some place far away and far different.

They were not fifty feet from the customs station when they saw long lines, not only of men but of various sorts of fairies and creatures from unknown places, all shifting cargo under the watchful gaze of a number of tough-looking military types, some of whom had whips and others with mean-looking crossbows, loaded and held on the workers. It was clear that these were hardly volunteer labor; and this close to the border, with ships from the free north putting in and needing service, the local authorities were taking no chances.

Likewise, it seemed as if there was a uniformed soldier on each street corner, keeping an eye on everything and everybody. The few ordinary citizens on the street looked cowed and terrified and were being stopped every block for some sort of credentials check. The travelers were waved on, since they had an escort. They finally reached their hotel, a small, three-storey structure that badly needed repair and several coats of paint.

In point of fact, the whole town looked as if it needed a great deal of repair. Hitching rails seemed rotted or fallen everywhere, wood sidewalks were dangerous to walk upon, and the shops were dingy and grim-looking.

The hotel was as bad as the rest, inside and out. It stank and looked so rundown that it reminded Joe of more than one bad flophouse he'd seen in the older cities of America. The bathrooms were on the first floor and barely better than holes in the floor, not cleaned or sanitized in ages, and smelling so bad that no one could waste any time in them. The flies, too, were awful, not just in the bathrooms; and everywhere roaches and other insects scampered about. The desk clerk and a few of the people in the lobby looked just like the hotel—dirty, worn out, and hopeless.

Marge shook her head in wonder. "We'd need the entire race of Kauri to do anything here at all. And the soldiers are worse. They all feel so—*dead* inside, beyond all hope."

"You be careful around here, no matter what your impulses," Joe cautioned. "You saw how all those 'dead' soldiers were looking at you out of the corners of their eyes. I can just imagine what would happen if you fell into their hands."

"Worry less about me and more about us," she cautioned. "I wonder how long we'll be stuck in this great pigsty of a town?"

The answer was quite some time, with no way of telling exactly when they would leave. The soldier outside refused permission for them to inquire of the shipping agency, but also could not inquire for them without getting approval from her superiors. No, they couldn't contact her superiors without the proper forms and permissions. No, she couldn't supply the proper forms and permissions. It was one of those bureaucratic nightmares and it meant they were kept bottled up.

Tiana, in particular, didn't like it. She was in her home territory now, but there was a pretty good fugitive warrant on her that their simple cover names and stories would not hide for long. How many beautiful and exotic women six feet six inches tall would there be trying to get into the country? They discussed their options, which included fighting their way out, waiting for capture, or just sitting around, and grew itchier and itchier as they did so. Joe, in particular, was not enamored of the enormous prices they were being charged for the stale bread and half-rotten meat they were being served by the hotel.

Finally, though, just as they had decided to force a move, a soldier arrived and informed them that their ship was now in and that it would leave in just one hour. They were to accompany him immediately, or they would be stuck for two more weeks.

The inn, which, it turned out, was owned by the local government, quoted an outrageous room rate and they couldn't afford to haggle. They either disputed the bill, they were told, in which case the dispute would be heard by a local magistrate in "six or seven weeks," or paid up now and got their boat. Snarling, they paid up.

The boat, another shallow draft freighter, was also a patchwork affair, and it was clear that this, more than anything else, had thrown its schedule into disrepair. The oarsmen on this one were chained in place and supervised by tough-looking soldiers; the sail had been patched so many times it was impossible to see anything that looked original on it. But the boat clearly had been built by the same company that had constructed the *Tolah* and the *Pacah*, and the cabins, while not very comfortable, were at least an improvement over the hotel. The smell, however, was overpowering at times, since the entire central flat carried, not standard freight or amphoras, but goats. Hundreds and hundreds of goats.

Still, if a decent place to look could be found and the wind was right for the passengers and wrong for the goats, the scenery was spectacular.

The heights of Sogon Gorge reached almost a thousand feet on both sides, making the travelers feel as if they were moving through a small Grand Canyon. The gorge emptied into the third and last of the lakes leading to the River of Dancing Gods, Lake Ogome, a very deep natural reservoir that looked as if it should be fished as well—but they saw no craft of any sort on their passage southwest. Although there were no falls at its outlet, there were violent and swirling rapids, and a great deal of work had been done to dig an elaborate canal with locks to get the boats around them. It took the better part of a day to clear the locks and rejoin the river once more.

Everywhere now, there was a strong contrast from the opposite shores. To the north was still Marquewood, with small, brightly colored villages and lush farmland; to the south was Zhimbombe, rough, ugly, and overgrown, the few villages in sight looking either deserted or unfit for animal, let alone human, occupancy. Obviously the area along the border, perhaps all the way, had been cleared of people by the Barony and allowed to overgrow into wilderness, but there was no doubt in the minds of the three passengers that the riverbank was heavily patrolled, and it wasn't to keep Marquewooders out, either.

For Joe and Marge, what took place on the boat itself was an education. Neither had ever really experienced slavery and its cruelties firsthand, nor seen human beings chained and beaten as expendable draft animals. It was repulsive—and, worse, it was beyond their abilities to do anything to help the poor wretches. Captain, crew, and military, which were of the mixed races that seemed standard in the Barony, were crisp but not friendly or approachable. They handled their three passengers like carriers of some dread disease and spoke only when necessary.

The boat crossed the joining of the Tofud and the River of Sorrows late in the evening and moved into the mainstream of the now great and powerful river. The trio knew that they soon would be reaching their departure point, which might be more of a problem than it had sounded when Ruddygore sketched it out.

They were to leave at the junction of the River of Sorrows and the Corbi, the closest point to Witchwood and on the main road to Morikay. It would have been along this road that the troops of the Barony had marched for their crossing into Marquewood for the fatal battle not many months past, a battle those troops had almost won.

They passed the spot, still littered with the remnants of temporary bridges and abandoned equipment, late in the day, but decided to ride a bit farther downstream. Darkness would be a better ally here, and it wouldn't do just to jump ship near the road that was probably the most heavily guarded in the entire Barony.

It was still fairly easy to slip over the side, despite all the military aboard. The goats, for once, came in handy, covering any sounds they might make, and nobody really paid the three passengers much heed, anyway. The idea of jumping ship at *this* point was obviously ridiculous.

The water was surprisingly cold and the current rough. Joe cleared the ship and then, half swimming, half drifting with the current, made his way toward shore, with Marge slightly overhead to be sure he made for the right one. She had already scouted the immediate shoreline and found no signs of a patrol.

He reached the bank and pulled himself up onto muddy land and into the brush, then just lay there, getting his breath, while Marge went back to make certain Tiana would not get separated from them. She was gone a fairly long time, and Joe began to get worried, but finally Marge returned. "She's about a hundred yards down from here," the fairy told him.

He nodded, got up, saw how muddy he was, then made his way along the bank. "What was the hang-up?" he asked her.

"The sword belt, apparently. Getting it freed from herself so she could swim, she ran into some brush drifting down and had to get herself untangled."

He nodded understandingly. "Yeah, I had some hairy moments myself with Irving. Lost my new sandals, too, damn it."

Marge chuckled. "Well, she lost more than that."

They soon joined Tiana, and Joe saw what Marge meant. Tiana was sitting there, breathing hard and looking disgusted, wearing only mud.

"What happened to you?" he asked, trying not to chuckle.

"I was not born with three hands, that is what happened," the large woman responded disgustedly. "I tried carrying sword and belt and whip and wound up losing my clothes to a floating bramble. Scrambling for them, I lost the rest. Damn." She got up and walked a little way forward.

"Where are you going?"

"Back in the river. I *have* to get some of this mud off." This she did, taking several minutes, then sighed and came back out again. "I don't really mind losing the clothes, but the sword, belt, and whip are a real loss."

Joe thought a moment. "Well, maybe we can replace some of it, anyway. Let's take advantage of this darkness while we have it and see if we can find that road. Marge?"

"I'm off," the Kauri responded and flew into the night. It

was not long before she returned. "I'd say three miles, no more. There's an old village right on the river that's abandoned, except by troops. Nasty-looking bastards, I'll tell you. Big eyes and beaks, of all things."

"Bentar," Tiana said. "They are birdlike humanoids, very large, very fierce. Mercenaries all. Their eyes see like cats in any light, and they are swift and powerful."

"Can they fly?" Joe asked worriedly.

"No. They have arms and four-fingered hands, although their feathers give them protection almost like armor against the elements and even all but the most powerful and true of blows. I would be surprised, though, if they don't have winged scouts out. They have a communion with the birds that is hard to explain; often ravens and condors work with them as their protective shield, as well as several species of owl. You saw no birds?"

Marge shook her head. "At least none that I noticed. A few bats and a lot of insects, that's all."

"Any patrols?" Joe asked.

"Yeah, two that I saw. Parties of five, all on these big mothers of horses."

"That's too many, particularly with only one weapon," he said, almost as much to himself as to the two women. "Our best bet, I think, would be to parallel the road if possible and wait for a better opportunity."

They both nodded. "I agree," Tiana told him. "Things will have to wait. Still, Witchwood is but fourteen kilometers in from the river. Once we reach it, the risks will be less from the Bentar than from the wood itself, with the Dark Tower in the center."

"Hmmm . . . Yes, Esmerada. But won't those troopers be under her control and supervision?" Joe asked.

"They would be. She runs the entire area between the Corbi and Zhafqua, west to the Dancing Gods. However, within Witchwood she will need no troops. In there, she rules by magic."

Joe groaned. "Another magical grove. Is there no end to them?"

Marge grinned. "Probably not. So far, they all seem to be run by women."

Tiana nodded. "It is true, in a general sense. But Witchwood is much more than those you have seen so far. It is a seat of government for a much wider area, for one thing, and it is a place of black magic, not white or fairy."

Joe sighed. "Well, the object wasn't to storm the place, just to get invited inside. Let's get closer to it while we can move, and we'll talk about the fine points when we get there." He paused a moment. "I hope she's home after all this. I think she was still at the conference when we left."

"Oh, she has returned by now. Remember the delay on our part," the big woman assured him. "She has the advantage of fast flight."

"Huh? I caught sight of her back at the hotel and she looked human. Kind of imposing, but human."

"Oh, on her broom, of course. All wicked witches fly on their brooms. Surely you know that much."

"Hmmm . . . I should have known. Time to switch frames of reference," Marge put in. "So long epic fantasy, hello Brothers Grimm."

CHAPTER 12
WITCHWOOD

Since a witch's broomstick is for life, care should be taken to select one that will support not merely current but also future size and weight conditions.

—Rules, XVIII, 27(a)

MYRIAD SMALL SHAPES BROKE THROUGH THE DAWN, FLYING on long, tireless wings. Their leader wore around his neck a small golden charm, although never before had any of his tribe allowed such symbols of subservience to man or those of faërie. He allowed it now because he owed a debt of honor, and he and his would play their part in the drama for no reward other than honor, for that and the free skies that none could chain were all that was of real value in the world.

The magic charm about the leader's neck continued to give off a soft buzz that was not irritating but insistent, so close to his small earholes it was. Suddenly the buzzing sound was diminished, although it did not fade entirely, and over the sound was a very tiny, unnatural voice.

"I am in place on a small plot of what seems to be safe ground about three hundred yards from the side gate of the tower," the tiny voice said. "I have them located roughly at the edge of the wood, just off the road. I hope they have the sense to stay near it."

The leader looked down along the great expanse beneath him and saw the little road the groundlings made and of which the voice spoke. It was relatively straight and paved with loose white granite that made it stand out, even from this altitude, as a white line through the otherwise unbroken greenery. He saw now where it entered the witch's wood and became then only visible in little bits as it made its way in a nearly straight path toward the center of that wood. In the center, he saw, was a perfectly circular clearing in which sat a great structure of dull black stone, a single tower, only slightly tapered to its flat top, surrounded on the ground by a low, star-shaped outer wall. The road was clearly visible there, as it divided at the clearing and circled the Dark Tower before coming together once more and vanishing back into the dense wood.

He cursed the groundling agent mentally. Where was the side to a round structure? Or, for that matter, to a star-shaped one? Still, it would be easy to find the groundling when the need arose, but more difficult once the message had to be carried.

He heard a warning shriek from his point, and looked around to see a small swarm of blackish creatures rising from the village near the river. Clearly they meant to challenge, but just as clearly they could be ignored. Ravens. Was that the best the Bentar could send against the royalty of free eagles?

The flock slowed and circled to meet the oncoming black tide. The ravens approached brazenly and with great confidence, as they always did. When their leader reached hailing range, he called out to the soaring, great white and brown birds who awaited him.

"You trespass, eagles, far from range and eyrie. What seek you here in the land of the Barony?"

"And who are you, crow, to challenge us?" the eagle chieftain shot back. "Will you bind the skies as your foul masters who hold your leashes bind the earth? We recognize no boundaries here, nor any crow authority over our whereabouts." But lower, in the royal language understood only by his fellow eagles, he said softly, "None, not even one, should return alive or dead to the camp."

The ravens seemed so cocky and confident that they didn't even notice the eagle formation fan out and slowly and subtly take up the most advantageous battle positions. The chief raven replied, "The bird crumbles as victim to man. We are shot by the hunters and eaten by all manner of man and beast. We are captured, leashed, enslaved, even set forth by those slavers to catch and kill our own. We follow this cause out of choice, not from bindings, for the air must be liberated and purified as the ground will be."

"And this you propose to do to us here and now?" the eagle chieftain scoffed. "All ten of you against twenty-four eagles?"

By the time the ravens realized the import of that statement, the circle had closed and the eagles were upon them.

"Magic," Marge said, "flows toward you. I should have seen it before, but I never really got into the habit of shifting to the magic bands, particularly after spending so long in a city full of magicians. Now, however, I see it clearly. Bands of black and silver and bright green, they're slowly moving at you as if you were a magnet."

Tiana nodded worriedly. "Can you describe the pattern?"

"If I had pen and paper, maybe I could, but not much longer. As we move inland, more and more pieces are added, forming increasingly complex formulae."

Joe had that look that he always got when magic was being discussed, since he lacked not only the ability to see such things but even the proper frame of reference to imagine them. "In plain words, what are you two talking about?"

"A spell. No, several spells, all coming at me," Tiana told him.

He frowned. "I thought you were supposed to be more or

less immune to that sort of thing while under Ruddygore's protection."

"Only fully when I am with him. I fear our little deception at the convention did not last. Kaladon was quite clever about it, though. In a sense, Marge is correct—I was, in a way, magnetized by Kaladon. Since it was not, in and of itself, a spell, it remained totally undetected and undetectable by anyone. Basically, he laid half a spell on me, then randomly scattered the rest through Zhimbombe. Were I never to return here, there would be no problem, but once I did return, the opposite pieces of the spell are attracted to me, and only to me, wherever I am in this country. I see now that the loss of my clothing and weapons was not an unhappy chance, but the workings of the usurper's evil mind."

"Huh? He seems a little nuts, then. All that just to have you disarmed and naked? You can always find something for a weapon; and even if you have to wait a while for good clothing, you weren't exactly inconspicuous to begin with."

She smiled. "Poor Joseph. You are so totally practical. Kaladon is teasing me. What is more demoralizing than to make someone both naked and unarmed in a hostile land? It is his way of telling me who is boss and just what power I am facing. I suspect, too, that bad things will happen should I try clothing or weapons again. The spell is not a one-time thing, like your pirates' fireballs, but a true creation of the mathematical art of sorcery. And, as Marge tells it, I am to be greeted with even more annoyance as we grow closer to Kaladon."

Joe frowned. "Then you should get out of here and let us handle it. Get back out of range."

Tiana leaned over and kissed him gently on the cheek. "That would do no good. Whatever spell I wear, I keep until dissolved by my own resolution, which is unlikely, or by one greater than Kaladon, which means weeks of northward travel without clothing or arms to Terindell, or by the death of Kaladon. Besides, are we not supposed to be targets? The three of us are hardly inconspicuous. All Zhimbombe must know of us by now, I would think. As you yourself said, we are simply to get inside the seats of power, not storm them."

He sighed. "All right. It's kind of like my own, ah, problem. I don't like it, but I can live with it—if you can."

She nodded. "I am committed to this. Did you ever consider that nothing like this has ever been attempted before in the whole history of this world? To assassinate top members of the Council, whose power is just a little less than that of gods?"

"That's probably because they never found any suckers stupid enough to do what we're doing," he shot back.

Marge looked around. "Dawn is coming. Shall we press into the wood or wait for dark again?"

Joe looked over at Tiana quizzically, and she responded, "We may as well press in, at least as far as we can. There are far less dangers in Witchwood in daylight than in darkness."

With that, Marge, who flew and had only one piece of baggage, unclipped her sunglasses from the necklace and put them on. They started into the wood, keeping just to the right of the road in the brush.

The forest was full of the sounds of tens of thousands of birds awakening to meet the new day and of insects changing shifts from night to day, but the road remained deserted. The trees, however, began taking on a sinister appearance as the three travelers pushed deeper into the seat of power, with huge trunks looking like the ghosts of tortured souls. Vines and underbrush, too, grew thicker and harder to navigate. Many seemed to have thorns or brambles that caught and scratched.

"I think we're going to have to risk the road, at least for this part," Tiana said.

Joe shrugged. "It's a little rugged, I agree, but—*what*?" That last was caused by a nearby bush with long, vinelike branches, one of which managed to snake around Joe's foot and start pulling. He found himself suddenly crashing to the forest floor as yet another branch, then another, threw themselves around whatever parts of him they could, and all then began pulling him toward the large plant. With a yell, he managed to draw his sword, but had some trouble keeping enough balance to slash away at the tendrillike branches that held him. Tiana rushed over, trying to keep out of reach of more of the things herself, and grabbed him under his shoulders, creating a tug of war with the plant.

"Hey! Let go and push me up!" he shouted. She did, and Irving came down again and again, slicing through the vines and causing the bush to issue loud, high-pitched screams. Suddenly all vines were withdrawn, and he managed to get to his feet. Only Tiana prevented him from rushing in to take the sword to the bush itself.

"There are too many of them!" she shouted at him, and he calmed down and saw that what she said was true.

"Let's get over to the road," he suggested nervously. "Marge—take the high road as far up as you can without getting into the trees. Better they not see you until they have to."

Marge nodded and rose into the air, then paced her companions there as they limped out to the road. Joe found he had some fairly nasty welts where the vines had grasped him, but they began to fade almost immediately. Tiana looked at them and said, "Perhaps it *is* well after all that you have this curse. The poison those things have is often strong enough to paralyze a horse."

"I'll be all right," he assured her, standing and stretching. "But anybody we meet on the road, I'll face with the sword, I think. I don't like those green uglies."

With Marge softly humming, "We're off to see the Wizard," they started nervously down the road.

Joe felt better after a while and chuckled dryly. "You know, here I am surrounded by sexy naked ladies, and the only thing I can think of right now is that I haven't eaten anything since we left that damned boat. Must be really getting to me, though— I could swear I smelled something cooking right now."

Tiana sniffed the air. "You are not imagining things. It seems to be coming from just over there. Let us see what this could be."

They walked over and saw a small path through the trees and brush leading back to what looked like a fairly large, two-storey Victorian house. Or, rather, it looked like a cast of one. It was perfect in every detail, but clearly it was a solid block of some dark brown substance. They approached it cautiously; then Joe went up to the front steps, sniffed, and said, puzzled, "Gingerbread?"

Both Tiana and Marge approached and checked it out, then they nodded. "Gingerbread." Marge giggled. "It really *is* a huge gingerbread house."

"Yeah, but for whom? First time I saw two tons of gingerbread in my whole life," Joe noted.

Tiana was the only one who did not find it amusing. "This is one of Esmerada's famous creations. It appeals to her warped sense of humor."

"Huh?"

"She creates these things, then sentences those taken for crimes to work on them. Soon there will be prisoners here, forced to eat according to their offenses."

"Forced to eat? You mean it's not poison or something?"

Tiana shook her head. "No, not poison. But do not take it so lightly. For a major crime, you could be sentenced to eat out an entire living room, parlor, and two bedrooms. With a minor witch inducing a spell of gluttony, you could literally stuff yourself to death. It has been a traditional punishment with her ever since her great-grandmother was killed by a pair of bratty kids."

"Hmmm . . . Well," Joe said, "I don't know about punishment, but I feel hungry enough to eat out a room or two myself. Shall we try it from the back? They'll never miss it."

Tiana shrugged. "We must have something. Why not? Marge, will you watch, just in case the prison gang approaches?"

Marge did, not being able to suppress a bad case of giggles, and they had gingerbread for breakfast. It wasn't very nutritious, but it was filling, and a small creek that ran through the clearing provided a little water with which to wash it down.

"I suppose that somewhere around are the poisoned apple groves," Marge commented when they were done.

"They are to the north," Tiana told her matter-of-factly. "Not all are poisoned, though. There is one, for example, that is the most powerful aphrodisiac known. A fair amount of business is done by selling those throughout the region."

"Sounds like fun," Joe remarked.

"Esmerada has been known to feed them exclusively to people in adjoining cells of the tower dungeon, within sight of each other but just out of reach. They kill themselves trying to get at one another."

"Pleasant character. Was she here when your father was on top?"

Tiana nodded. "Oh, yes. Witchwood was then essentially a buffer, and it was simply regarded as an autonomous region. The road was guaranteed, in exchange for Esmerada's having her own way in the balance of the place. Once this was the seat of power for a great region and the place of learning for all black arts witches, but my father more or less limited her activities. Still, he thought they were as friendly as two great powers ever get, and there was a general compromise. She gained the Council with his help and support, as part of the deal which protected her and her order from others in Husaquahr. And look at how she repaid him!"

"Well, let's see how—oops! Somebody's coming!" Quickly the three of them checked out the brush, picked their spots, and barely got under cover in time. Joe hoped fervently that there were no more nasty vines around or other unpleasant surprises.

The big surprise was what was passing along the road. They had expected an occasional Bentar patrol, but this was a fairly long column of twos, all human and obviously very military, yet all wearing ordinary clothing and carrying standard knapsacks or bedrolls on their saddles. With varying growths of hair and beard, they looked very much like the sort of people who might be met anywhere in this world, despite their bearing.

When they had passed, the trio emerged from hiding. Joe scratched his head and frowned. "Now what the hell was *that*?"

"There is no way to tell," the big woman responded, "but clearly they are heading for the river and are in disguise. Something is going on, I will say that."

"Do you suppose it fits with the shortage of boats on the River of Sorrows?" Marge put in. "The pirates caused the delay upstream, but we had to wait almost a week for ours from Zhimbombe. The Marquewooders just about said that the Barony was in league with the pirates. They have all this, so it's not the cargo they were really after. Maybe it's the riverboats they want."

"Now why would they want riverboats?" Joe asked her. "They'd have to take 'em apart and shove them overland to get them to any place useful to them."

"That may be, but it's still an idea. The Zhimbombean boat looked just like a worn-out Marquewoodian one. Maybe they're using their own boats for something else, huh?"

"Yeah—but for what?" he mused. "Something's funny here."

They pressed on, speculating but unable to add anything to

the mystery. They still lacked too many pieces of the puzzle, and that was supposed to be Ruddygore's problem, anyway. They had other jobs.

They finally found a spot concealed from the road that seemed safe enough to use as a camp and got some sleep. Joe stood first watch, then Tiana, and finally, as shadows fell again upon the wood, Marge took her turn. It was well into the night before all were rested enough to continue, and the two humans were feeling very, very hungry.

As they made their way again along the road, Marge suddenly called, "Joe—look out! Above you!"

He stopped, turning and drawing his sword at the same time, and saw a menacing black shape leap at him from the treetops. Marge's warning had been well timed, and the thing missed Joe's dodging form and virtually impaled itself on his sword.

It twitched a few times, then was still, and they all stared at it. "An impaka," Tiana told them. "It is a vicious, meat-eating rodent."

Joe looked around nervously. "Do they hunt in packs?"

"No, they are usually solitary hunters. This one is a male and is probably a forager for a den. We might meet others, but we might not. Still, this is a very good omen for us."

"How's that?"

"They are tough and gamy, but they taste very much like a cross between rabbit and squirrel."

Joe looked at its nasty snout and dirty black hair and wondered just how hungry he was. Still, with Marge's scouting, they found a safe-looking spot and some branches for a crude spit. Tiana, using a spell she called a very simple thing, made a fire and then instructed Joe in the proper skinning and mounting of the beast.

Although they were nervous about the fire being seen and reported, both Joe and Tiana were too hungry to care at that point, and the thing yielded close to eight pounds of meat. Marge found a plant with a bell-like flower that was stiff and permanently open, it seemed, and managed to locate and fill two bells with water and fly them back to the camp.

Satiated, they proceeded along the road once more through the night, occasionally having to dodge an isolated patrol. They were aware of strange sounds within the wood and odd chants.

Once in a while, white ball-like things floated through the trees deep inside the forest.

Although they went mostly by night and slept most of the day, Tiana showed an uncanny ability near dawn and sunset to become perfectly still, often for up to an hour, waiting for a small animal or bird to come near, then quickly pounce and capture it. She came up with several rabbits, squirrels, a few unfamiliar but edible small animals, and even two fair-sized birds. When Marge and Joe asked about it, she simply told them to spend several years among the barbarian tribes of the north. There one learned such things or one starved.

After more than three days of this, they reached the center of Witchwood and the Dark Tower. It lived up to its name in every respect and seemed not only ancient but downright sinister.

The fortification surrounding it was shaped like a five-pointed star and rose about ten feet from the ground. There were gates in the wall at each of the inner angles, but it was clear from the paths to them that only two were actually in any sort of use these days. The walls themselves were patrolled by nasty-looking Bentar sentries and by what sounded like a roving pack of equally nasty guard dogs. The tower itself stood in the center of the fort, rising over three hundred feet into the air. Here and there, windows were occasionally lighted with an inner glow.

Marge tried flying up to the top and approaching the uppermost window, but she found that, as soon as she got to the start of the fortification part, there seemed to be an invisible wall that was impenetrable by living beings of any sort. This, then, was the sorcerous barrier that could be crossed only with the permission of those inside.

Joe sighed when told the news. "So what do we do now? Go up and knock?"

"She is much too clever to fall for that," Tiana responded. "Our identities, or at least our descriptions, must be known to them. She would understand in a moment our objective if we did that."

"That would go for being taken prisoner, too, then," Marge put in. "So what do we do?"

Tiana suddenly had a thought. "Joe—how long has it been

since you were bitten? The moon looked almost full last night."

He thought about it. "Let's see . . . Two days later, we were still in Sachalin, then three days down the lake, another three laying over in Zichis, then four down to Tochik . . ."

"Seven more stuck in that hole, then five downriver," Marge continued the count. "How many is that?"

"Twenty-four," Tiana told them. "And we have now been five more in this land. Tonight will be the first night of the full moon, then. Marge—can you not see the curse coming forward?"

Marge looked at Joe, and, sure enough, in the bottommost part of the magic band, there was a faint but discernible black pattern. "Yeah. What have you got in mind?"

"First we spend the day here, within sight of the tower. Let us see who and what goes in and out of those gates. When we know that much, we can better make our plans."

They did as she suggested, finding an uncomfortable but adequate concealment near the gate facing them, while Marge, grumpy about being kept up all day but nonetheless curious, staked out a convenient tree near the other gate. In midafternoon they met to compare notes.

"Well, let's see, not counting the dozen or so witches on broomsticks flying in and out from the top of the tower, we have a half-dozen Bentar, two ogres, five humans, and four fairies of unknown but various types," Marge summed up. "Where does that get us?"

"In, perhaps," Tiana said. "I do wish we knew the exact time of sundown, though. It would be a great help." She looked at the sky. "Perhaps three more hours. The moon is already full, so the transformation will be directly at sundown, which is a help. Marge—more work, I fear. We must pray that the good spirits remain with us and that a target of opportunity presents itself."

They fell back about a quarter of a mile from the tower and waited while Marge continued to scout the area. She returned as sundown was almost upon them and they had just about given up being able to put the plan into operation that night. "Rider coming. Bentar on a big black horse. I think it's one of those that left earlier today."

Tiana nodded. "It will have to do. Joe, get into position. I'm going to lure it your way if possible."

Joe drew his sword and got behind a tree just inside the forest. Tiana and he had gone over this many times, but he was still uncertain about it and still apprehensive about all that could go wrong. The sun was almost gone, and it would be cutting things very close indeed, even if all went well.

The Bentar came along the road, dressed in full armor, a huge, muscular, man-shaped bird with nasty eyes. It was looking pretty well straight ahead, but Tiana made enough of a commotion to attract it by the simple expedient of seeming to trip over a vine and cursing.

The Bentar officer glanced quickly in her direction and did not hesitate. Dismounting and drawing its sword at the same time, it proceeded cautiously into the woods, being as quiet as a creature as large as it was could be.

Tiana had gotten up and taken cover behind a tree, but she was careful to leave just a part of leg exposed to view. The Bentar, after checking the area, suddenly spotted it; while the great birdlike head remained expressionless as always, a tiny forked tongue ran out of its mouth and along its beak in anticipation. Slowly, carefully, the Bentar soldier crept toward the tree that almost concealed her, passing several other trees at the same time. After it passed one particularly large specimen, Joe, still unseen, brought down the flat of his sword on top of the Bentar's bronze helmet, and the creature toppled over, groaned once, then lay still.

Tiana quickly rushed over to the fallen soldier, checked, and nodded to Joe. "Hurry," she told him.

"I'd still rather be the Bentar," he muttered, but he went out to the road all the same. They had gone over and over this, and the way they were doing it was the safest and surest way to do what had to be done.

Marge held and pacified the large horse, but backed off when Joe approached. He looked around nervously, not quite knowing what to expect, or even whether this wasn't something rather stupid. It certainly looked dark enough to him, if this curse thing were really true. He just stood there, petting the horse, and hoped that all would go well.

There was a sudden, odd blurring of vision and the fleeting feeling that he was on fire; then it was over. Marge rushed out, looking very happy, and she and Tiana hurriedly removed the saddle, pack, and bridle from the Bentar's horse—and put them on Joe, who was now that horse's twin.

Only his prior experience as a bull, when he'd had an encounter with a Circean, kept him calm and cool. In point of fact, being a horse felt, well, *right* somehow.

The two women barely got the original horse out of sight before there was a great stamping and cursing in an inhuman language issuing from the brush. Joe turned his horse's head and saw the Bentar, dizzy and rubbing its head, manage to make its way out to the road. It headed for what it believed was its horse. Just before mounting, it turned unexpectedly and shouted, in the universal language, back at the forest, "All right—you have had your little victory! Enjoy it! None of you shall leave Witchwood alive, and your fate will be most unpleasant!" With that the Bentar mounted the horse and urged it slowly forward.

Joe had been uneasy that he wouldn't know how to react, but he found that his duplicate horse's body felt like and reacted just like the original. They approached the gate nearest the ambush spot, and the Bentar reined him in and called out, "Guards! Open the gate! I have important news!" This was followed by several under-the-breath curses in the odd-sounding Bentar tongue, but Joe didn't think he needed a translation.

Despite the sorcerous protections, the place was as well guarded as any fort, and two sentries appeared atop the wall with crossbows aimed at the outsider, while a small peephole in the gate itself slid back to reveal a pair of eyes, then slid shut again. There were muffled commands given, dogs barked furiously, and the double gate of bronze and wood opened inward. The Bentar rode into the castle at this, and Joe was relieved to find no barrier to his own passage. He had been worried about what constituted an invitation and had feared that he would be stopped at the entrance while the Bentar sailed through.

They entered a courtyard that was larger than Joe had expected by what could be seen from the forest. Two female grooms ran to take the bridle and halter as the Bentar dismounted. The soldier then went immediately to a nearby tower entrance and stalked inside, while the grooms led Joe to a stable area.

Within a short time, he was unsaddled, given a wipedown and brushing, then taken to a stall where a fresh bale of hay had been prepared. He was mildly annoyed that he'd found that the wipe and brush felt really good, and he started in on the hay without thinking about it. In fact, it wasn't until he'd eaten his fill and relieved himself in true horse fashion that he bothered to think much at all. He tried the welcome invitation, but found that only a contented *neighing* issued forth; that brought a curious groom, who petted his head and fed him a lump of sugar, but nothing else. There seemed little to do but try to catch some sleep and hope both that he awakened before dawn and that the Bentar didn't want to go back out that night on him.

In point of fact, he expected a hue and cry and a full-force patrol to be dispatched and didn't know whether to be relieved or apprehensive that neither occurred. He vaguely guessed, since the Bentar talked to and used birds, that the message was being conveyed by swifter means and that the avenues of escape would soon be closed off in the immediate area, with perhaps a bird search for the strangers in the forest. He hoped that Tiana and Marge could withstand the search until dawn.

Joe awoke and looked nervously around. He was human again, and that was definitely sunlight coming in through the wood slats of the stable. He was stark naked and unarmed, of course—there had been no way to take or transform his sword or breechclout—but definitely in control. Except for stepping in a little horse excrement and reflecting embarrassingly on where it probably came from, he was in fine shape. First business first, he decided, reaching up to his left ear. The device, somewhat to his surprise, had been transformed with him and was now still there. Keeping his voice low to avoid attracting a groom, he took hold of the earring, rubbed it, and said, "Throckmorton P. Ruddygore and any in your service, you are free to enter the Dark Tower of Witchwood and invited to do so."

There was no apparent change, and he only hoped that the message had been heard and that the wording had been sufficient. If so, then Marge could reach him if need be by flying, and whatever the system was of getting word to Ruddygore would go into immediate action. If not, then he was in for a pile of trouble.

He wondered how late it was. The cool dampness he felt

told him that it was still quite early, perhaps just beyond sunrise, which was fine with him.

He heard someone enter and ducked down, then crept to the front of the stall, crouching in expectation of an attack.

"Joe?" came a familiar whisper.

He stood up, cautiously looked out, smiled and nodded, then reached over and undid the latch. "Good to see you, Marge," he said, keeping his voice low. "And thanks."

She dropped a bundle at his feet and looked greatly relieved. "That's *heavy*, damn it, and that sword hates me. I hope you appreciate what I did for you just now! *I carried iron!*"

He nodded and quickly re-formed the breechclout and put it on, followed by sword and belt. Marge had taken a great risk carrying Irving, and not just from the terrible weight, even though Tiana had another simple spell to help her for the short haul here. The glorified loincloth, tied around the hilt and scabbard of the sword, was all that had been protecting her from the deadly iron blade. Only the ornate gold and bronze hilt, which covered the true iron base of the sword, had made it possible at all.

He hugged her. "Now I think we better get out of here. Those grooms or Bird-face and his friends will be here any time."

She nodded gravely. "But where? There are sentries on the wall that I really had a time avoiding to get in here—that sword dragged me down a lot—and every place else is their barracks, the kennels, and the tower."

"The tower, then. We might as well take risks here. If the old boy doesn't come through, I'm done for, and probably Tiana, too." He paused a moment. "She's okay, isn't she?"

"When I left her, anyway. She's dug in within sight of the gate, figuring that's the last place they'll look for her. There were owls everywhere last night, and at dawn a huge flock of ravens lifted off from the top of the tower and fanned out in all directions. I thought I even saw some eagles up there, believe it or not. The hunt's really on, so her best bet is to stay still."

They made their way back to the stable door, and Joe peered nervously out. The sentries were visible on the wall, but they seemed to be looking either out or straight ahead, and the courtyard itself appeared clear.

At that moment there was a wild, maniacal cackling sound from the direction of the tower's upper levels, and the sentries turned and looked up. There was a sudden roar, and then all eyes followed a black figure on a broomstick riding out over the wall to the west.

"I wonder why they always cackle like that?" Marge mused.

"Probably in the Books of Rules," Joe grumbled. "Let's move before this one turns around for another launch."

They made the barely twenty feet to the tower door with no trouble, and Joe was relieved to find that it opened when he tried it. Quickly, both were inside and they shut the door quietly behind them.

Clearly the tower was a complex place, and they had entered on the ground floor. Stairways led around the whole outside, both up and down, and vanished in both directions through cavities in the floor and ceiling. This level in general looked barren. There was, however, illumination from torches around the hall, and a stone altar in the center.

"I don't think we better stop here," Marge said nervously. "That altar's stone, but it has a reddish look. Before long, this might be Grand Central Station."

Joe nodded. "Up or down, though?"

"Well, down's probably either the dungeons or Esmerada's workshop, neither of which I particularly want to visit. I'd say up. If we hit some novice witch, I might be able to deflect some of what she has, although my power's not much against women."

"Up it is," he agreed, and they cautiously crept up the stairs. The next level was a warren of rooms, but they had no desire to find out whose. There were definite snores coming from the darkened level, lots of snores, and some of them sounded decidedly nonhuman.

They went up through several more levels. These contained everything from rooms full of various sorcerous paraphernalia and wardrobes to an entire level in which young women were preparing meals. That one was not as hard to get through as they had feared, since the girls were busy and there were few of them.

"What happens when we get to the top?" Joe whispered to Marge as they climbed and climbed.

"We don't get that far—I hope. I think maybe we ought to

find a hiding place and just camp out. The top level's the home
of those packs of birds, I'm pretty sure."

"The storerooms would be handy," he suggested. "Shall we
go back down?"

"One more level. I'm really curious about this place."

He shrugged and followed. They emerged into a brightly
lighted room with a polished and stained oak floor and walls
that squared off the chamber, made of some sort of paneling.
There were no furnishings, but at the far end of the room,
flanked by two floor-to-ceiling red satin curtains, was a huge
and hideous multi-armed idol, seated in the lotus position. Its
face was a travesty of a human woman's face, and it had eight
human arms coming from its somewhat distorted human torso.
Each of the hands held a different deadly weapon—dagger,
sword, crossbow, garrote, and the like. While it seemed made
of some black stone, its eyes were blazing red rubies of nearly
impossible size and perfection.

"Looks like something out of *Gunga Din*," Joe noted. He
wasn't much on books, but he loved old movies.

"The goddess of death, all right—or what passes for Kali
here," she agreed. Together they approached the altar and its
statue and examined it. "Look at those stones! Wouldn't Macore love it?"

"I, for one, wouldn't touch it. It's probably cursed a thousand ways from Sunday."

"Actually, I'm not," the idol responded. "If you looked like
this, would you need much in the way of curses?"

They both jumped. Joe started to pull his sword—and found
that it would not come out of its scabbard. He pulled and
strained at it, but it just wouldn't come. There was a chuckling
behind him, and he and Marge whirled to see a tall, attractive
woman standing there. She was dressed in a black satin robe
and, except for snow-white hair, looked very young and pretty.
Both, in fact, had seen that face only weeks before.

"Esmerada," Marge said, feeling trapped.

Joe stopped tugging at Irving and just stared at the witch
queen. Swords wouldn't do for somebody like her. It would
be like going against an elephant with a peashooter.

"This is all quite amusing and interesting," Esmerada said
conversationally. "How in the world did you two get in? Well,
never mind that for now. I assume the plot was to get inside

somehow, then issue an invitation to Tubby Ruddy for a show-down. How droll. Well, you're here, but old Tubby's nowhere in sight; and since the invitation must pass from inside to outside, I hardly think you'll get the chance." She turned and shouted down the stairs, "All right, boys—bring her up!"

There was a commotion below, and Tiana was brought up, flanked by half a dozen Bentar. She had her hands tied behind her back and her arms lashed with heavy rope around her chest. She looked at her friends, shrugged, and said, "Sorry."

"Since you two were taking the tour, come on up one more flight," Esmerada invited Joe and Marge, still being casual.

They followed her, with the Bentar and Tiana bringing up the rear. The next level proved to be a comfortably appointed apartment, obviously the witch queen's private quarters.

"Untie the woman," Esmerada commanded the Bentar. They hesitated, and she added, "She's no threat—now."

The rope and hand ties were swiftly cut, and Tiana massaged her wrists for a few moments.

"You can go," the witch told the Bentar. "I'll handle things from here on in." They looked uncertain, but left.

"Please, take seats, all of you," the witch urged. "We might as well be as comfortable as possible for a little while."

Figuring that they had no other choice, all three of them took seats. There really wasn't much else to do. Esmerada seated herself in a large, high-backed plush chair opposite them and crossed her legs. "So, now. What shall we talk about?"

"That idol—is it really alive?" Joe asked, genuinely curious.

She chuckled. "Oh, yes. A former adept of mine who got too big for her robes. I changed her into the statue because it was amusing. She's totally frozen except for her mouth. She's a useful object lesson, though, to the newer girls, don't you think?"

"Charming," Tiana muttered.

Esmerada smiled. "So glad you approve. I'll try and make things equally entertaining in this case. You, Kauri, are simple. Just neutralize your therapeutic qualities, remove your ability to think, and give you to the soldier boys. You and they will have a continual ball. Nothing but animalistic sex until the end of time."

Marge shivered but said nothing.

"As for you, big boy—you're more of a challenge.

Hmmm... Let's see... We really shouldn't lose the properties of that magic sword, I think. Maybe a gargoyle. Yes, definitely—a big, lurking, hulking gargoyle with bat's wings to guard the gate and attack any who enter that I wish eliminated. No, too ordinary. Well, I'll think of something." She sighed. "I wish I had the complete set. Too bad I can't play with both you *and* the amazon here."

Joe looked up at her. "What's that mean?"

"She's due on the ten o'clock broom to Morikay. There's a friend of mine there just dying to meet her."

Tiana bristled. "You would not do this!"

"Why not? Then he owes me one." The witch chuckled. "Seeing your reaction, I think it's the absolutely perfect thing to do."

Tiana started to rise, but Esmerada gave an idle flick of her hand, and it was as if a giant's hand pushed the big woman back into the chair. The witch smiled sweetly, then made a few gestures in the air. Marge switched to the magic band and was startled to see just what a riot of color and complex patterns filled the room. Still, she could see the witch's hand actually trace out a basic pattern of new material. It shot out from her rapidly moving fingers like spider's silk, reaching and covering the big woman. "Just stay there for a few minutes, won't you dear? I have to stick these two in storage for a bit."

Tiana struggled, but she was bound tightly and securely to the chair with a pattern so complex that neither she nor Marge could have understood or duplicated it in hours—and the witch had done it almost as an afterthought!

Esmerada got up and gestured to Joe and Marge. "Come with me." She paused. "Oh, take the sword off first and just leave it over there on the floor."

He hesitated, and she gave another seemingly random series of finger motions. Abruptly the sword belt tore on the side opposite the scabbard, and both it and Joe's breechclout were flung against the far wall by a force invisible to him, but all too visible to Marge.

The witch smiled her sweet smile once more. "Now, follow me and don't dawdle, or I'll have to get a little unpleasant," she warned them. It was enough, and they followed her.

To their surprise, they went not down but up. "I put the

dungeons up here when I redecorated," Esmerada told them. "In the basement, escape was unlikely but possible. Up here, you not only have to break out but must get down through all the lower levels. Or fly, of course."

The dungeon level, as she called it, was second from the top and contained about two dozen small cells. They walked along and saw some pitiful remnants of humanity and fairy people in them, most certainly no longer sane. All were naked, but one wore on his head a helmet that totally enclosed it. As they passed, he rushed forward, crying, "You *must* listen! I *am* King Louis! I *am*!"

Marge frowned and hesitated, then shook her head and went on.

They finally reached the end of the cell block, and Esmerada opened a cell door. "In here, big man."

Joe hesitated, there was the hand motion, and he felt himself violently shoved inside the cell. The door clanged shut behind him. Marge made no resistance to entering the next cell. The doors, while of metal, bore no clear locks. They were made fast by Esmerada's spell, and that was better than any lock.

The witch looked back at the Kauri and thought a moment, then made a few more motions with her hand. Marge saw long threads of gold and silver emerge and bind her in a pattern even more complex than the one that held Tiana downstairs. "What is that all about?" she asked.

"You're grounded, dearie," Esmerada replied. "In technical terms, I just increased your density and altered your specific gravity. You won't notice it, because I've compensated you for it, but if you try and take off, you'll get nowhere. You now weigh two hundred pounds, you see. I also removed your wings so you wouldn't smash them, although I fear that also removes any power you might have."

Marge gasped and raised her arms; they were totally free once more. She now must look pretty much like a wingless, naked, burnt orange version of Disney's Tinker Bell.

"Well, goodbye for now, darlings!" the witch queen called as she walked away. "I have much to do today, including getting our big beauty off to the city, but I won't forget about you, never fear. Ta-ta!" With that, she was gone down the stairs.

The cells were made of solid stone blocks, bound with some very hard mortarlike substance, and it was clear that escape was all but impossible from them.

Joe looked around his cell. There was a large pile of straw that served as a bed, he supposed, and what looked like a bronze chamber pot. That was about it. The old girl took no chances with her prisoners, that was for sure.

He walked to the only opening, the barred door. It was far too tight for him to do more than get a hand through between the bars, and there was no lock even to try to pick or reach. It was hopeless. "Marge?" he called.

"Yeah, Joe," came her voice, sounding a little far away. "I'm sorry I have to stay back a bit, but those bars are iron."

"I understand." He sighed. "Well, I guess we just pray for rescue before she remembers us again, huh?"

"I guess so," Marge responded dejectedly. "I hope it's a rush job. It wouldn't take more than a few flips of the wrist for her to do to me what she said she would."

"Yeah, I know." He sighed again. "Wonder why she even waited?"

"It's no fun to her unless she lets you stew for a while," came a man's cultured voice from the other side.

Joe was startled. "What? Who's that?"

"A fellow prisoner, I fear," the voice replied sadly. "I've been here quite some time. Months, actually, although it seems like years."

"Huh? How come she hasn't turned you into a toad or something?"

The voice sighed. "She doesn't dare let me out of this box. I am held, my friend, by the strongest, most diabolical set of locks you can imagine, and I'm actually inside an inner box as well. She is very evil and very clever. My inner box is but a scant foot from the outer one, which is only a fraction short of what I can reach. She is diabolical."

"Why two boxes and locks?" Joe asked.

"One finger," the voice said mournfully. "If I could just get one finger *fraction* outside the cell, all would be changed. She knows that, and she's tortured me with this arrangement."

"Who's that, Joe?" Marge called. "I can hardly hear him."

"Yeah," Joe pressed, "who are you, anyway?"

"I am Count Esmilio Boquillas," the voice replied.

CHAPTER 13

OF FRYING PANS AND FIRES

No thief shall ever travel without all the necessary tools of his or her trade.

—Rules, VIII, 117(b)

"It was the Baron who did it," Boquillas told them as the morning passed. "I believe in the necessity of social revolution, but the battle should be for the minds and hearts of the people, not their lives. Yet what could I do? As a theoretician, both of social principles and of the magical arts, I was no threat. I have no vast armies nor great cults. By common agreement, the City-States remain neutral territory, lest all Husaquahr strangle for lack of trade. I gave my word to them. I would be free to speak out against this terrible war, but I would not actively intervene on either side. As neutral, then, as morality would permit me. For a while it was enough."

"The Baron thought you stabbed him in the back, huh?" Joe responded.

"Indeed. The Baron was convinced that his battle plans in the Valley had been betrayed, so that his flanking maneuver was in itself outflanked. He felt, too, that certain of his powers had been neutralized; and since he was facing Ruddygore, the only sorcerer with the guts to defy him openly, he felt that the additional sapping of power had to come from an outside source. He blamed me, but I didn't know it at the time. He was, in fact, quite cordial. He told me he was investigating his own lacks in that affair and, since I was the foremost theoretician in the area, he invited me to what amounted to a magical postmortem of the battle. Naturally, I accepted; even though I opposed the war, the idea of being able to study and analyze this methodology firsthand was a once-in-a-lifetime opportunity. I had no reason to suspect his motives, as we had had many such meetings on a friendly basis before—and I've also met with the other members of the Council from time to time."

"It was three to one, though, and you got trapped," Joe guessed.

"Precisely. This box had been specially prepared for me. I am far too good for them to destroy, even all three, but they did manage to knock me cold for a period. My defensive spells were too much for them to unravel in the short time remaining, so I was carried up here and put inside. It is a bizarre and humiliating experience, and a humbling one. It must have taken them months to construct this cell, but it is tight. Within the inner box not a single spell can be cast, not a single thin strand of magic can penetrate in either direction. I am totally and completely powerless within it. The locks are elaborate and made of dwarf-forged steel, taking three keys that must be moved together and in certain ways to unlock them."

Joe had to chuckle. "Crazy. Here I am in a magic box, and there you are in a nonmagic one. Each of us is helpless where we are, but might do something if our positions were reversed."

"You know the picking of complex locks?"

"No, but nothing mechanical is foolproof, particularly in this world. That's why thieves still do a good business. They're just the local equivalent of truck mechanics."

"What mechanics?"

"Oh, never mind. I— What the hell is *that*?"

From the floor above them came terrible screeches and squawks and a great deal of thumping around. The noise lasted for some minutes while they waited to see what might be coming next. Finally things seemed to quiet down once more, and they heard someone slip down the stairs and land on their floor. Who or what it might be they couldn't see, but the upstairs commotion had started the predictable outcry in all the cells, and so it was impossible to do anything but continue to wait.

A few minutes passed. Then finally someone approached the door of Joe's cell and looked inside. "Joe? Is that you?"

The big man was thunderstruck. "Macore? Is that really you or is this some witch's trick?"

"Oh, it's really me. I was just holding down the fort, so to speak, when I saw Tiana come out on that broom, captive of one of those harpies. I figured I better get in here before it was too late."

"But—how?"

"Let's just say I have a lot of fine feathered friends. Hmmm... Where's Marge?"

"Next cell—no, the other way."

Macore went over, looked in, then returned. "Fast asleep. Well, we'll wake her up when we have to. Hmph! Spellbound doors. This will be a tough one. Even if I work on the hinges, the damned thing might stay in place."

"Wait a minute! In the cell next to me is Count Boquillas. He's in a nonmagic cell, and that means locks. And here we were, just wishing for a good thief!"

Macore walked over and examined the outer door. "That you in there, Count?"

"Yes, it is me," the cultured voice of Boquillas responded. "Can you do anything?"

"Let me study the situation for a minute. The outer door's pretty standard. I'll get my small pick and jeweler's hammer out and do some probing." For a while there were only small picking and hammering noises, with all comments and questions shrugged off by the thief as distracting. Finally they heard a decisive, hard metallic *tap* and then the sound of creaking hinges.

"You did it!" Boquillas breathed, not really believing it. "But—can you take the inner locks?"

Again Macore set to his work, at one point actually closing the outer door so he could get rid of the annoying other noises from the prison area. He began attaching a series of small magnets around various points in the door, then maneuvering them with his ear to the inner cell door. Finally he seemed satisfied, and out again came the pick and tiny hammer. There were three hard taps, then two more, then one more. "All right—push on the door now, Count."

Boquillas did, and the door swung open. Macore found himself facing a wan, elderly, and very scrawny-looking man with long, matted, white hair and beard and hard lines in his face. He didn't look much like the picture Ruddygore had shown them, except for the eyes, which were the same energetic, almost electric brown eyes of the portrait.

"I can't believe you actually picked the locks so easily," Boquillas said wonderingly. "If you only knew how long I studied them . . ."

"Oh, it's a talent, just as you have talents," the little thief responded modestly. "However, a thorough knowledge of all kinds of lock mechanisms, years of on-and-off practicing on them, and the right tools help. Come on—let's free the other two."

Boquillas nodded and made his way out to the hall. At this point, he stretched and seemed to gain in both strength and stature as Macore watched him. Before the thief's startled eyes, the frame filled out and both face and form appeared to grow younger. Finally all that was left of the old man he had freed was the hair and beard; the rest was unquestionably the Count Boquillas of the portrait, his face full of determined self-confidence. He walked to Joe's cell, looked at the door, chuckled, then began a series of tracing motions with his left index finger. The door creaked and then opened a trifle. Joe went over to it, pushed it, and entered the hall. "You don't know how glad I am to meet you, Count," he said sincerely.

Boquillas nodded, then walked down to the next cell. "Humph! The old girl's getting sloppy. Same damned simple spell." Again the finger traced and again the door unlocked itself.

Marge was still fast asleep, but it was a shock to see her. Without those grand wings, she looked very frail and childlike.

Boquillas stepped inside. "A defrocked Kauri. Amazing."

"Can you restore her?" Joe asked hopefully.

"Certainly, but it will take time. This is a far more complex spell; if I don't get it right, she'll wind up worse than she is now. Best I simply *add* something, which is easy, and take care of the restoration later." Again a few finger gestures. "This will give her a jolt of energy to get going and also rearrange her time sense and eyes to daylight. For the moment, I think we'd best just get the hell out of here. I assume Ruddygore is coming?"

"Yeah," Macore told him, "but it won't be quick. These communicators don't have much of a range, so the message is going north by eagle."

"Then I don't think we dare wait for him. I couldn't protect both of you people, even though I have no worries about myself any more. I think, also, that I want to go to some place that is mine and get myself back in shape before going on with this. Thief, can you handle Ruddygore's amenities?"

"Sure. No problem. But where will you go? And how?"

"Up. Up and over, the same way you came in."

"But eagles can't carry you!"

"No, not eagles. Me. As much as I would like to stick around for the showdown for personal reasons, these two need me to get clear not only of the tower but of Witchwood. We'll go to my retreat on Wolf Island. When Ruddygore is finished here, send one of your eagles to tell us the news, and we can plan from there. Agreed?"

Macore nodded. "Sounds fair to me. Oh—Marge is waking up."

She turned and groaned, then opened her eyes and looked around, puzzled. "Joe? Macore? Am I dreaming?"

Quickly things were explained to her. With Joe carefully holding the door open wide so that she would not contact iron, she walked out and glanced around. "Now what?"

"To the top!" Boquillas said, and they started upstairs.

The rookeries and aviary inside the top level looked like the remnants of a war zone. There were dead birds, feathers, and blood all over the place. "The boys were a little messy," Macore told them.

A ladder and trapdoor brought them to the top of the tower and outside into the midday sun. Marge was startled. "It's been a long time since I could look normally at a day like this."

Macore turned and looked upward, then made a series of motions with his arms. "I just told them everything was fine."

Boquillas nodded. "Good. Let's waste no more time. Stand back against the far wall, all of you."

They did as instructed and watched as the sorcerer went to the very edge of the tower's top, then got up on the narrow ledge. He seemed in intense concentration; then he stretched out his arms, and they all gasped as he apparently plunged off the cornice.

But Boquillas did not fall. Instead, rising back up to the top was an enormous bird, the largest and perhaps the ugliest any of them had ever seen. It had to weigh close to a ton, and it seemed impossible that such a thing could fly. It landed back on the roof, completely blotting out the sky and giving them little room to move. "Get on my back," Boquillas' voice came from the giant, misshapen beak. "I will carry you all to safety. Be quick. A giant roc is bound to cause a great deal of attention below."

They needed no urging, but it was scary getting up on that broad back. They finally did, though. "Now just hold on and do not panic," Boquillas told them. "Grab one another around the waist and dig in hard with your feet—quickly!"

They followed his instructions and then felt a tremendous jolt and bounce. They were airborne.

Boquillas settled down and hovered unnaturally at treetop level. "Hop off now, thief. You should be able to make your way down from here."

Macore let loose and looked nervously at the top limbs. "Yeah, if I don't break my fool neck. Well, here goes." He slid off and managed to grab onto a branch that held, finally pulling himself in. The roc then flew away, gaining altitude and speed as it went. Soon they were high in the warm air and rapidly heading southwest.

"Over to the right, there is Morikay," Boquillas told his passengers. "You can see the great castle directly in the center of town, rising on top of the mesa." They looked and saw a large city spread out along the banks of a river at the junction of the main river branch with what had to be the Zhafqua. The land was quite level; but in the center of the densely populated area, a single reddish hill with a flat top stuck out, and atop it was Castle Morikay.

"It looks like Disneyland," Joe commented. He seemed suddenly struck by other, darker thoughts. "Tiana's in that thing somewhere."

Marge gave him a squeeze. "We'll get her out. Don't worry about that. First things first."

He nodded, but was mostly silent for the rest of the journey.

He had no idea of the speed they were making, but it was in the best tradition of jet airplanes, despite the heavy breeze and lack of comforts. In only a couple of hours the flat land gave way to what appeared to be a seacoast. This was Lake Ktahr, and soon they could see two large islands. The roc banked toward the southernmost of these, a heavily forested wilderness. Near the southern end, though, on a bluff, they could see Boquillas' retreat—a castlelike structure that was not large as castles went but looked very much the part. Boquillas descended toward it, landing just outside the low castle walls.

Joe and Marge slid off quickly, then stood back as the giant bird reared up, stretched out its massive wings, and seemed to dissolve and shrink into human form once more. Soon only the Count himself stood there, looking much as he had looked back at the Dark Tower. He smiled and nodded, then came over to them. For a moment he examined them with a critical eye, then noted Marge's golden necklace and Joe's lone earring. "I assume that these hold the communicators the thief spoke about."

Joe nodded. "So we're told."

Boquillas reached out and took the necklace in two fingers, then pulled. It was still intact, impossibly so, as if it had come right through Marge's neck, but it was off. With a quick motion, he reached up and pulled on Joe's earring as well. It, too, came off. "Hey! What?" Joe managed, but Boquillas silenced him with a nonmagical gesture, holding up his hand.

"A thousand pardons for this, but, you see, although I trust you just fine, I can not really trust Ruddygore. These will be put in a safe place and returned to you, I promise, when you're ready to leave the retreat. I simply can not afford to have you even inadvertently invite him in without my permission and restrictions. You do understand, I hope."

They didn't really like it, but they had little choice, and it did seem reasonable. Both, though, remembered that Ruddygore had not really trusted Boquillas, even though the two were on good terms with each other. No top sorcerer ever could fully trust another of at least equal and possibly superior powers.

Boquillas turned, said, "Follow me now," and walked up to a small gate which opened inward as he approached. There had been no hue and cry at their arrival—in fact, the place looked deserted—but Boquillas wasn't in need of a lot of servants. He had a large place in the City-State of Marahbar for that, after all. This was his place and his alone.

They entered the courtyard, which looked somewhat overgrown and unused, and headed for the small castle's main door. Marge glanced down at the soft earth and gasped, which caused the other two to stop and turn in puzzlement. "What's the matter?" Joe asked her.

"Look at the prints I'm making in this wet ground! I'm practically sinking in it!"

"That is Esmerada's spell, or part of it," the sorcerer explained to her. "Kauri normal construction is far less dense than that of humans or even most other fairies. The spell is actually a transmuter, altering the atomic structure so that you are made up of much heavier stuff. Don't let it trouble you. I will examine it in more detail tonight and see about unraveling it. Esmerada is quite good, though, at that sort of thing. We may have to wait until Ruddygore does her in before the spell is loosened enough to be worked on. Still and all, it's temporary. Come in and let's get cleaned up and have a decent meal."

They entered. As Boquillas went along the dark castle halls, torches burst spontaneously into light, and even fireplaces began to roar. Marge recalled Ruddygore's comment that Boquillas had a penchant for cheap magic and theatrics. She wondered who was expected to cook this meal and how fresh the food would be. That startled her, too—thoughts of a meal. She was starting to get hungry for real food, she realized, although she hadn't needed to eat since plunging into that molten pit back in Mohr Jerahl.

Boquillas led them to a combination dining hall and study, the walls of which were lined with copies of the Books of Rules and other volumes. He stopped by one wall briefly, then took them up a flight of stone stairs to a second floor area.

There were only two rooms and a large alcove upstairs. The Count led them to the far room and opened the door. It was a spacious bedroom, with thick carpeting on the floor and carpets of various designs hung on the walls as well. A window looked out on the lake, providing a nice view, once the thick shutters were opened.

"Things are a trifle dusty," the Count said apologetically, "but I'm afraid it's been a while since anyone was here. The small door over there leads to an operable shower and toilet, which you share with my own room. I have begun the fire under the cistern above, so there should be hot water. Soap, shampoo, and all the amenities are there as well, and I will allow you some time to clean yourselves up. A bit of conjuring has permitted me to take a look at you and shape some appropriate clothing, which you'll find in the chest over there. When you're washed, dressed, and relaxed, join me downstairs in the main hall, and we will eat and talk."

With that the Count left them alone. Marge looked up at Joe. "What do you make of all this?"

He shrugged. "I don't know, but it's a damn sight better than a cell in that witch's tower. I do know, though, that I'm in bad need of a cleanup, a good meal, and a nice, long sleep."

"I'll go for that," she agreed.

The shower, which used a rooftop container that apparently caught rain and held it, was ingenious and practical. There was even hot and cold running water, from two separate tanks, although it took a lot of experimentation to get the balance right. The soap was the heavy lard soap so common to Husaquahr, but there was also a liquid soap that made a good shampoo, and both Joe and Marge used it.

The climate here was tropical but damp, and the stone of the castle made things a bit chillier than they normally would have been.

The clothing Boquillas had conjured up for them had to conform to the Rules on such things, of course, so Joe found a clean breechclout and a pair of well-made sandals for himself. Marge, who had not been able to wear clothing since getting her wings, now could once again and found that Boquillas had interesting tastes. He had provided a loose slit skirt of some satiny yellow material that hung on her hips and a halter top of the same material, as well as a pair of matching, open-topped, high-heeled shoes that gave her a couple of inches in height but also quite a wiggle to her walk, due not only to the shoes themselves but also to the excess weight they had to bear.

When Marge had finished dressing, she paraded in front of Joe and asked, "Well? How do I look?"

"Beautiful. I'm turned on already."

She laughed. "At least I come up to your thick neck now."

She looked at him playfully. "Sir, may I have your arm?"

"Delighted," he responded, and they went out and down to the main hall.

As far as they knew, there were only the three of them in the castle or on the whole island, yet the table was set with fancy tableware and covered tureens and dishes. Boquillas, sitting in a high-backed chair trimmed with gold, rose and greeted them with a smile, closing a book he'd been consulting. It looked very much like one of the volumes of Rules, but since neither could read the language, they couldn't tell which volume it might be.

"You look wonderful," he told them. "Please be seated."

"You look pretty good yourself," Joe replied, and it was true. Gone were the last vestiges of the scrawny, bearded prisoner of the Dark Tower. Boquillas wore the fine clothes of a civilized gentleman, reminding Marge, at least, of some Spanish don, complete with ruffled shirt. His beard had darkened to black with only a fleck or two of gray here and there, and his hair, now washed, trimmed, and combed, matched that coloration. On each hand he wore several large golden rings in which were set precious stones.

Boquillas took them through the meal, from appetizer to salad to soup to main course, which was a whole roast pheasant perfectly done, all accompanied by very fine wine, but the talk they had was mostly small talk. Marge found herself eating ravenously, as much as or more than Joe, and she had to ask about it.

"When Esmerada took your wings, so to speak, she took with them the powers of Kauri," the Count explained. "That meant your very unusual biochemistry had to be changed, and this was done. With a structure that is three times as heavy as that of a human or earthbound fairy—about the density of a dwarf or a kobold, actually—you require more to fuel it. You see now why these spells are easier put on than taken off, I think. It is not enough just to change one thing. When you change that, you also change thousands of other things as well by sheer necessity. To put on the spell is easy, as much of this follows automatically. Magic runs by natural laws as fixed as any in the world. But to remove the spell, one must decode it. I must crack Esmerada's personal secret code, then undo the spell in such a way so that you aren't killed in the process of restoration."

That seemed to make sense. "Just how—dense—am I?"

"You mean weight? Well, if you were human, someone your size would weigh, perhaps, eighty pounds. She tripled your density without adding to your apparent size, so that would make you about two hundred and forty pounds. It's not as complex as you make it out to be. Just imagine a feather. Light, airy, a floater. Now transmute that feather's atoms by adding a bit here and subtracting a bit there so that those same atoms, the same number, are atoms of lead. That's what was done to you."

She nodded. "But I still feel the same. I still have the same, well, urges and inclinations."

The sorcerer grinned, and Joe looked at her curiously.

"You are still you, that's why," the Count told her. "Why not just relax and take things as they come? It is always best in this crazy world."

They continued to talk after dinner, this time on more substantive topics. Boquillas wanted to know their basic histories, background, and details on the scheme. They decided to keep as close-mouthed as possible, but he had surmised much.

"Of all the sorcerers of this world, Ruddygore is the most complacent and satisfied with things as they are," he told them. "I suspect this comes mostly from his being able to move between the worlds, almost at will. You know—the man who can travel anywhere, see, enjoy, and experience anything he wishes, then comes back to his comfortable, stable home to rest. The trouble is, for the rest of us it's not all that simple. This world is, after all, comfortable only for those with wealth or magical power that brings such wealth. The vast bulk of the population, both human and fairy, toils under a system where muscle is the only thing that matters. It is their labor that makes the comfortable lives of the few possible, yet they share very little of the rewards. Nor can they—for if they stopped their unceasing toil, the whole world would grind to a halt and collapse. It is not the magicians and kings of this world who are essential to it, though—if we all vanished overnight, this world would probably be the better for it."

"You sound as if you feel guilty for being one of the leaders here," Joe noted. "It seems to me that you're talking one side and living the other."

"A fair point," Boquillas conceded, "but any social revolution here will never come from below. It can't, as long as magical talent is the measure of authority. It must be imposed from above by ones who are firmly committed to changing things."

"A benevolent despotism," Marge said.

"If you like. The alternative is either a malevolent despotism or a totally amoral one that doesn't care about anybody and has a stake only in keeping things the same. Esmerada is a good example of a malevolent despot, and your friend Ruddygore is the amoral one. In a way, he's worse than the witch queen."

"Huh?" they both said at once.

"Yes, I know that's a shocking statement, but consider that even the evil ones are committed to change. Not the kind of change we would want, I grant you, but change all the same. It is Ruddygore who stands against change of any sort. Any society whose intelligentsia knows atomic theory and structure, to name just one example, is one with the potential to grow, to create machines to ease people's labor, to produce, in fact, a system whereby everyone profits from his labors according to his contributions. We have a complex, multiracial society here with everything it needs to become a great civilization, yet we find innovation stifled, invention wiped out. Even in the magical arts, which create the elitism and maintain the feudalism, there is room for expansion. Look at those Books of Rules on the walls around me. Absurd, aren't they?"

"From what we've seen, I'll grant you that," Marge admitted.

"With guts, a benevolent Council could eliminate those Rules—wipe 'em out instead of continually adding, deleting, modifying, and changing. That alone would totally liberate society from its stratifications. You could change. Barbarians wouldn't continue to be barbarians unless they wanted to, nor would dwarfs have to toil in the mines, or Bentar be mercenaries. Each might also learn what of the art they could, so that all would have a measure of power, and their collective power would be enormous. The Rules are nothing more than those of the privileged elite keeping things forever static. The steam engine was invented at least eighteen hundred years ago, yet, thanks to one of those Rules, it is nearly instant and horrible death to build one. You see what I mean?"

They thought about it. Finally Joe said, "I don't know. I've seen the other side and it's not so great."

"Oh, you've been to Earth, then? Ruddygore must indeed favor you."

Joe shot a glance at Marge, and she got the look. "Yes, we've both been there. Every time they have a revolution with noble goals, it seems to wind up just the same—dictatorship, the workers working just as hard for just as little, while somebody new gives the orders and lives the good life. The only difference is, those new leaders kid themselves that it's okay, that one day it will all be different. But it never is."

"You sound like Ruddygore, which, I suppose, is to be expected. And, in fact, I agree that things usually work out for the worst in such movements. That's why the Council is so important. If, right at the beginning, it writes the new, simpler, more free and democratic rules, progress *can* work here. I've devoted a good deal of my adult life to determining those ideal rules, and they are very simple and very basic indeed."

"It's an interesting idea, but I'd hate to see all this spoiled if you made one mistake. I guess you've never gotten the rest of the Council to go along?"

Boquillas chuckled. "They're all stick-in-the-muds by the time they reach their positions. It takes decades of work, dedication, endless practice, and stress to get to the top in my profession. By the time most of them reach that position, either they're too old and set in their ways or they feel they are getting their just payment for all the agony they went through getting there. It does tend to give you quite an ego."

"Sounds like doctors," Marge muttered, but he didn't hear her.

"Yeah, but what if it's the Baron who gets to rewrite the rules instead of you?" Joe asked him. "I'm not sure I'd like *those* rules, considering the company he keeps."

The sorcerer shrugged. "In many long conversations with the Baron, I have never been absolutely clear on what he wants. So far, it's just getting control that matters. It was my hope that I could influence him, should he win."

"Could be," Joe said, yawning. "But I doubt it. Sorry about the yawn, but I'm dead tired."

The Count was suddenly all courtliness. "Oh, I beg your pardon! Please—both of you. Go on up and get some rest. Sleep off the whole of your ordeal. Tomorrow we will get down to what happens next."

As much as Marge wanted to keep talking, she, too, was really feeling the exhaustion of the past few days. With a few more words, they excused themselves and went upstairs.

Joe looked around the room. "Well, what do you think of him?"

"I don't really know," she admitted. "On the one hand, I like him. He's got tremendous charm and a real sincerity about him. On the other hand, I don't think I'd trust him too much. I had the feeling he was keeping a lot from us, and I don't like his taking away the transmitters, even if Macore and Ruddygore know where we are."

"We can't worry about it," he told her. "Hmmm ... Only one bed. I hope we'll both fit on it."

"Oh, we'll fit," she assured him, and they both undressed and got in, after brushing a bit of dust off the sheets. Joe just lay there a moment, thinking, and she knew what the problem was.

"You can't forget Tiana, can you?"

"No. I keep thinking of her in the hands of that bastard and I want to go charging off to the rescue."

Marge sighed. "I wish I still had all my powers. I can feel the hurt inside you, Joe, and I wish I could help."

He turned and pulled her close, then kissed her. "Maybe you still can. Want to try?"

She smiled. "You know I do." They embraced and kissed. *"Damn!"*

She pulled away and stared in confusion at the other in bed with her. Where Joe had been only a moment before, there was now an exact duplicate of herself.

The duplicate rolled onto her back. "Damn!" she echoed. "It must be sundown."

Marge sighed, remembering the curse. "Well, we might try it anyway."

The transformed Joe shook her head. "No, it's no use. When I was a horse last night, I was every inch a horse. It's an exact physical duplication. Exact."

"Huh? You mean...?"

"Uh-huh. I want it as much as you. I want it from Joe, though, and, hell, *I'm* Joe."

Marge sighed, knowing exactly how Joe felt, and pulled up the sheet. "Well, at least we both fit on the bed."

They awoke at almost the same moment. It was quite dark and all seemed still. Both just lay there, not really aware that the other was awake, lost in thought.

For Joe, it was an interesting experience. Not merely the physical change, but the change from human to fairy. It felt— well, not better or worse, but *different*. Without even realizing it, he shifted his Kauri eyes from the regular band, which saw only darkness, to the magic band, and suddenly all was alight with intricate and colorful patterns. It was all over the place, in, around, and through them and all the objects in the room, as well. For the first time he saw as Marge, Ruddygore, and Boquillas could see, and he understood just what this world was really all about.

He got up from the bed and went to the window, something he couldn't have done under normal circumstances without breaking his neck in the dark, and found it unusual to have to strain on tiptoe to the utmost to see out of it. It had seemed relatively low to him the day before.

There was a storm off in the distance. He could see the night sky occasionally light up, and every once in a while a distant, jagged pencil stab of lightning. A breeze whipped up by the storm made the lake surface rough and caused breakers to smash themselves against the cliffs far below with repeated dull roars.

Marge got up and came over next to him, also looking out. "It's very pretty, a night like this."

He nodded. "This magic band is kinda wild, though. Jeez! It's all over the place! Even the lake has it!"

"Well, it's a little more crowded around here than it is with the usual spells, but, yes, there's magic in everything and everyone here. Both the Laws and the Rules are magic, and they determine just about anything."

"You know, it sort of reminds me of that night in west Texas, except for the water. Same kind of far-off storm, same pitch darkness. We sure have been a long way since that night."

She took his hand and squeezed it hard. "Yeah, we sure have." They both lowered themselves and hugged and kissed each other. "You know, it seems that we should have been a pair rather than just a team. Things never worked out the way we figured."

Joe chuckled. "Yeah. Even tonight. Seems as if something's always working against us, doesn't it?"

There was a tremendous rumbling sound echoing outside, and they turned back to the window and again looked out. As the lightning lighted up the southern skies, Joe said, "Funny."

"What's funny?"

"Those big clouds out there. When the lightning goes off, they almost look like demons' faces."

"Huh? Let's see." She stared out, waiting for the next flash. It seemed as if it would never come, but then it did, and she saw that he was right. "Yeah, I see it. Looks almost like that hideous thing we met in the tent just before the battle." She looked again, making adjustments. "Joe—I don't think this is imagination. Shift back to the magic band."

He did, and looked again. It took a while waiting for the next flash, but then he saw just what she meant. When the face in the cloud was illuminated in the magic band, it seemed framed in shades of crimson and lavender, but there was no pattern. All the other magical things had patterns. "What's it mean?"

"Solid magic, Joe. Pure magic. A pure magical force, not the kind of things we see here. Joe—that isn't a dream. It's real. That *is* the demon we met. The Baron's demon, coming toward us under cover of that storm."

Joe frowned. Although frustrated in one respect, Marge found it fascinating to see herself as everyone else saw her, and she liked what she saw. "What are you thinking of?" she asked.

"Didn't he say the bathroom connected? Want to try a peep and see if he's there?"

"He may have a spell on the door, but let's try. You stay

here. I'm more used to this than you are and I'll know what
to look for. If I can get a peek into his room, it's going to be
tremendously crowded with magic."

He nodded and watched as she entered the bathroom and
crept to the door on the other side. After listening for a moment,
she tried the door and found to her surprise that it was open.
She peered in, then quickly shut the door again and returned.
"He's not there."

"It doesn't mean anything. He could be downstairs, anywhere."

"I think maybe we ought to find those little transmitters and
turn them on," she said. "Just in case."

Joe thought a moment. "He had 'em in his hand when we
came in, but not when we went upstairs. I don't think he
dematerialized them or anything, so they're probably downstairs in the den. That's the one place he could have stopped
for a moment before coming up."

"Right. Let's go."

Joe sighed. "I don't know how we're going to explain my
looking like this if he catches us."

"If he catches us, that will probably be the least of our
problems."

"Good point," he conceded and followed her out into the
dark hall. The magic gave enough of a glow to the place to
guide them to the stairs. The torches were still burning dully
below, enabling them to proceed on normal visuals.

They crept down the stairs and peered into the den. Several
books were open and scattered around the table, but there was
no sign of Boquillas. They walked in and started looking carefully for any place that the Count might have put the jewels,
but not discovering any likely one. Joe was also finding it hard
to adjust to being far shorter than he'd ever been. Things that
had been within easy reach of him before now seemed unat-
tainable. He began to understand why Kauri had the ability to
fly.

They looked over the area for the better part of an hour
without finding anything. Then the storm hit outside, and Marge
turned to him. "We'd better give it up and get back upstairs.
If the storm is here, he's probably finished."

Joe nodded, and they scampered quickly upstairs. The rain

was blowing through the windows in great sheets, and only by dragging over a stool could Joe get enough height to close the shutters.

Marge took one of the long sulfur matches from a holder and lighted the lamp, illuminating the room with a ghostly glow.

Joe got down off the stool and sat on it, oblivious of the wetness. He was wet enough anyway. "So what do we do now?"

She shrugged. "Wait it out. I just can't believe he's the Baron. If he's the Baron, then what was he doing in Esmerada's prison?"

Joe suddenly felt a burning sensation once again, and knew now just what that meant. "How about that? Sunrise, I guess. I'm me again."

"Welcome back, Geronimo. Speaking for myself, I like you this way a lot better. But I still can't figure it all out."

"I agree with you. If he's the Baron, then everything that happened yesterday was a sham. It meant they knew we were coming, what we were there for, and that he planted himself in that cell next to us so we'd fall into his hands."

"Yeah, but even if we buy that, how could he possibly know that Macore would be there and the right man to break us out?"

Joe had an uneasy thought. "Maybe it wasn't Macore. Ever think of that? We saw somebody turned into a crazy statue, and I've sure been turned into stuff lately. Even you were turned with a few finger motions, and the Count became a big bird with no trouble. So what's to keep him from turning somebody into an exact copy of Macore, or even Esmerada herself doing it?"

"It just could be. But—why? I'm sure neither she nor Boquillas knew about the transmitters. If that's so, then Ruddygore's still going to get in and find her. Certainly the Count didn't have a chance to tell her."

Joe shook his head sadly. "I don't know. Maybe he just didn't need her any more. Maybe she was even in the way."

"Not quite right, my friend," a familiar voice behind them said. "She was of great use to me." They whirled and saw Boquillas standing in the door to the bathroom.

"Don't look so shocked," he told them. "You think your

wanderings of the evening would go undetected here? I left a lot of magical strands to see just where you went. For your information, the transmitters are in a small chest on the top shelf of the den, masked by a few books. If you had had more time, you probably would have discovered them. It was an oversight on my part, but not one that was fatal."

"I have a feeling that the reason you're telling us this is because we won't have a chance to get back there, right?" Marge said uneasily.

Boquillas grinned. "Alas, no. However, as long as those devices remain there, they will give out an all's-well signal to Ruddygore's eagles. Your thief friend, who should arrive nearby in a day or two just on suspicion, will be lulled. I may even trot you out under a spell to tell him how wonderful it is here, if it's still necessary by that time."

"What do you mean, still necessary?" Joe asked. "What the hell is going on here, anyway?"

"A very complicated plot, or series of plots, I fear. My original plan was already under way, but I still lacked a key element. I had to get Ruddygore out of the north. I had to bring him south, the farther south the better. There were any number of ruses, of course, but when he launched his own little plot against the Barony, it all fell neatly into place. Although I still don't know how you got into the tower, I had no doubt you would. Because I had to know the mechanics of Ruddygore's little plot, I contrived that imprisonment scenario. Thanks to it, you not only came willingly here with me but also told me about those interesting little devices. That was what I needed to know."

"Was that really Macore?" Marge wanted to know.

"Oh, yes. It would hardly have the ring of truth, not to mention giving me a nice alibi, if it wasn't. He has quite a— record, I suppose you might say—and is rather well known up and down the rivers of Husaquahr. I had no doubt that he'd come running when he saw Tiana flown off as a prisoner, or that he could pick those locks. If he hadn't, though, I had other rescues arranged. So now, today, Ruddygore enters Witchwood and faces down Esmerada, who is convinced that I will come to her aid. Poor Esmerada. She has style, but she always was a second-rate politician."

"You intend for Ruddygore to kill her, then?" Marge responded, somewhat appalled.

Boquillas shrugged. "I have far more vital things to attend to today and tonight as the Baron. Ruddygore is very powerful, as well I know, and I would prefer to face him on my own terms at a later date. That, however, might be rather soon. You see, Ruddygore will attain the seat in Witchwood, but at the expense of Terindell."

"What!"

The Dark Baron grinned at them. "For the past few months, in small groups and under civilian cover and disguise, a rather large force has been moving north on riverboats. Even now they are beginning to assemble for their individual marches, closing in on Terindell. Another army is north of Lake Zahias, set to strike at Sachalin. Yet a third will besiege Halakahla at the same time. The Sachalin attack will tie down my only sorcerous threat in the region, while I take the key cities and transportation hubs. I personally will take Terindell, then attend to my brother wizard to the east."

"Big talk," Joe told him. "If Ruddygore can't set foot in here, what makes you think you can set foot in Terindell?"

The Baron laughed. "Alone I can not, but I have a rather powerful ally. You saw him earlier this morning, I would guess."

Marge just shook her head. "So all that talk about the horrors of war and a great moral crusade was just so much wind for another brutal dictatorship."

"Oh, no! All that I told you last night I fully believe, I assure you. I am bringing revolution to this world and I will change it for the better, make it free and great. But I grew weary of trying. I was a voice crying for sanity against a world oppressed by powers who would fight all change. It was obvious that no change was possible except by using the one thing they respect—brute force in all its ways. But come. We must attend to you for a while." He made a few hand gestures, and both Joe and Marge felt their bodies below their necks go completely numb. With no control at all over themselves, they found themselves getting up and walking out into the hall, then down the stairs, the Baron following.

Their heads were still their own, though, and they continued to press the conversation.

"All your allies are evil sorcerers and a demon from Hell," Marge pointed out. "I don't think they have the same visions as you do. You've fooled yourself."

The Dark Baron chuckled. "Well, Esmerada's going to be a vacancy soon, and I will appoint the next candidate, one who thinks as I do, because I will control what's left after all this. There will be other vacancies around as well. In fact, I have a number of friends already on the Council who are simply dubious about my chances. It's been figured out pretty well, my friends."

"You mean Kaladon has your idealism? I doubt it," Joe spat.

"No, Kaladon is playing out a very long game of his own, a game that seems to involve your girl friend in an integral way. He will support me as long as it serves his purposes, then try to dispose of me when I win."

"I thought he was the weakest on the Council," Marge said as they walked down to the cold, damp cellar of the castle.

"He is, but he knows it. Magic is a curious blend of art and science, you know. Sort of like mineralogy and a symphonic composition at the same time. Kaladon is very strong on the science, perhaps the most knowledgeable man in the business, but weak in the artistry. As I understand it, years ago he worked out a very strange plot, partly by duping the girl's father. She was in Kaladon's keeping when she was quite young, and he performed some mental games with her, stuff that her father would never notice unless he really suspected something. When her mother died in childbirth, her considerable powers were transmitted to her daughter, and the old boy continued the process, weakening himself in the bargain to where Kaladon, with a little help from Esmerada, could knock him off. So Tiana has more of the artistic side of magic than any other alive, I'd say. She is potentially the most powerful sorceress in the history of the world, from what I've been able to understand—but, thanks to Kaladon, she suffers from a very minor bit of selective brain damage."

"What!" Joe roared.

"Yes. All that potential is wasted without the ability to form spacial abstracts and complex mathematical formulae. Poor Tiana couldn't count past her fingers and toes, I fear, nor draw even a cube in perspective. You can see Kaladon's problem, can't you? For twenty years and more, he put together his scheme whereby he'd be the only one able to use and in complete control of the most powerful sorceress the world has ever known. And then she went and escaped from him!" Boquillas chuckled. "The man's been paranoid for years, afraid he would be deposed before he found her again. He grasped at my offer for protection in exchange for absolute service like a drowning man clutching at a branch."

"Aren't you afraid that, now that he's got her, he'll turn on you?" Joe asked. "Not that it would be much of an improvement."

The Dark Baron shook his head. "No, Kaladon simply has no idea that there's a demon prince involved in all this, capable of negating the power of three or four Kaladons, even augmented. I intend doing things the same way Ruddygore hit on—one sorcerer at a time, although I must work faster than he. Ah! Here we are!"

In a few moments, deep in the dungeons under the castle, the two captives found themselves actually cooperating in getting into manacles stuck in the wall. Boquillas closed the locks on each of them, then also closed locking waist bars and leg manacles. Both now hung helplessly on a stone wall, about five feet apart. The sorcerer stepped back and looked at them with satisfaction. He then used a small wooden stool to get up next to Marge first, then Joe, and attach something to a small rod which he brought out. In front of each, about two inches from their mouths, hung a loaf of bread and a hunk of smelly cheese.

"I'm sorry. I had hoped this would wait until after breakfast, but at least you won't starve. You can manage the bread and cheese with a little effort and practice. There's a small trough just above you both that's rather sensitive to loud sounds. If you just shout, it will tip over and produce a stream of water for half a minute or so. After the rain last night, it's quite unlikely to run out." Boquillas stepped back, took the stool, and walked to the front of the cell. "I'm doing this only because I can't be here for a long period. However, I'm not like the fool in the stories who takes it for granted that he has his enemies trapped and then ignores them." He walked out and clanged the cell door shut, then locked it with a large key which he put in his pocket. He concentrated for a moment and made a few more gestures with his hands.

"There," he said, satisfied. "I have transmuted the cell floor so that it is now an iron alloy. So is the ceiling, and so are these bars. There are no windows—you are deep within the rock itself. So, if by some chance you break the control spell on your bodies, you, at least, my lady, will still have to hang around. I suspect that this alone will keep our big friend put, but since iron is no problem for him, I'll cast one little insurance spell." Again he flicked his wrist, and Joe yelled.

"Hey! You're not going to leave us in the dark!"

"It is no matter," Boquillas responded. "You see, you are totally blind until I return. Do hang around and have fun. I have many questions to ask you under less pressing circumstances, and I know that Hiccarph, too, wants to question you on why you don't seem to exist for him. Until happier times, then—bye!"

With that, Esmilio Boquillas walked off, and they could hear him ascending the stone stairs to the cheerier part of the building.

When all sound of him had faded, Marge called, "Joe?"

"Yeah?"

"Is it true? Can't you see at all?"

"Not a thing. It's pitch dark to me." He turned his head toward her. "Can you see my eyes?"

She strained to see. There was only one torch, and no certainty of how long it would last. She gasped.

"Bad, huh?"

"Joe—all I see are whites. You don't seem to have any pupils at all."

He sighed. "Yeah. He sure wasn't taking any chances, was he?"

"There's still tonight, if he's gone long enough."

"Huh? What do you mean?"

"The last night of the full moon. Remember last night?"

"How could I forget it?" he responded grumpily.

"You'll change again. The spells will be off."

"What good's that gonna do? You're the closest living thing to me, so all I'll be is you again, right? Hanging here without any painkiller. Okay, maybe the iron wouldn't kill me, only silver, but what good does that do? Even if I slip out of these bindings by getting smaller, I still am no Macore."

"It's a chance, though. One we must take. This madman is going to destroy the whole world. Our only hope is to get Ruddygore in here before the Baron comes back. Otherwise Ruddygore will have nowhere to hole up, no safe seat of magic. The Baron and Kaladon will pick him off easily, even without their demon."

Joe sighed. "Yeah. Thanks a lot. It seems that an awful lot is hanging on very little here."

"That goes for both of us," she said glumly, looking at the manacles.

CHAPTER 14

OF MICE AND MEN

Castle dungeons must be dark, damp, and infested.
                              —Rules, XVII, 114(d)

WITH NOTHING TO DO BUT HANG AROUND, THEY TALKED.

"Joe, do you think that even Ruddygore could take Boquillas on? With his demon, I mean?"

"I don't know. Ruddygore seemed to think so, so we have to go with that. I'm still trying to figure out how the Baron could move several large armies all the way up there without anybody noticing. At least that explains the squad we saw."

"And the missing and pirated boats. I wonder, though, if he really can pull it off."

"He probably can, at least the military part of it. They aren't ready for him with massed armies this time and a couple of weeks' notice on where he'll march. Oh, he'll do it, all right. What he probably can't do is win the peace the way he thinks.

I wish that demon had brought him over some history books along with that Marx and Hitler stuff."

"That's true. Lenin in particular was a well-meaning visionary with real hopes for the future, but his system gave us Stalin instead. And there were a bunch of Hitler's friends and supporters who thought he was just a social reformer. By the time they found out, it was too late. Boquillas isn't Hitler or Stalin, but there's one around."

"Kaladon?" Joe mused. "I wonder if that's the plot."

"Maybe. Certainly he would be a better friend to demons than Boquillas in the long run. Do you think Ruddygore knows about Tiana's power?"

"I doubt it. If he did, he'd never have let her risk it all by coming with us. Damn! So much depends on your getting out of here! It's the Baron's only real mistake. That and bragging about where the transmitters were hidden. If he wasn't just putting us on. Anybody with his kind of mind can't be trusted to say his own name right."

"Oh, I think he was telling the truth. As he said, he needs to have them on and operating or it will tip everything off. Let's just be thankful he didn't return a few minutes sooner this morning, or we'd have no chance at all. He'd have discovered two of me in that room, and that would have been it."

Joe sighed. "Yeah. But I still wish I knew how to pick locks. How's that torch coming along?"

"Still going. I think it will last a while." Marge paused a minute. "Say, do you hear something?"

He cocked his head. "Water dripping."

"No, a little *scratch, scratch, scratch* type of sound."

They both kept silent for a long while, and finally he heard it, too. "What the hell *is* that?"

She thought a moment, then had it. "What else? Rats. Ugh!" Suddenly it struck her. "Joe! Rats! Around here!"

"Big deal. So we'll get nibbled to death."

"No, no! If we're very, very lucky, we might be able to attract them by biting off some of your cheese and letting it drop to the floor!"

"*My* cheese? Why not yours? At least you can see."

"No, I mean at the proper time."

He finally got the idea. "Fine—if we had a watch or a view

of the sun. I don't know if we've been here for ten minutes or ten hours. The odds are just too slim. Besides, becoming a rat might get me out of here and even upstairs, but I couldn't activate the transmitters."

"You wouldn't have to. Just escape, find them, then wait until dawn. When you turn back again, you can use them."

"No good." He sighed. "When I turn back again, I'll be paralyzed and blind again, too, remember?"

She thought furiously. "Maybe not. At least, not paralyzed. I looked you over. The paralysis is a simple spell analogous to an injury. All your injuries faded, right? I think this will wear off, too."

"And my eyes?"

"That's fifty-fifty. It looks like a transmutation spell there, rather than an injury. If he'd just rendered your optic nerves inoperable, that would be one thing, but he took no chances. He changed the composition of your eyes. The curse isn't clear enough to allow me to guess on that one."

"Oh, great. So we have to hope that you're right and that I'll be able to move afterward. Uh-uh. Too risky. I'll try picking the cell door lock. Just as likely to fail, but more of a chance than the other way."

But as it turned out, he had little choice in the matter. After a while the skittish rats grew bolder, first showing themselves, then scampering about here and there, and finally checking out the leavings that had dropped on the cell floor from the prisoners' attempts to eat.

It seemed like an unpleasant eternity that they hung there, but finally, when both had more or less lapsed into sleep, sundown arrived.

The first Joe knew about it was when he was falling. Then he hit the floor with a force that hurt. Dizzily he got up, opened his eyes, and looked around. He was awfully low to the ground. He turned on four legs and saw behind him a long, bare tail; he knew for a fact that he had indeed changed into a rat.

He looked up at Marge, who seemed incredibly gigantic to him, and saw that she was still sleeping. He decided to leave her that way, since he'd be gone a very long time, anyway, and she would take a lot of comfort from his absence, far more so than from his presence.

In rat form, he found it absurdly simple to get between the bars and out into the corridor. His rat's eyes were quite good, he discovered, although that stairway was one hell of a gigantic obstacle.

It took him three hours, stretching and groaning and aching all the way, to manage the climb. He knew, somehow, that there was a far better and easier way, but he decided that the other rats might not take kindly to him, and probably couldn't tell him where it was, anyway.

Once on the main floor, which was mostly dark now, with only a few isolated torches left going, he made for the main hall and discovered that, while the previous evening he'd been short, now he was in a world where giants loomed.

Being four foot ten was a hell of a lot easier to live with than being six inches off the floor.

Disgusted, he relaxed and let the rat in him dominate. He began exploring, almost without thinking about it, and found a long, tasseled bell rope at one side of the bookcases. Using his handlike clawed feet, he tried several times and finally got a grip, wondering where and what he might be ringing, and started up.

It was a hairy task, and he fell several times, but eventually he got the hang of it and made it to the top row of shelves. Judging the distance as best he could, he made the leap, grabbed a volume of the Books of Rules, and almost pulled it off the shelf and himself with it. Fortunately, there were so many of the things that they were very tightly shelved, and he managed to pull himself up on top of the books and start to look behind them.

It didn't take him long to find the small jewelry box, hidden behind a row of the Rules; but after pushing several volumes out from the back and having them fall and crash to the floor, he waited nervously. He'd never really believed the place was deserted; but when a reasonable time had passed, he decided that it might be true.

He got behind the box now and started pushing it out with his head, using his neck muscles. It was tough going, but finally it reached the edge of the shelf, then dropped to the floor. It somehow managed to miss the pile of books down there and hit on a corner, coming open in the process. Among a lot of junk spilling out, he spotted both the earring and the necklace. *Halfway home*, he thought to himself.

It took him a lot longer to get up the guts to climb down, but he finally decided on the rope approach in reverse, and it worked, although he fell the last three feet to the floor. He was by this time one battered and bruised rat.

He scampered over to the two small pieces of jewelry and, taking them in his teeth one at a time, he arranged them in a clear space, then settled down to wait until dawn. He was determined that, no matter what, he was going to wake up with those pieces near his head.

Marge heard sounds of somebody coming and moved her head to look. The torch was dying now, but it still gave off enough light for her to see by. She was apprehensive about those sounds, and she had no idea how long she had slept or whether it was night or day. The figure moved with agonizing slowness, closer and closer to the cell, and finally appeared.

"Joe!"

He grinned. "Yeah. You were right, kid. When I changed back, I moved perfectly. I sent the signals with no trouble at all. If there's anything out there, they're hearing it now. Just to make sure, I gave as much information as I could into both transmitters, along with the proper invitations."

"And your eyes?"

"I'm still blind," he told her. "That's what took me so long. I damned near broke my fool neck coming down those stairs."

"You shouldn't have tried. You should be up top in case Macore or somebody else comes. You can't get me out of here, anyway. Even if you had sight and a key, there's too much iron here for it to be safe, and besides, I'm still paralyzed."

"I had to," he told her. "I couldn't just leave you here not knowing. Don't worry, though. I can make it back up now. Even blind, I can do it a hell of a lot easier than as a rat."

She laughed, and he quickly filled her in on the night's work.

"Well, I'll go up now, for all the good it will do. Just stay here and pray the message gets through before our mad Baron returns."

"It will, Joe! It has to! After all this, we can't have failed in the end!"

"Well, we'll see."

"Be careful!"

"I will. Just stay here until I come back."

"Ha, ha," she responded sarcastically.

He stumbled a couple of times, but made it to the top without any real disasters. He felt lucky that the place was so small and therefore fairly easy to remember. That didn't keep him from stumbling and tripping over things he didn't quite remember, but it helped him get around.

Flags fluttered in the mild breeze, and the army, more than two thousand strong, now resplendent in full uniforms, waited in the fields outside the tiny town of Terdiera. The town itself seemed unnaturally quiet in the early morning sun, but it was often so just before a battle. Although tense, the men-at-arms appeared boldly confident. All had gone well up to this point. The really dangerous part of sneaking in undetected and then assembling was over. Through the night, supply barges had shed their protective freighter's camouflage and offloaded all that was needed. Unit after unit had turned from ordinary civilians back into menacing military men.

The Dark Baron himself had arrived an hour before dawn. None had seen him arrive nor knew whence he'd come, but now he was here, resplendent in his shining black and gold armor atop his great black horse. With him, too, was his mysterious and equally armored adjutant, known by reputation only as the General. Few had ever seen his massive figure on its white horse before, but now they watched as both rode forward to inspect the field of battle.

The Baron looked out on the town. "I do not like this. It's far too quiet. Not even a rooster crowed, nor has a dog barked."

The General nodded. "We've sealed off the bridge on the Marquewood side, so they've no place to run to. The trolls have been raising Cain all night, but they'll quiet down. Send a patrol into the town and let's see what we're up against."

The Baron rode back and conferred with a leading officer. Six soldiers drew swords and proceeded slowly forward, followed by a dozen spread-out infantrymen armed with powerful crossbows. They met no resistance nor saw any sign of life, except an occasional bird and butterfly, as they advanced on the town. When they reached the first of the buildings, the cavalry stopped, and the infantry fanned out both to scout and to protect the mounted men. Only then did they proceed into the town.

It took them almost forty minutes to do a thorough search, but after the first quarter hour, they were pretty sure that no one remained behind. It was, in many ways, an eerie sight. Although a few things were missing in one place or another, there were still half-eaten meals on dinner tables and half-consumed tankards at the inn. All food and fires were cold, yet there was the distinct feeling among the men that the town's hasty abandonment could not have occurred earlier than the previous afternoon or early evening. In fact, dinner had clearly been at least in preparation when the alarm came. The captain ordered one of his men back to inform the Baron.

"I don't like this," the General noted. "It has a bad feel to it."

"It was your plan, remember," the Baron responded, knowing that the truth of the statement would make very little difference now.

The army marched into the town and quickly secured it, while the bulk of the infantry was told to establish safe perimeters to guard against an attack from the rear and to seal off any breakout.

Detaching a hundred and fifty battle-hardened cavalry from the main unit, the Baron and the General rode on down the road toward the dark towers of Terindell.

"Could they have all retreated inside the castle?" the Baron speculated.

"It's possible," the General responded, "even probable, if it were just the people who were missing. But they took their livestock and pets as well when they went, and that I don't like. The wind is right from the castle now. Such a crowd of people and animals should make an awful racket, yet I hear nothing save the birds."

They came around the bend to the castle gates and stopped. The gates were wide open. Inside, they could see no sign of a living thing.

Another patrol was dispatched, moving forward with agonizing slowness. Finally it reached the gates and halted for a moment. The officer in the front turned back to his leaders and gave a massive shrug.

"I'm going forward," the General told the Baron. "Stay here and wait for my signal." He rode confidently ahead, soon reaching the forward patrol. He stopped then, his huge, oddly cast helmet, which concealed every bit of his features, looking this way and that, as if giving some sort of impossible inspection of every stone. Finally he eased his horse across the bridge and entered the outer castle, the patrol nervously following. They passed through into the inner castle and then into the beautifully manicured inner courtyard and looked around. Nothing stirred.

"There is no life here except the usual parasitic animals," the General told the patrol. "No ambush. Nothing. Signal the Baron to come in and have guards posted on outer and inner gates."

The patrol quickly did as it was instructed, and the Baron moved forward and joined the General. They dismounted together and walked over to the simple, two-storey block building at the far end of the courtyard. On the door was a large scroll, held with two heavy nails. The Baron took it down, unrolled it, and read it with mounting anger and frustration.

"My dear Baron:

"Welcome to Castle Terindell. I hope that you and the boys won't make too much of a mess of it, since it's a very nice castle in a wonderful location. You can safely put up your troops here and be comfortable about it, as I will have no need for it in the immediate future. You should have no difficulty in defending it, as there is no enemy army anywhere nearby.

"I must thank you, though, for that brilliant infiltration plan. I admit that my military education is sadly lacking, and I would never have thought of it on my own. Of course, you must have realized that moving such large forces, even in small groups over a long period, would inevitably attract somebody's attention, and it did. When I saw just how ingenious the whole thing was, I embraced the plot wholeheartedly.

"It should be immediately obvious to one of your talents and intellect that it is far easier to move such forces downriver than up, and far faster. It therefore occurred to me that if you really wanted this place so much, it would be absurdly easy to swap. By the time you read this, Esmerada will be disposed of and Witchwood will be under my domain, but I suppose you expected that. However, at almost the same time, my forces will have seized control of the roads and river routes between Zhafqua and the Khafdis, giving us effective mastery of all Zhimbombe except for Morikay itself, which is totally besieged and cut off.

"In the meantime, my agents in and around your three armies have the ability and means to poison meats, fish, fowl, and water selectively, by nonmagical means. As long as your armies remain in and occupy the places they took today, all will be well; but should you take to the march, you will find the pickings slim. I'm afraid, too, that our effective blockade of the Dancing Gods at the River of Sighs has already captured more than a third of your fleet. The rest can not come up, while those that you have are trapped, as we sank a number of old ships in the main channel of the Rossignol after your supply boats passed and I'm afraid there isn't enough draft left to allow travel. Feel free to start removing my obstacles, but we sank a tasty cargo with them, so you'll find the river monsters rather dense, shall we say? And, naturally, I'm saving some other surprises so as not to spoil your fun.

"The civilian populations you now hold have all been given an effective poison antidote, but they remain your hostages, of course. I might remind you, though, that your attack on Sachalin has brought an additional and formidable sorcerer into the fight against you, so if *you* leave, you'll give our brother free rein to trample your army with all sorts of delightful scourges.

"I believe I have given you only one way out, and I shall be delighted to meet you in some neutral place to settle this. Bring your friend, too. Otherwise, have a nice day. Love and kisses, Throckmorton P. Ruddygore."

The Baron shivered in cold fury, then handed the scroll to the General, who read it without any visible reaction.

"Now what?" the Baron asked him.

"Well, I would say that we certainly underestimated the man," the General responded. "From a military standpoint, he's got us cold. He is quite right that it is far easier to enter a place than to leave it. We can't even depend on treaty to keep the waterways open, since nothing says he cannot blockade his own lands. We could certainly consolidate our forces into a formidable army, but we would then face a fighting retreat of over a thousand miles. There are harsh and difficult measures that could be taken, of course, including the wholesale elimination of the civilian population, one bit at a time, attempting to force terms, but we don't have enough force to hold this vast north country well enough to keep the majority from fleeing to the wilds and waging an endless guerrilla action In any such war of attrition, the carnage would be horrible, and we would lose."

"We could always retreat inland through Marquewood under a pledge of safe passage," the Baron suggested hopefully. "They would go for it, I think, just to eliminate the devastation we could cause."

"To what end, though? Ruddygore would be under no such constraints. It would be the Valley of Decision all over again, with all the elements in the enemy's favor."

"I suppose. Damn Ruddygore! He's thwarted us at every turn! Only my slow subversion by means of the books you imported from Earth through Hell has shown any measurable effect, and that will take decades, perhaps, to have any real impact!"

"He cannot take Kaladon now. Morikay may be besieged, but its seat of power is safe. The Council will be shocked enough by Ruddygore's audacity in eliminating Esmerada. They will not be kindly disposed to helping him topple yet another member. Even his friends will be feeling their own necks by now."

"True, but Kaladon is loyal to me only because he sees me as the way to expand his power. If he is in fact besieged, he knows that we have lost another round. I hardly think he will welcome me with open arms, or, if he does, with empty ones. No, if we are to recover from this, it must be as Ruddygore himself suggests. If I can eliminate the fat man, I can turn things around immediately. Then he has an unsupported army in the south, while we control a strong series of bases here. Eliminate Ruddygore and we win. Anything less and we lose. It's as simple as that."

"I concur. However, do you think he can be defeated? You faced him once in the Valley of Decision and fought to a draw. It was my analysis at that time that you would both have died, had the engagement not been broken off."

The Baron chuckled. "*You* are worried about *my* health? Kaladon would probably be more to your liking."

"Kaladon is as surely mine in the end as you are; but, unlike you, he wishes no meeting with Hell until forced to do so. He is a good schemer, but he is vain and egomaniacal in the extreme, without the intellect to control what he would have. Politically, the surviving Council members would move to fill the weakness. As I said, our fortunes are linked, and I believe that you are right. Where will you fight him?"

"No question there. I have the means to bring him to Wolf Island in a hurry, for I have two of his most favored agents there and a third certainly lurking nearby. I meet him there, on familiar ground to me, with hostages who just might distract him." He thought a moment. "Have the Bentar dispatch messages by their birds to the other units to secure and hold their positions but not advance until further orders come from you or me. Our unit here will take Ruddygore's suggestion and enjoy the comforts of this castle and the town. We will return to Wolf Island to prepare for the arrival of our fat friend. 'Love and kisses' indeed!"

The General laughed. "You must admit the man has real style and flair. Come! We will tend to the business that needs to be done, then fly to Wolf Island. With any luck, you can be home by midnight. *Then* we shall prepare to decide this thing."

CHAPTER 15

A FALLING-OUT BETWEEN OLD FRIENDS

Never give a sorcerer an even break.

—Rules, VI, 307(a)

It was well past midnight when Esmilio Boquillas swooped down on the familiar shores of Wolf Island once more. He could see at once from the air that things had changed, and he didn't like it. In his flight back, he had diverted to check on the progress of Valisandra's southern expeditionary forces and he hadn't liked what he'd seen there at all. The border with Marquewood was now a very open one, with that nation's army pouring in behind the protection of the Valisandran advance parties, and the nearest really effective troops the Barony had were in Leander. The bulk of the regular and mercenary forces of Zhimbombe not involved in the north had apparently fought well, but had finally been forced to retreat to secure defensive positions within the city limits of Morikay. The majority of the forces south of the Khafdis could not be spared, or the region would rise in revolt behind them.

In other words, the Barony was in deep trouble.

And now, he saw, even Wolf Island was not secure. The castle he had left virtually shut down now blazed with light and warmth, with smoke coming from the two main chimneys. There was, in fact, a boat docked just down the island from the cliff side, a boat such as he'd never seen before, and decorated with strange writing and symbols. It looked large enough to have transported a small army, but the signs of such a force in and around the castle were absent. He was pretty sure whose boat it was and what was waiting for him. He was more or less ready, but he had wished for a night's sleep first. He was dead tired, and that was no way to go into a fight.

He landed just outside the castle as he always did and quickly transformed himself from great bird to his normal self. He was dressed now in his own formal clothes and he hoped for the courtesy of a switch of robes, at least. Hesitating only for a moment, he walked up and entered through the familiar gate and then the front door.

All the torches were fully refueled and lighted, but there was no sign of any large force. There was, however, the sound of habitation from the main hall area, and he headed for it.

A lone, huge man sat at the dining table, which was littered with the remains of a meal that might have fed four lesser men. The big man looked up, smiled through his white beard, and raised a wineglass to the haggard-looking newcomer. "Esmilio! Please, do come in and have a seat. You look dead on your feet!"

"Hello, Throckmorton. I see that you've made yourself at home here."

Ruddygore beamed and drained the wineglass. "I really must compliment you on your wine cellar. It is surely the finest I have ever seen, and certainly not what I expected in this remote locale."

"Glad you enjoyed it. Did you leave a bottle for me?"

Ruddygore chuckled. "But of course! I couldn't help noticing the Hobah '99. Really remarkable! I had thought I'd seen the last of that enchanting vintage. I took the liberty of bringing it up but wouldn't dream of touching it. Still, don't you agree that this is a fitting occasion for it?"

Boquillas was forced to smile. "Yes, I believe it is. However, I hope you will allow me the luxury of changing into something more appropriate and perhaps even a shower first?"

"But of course, my old friend! Of course!"

Boquillas looked the big man over critically. "You seem remarkably hale and hearty. I *had* thought that Esmerada would give a better account of herself than that."

Ruddygore shrugged. "It just must have been my day. Actually, I managed to get a little sleep through it all, so after that, plus a good meal and fine wine, I've never felt better in my life."

"I wish I could say the same. I assume your young friends are free?"

"Oh, yes. The blindness was a bitch to straighten out, though. Nice piece of work."

Boquillas sighed. "I should have put them both in suspended animation and have done with it. The result would have been the same, but at least I'd get a decent night's sleep."

"I am a bit surprised that you arrived this evening, despite seeing my boat. You could have waited until morning, after all. If it makes you feel any better, though, even the suspension wouldn't have helped in the long run. Not only are they smart and determined, the best I have, but one of them is a were."

Boquillas started to laugh at that, and then the laughter became louder and more prolonged. It was a minute or so before he got his self-control back. "A were! And last night was the last of the full moon! That's very good, Ruddygore! No, it is more than good. It is *genius*!"

"Yes, well, I wish I'd thought of it, but he managed to catch the curse all by himself. It did come in useful, though. Got him into the Dark Tower and out of your little jail. If you have to have a curse, I think that's the one to have." Ruddygore sighed. "I must say, however, Esmilio, that even with every signpost pointing to you, I continued to refuse to believe until the last moment that you, of all people, could be responsible for such carnage, cruelty, and destruction. It wasn't just an act. I'm sure of that. What changed you, Esmilio?"

"Frustration! Perhaps a little guilt, too, at having so much while the masses were in bondage!"

"But what do you know of the masses, Esmilio? You were born to wealth. Even had you not had the talent or the intelligence, you still wouldn't have had to work a day in your life. You're like every social revolutionary I've ever seen. You know no more of the masses, what they're like, how they think, act, and live, than a hereditary king."

"One does not have to be a woman to understand women's oppression. One does not have to be a soldier to know the horrors of war. Often I've gone out in full disguise, mingled with people from all walks of life all over Husaquahr, lived with the farmers and the merchants and the stevedores on the docks. I know more of them than you!"

"Indeed? So the rich boy went off in disguise and played at farming, or played at loading ships, all the time knowing that at any time he could materialize what he needed or, if need be, slink back to his family's banquet hall. You have never felt, nor can you ever feel, the hunger that comes from having no such fallbacks, no resources. You can never know the anguish of being a continual victim of society, pushed and shoved, without influential friends to bail you out or stay the whip's cruel hand. Even your emotions are intellectualized. The masses are a conceptual model, a mathematical construct like a good spell or an accountant's ledger. You can never know the human individual, for you can never experience what he or she experienced. As any actor, you can play the part, but you cannot be the man."

"And you can?"

"My mother was a prostitute. My father, I was told, was a common sailor, looking for a good time while in port in Todra. I grew up in the filth and squalor of the docks of long ago, which were worse then than now by quite a bit. I scrounged through the garbage for scraps to eat, but I was ambitious. Oh, yes. I could see the magic and I understood what that meant. Back in those days, Todra was a republic, and imported tutors taught the very rich and powerful in small groups on the tree-lined estates of the wealthy. One day, while still a mere lad, I was casing one of those places for a possible robbery when I happened on such a class. I was fascinated. I never did burgle the place, but I came back, day after day, for weeks and months, hiding in the trees and hearing the lessons. Basic mathematics. The classics, frustratingly discussed but which I could not read. Oh, yes, I can indeed, my friend, I can be such a man."

Boquillas was shocked. In all their conversations over the years, he had never heard this before. "But—how did you rise?"

"Every society requires one thing to keep it from exploding. It requires a measure of social mobility. Surely you know that. In some countries it is the degree of literacy, or some sort of merit system within a political structure. For some, it is money. Here it is both money and magic, but you know that magic brings wealth. By my tutorial eavesdropping, I was able to manage and master some small spells. With that, I was able to demonstrate the art to certain magicians in the bazaar, who seemed impressed. They continued my education, as well as taught me to read, and from this I attained membership in the Society. From that point, I began truly to learn and to rise. I really never regretted my origins, nor my pride in my attainments. Perhaps my only regret is a lifetime of overcompensation for those early days of near starvation."

"I never knew."

"It was very long ago."

"But—you should have been my natural ally, not my enemy in this! Together we could have changed so much!"

Ruddygore sighed. "I see now my mistake, one that must be paid for. At some point I should have put aside my reservations about taking a fellow ranking sorcerer across and given you a tour of Earth."

"Is it so terrible?"

"Well, yes and no. But with all the modernities that technology brought them, there is more true happiness there than here, I would say. Many people yearn for our world and our life. Some of what we have here comes across to them as dreams, and they write glorious books with wizards and sorcerers, and all have their fairy legends. Most would be very disappointed with the reality here, I grant you, but as long as we remain fantasy, we remain an ideal they yearn for. It is ironic, I think, that they yearn for us, while just the opposite has happened to you. No, old friend, it's not worse than here over there, only very different. But, on balance, it is about even in its good and bad points. Those two you held here were from Earth, and from a particularly progressive part, and they both seem to be doing better here than there."

"So that explains...Never mind. You talk of Earth, but this is not Earth. Here we have magic! We need not fight, Ruddygore! Together we can blend technology and magic to build a perfect world!"

Sadly, Ruddygore shook his head. "No, it cannot be. You would see it for yourself, were you not blinded by a beautiful but impossible vision. Technology and magic do not mix. The more of the former, the less powerful the latter becomes. There were as many fairies on Earth at the start as here, you know. They are mostly gone now—dead. They died from obsolescence. Their forests were cut down, their rivers dammed, their true work replaced by devices. You would kill them here as well, for they cannot change. They are not meant to change. And, with their going, our power, too, will vanish, for all new magic comes from faërie and its values and traditions and work. It happened on Earth, which once also frolicked with the djinn and had sorcerers and witches as great or greater than ours." He sighed. "I will make you an offer. I will send you to Earth, to a system run according to one of those books you got hold of. Live there as a commoner and see how far you get and whether you want it for Husaquahr."

It was Boquillas' turn to shake his head sadly. "It is much too late for that, even if I believed you, and you have been too full of tricks for me this day. I can neither give up my dream nor abandon my people who believe in it. Surely you must know that."

Ruddygore nodded. "Yes, I knew, but I had to try first. Why don't you go upstairs, shower, and change? Then we'll crack that fine old bottle and smoke a couple of good cigars. I do have your word that you'll be back shortly?"

Boquillas smiled and nodded. "Yes, of course. There is no purpose to prolonging this while good people are dying on both sides." With that he arose wearily from the table and made his way upstairs to his room. Ruddygore just stared after him, a sad look in his eyes and perhaps just a glint of a tear.

They stood facing each other on the wall, the tall, handsome Boquillas in brown velvet robes, trimmed in gold and silver, Ruddygore in his sparkling golden robes. Below them, waves lapped at the base of the cliffs several hundred feet down the sheer drop. The sky was clear and star-filled, the nearly full moon eerily illuminating the great lake.

Boquillas looked at the huge figure of Ruddygore and shook his head. "This shouldn't have to be. If I win, I win it all. If I lose, you merely abandon this world to Kaladon, who will do it far worse than I."

"I think it does have to be," Ruddygore responded. "As for Kaladon, I will tend to him at the proper time. Come. It is time to put an end to this thing."

Boquillas bowed silently, his face grim, but he said nothing.

It began.

There was a seamless growth in the Count's figure, until it rose up and towered over Ruddygore, fluidly taking the form of a great and ferocious beast that stank and howled and gibbered and drooled. Ruddygore watched, but did not seem impressed. "Magic tricks," he muttered. "Ghoulies and beasties. No, Esmilio, we met this way on the fields of the Valley of Decision and settled nothing. Now face the curses you would bring to our land."

Massive explosions sounded all around the monstrous, gibbering shape, the concussion from their charges echoing menacingly against the castle walls and then out onto the lake like some eerie thunder. The creature became confused, disoriented, and began to swat at the explosions, then realized that it was on the wrong tack. It leaped upon the form of Ruddygore with a snarl, but he was not there. In his place was a massive, horrible machine, all gaseous fumes and grinding gears, sucking in the monster, sucking in and grinding it in sharp and nasty gear teeth.

The creature changed and became a terrible whirlwind, a tornadolike funnel cloud that sucked up and broke apart the machine with a thunderous roar. Overhead, immediately atop the whirling mass, appeared a great orange explosion that rapidly spread and grew until it covered the whole of the sky, setting, it seemed, the very air afire. As it descended, a blazing blanket, it drew up into it the very oxygen below; with its force, it dissipated and swallowed the whirlwind. But it did not reach the castle proper, vanishing just above it and leaving the region oddly quiet.

From the sudden, deathly stillness came a huge shape, the great roc of ancient and terrible legend, its condorlike beak snapping furiously while from deep within its massive throat came horrible shrieks. It swooped and whirled around, searching for an adversary, and it found one, also coming out of the sky, a strange blackness that approached at impossible speeds and was gone again before even the tremendous explosive sounds of its passing struck the great and terrible bird of old.

But the newcomer had not passed in demonstration but rather had laid its eggs, dozens of them that now sped toward the roc from all directions, including from above and below. Frantically the bird tried to zoom up, then straight down, then from side to side, but those horrible eggs kept matching its movements and all the time coming closer, closer...

At least five struck the roc in its massive underbelly, exploding with incredible force, driving white-hot bits of metal into its flesh along with flaming jellied liquid that seemed only to eat into the creature while refusing all efforts to be extinguished. The roc reeled as seven more struck it, one in the head, and the force of the explosion there and the spread of the terrible burning jelly struck its eyes, rendering it blind. In panic, burning, it raced for the surface of the lake and dove beneath the placid waters, sending a plume of water thirty feet into the air as it did so.

Ruddygore, his face and eyes showing tremendous strain and concentration, stood on the castle wall and looked outward to where the roc had entered the water. Within a short time, the water was smooth once more, with no sign of the huge entry.

Now, though, great bubbles issued up along a wide area below the castle, as if some enormous creature was surfacing. When it did, it was more terrible than anything of the old legends, a monstrous mass of living green slime from which issued thousands of wriggling tentacles as needed. It continued to rise, its bulk so vast that it was soon almost the size of the entire castle. Ruddygore faced it impassively, not moving a muscle as stench-ridden, sucker-covered tentacles reached out for him.

From all around the beast, small white contrails broke the surface of the water, dozens of them coming in a semicircular pattern toward the beast's bulk. Just as the first tentacles of the kraken closed upon Ruddygore, the objects struck, all within a fraction of a second, sending up tremendous plumes of water as each exploded with a roar that made all previous detonations look like firecrackers. With the water, pieces of green slime went up as well, and the kraken roared its terrible agony and writhed in pain, its two giant eyes on great stalks glaring in hatred.

Ruddygore reached down, picked up a strange-looking object, and aimed it at the eyes. The thing shot more of the jellied flame, which this time burned on and into the water, and the creature groaned and thrashed in an unsuccessful attempt to quench the spreading fires that covered it.

Suddenly the kraken vanished. For a moment, all was silence again. Then there was a roar from the castle roof, and Ruddygore spun around to face an enormous dragon that reared back and shot hot, smoky flame at him. Boquillas was fighting fire with fire.

Ruddygore flung back his right arm as if about to throw something, but when he brought it forward, an enormous stream of water rose out of the lake and struck the dragon full force in the mouth. Suddenly the fat sorcerer was standing right on the castle wall, holding and guiding a gigantic pressurized hose that quenched the dragon's flame.

The dragon, its flame so easily extinguished while Ruddygore's fires had been unquenchable, roared defiance and leaped upon the man below, but suddenly the man wasn't there. The dragon missed and plunged over the edge of the castle wall, but there was no sound of an object striking the water.

Both men again stood facing each other on the outer wall, neither actually hurt, but Boquillas' fine robes looked slightly singed.

"It's called napalm," Ruddygore told him. "Just one of technology's little gifts to mankind."

But Boquillas was no longer there. Instead, the whole castle shimmered and seemed to change into a terrible, menacing jungle of carnivorous vines and animated plants. The transition was so swift that Ruddygore found himself suddenly held by strong tentaclelike vines that tightened and pulled in all directions toward gaping plant jaws. The abrupt change had obviously surprised him, and he showed real pain and discomfort, but only for a moment.

There was a sound like a thunderclap, and down from the sky rained a suffocating, yellowish cloud of gas. It quickly covered all the plants and the sorcerer himself; but at its first touch, the vines recoiled and the gaping mouths of the huge plants seemed to scream in dreadful agony. The jungle was suddenly in frantic, insane movement, screaming and tearing itself to bits as it died. The more it writhed, the more it opened its wounds to the yellowish powders.

Freed, Ruddygore, although slightly injured, did not pause.

"Now smell the world of the perfect future! Breathe it and weep!" he cried. The air changed, and the stars and moon were blacked out. All around was a dense, wet fog that choked anything it touched, a fog filled with the metal particulates from a billion smokestacks and the noxious fumes of a hundred chemical and power plants. It was the condensation of all that had been pumped into the air by mankind's progress through the centuries, and it was more horrible than any monster of Husaquahr.

Again Boquillas was disoriented by the tactic, which was more terrible and incomprehensible to him than anything he had known. He tried to fight his way out of it, to rise above it, but it was so dense and so horrible that he could not seem to find a break in it.

Suddenly the way was clear, and he made for it, but it was not a pleasant clearing. Although the pretty farms and fields appeared lush and green and the little town looked both alien and very familiar with its small cottages and dirt main streets, it was a scene of total terror. Two armies, it seemed, were going at each other, but not in any formal way. The entire pastoral vista was one of pure carnage and disorganization, and men were falling from bullets so thick in the air that the entire countryside seemed infested with some sort of locust. When any man showed even a part of himself, though, those locusts struck and tore gaping wounds open, causing terrible pain and agony. Men fell by the hundreds, by the thousands, in an impersonal carnage that turned the little creek that ran through the fields and then through the town into a river of blood. Antietam Creek had become Bloody Lane.

Just as abruptly, the scene changed, yet somehow stayed the same. It was a horrible wasteland now, any trace of what it might have been before having been long obliterated. Shells burst in the air in an almost constant barrage of concussion and shrapnel, while men huddled in long trenches and died every time they tried to advance *en masse* just a few yards from those holes . . .

Then the sky was filled with a shattering roar as machines of destruction flew over in so dense a formation that the city below seemed blocked from sunlight. Most of the people were below, in shelters against the rain of bombs, but nothing could protect them from this onslaught of explosions that created a firestorm above, rather than on the surface, sucking out the oxygen and killing them, men, women, children, old and young, dogs and cats, soldiers and bankers and janitors, as they huddled in their shelters . . .

Boquillas whirled, but the place now was a new place, without explosions or bombs. He saw rows upon rows of men so thin and emaciated they looked like what the line marching the road to Hell must look like, only these were human beings, some being forced to shovel out piles of human remains from enormous ovens, the remains of men, women, children, and none of them soldiers . . .

The sights sickened and appalled him at first; but after a while, their very sameness brought him a measure of respite, a crack in the chamber of horrors, allowing reason to resume command. Ruddygore was effectively showing him the evils of technology, but without any of the benefits, and he fought back in this Never-Neverland of the mind.

Gleaming cities of steel and stone . . . Highways that were ribbons of concrete stretching from coast to coast, spanning continents, filled with horseless vehicles in astounding numbers . . . Homes, powered and heated by oil, gas, even the sun itself, in tremendous profusion, and not a castle in sight . . . Huge symphonies in large, well-lighted halls of acoustical perfection, playing wondrously beautiful pieces . . .

Ruddygore, ready, counterattacked . . .

Family units all grouped around boxes from which issued moving pictures in full color, all hypnotically staring at the screen for hours on end, all watching incredible drivel . . .

A band on a huge stage entertaining tens of thousands of young people, but the band was dressed in weird, half-naked fashion, its lead singer's jewelry including razor blades for earrings; all their faces were terribly made up, while their hair was shaved in strange ways and dyed in greens and blues and reds. They were singing of death, destruction, and hopelessness to a crowd that was at one and the same time worshipping them, emulating them, and watching with that same hypnotic fascination as those in front of the little boxes . . .

Inventory, Boquillas commanded. And in his mind appeared fallout shelters, missile silos, satellite guidance systems . . .

Mutual Assured Destruction . . . the hydrogen bomb . . .

He located what he needed, targeted it, and aimed it properly. The great missile broke back through the atmosphere, targeted not on a city but on a single individual, its lenses and computers interacting to locate that one man, who, when spotted, turned to the onrushing death from the sky . . .

Only it was not Ruddygore. It was a small, helpless beggar child with pitiful eyes, his hands still grubby and stained from rooting through dockside garbage. He looked up at the missile with sad, fatalistic eyes, then turned to Boquillas, who watched, horrified. The boy reached out, pleading with him, pleading . . .

Count Esmilio Boquillas screamed and fell back against the battlements. Again back in his own world, under a starry, moonlighted night sky, he was not alone. The poor beggar child was still there, still approaching, those sad eyes boring down upon him. And now the child spoke, a halting, hurt sort of tone. "Please, my lord, why do you wish to kill me?"

Only a child, only a little child now. He could reach out, crush that child, beat in his brains, and toss him from the battlements to the cold waters below. He could, he could . . .

"I cannot!" Boquillas sobbed. *"Hiccarph! Save me! Save me from the child!"*

Behind the child, abruptly, a ghastly shape formed, towering over both child and man, a rotting, stench-filled body filling out a grand costume of crimson and lavender, its eyes consumed with hatred and contempt. A gnarled, clawed hand reached out for the boy, then picked him up. The boy screamed as he was pulled into the air and mercilessly crushed in the foul hand of the demon, his body quickly limp and then reduced to a bloody mass of tissue which the demon contemptuously discarded. Then the demon stood there, looking down on Boquillas, and shook his head from side to side.

"Well," Hiccarph said casually, "he certainly had your number."

The Count, breathing heavily, pulled himself weakly to a sitting position and for a moment just buried his face in his hands. Finally he looked up at the demon and sighed. "It—it was horrible! Horrible! If he was that strong, why did he not take me in the Valley months ago?"

"Because he cheated," the demon told him. "First of all, he knew you very well indeed, while out there he was fighting an unknown enemy. But, most of all, he cheated. He brought in the weapons of Earth to face the magic of Husaquahr, and that was something he could never do in public, where all could see or feel or sense it. There would be those who would get ideas, and others who would like what they saw. Out here, it was a safer bet. Now, though, his soul is lost to the world. A pity, for I'd hoped to have him myself."

Boquillas looked up at his demon general. "He is dead, then?"

"I search high and low and cannot find him in the world. He is vanquished by his very trap that really won him the contest. He knew you well, knew that you were powerless to face down someone totally vulnerable, innocent, and defenseless. But when he chose that path for the coup de grâce, he also was most vulnerable to outside forces not so easily swayed."

Boquillas tried to get to his feet, failed, then tried again, clutching the battlement stones for support, and finally made it. He gasped and coughed as he did so. After a few seconds, he got some strength and took in several deep breaths. Finally he said, "Then we've won."

"Yes. We've won," the demon agreed.

"Well, not exactly," came a voice from the window nearest them. They both turned. Sitting in the window, looking fairly relaxed, was Joe de Oro, clean and rested, dressed in a breechclout and sandals, and wearing his great sword.

CHAPTER 16

WHEN THE HURLY-BURLY'S DONE...

A woman has no fury like Hell scorned.
> —Old Husaquahrian Saying

BOTH THE BARON AND THE GENERAL WERE STARTLED, BUT not particularly worried. Hiccarph reached out a long arm to Joe and swiped at him as if swatting at a fly. Joe flinched, but the demonic hand passed right through him without effect, and he relaxed and smiled. "Having problems, fish-breath?"

"You're the one from the tent back in the Valley," the demon recalled. "I understand it all now. You're from Earth, aren't you?"

"Give that devil a cigar," Joe responded, gaining a little confidence.

"You are subject to the magic of Husaquahr, so I wouldn't feel so confident. You have no one left to protect either you or your female companion, who, I assume, is also from Earth."

"You're right on that," the swordsman conceded, "but not on the other. Ruddygore didn't think that a battle between two such illustrious sorcerers should go unappreciated by all except vagrant travelers from Earth and a notorious thief. He issued some invitations, and, what do you know, everybody accepted. You see, he sort of made a bet with each one, and even though you did him in, for which I will cheerfully see you in a worse hell than the one from which you came, he still won the bet. He was very busy at that convention making deals, you see."

Both the exhausted Boquillas and the demon were fascinated but hardly worried. "Indeed?" Hiccarph responded. "And what sort of petty magics can you find against *me*?"

"Just one," came a thin, nasal voice from behind the demon. The two on the battlement turned. While Boquillas simply frowned in puzzlement, the expression on the demon's face was terrible indeed to behold, and he uttered a groan that sounded like the death cries of a million damned souls.

The object of this was a small, pudgy little man in monk's robes, clean-shaven even to his very smooth scalp. He looked quite cherubic, but his expression was anything but amused.

"Mephistopheles," Hiccarph whimpered. "Wait! I can explain . . ."

"Explain what?" the little monk asked. "That you, a minor nothing over here in the backwaters, could unilaterally break the Compact and risk Armageddon without even his Majesty knowing of it? *Well, he knows now, Hiccarph!*"

"No!" the demon wailed. "How—how did you find out . . . ?"

"Ruddygore does a fair amount of business our way, usually with the minor elementals, of course, but enough to get messages where he needs to. He's been complaining about this for years, but we never believed him. We never believed that *anyone* in the demonic hierarchy could be both so clever and so utterly stupid at one and the same time. Finally, he offered a wager to us. Himself, his soul, all that he had, to the total and complete service of Hell, if he couldn't prove it to my satisfaction tonight. It had the approval of the Old Man himself, in fact. We usually get the average soul without bargains, as you know, but one of Ruddygore's caliber, right away and now, is very rare. The Old Man's going to be as pissed by missing that as he is with your rampant and reckless risk of the status quo."

"But I could have delivered this whole world to Hell!" Hiccarph whimpered.

"Bah! You idiot! We're winning *now*! We could lose the whole thing if we're forced into a premature Armageddon. Well, you'll spoil things no more, now or in the future, until Armageddon truly comes. An example will be made of you, Hiccarph, and a most terrible one indeed, I promise you, by the Old Man himself. Let's see how you like an eternity stoking fires in the dung pits we reserve for the religious zealots! And not as supervisor, either—as a common demon ninth class! And when Armageddon arrives, guess who's going to be right out front leading the first charge into Heaven!"

"No! Wait! I—" the demon screamed, but there was a sudden, near-blinding flash of light and both figures were gone, leaving only a very slight smell of sulfur behind that the wind quickly carried away. Again there was silence.

The silence, though, was broken by a low chuckling. Joe turned and saw Boquillas sitting on the battlement wall, looking highly amused. Finally the sorcerer said, "Well, that's that. Actually, I have to thank old Ruddygore, wherever he may be. Now the Dark Baron will put his plans into action without the meddlings of any Hellish princes—or ex-princes. Yes, indeed, it was quite a favor you just did me, and I appreciate it."

"Don't appreciate it too much," Joe cautioned him. "Old monkey wasn't the only onlooker, and I think it's time you met the rest."

Marge appeared now, looking every bit the Kauri once more, grand with her wings of power, flitting along the stones in true fairy fashion. Behind her came a rather large assemblage of people, all wearing varicolored robes that were made of fine materials and beautifully tailored.

Marge went over to Joe as Boquillas gaped. "You know the folks," she said lightly. "Fajera, Docondian, Sargash, Mathala, Brosnial, Careska, Jorgasnovara, Yiknudssun, O'Fleherity, Kaladon, and Esmerada?"

The Baron gasped. "*Esmerada!* But I thought Ruddygore had killed you!"

Joe looked at Marge quizzically. "O'Fleherity?"

"*Darling* Esmilio!" Esmerada oozed. "You know me better than that! I mean, given a choice between a fight to the death you might not win and a partnership, which would *you* choose?"

"So that's why he was so well rested," the Baron muttered. "You traitorous bitch!"

She laughed at him. "Oh, darling, you say the *sweetest* things!"

"To business! I have already delayed my departure from this rotten continent long enough," snarled a huge and powerful-looking black man in robes of red and yellow. "Although, I admit, the show was more than worth waiting for."

Boquillas was frankly too tired to care. "So what happens now, my fellow members of the Council?"

"You've been a *baad* boy, Essie," Esmerada scolded playfully. "Got to pay the piper. Playing with real demons in the real world is a no-no, and you know that."

"You and Kaladon in particular didn't seem so upset at the Barony when it was going your way," he noted sourly. "And you, Careska, surely didn't mind when we handed you Leander on a platter. Fajera, you weren't exactly turning the other cheek when you helped recruit the Bentar mercenaries. A fine lot you are! Most of you are blacker than I am!"

"Which is precisely the point," Fajera, the big black man, shot back. "You heard Mephistopheles. We've a long way yet to Armageddon, but you provoked it prematurely. At least half the Council is on the dark end of the art, and the other half doesn't know which way they'll finally go, but has some idea that you don't get this far and receive wings, a harp, and eternal thanks. Maybe Ruddygore got away with it because he was willing to give his life to stop you, but that's too high a price for me. You and your damned visionary dreaming almost got us screwed for eternity! Now you have to pay."

Boquillas sighed. "Yes, I bet Kaladon and the rest of you love that. Two vacancies to fill on the Council, and Husaquahr is yours with its armies in place. You like that idea, Sargash?"

"Enough. Temporal problems are for temporal resolution," a distinguished-looking woman in silver robes said. "The vote has been taken after evidence was presented on a proper complaint by a member of this Council, now deceased. Shall we agree on the sentence?"

"We are agreed," the rest chanted.

"Very well, then. Esmilio Boquillas, the problems of the world and how much or how little each of us gets involved in them are none of the affair of the Council as a whole. The Council is agreed that you have made a most grievous breach of the ethics of the art and hereby expels you from the Council, with loss of all rank and privileges, and from the Society, whose covenant you so violated. So say we all, and so do we all act in concert."

Boquillas just sighed and nodded.

The Council was quiet for a moment, each member's head bowed as if in prayer. Then they looked up again at the man who had been the Dark Baron.

"It is done," the woman in silver intoned. "Let us leave this place."

With that, they all turned and walked back along the wall, chatting pleasantly, and disappeared into the castle below.

Joe was disappointed. "That's *all*? They cashier him and that's that?"

"You don't understand, Joe," Marge told him. "They did the worst thing they could do to him."

Joe looked over at the man, who was still sitting on the stone wall. "He looks pretty good to me for a guy who just got scolded."

"Not just scolded, Joe. They took away his power. All of it! He has no more magical power than you do. Less, in fact. I doubt if he's even able to do a sleight-of-hand magic trick. They cut him off from the magic, you see. He's just an ordinary, totally human, totally nonmagical mortal now."

Joe brightened. "You mean I can bash him?"

"You could," Boquillas agreed, "but why bother? If you wish to kill me, then do so now. Otherwise, I am going inside and going to bed." With that he got up, then walked away from them down the battlement walkway to the small door, through it, and back into the castle.

"Damn!" Joe swore. "He kills the best man in this crazy world and gets away with it! And I don't have the heart to take him on, not when he's *that* beat."

Marge grinned. "Well, we could always do likewise, you know."

"Huh?"

"There's still the bedroom in there, and we're still here. It will be a while before Macore gets back with a longboat to take you off, probably tomorrow sometime. In the meantime, Boquillas can't get off the island any more than you can, and all the others have already gone."

"But it's still the middle of the night!" he protested. "You're not sleepy and I'm not tired."

"And there's no full moon, either," she pointed out.

"Oh—I *see* . . ."

Together they went in by way of the window.

The weather turned bad the next day, delaying Macore's rescue boat. Ruddygore had sent the little thief back to the mainland before the battle between the two sorcerers because he feared too many people would be noticed and because Macore had no demonic immunities.

Boquillas slept solidly for more than fourteen hours, but Marge and Joe finally heard him moving about upstairs as he breakfasted on leftover pastries from Ruddygore's last meal. Both Joe and Marge felt pretty good, their only dark clouds the knowledge that Ruddygore was gone and that Tiana was still in the hands of Kaladon. That last seemed more unassailable an obstacle than ever; although Marge could ease some of the ache, she wasn't able to remove the problem from Joe's mind.

When Boquillas finally came down, he looked years older than he had looked the night before—just a tired old man. Joe reached for his sword, but Boquillas raised his hand wearily.

"Must we still continue to go through this?" he asked. "Please understand that now I am as much on your side as Ruddygore would have been, although, alas, without his power."

Joe frowned. "What do you mean?"

"I may have done all the dark things that you say, and I will surely roast in that pit for it, but what I did, I did for the most idealistic of reasons. With what happened last night, things have turned upside down. Is there still a pastry, by the way?"

Marge, who no longer felt human hunger, passed him a gooey one. "What do you suggest, then?" she asked.

"I know Kaladon and some of his plans. I know Morikay, too, and what's involved there. More than that, I still know more magic than practically anyone else alive."

"But what good does that do you now?" Marge asked him. "I mean, you can't use it, you can't practice it, and you can't even see it or protect against it."

"Quite true," he admitted, "but beside the point. Kaladon really isn't very good, either. Esmerada helped him rig his contest for the seat he holds because she wanted a share in the take, you might say. She's now been badly burned. Ruddygore had to get a sacred oath out of her to stop the fight, and that oath certainly removes her from any politics inside or outside Zhimbombe. We are, then, dealing just with Kaladon, whose power resides not in himself but in his ward."

"Tiana," Joe said softly.

Boquillas nodded. "Exactly. She has the power, but is totally under his control. She doesn't even have the knowledge to break the simple spell that binds her to him, although she has the power to break half of Husaquahr. So we are in a cul-de-sac, as it were. I can analyze the spell and show anyone just how to break it, but I can't see the spell. Break the spell, and any half-baked magician could tell her how to fry Kaladon to ashes. Ruddygore's fairy adept, for example."

"Poquah! Sure!" Marge responded, sounding enthusiastic.

"Kaladon's bound to make his move very quickly, before the armies start getting ideas of their own. That means both he and Tiana will have to come out of that castle, and I can guess by the way his mind works what he'll pull. It will take a pretty good adept to resist the spell, and even that will be chancy. However, that sort of thing won't work on a true fairy, so somebody of true fairy blood, preferably somebody who can also fly and defend herself quickly, would have to go there and examine that spell, sketch it *exactly*, and bring it back to me."

"I think I'm beginning to see where you're headed," Marge noted.

"Uh-huh. The trick then would be to get into Castle Morikay, if need be. Outside the castle, the defenses will be too much for any but the best sorcerers in the land. That means somebody has got to pull Ruddygore's trick—get into a castle you can't get into without an invitation if you harbor intentions against any of the occupants, invite in Poquah, say, and dissolve the binding spell on Tiana. Give me a couple of weeks with him, and I can teach him what he'll need to know. If my analysis of her latent powers is correct, and I'm sure this is what Ruddygore had in mind, the proper spells directed against an unsuspecting Kaladon could do to him what was done to me last night."

"You mean—take away his powers?" Joe said hopefully.

Boquillas nodded. "Not permanently, I think. That would take four or maybe five of the Council to do. But, Joe, if you had Kaladon unable to use any magic whatsoever for several hours, what would you do?"

Joe grinned.

"That's what I thought. Now this is going to be tricky, and I assure you that the odds are very much against it all going our way, but Ruddygore seems to have picked you two very well. Somehow, with a superhuman effort, he's matched you to various arcane bunches of Rules, so that, no matter how hopeless the situation is, you seem to come through. How anyone could do this, even in a thousand years, is beyond me, but he managed it, and I have to go with that."

Marge thought a moment. "You know—Ruddygore was always going off to Earth at odd times. I wonder if, somewhere over there, he hasn't got one hell of a computer working for him."

"Computer? You mean an abacus?" the Count asked, confused.

"One hell of an abacus, you might say," Marge told him. "Joe? What do you think?"

"I think this is crazy," the big man mumbled. "A couple of days ago this guy blinded me and chained us both up in a rat-infested dungeon; then last night he killed the only friend we had in this world; and now *we're* working for *him*!"

"Will you do it, though?" she pressed.

"Oh, *sure* I'll do it, but . . ."

CHAPTER 17

. . . WHEN THE BATTLE'S LOST AND WON

When cults convert more than ten percent of a population, they are to be considered a religion and are covered by Volume XXVI instead of Volume XCI.

—Rules, XCI, 494(b)

"IT'S LIKE NOTHING ANYBODY'S EVER SEEN," MARGE TOLD the small council of war two weeks later. "I've never been so alternately fascinated and repulsed by anything in my entire life."

They sat there, Poquah, Joe, Boquillas, listening intently.

"First of all, the siege is over. In fact, the war is over for all intents and purposes. The Barony has been replaced by the spreading new world of the Goddess."

They nodded, knowing some of this, but not firsthand.

"Morikay has been rechristened the Throne of Paradise and is the center of this expanding movement. It's an amazing thing to see it spread so quickly in so short a time. The official line is that the Dark Baron, who brought Hell to Husaquahr, was defeated by Ruddygore at the cost of Ruddygore's life. They made him a saint."

Boquillas chuckled. "It's a wonder he doesn't come back from the grave over that."

"Anyway, with Hell vanquished, so the line goes, the Creator sent the Goddess of Husaquahr, a true angel, to watch over us and see that it never happens again. Three guesses who the Goddess is."

Joe looked at her and nodded glumly.

"Anyway," she continued, "the Goddess came to banish all war from the world and to carry out the Creator's plan for us. She appointed the wise and benevolent Kaladon as High Priest of the new One True Church and established her seat on earth at Mori—sorry, the Throne of Paradise. She raised the siege by merely walking through the lines and letting all the soldiers see her. They fell down and worshipped her, even the mercenaries and half-breeds like the Bentar. She has since appeared in dozens of major towns and cities, including Sachalin, Halakahla, and other places, and every time it's been the same. Instant conversion, followed by the immediate establishment of a temple under a leader hand-picked by Kaladon. There are already huge statues of her all over the place, all of which attract crowds of worshippers. By the way, Joe, all the statues are full nudes."

"Naturally," Boquillas put in. "If she's a true angel, then she is without sin of any sort, and clothing would be inappropriate."

"If the statues are from life, that means she's changed a bit," Marge went on. "From what I understand, she's just about ten feet tall; and if you thought her proportions were large before—*wow*! Her hair also seems much thicker and about ankle-length, and she looks, well, smoother. Really angelic in the extreme. Of course, I never saw her personally."

"What of the fairy folk?" Poquah asked. "How are they taking all this?"

"The ones I talked to are mostly divided. Kaladon has sent emissaries to all the key tribes, offering peace and harmony and assuring them that the temples will preach a line that they're the children of God and are to be treated with honor and respect. Most of 'em seem willing to suspend disbelief and go along. A few are even debating whether or not the Goddess might be the real thing. The ones who have seen her haven't fallen down in worship, but they report an enormously powerful glow of pure white within her, more than has ever been seen."

"Pure white. Good touch. Perhaps I *did* underestimate Kaladon," Boquillas noted, mostly to himself. "And what of the distinguished members of the Council?"

"Esmerada has been given her own seat at Halakahla, taking over from Ruddygore. She seems delighted to go along with it all and is working to make Terindell a holy shrine, of all things! Sargash is still fuming over the siege of Sachalin, but she's decided that the handwriting is on the wall. She's not helping, but she's not obstructing, either. Word is that Kaladon and Esmerada have offered to back her candidate for one of the two vacancies on the Council, and that's bought her off. Careska's head of the Church in Leander and she's been given a pretty free hand there, while Fajera is priming Todra for a visit by the Goddess real soon now. It's all happening so *fast*."

"But it's been planned for years, perhaps decades," Boquillas responded. "Kaladon is an incredible politician with an incredible mind set only on power. With the complicity of the rest, or at least noninterference, he'll soon have all of Husaquahr that's worth having under a single theocracy with himself at the helm. Oh, it will take quite some time to secure it all, but if the mere appearance of the Goddess can cause instant conversion and worship, then any time he gets a pocket of trouble, he just goes visiting. But tell me, what is this new doctrine like? Surely he has grandiose plans."

Marge nodded. "So far, the grand plan is limited to the

Throne of Paradise, and that's just getting organized, but the pattern seems clear. Each cooperating sorcerer is more or less being encouraged to write his or her own holy book for the locals, tailored to their own aims and conditions, so that keeps the people happy. Kaladon himself seems to have his own vision. Whole parts of the city are being torn down by eager volunteer converts. Parks are being developed, and a style of building that reminded me of ancient Greece—sorry, I know most of you won't understand that—is going up. Big marble temple-style buildings. People work five days on their regular jobs, then two for the Church for nothing. They also are expected to go to services each night and get more holy instructions and they do. Half of what they earn goes to the Church and gets poured into the building and developmental programs, while Church leaders are organizing syndicates for all major industries, including shipping and farming."

"An integrated economy. Interesting. Continue."

"Well, what he's getting is a world of willing, worshipful slaves who won't even sneeze without permission, but who will do anything they are told to do. They also seem bent on a plan they call 'efficiency of form,' where people are being willingly turned into other creatures to do their work better. The centaur population alone is growing by leaps and bounds, since that's an efficient farm form, and the mermaid and such-like population's going to grow under a harvest-the-sea program. There's a whole winged legion for transportation and communication, too. It's scary. And remember, I'm an empath—I can feel these people's insides. They're sickeningly joyful."

"That's to be expected," the former Dark Baron commented. "After so much war, suffering, and killing, they were ready for a savior, and he's given them one. Of course, Tiana's magic is reinforcing all this, but that just makes it easier. You were not, however, able to see her in person?"

Marge shook her head from side to side. "I tried to. Just missed her once. But she takes a leaf from your book and turns herself into a great white dove, or something similar, and gets places faster than I can."

"Hmmm . . . This complicates matters. Have you any idea how often she returns to the castle?"

The Kauri shrugged. "Hard to say. They're transforming the place into a really stunning supertemple, by the way, at least on the outside. All marble and spires."

Boquillas thought for a moment. "But you said Fajera was trying to arrange an appearance in Todra. Any idea when?"

"The Goddess is due to appear in the City-States—which are, by the way, mostly very cynical but very curious—next month. Does that help?"

"Yes and no. I hate giving him so much more time to establish and consolidate his program, but this has to go exactly right or it's no go. You'll be down there when she shows and give us a firsthand account, plus that all-important spell information. I've told you what to look for—the one string that ties her to Kaladon."

Marge nodded.

"I don't see why I have to wait," Joe put in. "I mean, in just a couple of weeks I'll be ready again to sneak in there. Should be particularly easy with all the workmen."

"Perhaps, but we can't take any chances we don't have to," Boquillas replied. "First of all, I don't want you meeting the Goddess. The spell would grab you, and that would be that. Secondly, we might catch Kaladon with the barriers down for a few days, even a week, but certainly not a month. He's bound to notice, busy as he is, that he has no protection. You're the key man, Joe, the only human we can afford to use in this operation. Marge and Poquah will handle the rest, but they can't get in without you."

"Okay, but I just get itchy sitting around here, that's all."

"Better itchy than lost forever," the Count warned.

Four weeks and three nightly transformations for Joe later, the conspirators held another meeting, this one far more pressing.

"I've seen her," Marge told them. "Man! Is she *something*! I tell you, I knew what was going on and I was immune from the spell she radiates and I still almost bought it. This empathic thing is a two-way sword. She radiated such, well, godliness that it almost overwhelmed me."

"It probably would have overwhelmed any other Kauri," Boquillas told her. "Your mind and your past are your strength."

She nodded. "Joe, she *is* ten feet tall and looks just like those statues all over the place. Also, every little blemish and imperfection is gone, and so is that great dark tan. She's almost blindingly smooth and white, and her hair's now silver—and I mean *silver*, not white or gray—and her eyes are a deep emerald green. She still has her slight German accent, but her voice is real soft and musical and super-sexy; yet it will carry in a square jammed with ten thousand people, somehow. You ought to see Kaladon, though. Wearing snow-white robes with silver trim, he looks just like an angel from an old religious movie."

"You have the spell, I hope?" Boquillas prompted.

She sighed. "Damned hard to do, I'll tell you. That white inner glow is almost blinding, and I had to do it in daylight. Bless old Ruddygore's dark goggles! I doubt if anybody without 'em could see through the glare enough to figure out the pattern."

"A smart move on Kaladon's part," Boquillas noted. "Just in case some of the other councillors get ideas."

Marge passed him her sketch of the spell in colored pencils. "Took me five different appearances to get it all down," she told him, "and each time it was harder not to join the cult."

Boquillas studied the incredibly complex pattern for several minutes, then grabbed a pad and began sketching his own series of lines, shapes, forms, and relationships. It looked like kindergarten scribble to Joe, but Poquah in particular was gazing over the former sorcerer's shoulder and nodding.

"Can you do it?" Boquillas asked the Imir.

"Of course," the adept responded. "It is not difficult when you diagram it that way, but I can think of no other mind save perhaps Ruddygore's that could have solved the pattern from so basic a sketch."

"I was a theoretician far longer than I was an activist," the Count told him. "In fact, Kaladon is cloddish enough or egomaniacal enough to have used a slight variation of one of my own designs. I suppose he no longer considers me a threat. Still, a wise teacher never tells his student *all* he knows." He looked up, smiled, and said to the Imir, "You have all the rest of the preparation. Joe, you have the latest reports from Poquah's and Marge's fairy friends about what's going on in

Morikay. Let's see . . . Your next cycle is in eight more nights, right?"

Joe nodded. "Yeah, that's about it."

"And we have here from Marge evidence that our dear Goddess will formally and personally dedicate Fajera's temple a week from tomorrow." He sighed. "That's pretty dicey, and cutting things rather fine, but I think we might manage. No, I think we *have* to. If we let this go on another month, we won't be able to get near the place without being converted ourselves. Let's do it. Eight nights from tonight, Joe, you will be in Morikay, and so will Marge and Poquah. If your phenomenal luck holds, nine days from today we will free this world from Kaladon, not to mention Tiana."

"I can hardly wait," Joe said truthfully.

It was easier to get into Castle Morikay, or the Palace of the Angels, as it was referred to, than it was to stomach two days in the city itself. The building boom was amazing, with all sorts of bright-eyed men and women, aided by the Halflings of equal fervor, working like insects in a hive for the glory of the Goddess. How so many statues had been made in so short a time without a production line was beyond Joe and the others, and they were probably magical products, but it was both stunning and disturbing to see them, not only as decorations but actual objects of worship.

The people drove themselves with total fanaticism, calling one another Brother and Sister and praising the Goddess all the while they slaved. Even though he lay low and kept away from much contact, Joe got blessed more times than a Swiss guard at the Vatican. He had to admit, however, that, if it wasn't for the sheer fanaticism of the people and the fact that they looked malnourished and horribly overworked, he approved of the face lift in progress. It was still hard to tell just what the final thing would look like, though.

The great castle on the flat hilltop in the center of town was getting a new marble facade, its towers extended, and, in front, a tremendous statue of Tiana was being installed.

Still and all, Joe had the same distaste for this cult that he had for the cults back home on Earth. About the only nice thing he could say for this one was that at least they didn't ask for money all the time. In fact, he couldn't pay for anything at all.

Not that there was an awful lot to be had. Restaurants and cafes seemed a thing of the past, and inns were closed and deserted. He had to depend on the charity of some of the bright-eyed converts for what food he could get, and they were sharing obviously meager rations. The economic and trading system had been given a lower priority than the building of Kaladon's dream city.

As for the castle, or temple, or whatever it was now, passing through into the inner courtyard proved quite easy in the evening, since work never seemed to stop. As a mule, though, Joe put in one hell of a tough night's work and almost had it all go for nothing when they moved to take the animals out come daylight. Fortunately, animals worked better when fed, and there was an area inside the courtyard where the horses and mules could munch on hay. Near sunup, he positioned himself in the middle of a large group of animals and managed to change back unseen, although he was almost chomped and trampled getting out of the mob.

He wasted no time issuing his invitation with the earring he still had, and he prayed that the batteries hadn't run down. They had worked fine in a test the night before, but one never knew.

His problem now was that he was naked and unarmed in the midst of the enemy camp and he had no real way out. Boquillas' memories of the inner castle, though, proved right on the mark. After a few hairy near misses with some of the people inside, who did not look or act completely entranced, he found the right section and also found, to his relief, that it was still used as an inner storage area. In fact, it had been stuffed with lots of junk left over from the siege, causing him no end of trouble to locate a comfortable place. He only hoped that Marge would find him, preferably with a roast turkey or a thick steak.

Fortunately, the night's work as a mule, powering a complex pulley system for the main steeple, had tired him out so much that he just passed out for the day.

Marge got in, somehow, before nightfall, with a large cold cuts sandwich and a small gourd of water. It was better than nothing, and he ate the food quickly. As planned, they remained together until the full moon was again in the sky, making Joe once more a twin of Marge; but this time a different Marge was involved. The last time she'd been just a pixiewoman, but now she was a full Kauri again—and could fly.

That gave him the double immunity of the were's curse and a fairy form, as well as flying ability.

"Poquah?" he asked her.

"By midnight," she told him. "He's using some of his magical talents and coming in as a pilgrim worker."

"I just wish Tiana were back," he said. "I want to get this over and done with."

"She is back. Came here in midmorning, as a huge white bird with Kaladon perched on her back."

"Something symbolic in that."

Marge smiled and nodded. They settled down to wait in the dark storeroom for Poquah.

"You know," Joe remarked, "it's a wonder they don't do this sort of infiltrating each other all the time. Esmerada, for example, would love to replace the Goddess with herself."

"They would if they could," Marge pointed out. "Remember, it's only these neat little transmitters that make all this possible. Kaladon's people are watching for any strangers, and they'd prevent anybody new from talking to anybody outside. They check every working person coming up here thoroughly, too. No, Ruddygore's beaten the system with a were and some Japanese transistors. Nobody else has even one, let alone both."

"Maybe I should rent myself out to bite specific people, if being a were is so important."

They waited nervously for hours, but it was almost dawn before the storeroom door creaked and a shadowy figure entered.

"I had real problems," the Imir told them as soon as they saw that it was indeed he. "The spells to detect other spells are very tight. This is a well-defended place, I'll have you know. I had to—radio, isn't that the term?—Boquillas for additional help."

"Boquillas! He's here?" Marge was both amazed and worried.

"He is. Hiding out in the cellar of a deserted inn just down the hill, and a good thing, too. He said either we do it or he might as well join the cult. There was no purpose in his staying away. I can communicate with him through Macore's little devices." He pointed to a small object, like a golden hearing aid, in his pointed left ear.

"Well, I just changed back, without even getting to fly once," Joe grumped. "Damn! What do we do now?"

Poquah paused, as if listening, then nodded. "The Count suggests that we either act straightaway or wait until dark once again. The rest of the time, the halls will be filled with functionaries."

"Take a chance and go now," Joe suggested. "I don't think I can stand another night in this place."

Poquah, nodding agreement, pulled up his hood and silently slipped away.

They almost went crazy waiting, but finally he returned after what not only seemed like but might have been hours. The impassive Imir was not in a better mood. "Problems," he told them.

"You couldn't get near her?"

"Oh, I located her, all right. The trouble is, Kaladon seems to be in the same room with her at all times. The moment I try to break the spell, he's going to be aware of it. Incidentally, you might be interested to know that, although the physical changes remain, inside here she reverts to her old height, which was still considerable."

Joe nodded. "That's a relief. But if Kaladon never leaves her side, we've got problems. How long will it take you to break the spell?"

"Only a minute or so. But that is a very long time if he knows immediately and can react. The lines of magic from me to her will be instantly recognizable to him and traceable back to me."

Joe thought a moment. "Well, we're in no position to have him called away. That means we have to distract or confuse him . . . Hmmm . . . Yeah. Why not? I've been Marge twice, so why not?"

"Why not what?" Marge asked him.

"Poquah, how hard is it going to be to sneak *me* into a place of concealment near where they're likely to be at sunset?"

"They handle business in a magnificently appointed throne room," the Imir replied. "Their bedchambers are right behind. A large study and apartment, actually. They take their meals there as well. Why?"

Joe told him his plan, and both Marge and Poquah were aghast at it.

"Still and all, it's an interesting try," the Imir said at last, "and our technical advisor recommends trying it if it is at all possible. I have a few spells of concealment and nonrecognition I've used before and just used now. I can get you in, and myself as well. But the Creator have mercy if you so much as sneeze."

"I'll take the chance," Joe replied. "Just be ready."

"Above all, do not look at her if you can avoid it," Poquah told him. "It is possible, even probable, that the conversation spell does not operate in here, when she is human and normal size, but we can't take any chances."

Poquah set up a watch and waited until the receiving room was clear of business and both Kaladon and Tiana had retired to the rear apartment for lunch. With the aid of Poquah's magic, Joe found himself able to reach the room with no trouble and he was impressed with the way it looked—like some reception area from the age of kings, with grand tapestries behind the velvet-lined throne of solid gold. He got behind the tapestries all right, then settled down as best he could for the long wait. Poquah would have to remain outside until after dark, lest Joe's curse go the wrong way. Even now there was a fifty-fifty chance of real problems.

Throughout the afternoon, it was maddening to hear the voices of both Kaladon and Tiana, the latter on the throne just in front of Joe, but he held onto what patience he could. As the afternoon wore on, though, he certainly wished he could go to the bathroom.

Tiana sounded wonderful but imperious. There was a lot of work to be done and lots of people to be seen. Joe was certain that the only reason he had escaped detection was because it would simply never occur to Kaladon that such a thing was even possible.

Several times, sometimes for long periods, Tiana would leave the throne, and many times both of them would leave the room and then return, causing Joe a great deal of worry. He had no clock, no window, no way at all to know what the situation was, and he could only wait and listen and hope.

Still and all, it worked. Tiana was, in fact, sitting on the throne at sunset, while Kaladon was tending to some paperwork across the room. Joe knew immediately that the change had occurred, smiled, leaned down, and picked up the small gold charm he'd taken in with him but not worn. "Go," he whispered into it, hoping that only the one on the other end would hear. He then got up, brushed back the impossibly long silver hair, and stuck the little gadget in his ear.

Outside, a door opened, and a man's voice said humbly, "Begging your worshipful Highness' pardon, but there is an Imir outside."

Kaladon was quick to get suspicious. "What? How did he get in?"

"I—I don't know, sir. I assumed—"

"You *assumed*! I should—no, wait. Send him in and leave us. I'm going to get to the bottom of this."

"As you wish, your Worship," the adept responded, then bowed to the woman on the throne and left.

Poquah entered without disguise, looking as impassive as ever. Nothing had ever seemed to disturb him, and he didn't appear to understand the meaning of fear. He bowed to the throne and to Kaladon. "I am Poquah, your Worships, formerly in the service of the late, sainted Ruddygore."

Here we go, Joe thought, knowing every possible meaning of fear.

"So you are Poquah," Kaladon responded. "I have heard a lot about you. How did you enter this castle without permission?"

"But, your Worship, I *had* permission," the Imir replied.

"Whose?"

The Imir pointed to the throne where Tiana sat, impassive as the fairy. "Hers," he said.

Kaladon turned to look, and as he did, Tiana rose and started toward him . . .

Then *two* Tianas were there, side by side, walking toward him.

"Wha—*what trick is this*?" Kaladon screamed, and Poquah

watched the thin yellow band connecting him to the real Tiana. Watched as it wavered, moved, and seemed unable to choose between the two absolutely identical Goddesses.

The Imir struck. It was something that even Joe could see, because he had the same relative abilities as Tiana at this point; although, since his soul was different, he did not have her great magical powers.

Tiana herself seemed to frown and rock to and fro. Kaladon became suddenly concerned with reestablishing his umbilical link, completely forgetting Poquah, who was rapidly rewriting the magical script.

Once the link had been broken, even for a few seconds, Poquah's opening had begun changing the rest of the pattern that bound Tiana so tightly, so that Kaladon's link with the big woman would not rehook to her. Instead it wavered, then attached itself to the one pattern it could grab hold of—Joe.

Realizing his problem, Kaladon screamed and rushed headlong into the Imir, bowling him over onto the floor.

Tiana shook her head as if to clear it and blinked several times, as if awakening from a strange and terrible dream. She looked around in complete confusion, then saw the two fighting on the floor.

The yellow umbilical was attached to Joe, but it had no pattern with which to mate and so it only tickled a little. Tiana gazed very confusedly at him, gave a gasp at seeing herself, but did not know what to do, so she just stood there. Joe quickly moved around to the other side of her, in the process knocking the yellow magic band away as if it were a cobweb.

The protective spells taught him by Boquillas worked well, but the Imir was no match for Kaladon and was quickly brought to heel. He lay there unconscious on the floor, and Kaladon picked himself up, then looked with a snarl of satisfaction at the twin Goddesses before him. He stretched out his hand, and from it flowed a pattern of yellows, greens, and reds, completely covering one of them and freezing her into immobility, while the other stared wide-eyed, then seemed to realize exactly what was going on.

"First the imposter, then the Imir," Kaladon snarled. "Here is the pattern. Do it! I command you!"

"She would if she could, usurper, but she is only a double

of me!" the unbound Tiana on the left said. "But thank you for the pattern!"

It shot out from her in blinding lights. Joe could only watch, unable to move or do anything at all, but no help from him was needed. Kaladon was trapped in the complex mass of colors and textures. They held him, froze him, and bound him all at once, and then they started slowly to constrict, ever slowly but steadily, until the veins began to pop from his skin. Vessels burst under the pressure, bathing the frozen man in his own blood and continuing to contract until the pattern met, then dissolved, leaving a gruesome mess on the rug.

As Kaladon died, the spells binding Joe seemed to snap and then dissolve away. He could think and move once more and he let out a loud sigh.

Poquah groaned, rolled over, and made his way to his feet. Both Tianas just looked at him. Finally he got hold of himself, glanced over at the pulpy mass and, for one of the very few times in his life, he gave a slight grin. It quickly vanished when he realized it, and he turned to the two large women standing there.

"What is this all about?" Tiana wanted to know. "I do not remember anything since I was forced into Kaladon's presence . . ." She suddenly paused. "Oh, God! It was not a dream, was it? This strange religion, all those people . . ."

The Imir nodded. "Not a dream. In fact, a more humane version of the system might be just what Husaquahr needs. I'm not at all sure that it can be properly dismantled with so many on the Council in on it."

"Quite right, my friend," came a voice from the door, and in walked Esmilio Boquillas. "The spells hold, for they are Tiana's, not the late, unlamented Kaladon's, and she doesn't even know how to undo them."

Tiana was confused. "What? Who?"

The other Tiana grinned a very uncharacteristic Tiana grin. "I'm Joe, Tiana. This is a night with a full moon. Remember?"

She gasped. "Then that explains it! And you, sir?"

Boquillas smiled and bowed. "Esmilio Boquillas, Count of Marahbar, at your service."

"How'd you get here so quickly?" Joe asked him. "The whole outer castle is guarded."

Boquillas chuckled. "Poquah did it. You see, while I can no longer *cast* spells, I can be the easy recipient of them. It was a trifle. I had him cast several good spells on me for practice weeks ago."

Marge entered from the back of the room, looking confused, and stopped at the sights she saw.

Joe eased away from Tiana and over to a side where two rapiers were mounted decoratively on the wall. Boquillas glanced over at him and grinned. "Oh, you have guessed it. Yes, indeed, my friends, we shall yet build perfection in this world. One of those spells you used in freeing Tiana, my dear Imir, also subjected her to my direction. Come! Come! Do not feel dejected! The Dark Baron's plans come to fruition at last, that's all. There is nothing you can do about it."

Joe took both rapiers from the wall and checked out the heft and balance. "I think there is, Baron," he said in Tiana's sweetest voice. "I think you should have been in this room rather than assuming your scenario."

Boquillas' face clouded. "What do you mean?"

"I mean that you'd better take this rapier, you bastard! Poquah did no more than break the link before he was otherwise engaged. *He cast no spells on Tiana—she used Kaladon's own!*" He tossed the rapier to the man, who caught it deftly.

"Joe!" Tiana cried. "No! It is not necessary! With Poquah's aid, there is no problem!"

"I can handle him without you," the Imir responded, and Boquillas looked nervously at the two of them.

"No! This *is* necessary!" Joe told them. "Just get out of the way, all of you! It's time for this murdering bastard to meet his fate in the real world!"

Boquillas glanced over at the real Tiana. "If I order you to fling the same spell on her—er, him—that you used on Kaladon, I don't suppose you'd obey, would you?"

"Not a chance, old man," she responded.

He shrugged, raised the rapier in a salute, then leaped at Joe.

Joe was fortunate that Tiana was about the same height as he normally was and that her body was also trained as a swordswoman, with the proper muscles and reflexes. Although he had to remember to protect his chest a bit better, he had height and reach on the older man, as well as youth. He also, unfortunately, had six feet of flowing hair that threatened to trip him up.

Boquillas was no slouch as a swordsman, either. In fact, he was nearly brilliant, and they dueled back and forth across the chamber with little effect to either combatant.

Ultimately, though, the Dark Baron's strategy held true, as he forced Joe into a series of gymnastic moves that could not be done without tripping on that damned hair. Joe fell, cursing, and lost his rapier.

Boquillas made no allowance for honor. The rapier plunged deep into Joe's chest twice, spurting blood, and the stricken were cried out in pain.

"I think that is quite enough," another voice said, and Boquillas whirled, froze, and literally gaped at the heretofore vacant throne. The rapier dropped to the floor, and still he stood there, looking like a man facing his own death.

Tiana, Marge, Poquah, and Joe all stared as well, and only the Imir remained in the least bit unaffected by the sight.

Throckmorton P. Ruddygore, looking about forty pounds thinner and with a neatly trimmed beard, got up from the throne, an amused twinkle in his eyes. He was wearing his formal clothes, complete with opera cape, distinctive cane, and top hat.

"Joe, don't just lie there feeling killed. The rapiers weren't made of silver, and he had no power to make them so. Wipe that damned blood away and get up!"

CHAPTER 18

COMPLEX EVER-AFTERINGS

Never consider a sorcerer dead for good until you have seen him die a minimum of three times.

—Rules, VI, 303(b)

"DON'T LOOK SO STARTLED, ALL OF YOU," RUDDYGORE TOLD them. "Come back into the apartment with me and let's find something to eat in this mausoleum. Yes, you, too, Esmilio."

"But—I killed you! Or, rather, Hiccarph killed you! We all saw it!" the Count protested.

Ruddygore chuckled. "Oh, I admit I got a real mauling, but only on the psychic level, like your kraken and dragon and my replay of Earth warfare. I will also admit that, had I been that poor, starving boy, you would have had me; but he was just a construct, like the rest."

"He *couldn't* have been!" Boquillas protested. "It was *you* there! You as a starving scavenger! I know the Rules better than you! No construct may have a direct relationship to its creator!"

"Could be you're right," Ruddygore admitted, "but, trouble is, Count, you're just too damned gullible. That life story of mine that I told you over good wine and better cigars was a total and complete lie. You're such a sucker for a bleeding heart I can't help but feel sorry for you, old boy. Come! Everyone! We must eat and relax and decide what to tell all those officials around here who are scared to death to enter the presence of the Goddess without permission, despite the commotion!"

"But where were you when you escaped the demon? Where

have you *been* all this time?" Marge wanted to know.

"Where I could rest and bind my wounds and regain strength?" the fat sorcerer responded. "Where else?" And with that, he launched into a chorus of "I Left My Heart in San Francisco."

It was daybreak, but Joe and Marge had talked through the night, telling Tiana of their adventures and briefing Ruddygore on what he had missed. Meanwhile, Tiana gave orders forbidding interruptions in her best imperious manner, while fanatical followers still worked on rebuilding the castle and the city.

Boquillas remained the most silent of the batch, rarely offering a question or comment. He looked, and was, a totally defeated man and he knew it.

Finally it was dawn, and Joe changed back to his old self. He was delighted, as was Tiana, who hugged and kissed him. He finally broke away, laughing, and noted that three of them in the room were stark naked.

"That brings up an interesting series of questions," Ruddygore said at last. "We have to discuss all our futures here."

Everyone was suddenly very serious.

"Boquillas, I certainly owe you for helping dispose of Kaladon, although, as I promised, I was ready all in good time. I find, however, that I can not allow you freedom, considering your activities of this night. I think, perhaps, that you will come with me for a while, and we will take a little trip together."

The Count's eyebrows went up. "A trip? Where?"

"I'll give you back your health and your youth, so that you will have a chance to see how things really are. I'll prepare you with languages and I will even bankroll you. You are going to work for me, on Earth."

"Earth? Doing what?"

"Research and correlation. It would be a shame to let one of your intellect and experience go to waste. You like technology so much, I will introduce you to my computer section. Without them, all this could never have been possible."

"I *knew* it," Marge put in.

"Alas, you are also ready to experience a far different world from what you've ever known, as well as the Bangkok flu, stomach ulcers, and all the other pressures of day-to-day living.

Still, it is better than you deserve." The sorcerer pointed at Boquillas, and he winked out and vanished. "Stuck him in storage until I have to go over again," Ruddygore told the others.

"And what of us?" Marge asked him. "What now?"

He sighed. "Boquillas was right, you know. Esmerada, Fajera, Sargash, and the rest will not be easily talked out of this cult thing. Nor, in fact, could you, Tiana, ever lead a normal life now. You have what you wished all along to have, much to my surprise. You are absolute ruler here. We can modify the harsh parts of this new religion, but the others won't let us kill it, I'm afraid." He chuckled. "Besides, I *like* being a saint."

Tiana shook her head in wonder. "You know, all that time in exile, I dreamed of this sort of thing, although tens of thousands of statues of me fully nude are a bit more than I thought about." She laughed. "Well, then, so be it. The climate is tropical, and I certainly can no longer claim modesty after so many have seen not only statues but me in the altogether." She paused a moment. "But the responsibility it now gives me is staggering. I had not thought in those terms. My dreams were always of taking back what was stolen, not of what happened after."

"Of course, there will have to be *some* modifications," Ruddygore told her. "Let them continue to think you an angel, for they will, anyway, but we must restore their free will and sense of perspective. We must get the economy going again. Adjust the new status to the old so that it all works, but without war or mass slaughter, at least for a very long time."

She nodded. "Of course. You need only show me how to do it."

Ruddygore turned to Joe. "And what about you? What do you want now, Joe? I mean, really want. Long-term."

Joe thought a minute, then leaned over and hugged Tiana. "I want a goddess."

She seemed delighted and excited, and grabbed and hugged and kissed him all over again.

Ruddygore smiled. "A slight modification is in order, then. There will have to be one, anyway, to explain Kaladon's demise. You sent him to his Heavenly reward, that's all."

"She sure did," Joe noted.

"Goddesses do not have consorts, of course, and I think Joe ill fits the role of high priest. Therefore, we'll reaffirm some old-fashioned values and virtues. The Goddess shall have her God. You certainly look the part, Joe."

"Hey! Wait a minute! You mean there's gonna be a million marble statues of *me* in the nude?"

Ruddygore laughed. "And why not? When they see the attributes of both of you, you will be the sex idols of Husa-quahr."

"But I have no godlike power, and Tiana can't use hers," he pointed out. "And you're expecting us to rule a country directly and a church that goes out who knows how far?"

"There will be little trouble there. First of all, your new high priest will handle the mundane magical chores and advice, accompanied by his faithful band of adepts and hangers-on. And, because the potential for this is so fascinating, there will be a backup. A simple microcomputer, I think, with a number of hard disks, should hold the basics. With some nice color graphics, of course, so you can see the spells and how they're formed when you punch them up. I'll bring one back when I drop off Esmilio."

"But how will you plug it in?" Joe asked him. "And isn't that violating your own ideas on technology?"

Ruddygore winked. "The power source will be a new type of battery tapping a magical source. As you know, sometimes cheating on one's principles is necessary. Without doing so, we would now all be dead, at the mercy of the Baron's armies."

Ruddygore turned to Marge, whose expression was solemn. "Don't look so glum, my dear!"

"Nothing in that bag of yours for me, is there, Mr. Wizard?" she responded sadly.

"Soon the inns will open, the shows will restart, and all will begin anew," he told her. "You are Kauri, Marge, and that is a great responsibility, but also an important one. Fly, Marge, into the night skies! Play! Sing! Dance! The whole new world is at your feet, and you are truly free to enjoy it!"

She smiled and got up and walked over to them. "I'll miss you all terribly, though."

"But you can return any time, and there is always time for you," Joe told her. "Always."

They hugged and kissed, and then Marge left. Going down a hall and seeing an open door, she walked in and climbed up on the window. The sun was bright, and she lowered her goggles to keep the sleep away, then leaped out into the cool sky.

Back in the apartment, Joe sighed. "Will we ever see her again for real, I wonder?" He leaned over to Tiana and kissed her. "I know and I'm sorry, but we were pretty close."

She kissed him back. "I understand."

Ruddygore grinned broadly and got up. "Well, Poquah, it's about time we saw what they've done to our old home. But we'll be back, children, rather quickly. Until then, don't worry about any problems coming about. Everybody here will obey every order the Goddess gives." He sighed, yawned, stretched, and made for the door, then turned back to the couple.

"Don't worry about not seeing Marge again," he told them. "The Rules still hold."

Tiana looked puzzled, but Joe smiled softly, and that smile turned into a big grin.

"Yeah, that's right, isn't it? We've got at least one more great adventure left, haven't we?"

"Oh, yes, yes. At *least*," agreed Throckmorton P. Ruddygore.

ABOUT THE AUTHOR

JACK L. CHALKER was born in Norfolk, Virginia, on December 17, 1944, but was raised and has spent most of his life in Baltimore, Maryland. He learned to read almost from the moment of entering school, and by working odd jobs amassed a large book collection by the time he was in junior high school, a collection now too large for containment in his quarters. Science fiction, history, and geography all fascinated him early on, interests that continue.

Chalker joined the Washington Science Fiction Association in 1958 and began publishing an amateur SF journal, *Mirage*, in 1960. After high school he decided to be a trial lawyer, but money problems and the lack of a firm caused him to switch to teaching. He holds bachelor degrees in history and English, and an M.L.A. from Johns Hopkins University. He taught history and geography in the Baltimore public schools between 1966 and 1978, and now makes his living as a freelance writer. Additionally, out of the amateur journals he founded a publishing house, The Mirage Press, Ltd., devoted to nonfiction and bibliographic works on science fiction and fantasy. This company has produced more than twenty books in the last nine years. His hobbies include esoteric audio, travel, working on science-fiction convention committees, and guest lecturing on SF to institutions such as the Smithsonian. He is an active conservationist and National Parks supporter, and he has an intense love of ferryboats, with the avowed goal of riding every ferry in the world. In 1978 he was married to Eva Whitley on an ancient ferryboat in mid-river. They live in the Catoctin Mountain region of western Maryland with their son, David.